"The authors should be commended for tackling a controversial era, and making it so intriguing. The characters are meticulously developed, the writing style is flawless, and the method by which the authors unfold the plot is unusually creative."

Carole Muir, *ForeWordreviews*

"Those who lived through the late 1960s will no doubt experience a sense of déjà vu, so clearly are the sights and sounds of those years presented."

Elizabeth K. Burton, *The Blue Iris Journal*

"Wonderful!"

Linda McDonough, Flower Films

"The authors handle the abundance of issues with grace and credibility . . . A gripping read."

Kristan Higgins, *Metroline*

"A novel of reminiscence revealing the often bizarre forces and pressures that shaped today's 'Boomer' women. A real page-turner evoking the heady confusion resulting from a cocktail of hedonism and hormones."

Linda Mason Hunter, author of
The Healthy Home and *Southwest Style*

"The characters are dynamic and interesting. The smooth narration and dialogue speed up the flow of events. Overall, this is a well-structured and well-crafted piece of fiction."

Writer's Digest

"An intriguing novel."

Diane Naber, *Boone News-Republican*

"A winning evocation of a hopeful, turbulent time, as well as a wonderfully juicy read."

Robert Rodi, author of *Closet Case* and *Kept Boy*

ON
THE
WAY
TO

Woodstock

Sheri Davenport
Elizabeth Warren

Published by Sisyphus Press
For information, please contact:
Sisyphus Press
1309 W. Albion Avenue
Suite 200
Chicago, IL 60626

This novel is a work of fiction. Any references to real people, events, establishments, organizations or locales are intended only to give the fiction a sense of reality and authenticity. Other names, characters, places and incidents portrayed herein are either the product of the authors' imagination or are used fictionally.

The lyrics on page 145 are from the song "I Feel Like I'm Fixin' To Die Rag," written and composed by Joe McDonald (c) 1965 renewed 1993 by Alkatraz Corner Music Co., are used by permission; all rights reserved.

The passages on pages 325-6 and 328 are from *Lysistrata* by Aristophanes, translated by Douglass Parker, copyright (c) 1964 by William Arrowsmith. Used by permission of Dutton Signet, a division of Penquin Putnam Inc.

The passage on page 324 is from *Letters to a Young Poet* by Rainer Maria Rilke, translated by M.D. Herter Norton, Copyright 1934 by W.W. Norton & Company, Inc. revised edition copyright 1954 by W.W. Norton & Company, Inc., New York, NY.

The passages on pages 34, 39 and 411 are from *The Courage to Be* by Paul Tillich, copyright 1952 by Yale University Press, New Haven, Connecticut, Thirtieth printing, August 1968.

ISBN: 0-9712648-0-5

Printed in the United States of America

ACKNOWLEDGMENTS

There are many people whose friendship and support have been essential to the creation of this book. The authors gratefully acknowledge their contribution and would also like to thank: Renee Adams, Sarah L. Bleeks, Michael Bodaken, Helen Brown, Candy Clough, Wendy Columbus, Mary Dahm, Helen Davenport, Richard DeJong, Erin L. Ferree, Linda Frosolone, Glenn F. Haines, Karla L. Heuer, Margaret L. Goss, Hillary R. Kalish, Nedra Kalish, Alonna Koehn, Marc Louria, Millicent W. Mackinnon, Shannon Madill, Merrilee Mitchell, Susan B. Mulvihill, Michael W. Phillips, Janet K. Syverson, Jeffrey E. Toevs, Bernice L. Warren.

To my sister, Millicent, and my sister-in-spirit, Sheri

To Doug and Betsy, and of course, to Elizabeth,
friend extraordinaire

I came to see the damage that was done
and the treasures that prevail.

Adrienne Rich

CHAPTER ONE

She dipped under the lavender scented water, slowly pushed the air from her lungs and waited until she felt the quiet hopeless pull of the abyss. She counted 10 seconds passing, then 20. From far off a phone made a muffled sound and she squirmed. I won't, she thought. I can't. Thirty seconds. The phone kept up its insistent wail, her lungs screamed for air. Finally, gasping, she exploded through the water and sent a wave skidding across the bathroom floor.

She lowered her shoulders back into the water, closed her eyes and dropped her chin past the line of bubbles and into the warmth. Finally the answering machine picked up. It would be someone from the office, or Eric. It didn't matter, she refused to talk to anyone after the day's disaster. She sat up, reached for her glass of chardonnay, took a long, full swallow and glared at the flames of a dozen candles on the tub's edge.

Jess Martin had fought her way to senior creative director of a major San Francisco advertising agency in just five years. Her swift climb was a major success by most standards, but her dour Midwestern upbringing always kept her from savoring her accomplishments. No matter how many credentials her resume listed she was always undone by failure, and today she'd failed miserably. The client's blunt words rang in her head: "The demographics are all wrong." The meeting had ended quickly and she hurried home to lick her wounds.

Jess dug out a cigarette from the half-smoked pack and picked up a candle for a light. Her hand was shaking. She quickly set the candle down but her hand slipped, hit another candle and sent it sizzling into the murky water. "Damn it!" She fished the candle out and set it, wet and useless, on the ledge. She'd lost so much, her job was all she had left. She took another swallow of wine and looked for answers in the soft bubbles that covered her slender legs. Yes, she'd missed the input meeting, but she and Eric discussed the objectives for the ProbTech campaign over dinner the night before he left for Hong Kong.

They shared a bottle of wine, no, two. He fed her information about earlier campaigns and she took her usual cryptic notes. They'd worked that way dozens of times, and Eric always said she had a knack for reading his intentions. Thank God he hadn't been there to see her self-destruct. But why had he scheduled the presentation for a Friday when he knew he'd be out of town? He loved being part of client pitches, especially when she was presenting. They'd often end a presentation day with passionate sex in his office. Jess dug her nails into the soap bar, remembering their last rendezvous.

She scooped a thousand bubbles and blew them across the tub. Another candle fizzled out. She'd make it right. She'd work the weekend, call in favors from her team and have a new strategy by Monday. Eric had recently been made senior account supervisor, and he'd quickly promoted Jess. Now she had to prove that she still had her edge.

Jess sprang up in the tub and made a splash. "Baby Boomers," she said out loud. Eric had told her the target audience was Baby Boomers, not Gen Xers. Hadn't he? She made a move to get out. This bath is a joke, she thought. Things need fixing.

She forced her body back into the water. "I guess I could try to get in touch with my spiritual side," she said without enthusiasm. She lit the cigarette and took a deep puff. It tasted hot. I'll quit for good when this is over, she thought. She squinted her eyes closed and began repeating a Buddhist mantra she'd learned decades earlier.

The doorbell rang and the squint turned to a frown. Eric wasn't due for hours; it was too late for mail. She wouldn't answer it. Whoever it was held down the buzzer for a good 30 seconds. Then the knocking began. "All right, all right," Jess muttered. She climbed from the tub dripping water, checking her figure in the mirror as she grabbed her white terry robe. Eric was right, all those business lunches were starting to register on her once-slim waistline. She made a mental note to schedule more sessions with her personal trainer.

The knocking continued in tandem with the bell. "I'm coming, I'm coming," Jess yelled. She picked up her glass and took a gulp. She returned it to the ledge too quickly and watched it smash to pieces on the tile floor. "Goddamn it!" She picked up the larger pieces, cut her index finger, swore again. The caller at the door was holding the bell down again. Whoever you are, you're about to get the brunt of my day shoved down your throat, she thought. Jess wrapped tissue over the cut, hurried to the door and peered through the security viewer.

"Holly?" She gasped as she opened the door. The apparition on the other side pushed it open wider.

"No, Holly's still dead. Why? Do I look like her?" The stranger was young, with irregularly cropped blonde hair. She was dressed in black, with three silver earrings in her left ear, a ring on the outside of her right nostril and another on her eyebrow.

"Who are you?"

"The daughter Holly O'Neal abandoned in 1970." Jess stood

transfixed while the apparition continued. "And you would be Jess Martin?" She didn't wait for an answer but came into the foyer, digging into her pockets. Her face was beautiful despite the piercings. She wore black stretch pants, a black cropped top with long sleeves pushed to her elbows and a thick silver chain around her neck. Her navel was pierced and tattooed, and on her feet were black platform clogs. The attire was uncomfortably familiar and the facial resemblance to Holly was astonishing.

"I have some questions about my mother. I was told you might have the answers." The girl pulled out a thousand-folded list handwritten in many pen types, a life's worth of questions scribbled on both sides. She unfolded it and began to recite. "Where did she live? Did she ever get married? What was her favorite color? Who was my father—"

"Wait a minute," Jess interrupted. The girl ignored her.

"Did she want to give me up or was she forced—"

"Stop." The girl fell silent and seemed to see Jess for the first time.

"Were you taking a shower?" The girl set her backpack on the floor. "Sorry. Can I start over?" Jess nodded, mesmerized by the face. "My name is Sar—my name is Zoe. Zoe Ryerson. And you're Jess Martin." Jess nodded. "Hello." She stuck her hand out and shook Jess's vigorously. "Sorry I barged in, but like I said, I have these questions."

"All right. But how did you find me?" Jess closed the door and turned to face the insistent bell ringer.

"So you'll talk to me? Good." The stranger seemed relieved.

"I didn't say that. First, you need to tell me how you got my name. But before that, I need to get dressed."

Jess led her uninvited guest to the living room and went to dress. Heart pounding, she closed her bedroom door and took a deep breath. She glanced at her rumpled unmade bed and suddenly wanted to lie down and sleep the weekend through. Who was this woman? Was she really Holly's daughter or was this some bizarre joke? No, she was definitely Holly's progeny. She looked like Holly, except she had a larger frame and her features were less delicate. And her name, Zoe. The people who adopted her must have kept it. Who were they? And what had they told her about her mother? Her father?

She shuddered. Jess Martin didn't like surprises, especially from her past. "I'm not up for this," she said out loud. She put a Band-Aid on her cut and looked for something to wear. Her entire week's wardrobe was piled carelessly on the chaise lounge. She went to her closet, put on last weekend's jeans and pulled on a turtleneck sweater. She drew a brush through her hair and pulled it back neatly with a large barrette. She never wore her hair down and loose anymore. Eric said it looked sophisticated pulled back. Sophisticated, practical and old. Like me, Jess thought. Her hair was sprinkled with gray, which she kept well hidden with regular trips to her hairdresser for a complicated and expensive color weave. It was past time for one now, and Eric would notice. Eric. She went into her office and played the message. It was him.

"Hey, Jess. Just got into LAX. I managed to grab an earlier flight, but I couldn't sleep on the plane, so I'm a walking zombie. I get into SFO at six, and I know we talked about drinks, but I'm too beat. I'm heading straight home. I'll try to call you in the morning. Maybe we can get together at your place tomorrow afternoon. Oh, and I heard about the ProbTech fiasco. We'll have to talk."

"Damn it." Jess hit the erase button and went back to her bedroom. Too late for damage control. "We'll have to talk." He'd sounded like a schoolmaster. She reached for the framed photo on her dresser and looked hard at Eric, tie askew, flashing his perpetually charming smile. It had been easy to fall for him. He was smart, handsome, successful, and married. And as usual, tonight, when she needed him, he was going home. Jess turned the frame face down and unzipped her makeup bag.

She quickly applied foundation to skin that looked drawn from long days and sleepless nights. In spite of the fatigue, Jess was a beautiful woman. Her bone structure was perfect, her nose straight and strong, her large, brown eyes were almond shaped, her lips naturally full. And there was a quality about her that made men take a longer look, a defiance coupled with a vulnerability. So Jess Martin still turned heads, even when she didn't feel attractive. And lately, she hadn't felt attractive or competent.

Her new position was incredibly demanding and balls had dropped. She feared senior management was having second thoughts about her promotion. Advertising was a game for the young and hip, and she wondered how much longer she could keep up. She was spearheading a big research project, driving the ProbTech proposal and the Clorox campaign. And the firm was in danger of losing the Celestial Seasonings account because she hadn't given it enough attention. But she'd keep up, she had to. Work was her life. Jess smiled at her reflection in the mirror, mustering her seasoned confidence.

Then she remembered her more pressing problem; she needed to rid herself of the stranger in her living room before she could salvage her career. She quickly applied lipstick and mascara, trying to ignore the lines around her eyes. She'd tell the girl she had work to do and could only spare a few minutes. She'd get her address and write a long, friendly letter, telling her about the years she spent with Holly. Those terrible, wonderful years. But she'd leave the terror out.

Jess found Zoe standing at the parsons table of photographs behind the sofa. When she saw Jess she leapt toward her, holding up a small square photograph in a distressed wood frame.

"This is her, isn't it?" The voice was aggressive, slightly bitter. Jess nodded yes. The picture was of Holly and Jess lying side by side in their brimmed felt hats on the banks of the Iowa River. It was the only photo of them that she displayed, taken before the deluge. "How old was my mother here?"

"That was the spring of 1969. We were freshmen."

"I can't believe someone really looks like me."

"You do, you look just like her." Jess didn't want to stare, but Zoe's face and energy were discomforting.

"What's the deal with those stupid hats?"

"Holly bought them for us one spring. Listen, I'm not going to be much help to you. Your mother and I were friends, but that was a long time ago. And you still haven't told me who gave you my name."

"Her sister, Maggie Connors. Over the phone," Zoe said with distaste. "I was going to fly to Chicago to meet her, then she called and said the timing was bad, something about a crisis with her brother. All I got from her was name, rank and serial number. She said if I had questions, I should ask you."

Jess remembered Maggie, and Holly's parents. I'll bet Ellen and Bill were shocked to hear about the family shame after all this time, Jess thought. They had probably long forgotten the skeleton in their closet. Jess felt secretly vindicated for Holly. She wanted to feel sorry for Zoe. But the way Zoe stood before her, scowling, she couldn't.

"Where do you live?" Jess asked.

"I go to school in Seattle. I'm getting my master's in oceanography. That's the plan anyway. But I grew up in Minnesota."

"How did you get here?"

"I took a plane. Listen, I didn't come here to answer 20 questions about my life. I came here because I need some answers. Now."

"Why now?"

Zoe hesitated. "A few years ago I got a letter from the Catholic Charities in Minneapolis, saying my birth mother was trying to find me. What was I supposed to do? I mean, after all that time, she finally wanted to see me? Why? I waited too long it turns out. I sent her a letter in care of the agency a few weeks ago. They told me she died in 1995."

"Yes."

"So now I'll never get to meet her, that's why I'm here." Jess said nothing. "I thought maybe you could tell me about her."

"Let me get this straight. You drop in out of nowhere and expect me to sit down on the spot and recount the details of a 25-year friendship? You don't ask for much, do you?" Jess quipped. Zoe laughed. A crack, Jess thought.

Then Zoe became persistent again. "Maggie said Holly sent you a box."

"A box? No, I'm sure she didn't . . . oh. Yes." Jess was embarrassed. The box had arrived after Jess returned from the funeral, her address written in Holly's sprawling hand. She'd barely opened it. "Yes, there is a box."

"I want to see it."

"All right. But I need a glass of wine first. Can I get you something? Wine? A beer?"

"I don't drink. But if you have some herb tea, I'll have a cup." Jess led Zoe to the kitchen and showed her a large jar of tea bags. Zoe dug through it, looking for something without caffeine, while Jess selected a bottle of merlot from her wine rack. When she turned on the gas under the teakettle, her mind wandered back to the presentation. Eric wasn't coming by, so she could get started tonight. She'd give Zoe the box and send her on her way.

"Are there any planes back to Seattle tonight?" Jess asked, she hoped, indifferently.

"Don't think so."

"Where are you going to stay?"

"Some friends live here. I'm staying with them."

"When are you going back?"

"I'm not sure I am going back."

"I thought you were in school."

"I am—I'm going back. Sunday. That's when my ticket's for."

Just what I need, a teenager on the edge, thought Jess. But Zoe was no child. She had to at least be in her late twenties, though she looked younger. Holly had always looked younger than her age, too. Jess glanced at Zoe, then away. Why all those rings? And that awful haircut? Jess pulled the cork on the wine as Zoe found the only herb tea bag, cinnamon apple.

While the tea steeped and the wine breathed, the women took the elevator to the basement. It smelled cold and dank and Jess hadn't entered it for several years.

Jess opened her storage locker and quickly located the large cardboard box. It sat on the top shelf, covered with dust. Zoe pulled it down, held it to her chest. Jess closed the locker door and the women rode the elevator up in silence.

Jess had never gone through Holly's bequest. When the heavily taped box had arrived, two weeks after the funeral, she had quickly opened it. On top was Holly's army jacket; seeing it, Jess had put her face into its musty fabric and cried. Then she replaced the lid and never looked again. Now she was suddenly angry at Holly. I'm not ready to do this, she thought.

When they reached Jess's apartment Zoe asked, "Where do you want me to put it?"

"The coffee table, I guess." Jess found her scissors and cut through the rewrapped package. Zoe pulled the lid off and a musty smell of age and incense wafted through the air. Jess took the lid from Zoe and set it under the coffee table. Then they stared into the box, stuffed to overflowing. There was Holly's army jacket; Zoe pulled it out and held it up, as if she were trying to guess its size. Jess took it from her, held it.

Zoe looked back inside and pulled out a large, heavy book. She removed it and blew dust off the cover. "*Sexual Behavior in the Human Male*," Zoe read. "Heady stuff."

"So that's where that book ended up," Jess said. Zoe opened the book, flipped through its pages. "It's the Kinsey Report. Your mother asked me to steal that from the library so she could do some research."

"What kind of research? Like for a paper?" Zoe asked.

Jess smiled. "Let's just say we weren't terribly informed back then about sex or men or—you know, I don't think sex should head the list of things you learn about your mother."

"Why not? It's not like I'm a virgin."

Jess ignored the comment and tried to focus on the overstuffed box. "Holly was such a pack rat."

Zoe continued removing objects and each sparked a strong visceral memory in Jess. There was Holly's POW bracelet, a dog-eared copy of *The Courage to Be*, a package of sparklers, Jess's Tri Delt pin. "Was my mother in a sorority?" Zoe asked.

"No, I was. But I threw that pin away. I don't know how she came to have it."

Zoe pulled out a package of red, white and blue rolling papers, a gold metal snake bracelet and a *Chicago Tribune*. Jess grabbed the newspaper. It was from May 1970, and the headline screamed: "Nixon Invades Cambodia." Zoe pulled out a McGovern button and handed it to Jess. "Was my mother a Democrat or a Republican?"

"She was neither."

"Oh." Zoe sounded disappointed. "My parents are Republicans. I was, too, until I got to college, then I became a

Democrat. But now I don't vote on principle."

"I see." Jess wanted to launch into a tirade about the responsibilities of American citizenship, but decided it would fall on deaf ears. Zoe continued rummaging and brought out matches from the Playboy Club, a glass Irish coffee mug with the words *Cliff House* on the side and a plastic speculum. Underneath Jess spotted a photograph of Holly standing with an old man in front of a cornfield. Floyd. How could she explain him?

"Her speculum!" Jess shouted loudly, hoping to distract.

"Was my mother a gynecologist?"

Jess laughed. "That's from our days at the Women's Center. We were going to save womankind by joining the SCUM movement."

"The SCUM movement? Sounds weird." Zoe lifted out the picture of Floyd and turned it toward Jess. "This must be my grandfather."

"No, he was a friend of Holly's." There was no way to explain Floyd.

"Did you know my father?"

The question caught Jess off guard. "No."

Zoe's lips formed a frown. Then, returning to the hunt, she pulled out soft-focus black and white photos of unrecognizable objects; a business card from Pandora's Box; a napkin that read "Brad and Jess Forever, June 19, 1982;" a blue felt hat.

"Hey," Zoe said, pulling it out. "She saved this. It's the one from the picture. Where's yours?"

"I lost it," Jess lied. Suddenly she wanted Zoe gone. "Why don't you keep the box? I'm sure your mother would want you to have it."

"All right." Zoe dug further and found some love beads, packages of incense and the video documentary of the Woodstock festival. "Cool."

"Well, good, now you have her things." Jess stood. "Once you go through everything, if you have any questions—" She started toward the kitchen.

"Hey, a gold mine." Jess turned back. Lining the bottom of the box were a dozen worn spiral notebooks with cardboard covers in various muted colors, Holly's diaries. Jess let out a gasp, then a sigh. She was absolved. Zoe could learn about her mother from Holly's journals. Zoe opened one and began reading, ignoring Jess as she continued to the kitchen.

Jess poured a glass of wine and removed the tea bag from Zoe's mug. She looked at the clock. 5:15. She'd hoped to be in Eric's arms by now, or at least hard at work on her comeback campaign. She hadn't planned for this, a woman who reminded her so much of Holly when she was young and her life was full of possibilities. Jess picked up the glass and mug and walked briskly back to the living room where Zoe was absorbed in a journal.

"Finding what you want?"

"Oh, yeah."

"I'll help you repack the box. Then I'll give you a ride to your friends' house."

Zoe looked up. Her eyes were wider than Holly's and bluer. But they held the same intensity. "You're asking me to leave?"

"Those diaries should tell you everything you need to know. More than I could begin to remember."

"No. I need to talk to you. You knew her, you were there—I need to know certain things."

"Listen, I wasn't exactly expecting you, I'm in the middle of a major project—I don't have time and I wouldn't know where to start if I did." Zoe sat, staring up at Jess, defiance and anger in her eyes. Damn you, Holly, Jess thought. What am I supposed to tell her? After a life of searching, you found a few years of happiness and then you died? Jess turned to the window, searching for an out. This young woman lost a mother she would never know. Of course she wanted answers. But Holly was gone and life was closing in on Jess. She had to stay focused and couldn't afford a distraction. She turned back to her uninvited guest. As if on cue, Zoe blinked back tears and Jess felt she owed her something. What, though? An explanation, a hope? "What do you want to know about your mother?"

"Tell me why she gave me away." Jess looked at Zoe, holding a stack of notebooks. So this was the baby girl they'd waved to outside the hospital nursery so many years ago. The baby girl Holly was never allowed to touch.

"I'll tell you what I remember." Suddenly, Zoe put her hand to her mouth and bolted from the room. She found a bathroom, and Jess could hear her vomiting before the door closed.

CHAPTER TWO

Jess stood outside the guest bathroom door, cradling a damp washcloth, wondering whether she should knock or speak. "Are you all right? Can I come in?"

Zoe's voice was low and quivering. "Okay." Jess found her hunched forward on the edge of the bathtub, elbows on knees. She pulled a wayward strand of bleached blonde hair from Zoe's brow and pressed the cloth to her forehead. "I'm really sorry."

"Are you sick?" She studied Zoe's waif-like frame, looking for her malady. "When was the last time you ate?"

"Oh, I ate." Zoe smiled meekly then stifled another episode.

"Do you want some toast and more tea to settle your stomach?" Zoe answered that if Jess had some crackers, they might help. "I may have some table wafers," Jess said. "Sit a minute while I look." Zoe nodded dully. What is it? Jess wondered. Drugs, anorexia? She told herself not to jump to horrific conclusions, a habit she'd been trying to break for a lifetime. Maybe it was something simple like the flu. She found some not-quite stale saltines and when Zoe entered she invited her to sit on the stool at the breakfast bar.

Zoe took a bite of a dry cracker, and Jess watched it shatter into a thousand pieces around her fingers. Zoe swallowed the cracker too fast and started to cough.

"Are you sure you're not sick?" Zoe shook her head no. "How do you know?"

"Well, maybe I am." Zoe focused her attention on the cracker box, examining its list of ingredients.

She's humoring me, Jess thought. She took a chance. "What's really the matter with you, Zoe?"

Zoe sat looking out the window toward the bay. Then she stood up. "I'm pregnant, okay? And I don't know what to do, I don't want to talk about it and I need some answers, okay?"

"Okay." Jess said slowly. She glanced at Zoe's hand. No wedding ring. Pregnant, unmarried. Oh, boy. "What kind of answers?" Jess asked, after an uncomfortable pause.

"You could start by telling me who my father is."

Another pause. A panic. An answer. "I don't know."

"Who knows?"

"I don't know."

"You were her best friend, weren't you?" Zoe stared hard at Jess, her eyes demanding more. Jess said nothing, but stared back, just as determined until Zoe broke the silence. "I just thought that she got pregnant and had me, so maybe there's something I can figure out from that, if I know why she decided to have me and why she gave me away. Maybe my father knows." She sat down, tears brimming again. "I don't even know my real father's name. I don't know anything about my mother. Unless someone tells me, I'll never know anything."

"I said I'd tell you about your mother. But first I'd like to talk about you for a minute," Jess stalled.

Zoe pulled herself up, forcing the tears back. "Well, I'm not going to talk about the joys of impending motherhood if that's what you mean."

"Then tell me about your family and your life in Seattle."

"I have some pictures."

"Perfect." It will give me time to formulate a plan, thought Jess. And I'll need coffee. She put a stopper in the wine bottle, then opened her cupboard and pulled out her coffee grinder and the designer beans she rarely used. While the Vienna roast ground to a fine powder, Zoe retrieved her backpack and several books fell out: *On Being Adopted*, *Lost And Found Chidren*, *The Adoption Maze*, *Aquatic Organic Geochemistry*. Jess watched and wondered whether Zoe's adoptive parents had been good to her. Was she sheltered and loved? Did anyone hurt her?

She thought of Holly and her search to find her daughter. It was after the tumor had returned, after Holly refused further treatment. Desperate to help, Jess flew to Chicago and took her on a road trip to Iowa City. Jess planned a tour of their old haunts, to remind them of happier, healthier times. She had hoped to reconnect with Holly, but as they drove through miles of cornfields, all Holly talked about was finding Zoe before it was too late. When she returned to Chicago, Holly wrote a letter to the adoption agency. She died waiting for a reply.

Well, Holly, she's here. But where the hell are you? Jess thought. She poured the scalding water through the filter into the single mug as Zoe broke her thoughts.

"Here they are," Zoe said, holding a stack of loose photographs. On top was a photo of a young man which Zoe quickly shuffled to the back. Jess sat down next to her at the breakfast counter.

"Joanne and Paul. The adopters." Zoe handed her a studio portrait of a handsome couple in their fifties. She was ringed with pearls; he wore a conservative business suit. Jess searched their eyes for kindness, for love, and thought she saw some in each of them. Then Jess remembered the way Holly used to talk about her parents, "Ellen and Bill." Was it genetic?

"The adopters with the adoptee," Zoe announced. It was a picture of a grinning toddler on a tricycle next to her parents. They each held one of Zoe's hands and they were smiling, too. Jess searched for signs of danger.

"And here's the whole family. An award winner for the adopted kids yearbook if I ever saw one." It was a shot of a picture-perfect American family on a sailboat in summer, father, mother, daughter and son, all healthy looking and tan.

"Did they adopt a boy?"

"Oh, no. After they adopted me, I guess they relaxed, and they were blessed with an heir of their very own. That's typical with people who adopt, you know. His name is Scott. The apple of Joanne's eye."

"Do I detect sibling rivalry?"

Zoe reddened. "Hardly. I'd hate that kind of pressure. Scott has to be perfect; but fortunately, he is. He's in medical school and doing the whole saviour son bit very effectively. Oh, and he just got engaged. Of course he made the announcement the same night we were celebrating my acceptance into graduate school. God forbid I should get any of the limelight in the Ryerson family! Joanne is all aflutter making wedding arrangements. With Stephanie. They spend every minute chattering about center-pieces, seating arrangements, nut cups. Stephanie's mother is conveniently dead, and Joanne is thrilled to be chief conductor of the entire event. Scott and Stephanie. And me, with a bastard in the oven."

"I take it you haven't told your parents."

"Joanne would freak. We aren't exactly close."

Jess was silent, thinking of the uneven relationship she had with her own mother and the lifetime she'd spent trying to win her approval: I've graduated; do you love me? I'm successful; do you love me? I'm winning awards; do you love me?

Recently, Jess's mother had changed tactics and had begun to comment on her daughter's single status. "It must be lonely in that two-bedroom condo." "You can't cuddle up to a wall of awards." And more blatant: "I guess I'll never have grandchildren." Jess had resigned herself to the fact that no matter what she did, she'd never fulfill her mother's dreams. But at unguarded times the comments still had the power to hurt her.

"I haven't told anyone but my friend Annabelle and now you. I could never tell Joanne."

"Why not?" Jess asked.

"The minute I turned fifteen she took me to the doctor for birth control pills. Joanne's very big on responsible sex. Which I find kind of ironic, me being illegitimate and all."

"Surely she'd come around. You made a mistake—"

Zoe stood and began pacing. "And embarrassed the family? No way. They'd either kill me or Joanne would take over and I'd disappear from the equation. Taking over is her favorite thing, whether you want her to or not. She's a control freak. Besides, they're paying for my school. Again. I admit I've had a few false starts. I thought I wanted to teach, but hated it, so I went back to get a master's in communications, but I really couldn't get into that, so I worked for a couple years. But oceanography is what I really want to do. I've always been great at math and science. That's the other thing that's so absurd, my getting pregnant now, just when I've found something I really want to do." Jess listened, amazed at how Zoe could talk. "So now, what the hell am I going to do?"

Jess wondered why she suddenly felt that Zoe's pregnancy was her problem, too. Zoe took a breath and sat down, spun out. Jess sighed too, wondering what to say next. "Well, you have a lot of options," she finally remarked, trying to sound optimistic. Zoe obviously needed to talk. But wasn't that what mothers were for, even adoptive mothers? Jess took a sip of coffee, steeling herself against being dragged into Zoe's turmoil.

"Three. I can have the baby and raise it myself, have an abortion—or have the baby and get married," she said with disgust.

"You wouldn't consider giving the baby up for adoption?"

"I would never do that to anyone," Zoe said slowly, as if Jess had suggested infanticide.

"What about the father?"

"A jerk."

"Do you have a picture of him?" Zoe flipped through the pictures and unveiled the photograph of the young man. He was of indeterminate ethnic origin and wore a flannel shirt, jeans, hiking boots. He knelt against a sunlit rock with his arm around a golden retriever. "He's very handsome."

"Well, looks can be deceiving. His name is Adam and that's Zeke, his golden. We broke up because he cheated on me—the guy, not the dog. It's very complicated."

"Does he know you're pregnant?"

"I already told you, no one knows but you and Annabelle. That's her." Zoe held up a picture of a young woman with pale skin pierced at the nose and mouth. She had cropped black hair and wore purple lipstick. She sat in a cafe smoking a cigarette and looking confident. "Annabelle thinks I should definitely have an abortion, no question. She's had one and she says she'll go with me."

"Let's go back to Adam. Were you two serious? How long were you together?"

"I met him eight years ago when I worked at Outward Bound—he was one of the guides. I was training to be one. I was supposed to learn survival skills so I could teach them to others, instead I fell in love with a Puerto Rican guy from Seattle. Well, his mother's Puerto Rican. His father's American—well, French,

English and a little of three other nationalities. We've been together since I moved out there. But none of that matters. This is my choice, not his."

Jess thought she should attempt to be objective. "Don't you think he should be a part of the discussion? You two must have feelings for each other." Zoe glared at Jess and she back-pedaled. "But, you're right. Ultimately, it is your body and you have to do what's right for you. It's never an easy decision."

"I have the 'right to choose,' isn't that what your generation was always chanting about?"

"We did more than chant." You little ingrate, thought Jess.

"You knew my mother. What do you think she'd want me to do?"

"I don't know."

"Didn't she even wonder about what happened to me?"

"She once told me she thought of you every day. She wondered whether you were happy, whether she had made the right decision."

Zoe stood and began pacing Jess's galley kitchen again. "Well, she didn't. And don't tell me how lucky I was to be chosen by my adoptive parents. The way I figure it, if you can be chosen you can also be un-chosen. Because when you're adopted there's no such thing as unconditional love, you know. That's something you can only get from your real mother, and mine apparently wasn't up to the job."

Zoe's spiteful tone angered Jess. "How can you say that?" she asked. And where did you get a chip that big? she wanted to add. Instead she said, "You don't know anything about your mother's circumstances."

"That's why I'm here, so tell me."

Jess fought the urge to send Zoe packing, and searched her memory for something to tell her about Holly, something bright and upbeat, maybe even charming, about their early years togeth-er. But all she saw was Holly's withering body, her yellow skin, the too-soon funeral. She began slowly, with the facts.

"We were dorm roommates freshman year. The university bureaucrats threw us together in the roommate shuffle and we were inseparable from that moment on."

"So you were a lot alike?"

"Not one bit." Zoe looked surprised. "Holly read books; I read *Cliff's Notes*. Holly played sports in high school; I was a cheerleader. She spent a lot of time alone; I pledged a sorority—"

"Wait, I just read something about a sorority. Hold on a sec-ond." Zoe hurried to the living room and Jess was sorry she'd never looked through the box, Holly's final gift. Zoe came rushing back with a tattered blue spiral book. She began reading and her voice sounded smooth and rich as she entered her mother's thoughts. Soon Jess was mesmerized by her tone.

November 6, 1968

Guess what? I'm going to be a Tri Delt! They still have to vote me in—but Jess says she'll be my advocate and it'll be a cinch. All this happened tonight while Jess and I were studying in the Union lounge. Jess made sure we were sitting in just the right spot—where we could both see and be seen—because she was hoping to run into a guy she'd talked to at a sorority mixer, Dean somebody or other.

I was reading *The Courage to Be*, by Professor Paul Tillich. Tillich says that angst and anxiety are inescapable. But I couldn't see one ounce of angst in the student lounge—a large open room filled with plush couches and chairs, oak coffee tables, new car-peting. The sorority and fraternity types study there and everyone wears the same uniform, slacks and skirts, button down shirts and V-neck sweaters. But even in that room filled with starched cotton, you could feel the underlying current. Sex. It was everywhere, in the looks across the room, the crossing and uncrossing of nyloned legs, the brushing against bodies in passing, the pins, the hand-holding. All there, just below the surface, sex, sex, sex. No angst. No inescapable anxiety. Sex.

Jess and I talk about sex all the time. She's already slept with Gene. I told her I thought it was a big mistake because if she'd gotten pregnant, she'd have to leave school and her family would disown her. I keep telling her that's what people in small town Iowa do. She teases me and says that people in Maywood, Illinois are just as bad. She keeps threatening to take me to a doctor for birth control pills so I can at least "have the option," as she calls it—she's big on options. She's on the pill but I'm going to wait until I get married. Randy isn't happy about it, but I'm not taking any chances.

We studied for a while, until the guy Jess thinks she can't live without walked into the lounge. He was tall and dark with curly hair and looked like he'd come from a family where his mother always made sure he walked out the door with ironed shirts and creases down the center of his pants. And he was really cute.

He scanned the room, taking everyone in at a glance—a king surveying his court. Then it looked like he was looking at us, at Jess. She made herself all tall and turned her face up to him from across the room. I could see the half smile on her lips, ready to crack into a full grin. Then the girl sitting next to us stood and waved to him. And he waved back. And the girl was gorgeous. I watched Jess's face pull back.

According to Jess, she's a Kappa Kappa Gamma, and Kappa's are supposedly the prettiest and smartest girls on campus. I tried to find some flaw to relate to Jess, so she wouldn't feel bad, but the Kappa had none. She was beyond beautiful. Her skin was even and pink, her blond hair fell into a perfect flip—a Breck Girl in the flesh. We watched him stroll over to her, scoop her up, whisk her away. It was over in seconds.

"He didn't even say hello to you," I protested.

"He didn't even see me." Jess was hurt.

"The creep," I offered, trying to lessen the sting. It didn't work. I tried again. "She wasn't that great, anyway."

"It doesn't matter." I knew it wasn't me she was trying to convince. "We've got to study."

I dove back into the abyss and the existential void. Professor Tillich says that because human beings are aware that they're going to die, they have this anxiety, which leads to emptiness and meaninglessness, to the abyss. Finding the abyss is important because otherwise you can't live authentically, with courage. There was no abyss in the sex-filled student lounge, so I tried to look for it inside myself, and closed my eyes. I'm going to die, I'm going to die, I repeated over and over in my mind. No anxiety, no abyss. Try to feel it, I told myself, try to really feel it. "I'm going to die, I'm going to die." I must have said it out loud because Jess elbowed me

"What are you doing?" she whispered, in an annoyed tone.

I opened one eye and looked at her. "Searching for the abyss."

"You're doing what?"

I opened the other eye, annoyed myself now. "Looking for the abyss," I said louder, and several coeds turned and stared, then turned away.

"Any luck?" she smirked.

I shook my head. "I must not be looking hard enough. I can't feel it, do you know what I mean?"

"If you want to know the truth, I think Paul Tillich sucks." Jess isn't big on religious philosophy.

"You can't say that about him; it says here he's a 'world-renowned theologian.'"

"That doesn't make him God," answered Jess. "Let me see that." I handed her my book and she read from the back cover. "Listen to this: 'His discussion of how to take this inescapable anxiety upon oneself has evoked warm praise from an exceptionally wide range of opinion.'"

"So?"

"So, maybe there's a 'how-to' section. You probably haven't read far enough." Silence. "Why do you want to feel inescapable anxiety, anyway?"

"Because it's inescapable."

"If it's inescapable, you should already be feeling it," Jess pronounced.

"That's just it. I don't feel it. But I want to. I want to feel every bit of everything. Jess," I said with bravado, "according to Tillich, you can't have real courage until you've faced the abyss, nonbeing, death."

"You want courage?"

"Of course."

"You're not going to find it in that book."

"Probably not." Jess handed my book back and I doubted whether I'd ever understand anything.

"Are you up for something to eat?"

"Always."

We walked downstairs to the basement of the Union, through the Pit, on our way to the cafeteria. The Pit has low ceilings and is always dark and dirty. It's as seedy as the train station in downtown Chicago, and I always walk through it fast, to keep the seediness from attaching itself to me. We bought fries and Tabs at the cafeteria and were on our way to the Wheel Room where the sorority and fraternity types eat, when Jess said: "Let's sit in the Pit."

"Why?"

"Better people watching."

"Why not?" I was suddenly game. "Maybe I'll find the abyss there."

Jess wiped off a wobbly Formica table with her napkin, then we sat on two orange plastic chairs. We looked around; not one head turned. Smoke hovered in the air, nobody had on penny loafers and there wasn't a V-neck sweater in sight. People were dressed like they were going to scrub floors. And instead of straight backs and sidewise glances, people were lounging, occupying the furniture with their bodies. There was a darker sexuality in the air there. It seemed dangerous, too. And that made it exciting.

Some people were studying, others were sleeping, but most had their heads tipped close in conversation. I imagined profound thoughts mingling with the heavy air. "People are really talking," I said to Jess. "It's not like that superficial bullshit upstairs."

"It's too smoky."

"I like it." Jess and I sat in our coed outfits, gawking at the counterculture. No one gawked back. I thought the people there looked smarter than the ones competing for the perfect flip—that this might be a place where what you thought was more important than how you looked. And the darkness and the squalor and the smoke were part of the scene. I was enjoying the intensity when two guys walked up. The guy with the short blonde ponytail spoke.

"Why, Jess Martin, what are you doing here?"

"Trying to stay cool. What about you?"

"This is my table."

"I didn't see your name on it."

"You're not looking at it with the right eyes." He was well-built and medium tall, with deep blue eyes. He wore blue jeans and a sweater with holes in it, with a dark green jacket over it. I wondered how many other holes he had in the sweater and why he'd wear a sweater with holes in it in the first place.

"This is my roommate, Holly O'Neal," said Jess. "Holly, this is Mark Bates. Mark's a Sig Ep."

"And this is David Delaney," Mark said. His shadow of a friend had white skin, shoulder-length dark hair and a mustache. He nodded hello, then stood there with a sheepish grin on his narrow face. He had the saddest brown eyes I've ever seen. I liked him immediately.

I wanted to say something witty, but all I managed was, "Hi."

"You girls look like you're at the zoo," Mark said.

"Yes, but we're the animals and everyone else in here is human," retorted Jess, and they laughed, and I wish I'd said it.

Say something, I told myself. Just say something. "I like your jacket." Dumb!

"Thanks," said Mark. "It's an army jacket. I got it at the surplus store."

"What's a surplus store?" I asked.

"The army-surplus store, in Coralville. You can get great clothes, cheap." I wondered why anybody would want cheap clothes.

"Here, try it on." Mark Bates took off his jacket and handed it to me. I stood and slipped it on over my V-neck sweater. It hung down almost to my knees, but it felt roomy and warm. "What do you think, Jess?"

"Looks interesting."

"I think it's cool," I said, posing.

"Tough. Really tough," said Mark.

"I like it. Can I keep it?"

"Sure," Mark said. "Why not?"

"I was just kidding." I started taking it off.

"Keep it."

"I couldn't."

"Why not?" Mark asked. "Nothing's really ours, anyway. It's all an illusion, owning things."

I took off the jacket and handed it back to him. "I can't. It's not right."

"Suit yourself," he said, throwing the jacket over his shoulder. I noticed then that his entire sweater had holes in it, as if it had been sustaining a closet of moths for a decade. "What's new and exciting with you, Jess?"

"Holly and I are down here looking for the abyss."

Mark laughed. "If you chicks really want to find the abyss, let's go back to our fraternity house and smoke some pot." I didn't say anything; Jess laughed nervously. "You have smoked dope?"

"Of course not—"

"But it sounds cool," I said.

"You really should try it. It's groovy—"

"Some other time," Jess interrupted.

"Let me know. We'd like to be the first to turn both of you on, right David?" David laughed, shuffled his feet and looked down. He was cute—but terribly shy.

"I bet you would," replied Jess.

"We have to go. Are you sure you don't want my jacket, Holly? It looks great on you."

"No thanks. But thanks."

"Say the word and it's yours. Good-bye girls." And he winked. At me. Jess smiled fakely at him as she grabbed my arm and pulled me toward the stairs. I felt like a universe had opened a crack, and I wanted to stay in that room. Jess had the opposite reaction.

"Those are frat boys turned drug pushers. I don't want you

hanging around them."

"I'll hang around whomever I want to," I informed her.

"You don't get it, do you?"

"What is the matter with you?"

"They'll have you hooked so fast, you'll be smashing Coke bottles against garage doors, and the broken glass will cut your mouth, and you'll pass out and bleed to death!"

"What are you talking about?" Jess can be so dramatic.

"I'm talking about pot, marijuana."

"Oh, and now you're going to tell me that smoking grass leads to shooting heroin? You're crazy. Besides, I almost got a jacket out of it."

"That's how they do it. 'I give you this and then you owe me that,' and pretty soon you're hooked. Why are you looking at me like that?"

I told her what a hypocrite I thought she was. "Where's Miss I'll-try-anything-once? Where's Miss You-only-live-once, you'd better grab every experience you can? You sound like an old lady. Why don't we just pull out the knitting needles and get to work making sweaters for our grandchildren?" That got her.

"All right, all right. You just can't be too careful these days."

"Give me a break." She laughed at herself as we came to the top of the stairs and re-entered the student lounge. I was 100 percent self-conscious feeling the eyes of a dozen coeds sizing us up as we walked to our seats. I looked around at the penny loafers and the good wool skirts and the homecoming queen smiles, and I thought about Mark Bates' jacket, earthy and warm. And I wondered where in the world Holly O'Neal belonged. Where was my Mr. Right? I had a feeling he might be in the Pit, but Mother Superior Jess would never allow me back there, so we'd never meet.

Jess started working on a rhetoric speech on capital punishment; I got sicker and sicker reading Paul Tillich. "The anxiety of emptiness drives us to the abyss of meaninglessness." Should I get out the gun? Is the bridge over the Iowa River high enough? I whispered to Jess that I couldn't last a second longer, and we left.

We walked up the hill to the dorm in silence and I felt like Sisyphus, destined to roll my rock forever, never arriving at the top. The only noise was the leaves crunching under our loafers, until Jess spoke.

"Holly, I've been thinking. You really ought to get out more. You ought to meet some decent people—"

"I get out plenty. I know lots of decent people."

"You hardly go anywhere. You need to meet new people."

"I don't want to meet new people." She ignored me.

"I was thinking, maybe—if you want—when second semester starts, some of the pledges won't make grades, there'll be another open house—and if you want—I'll recommend you to the Tri Delts. We could be sorority sisters, we could room together next year, you could meet new people, new guys, nice guys."

It was as if she'd taken the boulder I was pushing and tossed it into the air, where it floated light as helium to the sun. Goodbye, emptiness. Au revoir, anxiety. Jess would help me get it right. She was offering me a place, a home. I took in a cold breath and held it, afraid to let out the "yes" I wanted to scream.

I forgot all about the Pit and the people who'd intrigued me. I could be a Tri Delt! I could belong to a place where Jess would be, where I'd meet charming people and make friends, and maybe, just maybe, he would be there, the man for me. I thought, Yes, I can be a part of that. I could learn to do my hair in the perfect flip.

"It was only an idea," said Jess.

"I want to do it. I really want to do it."

"You do?" She sounded excited. "Holly, it'll be great. You

can pledge in the spring—we'll move into the sorority in the fall. In the meantime, we'll go to mixers and I'll introduce you to everyone. You'll love them, you wait and see . . ." Jess went on, and I kept nodding. She made it sound so simple.

I thought about the Breck Girl at the Union, the way her face lit up when she saw Dean walk into the room and the magic between them. That's how I want the world to be, like that look. And that's how it will be, every day. At the sorority I'll make friends for life—friends like Jess. I'll be Holly O'Neal—Tri Delt—successful wife—successful mother. I'll have a career, too, something I can fall back on when my children are grown.

We went to bed, but a dream woke me up, which is why I'm in the lounge writing this. In my dream, Jess and I were on a tropical island and our children were building sandcastles near the water—her brown-haired boy, my fair-haired girl. Nearby our husbands snorkeled, and she and I sat reading and talking and laughing under a big yellow beach umbrella. And Paul Tillich and Mark Bates and the abyss were cordoned off with a purple velvet rope far off in the distance, not allowed anywhere near our perfectly beautiful lives.

CHAPTER THREE

Zoe stopped reading and closed the diary. Her voice sounded so much like Holly's, even in its inflection, that Jess wished she hadn't stopped. She suddenly ached to have Holly sitting next to her. If Holly were here, Jess thought, she'd commiserate with me about life, tell me what to do about Eric.

Zoe broke the silence. "My mother dreamt of having a family. But she never did, except for me. And now she's dead and it's too late." Zoe pouted; Jess bristled. You never even bothered to answer her letter, she thought. How dare you miss her.

"Randy was my mother's boyfriend?" The question was curt, insistent.

Jess answered coolly. "Yes." Zoe waited. "He was her high school boyfriend, he was a year older."

"Did she ever sleep with him?"

"Yes."

"Is he my father?"

"No."

"So, I guess Holly changed her mind about waiting until she got married to have sex." It was the first time Zoe had used her mother's name.

"We threw out a lot of conventions back than; virginity was

one of the first to go." Jess smiled at the memory of Holly, shaking her awake that Monday morning.

"Do you remember something? Tell me."

"Nothing, really." Again, Zoe waited. "I stole the Kinsey Report on male sexuality from the library, and Holly stayed up all night reading it. The next morning she said she was going all the way with Randy. She'd read that most high school boys had sex, and she thought that was grossly unfair because she'd spent her high school days saying no. I think she decided to get even." Jess had told too much and turned away. She wasn't about to discuss Holly's sex life.

"Annabelle and I think that in this new millennium sex will be passé." Jess turned back and looked skeptically at her guest. "It's so overdone. It's sickening how sex is always used in advertising to seduce people to buy things."

"Be careful, I work in advertising. And we prefer to call it selling a lifestyle."

"No way. You're selling sex. There are men and women in their underwear on the side of every bus. People in jeans commercials practically have orgasms on television. You can have virtual sex on your computer. Victoria's Secret and *Cosmopolitan* tell us exactly what to wear and how to act to please a man in bed. It's so dishonest. I mean, when was the last time you had sex that was anything like what you see on television or in the movies? Why bother?"

Interesting commentary coming from a pregnant woman, Jess thought. She was about to defend her career choice when Zoe interjected.

"I stopped taking the pill five months ago."

The confession startled Jess. You idiot, was her mental response.

"I read on the Internet that some birth control pills are made from the uterus of a spotted leopard that's almost extinct, so Annabelle and I both stopped taking them, in protest. Anyway, this wasn't entirely my fault. Adam and I went camping. I thought he was bringing the condoms, he thought I had them. I don't even like to camp that much." Zoe looked away and blinked back tears.

Before Jess could come up with an innocuous response, the phone rang. She went to her office to answer it, leaving Zoe to her confusion. It was Jess's assistant, Carole.

"Yes, I know, it's nearly 6:30 on a Friday and I'm still at the office." Carole sounded spent.

"What's up?" Jess shifted the phone to her left hand.

"I was getting ready to leave when Bob handed me the Clorox proposal and I knew you'd want it. How are you doing?"

"I could be better. I'll be fine."

"Did you take a hot bath?"

"Bath salts, bubble bath, the works. I'll get over it, Carole. It was one pitch."

"Of course."

"Who's still there?"

"Dennis and Harper. She has that shoot tomorrow." I should have gone back to the office, Jess thought. Carole continued. "They're shooting the beach segment of the 501 commercial."

"Right. Well, you should go home and take a relaxing bath yourself. Fax me the proposal and I'll take it from there. And thanks, Carole, you're the best. Talk to you Monday."

"Don't kill yourself over this. You're right, it was one pitch. Oh, FYI, I lent the ProbTech file to Harper."

"You did what?"

"She just stopped by and asked me for it."

The last thing Jess wanted was Harper critiquing her fall. "You should have called me first."

"But you told me Harper could review any of your presentations. Has something changed?"

"Oh, right. But, hell, Carole, it's embarrassing enough to have failed in front of my own team. Well, from now on, she only gets to see the winners."

"Absolutely. I'm sorry."

"It's not your fault, you're still the best."

"If I were the best I could get you to take a weekend off."

"Not likely, work is my life. Have a good one." Jess hung up and frowned at the thought of Harper poring over the ProbTech mess.

At 26, Harper Wainwright was one of the brightest associates in the agency. She'd been with the firm a year and had already been promoted to creative coordinator. Figuring the best defense was a good offense, Jess befriended the rising star and offered to help her on two big projects. Unfortunately, Jess had also given her carte blanche to review her presentations. "Never again," she muttered. As the fax machine began its familiar hum, Jess picked up the first page and began reading.

Zoe entered the living room, took a sip of tea and began rummaging among her mother's treasures. She felt a rush of guilt. Why didn't you write back when you got her letter? she berated herself. She'd spent her life fantasizing about a reunion with the woman who gave her away. She always imagined that Holly would come for her one day and answer the questions she'd spent her life puzzling over: Did you love my father? Did he love you? Did you love me, and if you did, why did you give me away? And why, oh, why did you wait so long to find me? She felt the tears welling. "Stop it!" Zoe chastised herself. Maybe if she committed the diaries to memory she might conjure up her mother, and a ghost vision of Holly would appear, to rescue her. But that wouldn't happen. Life would always be tragic and there was no escaping from it. She sighed, picked up the worn blue journal and continued reading.

The phone rang again, startling Jess. It was Carole.

"I had my coat on and was heading out the door when Bob stopped by. He asked if you'd looked over the proposal."

"I'm reading it now, and there's something wrong with the numbers on the unaided awareness research. Do you know where he got them?"

"No, but hold a second and I'll find out." Jess continued reading until Carole returned. "He said he took them off the server. Aren't they right?"

"Shit. I was supposed to update that data last week. The new numbers are somewhere on my hard drive, I just forgot to post them. But don't tell him that, tell him I need more time to review his proposal. Tell him I'll fax it to him later, either tonight or first thing in the morning."

"You're coming in tomorrow?"

"No, tonight. God, Carole, I'm losing it. Everything is falling through the cracks."

"No way, Jess. You always manage to stay on top of things."

"Not any more. Look, I'm on my way. You go home. But do me a favor and get that file from Harper first. Tell her I need to work on it this weekend." Jess hung up and grabbed her coat from her office chair. She thought of Harper, Dennis, Bob and the rest of them. Young, fresh, talented, and on their way up.

Curled up on the sofa, Zoe took a sip of tea, then turned another page. She jumped when Jess appeared in the doorway. "Did my mother join your sorority?"

"No, she had other plans," Jess answered, her voice brusque. "I have to go into my office. I shouldn't be more than an hour. You're welcome to stay if you like. I can give you a ride to your friends' house when I get back." She set her business card on the coffee table and was glad to get away from the box filled with its distracting memories.

Jess climbed into her dark green BMW convertible and drove down Potrero. She turned up the volume on her Natalie Merchant CD and tried to ignore the uneasiness in her stomach. Holly would call it existential anxiety. Jess knew it was anxiety over fucking up royally. She raced through the intersection, just missing a turning car. The driver honked long and hard.

Everything was coming unhinged and Jess had no idea how to fix it. Work harder, keep your head down, that's what her mother would tell her. Work smarter, see the big picture, was always Eric's advice. The anxiety increased and she searched through her purse for cigarettes, then the glove box, with luck. Years ago she'd promised Holly that she'd quit, and she had, for a minute. But her demons always seemed to find their way back into her life, no matter how tightly she kept the doors locked and windows sealed. She'd made herself hundreds of incremental promises: I'll never smoke in the car, I'll never fuck Eric in my bed, I'll only have one drink after dinner.

What would Holly think of me now? she wondered. And what would she think of Zoe? "Overindulged" came immediately to mind. But that wasn't fair, Jess admitted. She didn't know much about Zoe's life, but it seemed she had parents who provided for her. Holly would be pleased about that.

Then Jess thought about Holly reading the Kinsey Report and smiled, remembering more of their first year together. As she drove down Market Street, she recalled the morning Holly tugged her awake to tell her she'd decided to have sex for the first time.

"I'm going all the way with Randy," Holly announced. "According to Kinsey, 70 percent of the boys in high school have sex. Just who are they having sex with? It isn't fair. I refuse to be a prisoner of my ovaries."

Holly wanted to be prepared for the big "twirl" as they called it, so Jess took charge. She bought her a short, see-through, white baby doll nightie with fake pink fur around the collar. When Jess finally coaxed her into trying it on, Holly complained about how much it revealed, but Jess insisted it was perfect. She took Holly to get birth control pills and showed her how to draw a sexy blue line of shadow across the top of her upper lid, complemented with a streak of black eyeliner on the lower. When Holly had sex for the first time, she was armed with all the facts and every boudoir accessory known to woman.

Jess smiled, thinking of their naiveté. Then she remembered that when Holly came back from her big weekend, she wasn't bursting with joy. She'd taken the pills, worn the outfit, put on the makeup. Randy loved it: Holly hated it. She said that having sex was a lot like shaking hands and that she'd never again wear any-thing to bed but her Iowa T-shirt.

Jess had wanted Holly's first time to be better than her own. She and Gene had urgent sex in his dorm room, with his room-mate passed out in the next bed. She remembered Gene's cold hands pulling at her and how her body had felt detached from her head. She'd always imagined that making love would be gentle and slow, and she was sure that if she'd had the right negligee and the candles, the romance would have followed.

The ash of Jess's cigarette fell onto the leather seat. She quick-ly snuffed it out and checked for damage. Then her mind wan-dered back to thoughts of sex. Romance. She thought of Eric, how gentle and romantic he'd been the first time they made love. She remembered their first kiss. They'd worked late the night before her first presentation to one of his big accounts, then shared drinks at Bix to celebrate. Back at the office, he kissed her in the elevator, tenderly, passionately, and she drove home feeling that she might finally get everything she ever wanted.

The next day she was on fire and the clients said they'd never seen such a dynamic campaign. They finished around 2:00 and she sent her creative team to lunch. Eric told her he wanted to go over some presentation points with her alone. They met in the bar at the Mark Hopkins, checked into a room in less than half an hour and spent the afternoon in a fiery embrace. He was passionate and made love to her every way: tenderly, intensely, insistently, but always lovingly. Afterward, she'd been breathless. She'd been won.

Then, as her self-appointed mentor, he'd helped Jess pass her rivals, and her career skyrocketed. After her divorce, Jess had been determined to restart her career, but it wasn't until she had Eric's help that she was able to break into management. She was indebted to him and he was always quick to remind her how hard he'd worked to make her a star. But that's Eric, she thought. He always has to take the credit. Eric said he loved her, but despite many late night promises, after several years they were still illicit lovers, sharing moments stolen from his wife, daughter, work.

Jess felt a cold chill as she thought about the ProbTech meeting. As she turned off Market Street she reviewed the night Eric left for Hong Kong. It was the first night in weeks they'd gotten away for dinner, and she'd been hungry to see him. He talked at length about the client, the project, the campaign goals and how important the account was to him.

She was sure he'd told her the campaign was geared to 35-to-45-year-olds. He'd seemed interested in some of her initial ideas. Hadn't he? She remembered taking notes that night, but her mind had wandered. The other couples in the restaurant looked so romantic. Watching them, Jess felt like Eric's workhorse.

After dinner, they'd gone back to the agency and made love in Eric's office overlooking the bay, something they hadn't done in a long time. Eric had been excited but distant and not at all tender.

Afterward, he stood up and closed the button on his slacks as though he'd just finished the last meeting of the day and was anxious to get home. They parted as they always did, in different elevators to alleviate suspicion. It wasn't the first time Jess felt cheap. But this time, she was also troubled by the detached look in Eric's eyes when the elevator door closed and she rode down first, alone.

She longed for the return of romance. Perhaps after she saved herself from this debacle, she and Eric could sneak away for a weekend.

Jess negotiated the turn onto California and headed for Sansome, to the agency's parking lot. She'd make it right and Eric would be proud of her again. She'd pick up the ProbTech file from Harper and start in immediately on the new creative strategy. As she slowed down, she spotted Eric's car pulling out of the lot and turning in the opposite direction. He'd said he was going straight home. Why had he gone to the office? He probably wanted to check on the day's fiasco himself. She really had fucked up.

Jess pulled into her parking spot next to Dennis's VW Jetta. She locked her doors and thought of Dennis and Harper putting in long hours, their creative juices flowing, still excited by big dreams and the material measure of success. She entered through the back so she wouldn't have to face their youthful exuberance.

Two women from the cleaning service were busy dusting plants and emptying trash from the sea of cubicles. They smiled as she passed through the glass doors into the executive suites. She turned on her desk lamp, preferring its soft golden glow to the overhead fluorescent light with its stark unflattering brilliance. She glanced at the mess in her office, then focused on her desk. No ProbTech file in sight. She picked up the stack of files from the credenza and flipped through them, without success. She looked in her In Box, overflowing with work shouting for her attention. "Damn," she muttered out loud, "Harper must still have it." As she headed toward Harper's cubicle she ran into Dennis, bouncing down the aisle, headphones so loud she could hear the song lyrics.

She pointed toward Harper's desk and Dennis answered with a loud, "Just missed her, she left about 15 minutes ago." He grinned and bounced down the aisle. Goddamn it, she thought. Once Dennis had disappeared into his cube, she searched Harper's desk, but found no file.

She'd have to borrow Eric's. He'll never know, she told herself. I'll have it back before he comes in Monday. Eric and the other account execs had offices across the executive suite from the creative directors. Jess opened Eric's office door and glanced at the familiar setting: dark mahogany desk and credenza, abstract art on the wall—original paintings by a well known local artist—the burgundy leather sofa with tapestry pillows where she and Eric had made love so many times. She opened the cabinet labeled H – T and looked for Eric's file. The hanging folder labeled ProbTech was there, but it was empty.

Maybe that's why he came to the office, Jess thought, to review the request for proposal so he'd know how badly I've screwed up. The knot in her stomach tightened. She'd have to start from scratch, come up with a new concept without any of the background information from the file.

Jess closed the drawer and quickly returned to her office. She turned on her computer, found the new data Bob needed and sent it to the main server. She made a note on his proposal telling him to recheck the data and faxed it to his home. All bases covered, she sped away, anxious to get started on the proposal and redeem herself. Then she remembered her unwelcome guest. As she turned off Market Street, Jess spotted a parking place in front of her favorite Thai restaurant. Perfect, she thought. I'll stop for takeout, feed her, then send her on her way.

CHAPTER FOUR

Jess shut the front door and Zoe sat alone. She closed the blue journal and tears rolled down her cheeks. She felt nauseous and she knew it wasn't from the pregnancy. It was the familiar feeling that she was hopelessly isolated and always would be. But now she really was alone, without Adam, without Joanne or Paul or Annabelle. Alone except for this thing growing inside of her. She hugged the pillow to her stomach and pounded it, cursing her life. "I don't want to be pregnant, I want to be home eating Chinese takeout in bed with Adam and watching music videos with Annabelle. I want to be anywhere but here, so pitifully alone. Damn you Adam!"

Zoe wiped her eyes, went to the kitchen, picked up the telephone receiver. The last time she'd talked to Adam, he said he was sorry for the hundredth time and asked her to forgive him. That was before she left for good, before Meredith took her place. She thought of Adam's toothy smile, his large soft hands, his boyish laugh. She dialed his number and let it ring twice, then quickly hung up. He didn't deserve to know. "You fucking cheater. I hate you."

She dialed Annabelle's number. After her message played out, Zoe filled the machine—she'd found her mother's friend, her mother had left these journals, tons of them, she was reading through them now, Jess said she could keep them. Had Annabelle had a chance to spy on Adam? Was he still with her? Zoe was tempted to call the Starbucks where Annabelle worked, but knew she wouldn't have time to talk. She clicked the phone off.

On a shelf she spotted the *Yellow Pages* and opened them, looking for an answer. "Abortion Alternatives." "Abortion Services." "Adoption." All of them advertised that they were "confidential, professional and caring." "Right," Zoe said, slamming the directory shut. Annabelle had taken her to abortion counseling. But when she was alone, the questions came flooding back. What if she regretted the decision? What if she had the baby and gave it away and regretted that decision? The adoption services advertised that they allowed the mother to choose the baby's new parents; that seemed so arbitrary. Could she do that? Would Holly have chosen Joanne and Paul? The abortion services had same-day service. All this torment could be over in a day.

She threw the book to the floor. She had to find her father, to learn why he'd agreed to the adoption and she needed to know how Holly could have given her away once she'd held her in her arms. How could that ever be the right thing to do?

Zoe pulled an envelope from her backpack and re-read the letter she'd received from Catholic Charities.

October 2, 1995
Dear Sarah,
My name is Holly O'Neal and I'm your birth mother. I'm writing to let you know that there hasn't been a single day in 25 years that I haven't thought of you. On every one of your birthdays I've made the same wish—that you are loved and that your life is happy and full of joy. I want you to understand why I made the choice I did. At the time, I

was so young and had so little to give you. It was the most difficult thing I've ever done, but I wanted more than anything for you to have a good life. I'm sure you've grown into a wonderful young woman, and I would love to get to know you—if that's your wish, too. If not, I'll understand. Please know that I have always loved you and I hope that someday you'll understand that giving you away was the right thing to do. And I hope you will forgive me for it.

Holly

P.S. I'm sending along a memento which I've kept all these years. I want you to have it. I know your name is Sarah now, but when you were born this is the name I liked. Zoe means life in Greek.

Zoe folded the letter away and retrieved the velvet pouch from the corner of the envelope. Inside was a tiny pink hospital bracelet, with the name her mother had chosen. Zoe was still living at home when she'd received the letter. It had angered her. How dare this woman try to endear herself after so many years of silence?

Zoe had taken her anger out on Joanne, who was trying hard to maintain her own equanimity. Finally, it was Joanne who suggested that Zoe contact her birth mother. That angered Zoe even more, and she accused Joanne of wanting to be rid of her. "All I've done is cause you trouble, so now you want to pass me off on her," Zoe said. "How convenient. Just pass the little bastard around." Zoe turned each of Joanne's attempts to comfort into a confrontation. When the undercurrent of anger became too much for either of them to bear, Zoe moved to Seattle to be with Adam.

Zoe stuffed the bracelet back into the pouch and buried it in her backpack. With a deep sigh she went back into the living room. She stared at the sofa with its pile of journals, then sat, opened the blue journal again and buried herself in her mother's world. She'd read until she understood who her mother was. Maybe then she'd know what to do. She tried to imagine Holly as a young woman, a college student, sitting in her dorm room, waiting for her best friend.

December 19, 1968

It's the night before we leave for Christmas break, and Jess and I are going to exchange gifts when she gets back—she's at the sorority, studying. I bought her the Beatles white album, which she's eager to add to her collection. It seems like yesterday that I walked into this room and saw Jess holding records stacked to her chin. Now it's Christmas and since I've been here I've lived in another universe. I think I've actually felt happiness.

I'm rereading *The Courage to Be* for finals and trying to find the truth in it. According to Tillich, the abyss is always nearby, threatening to undermine man's affirmation of himself. I think that's how it's always been for me. Until I came to school, I felt like I didn't exist, like if I disappeared tomorrow no one would notice. I don't want to go home.

Mother's mantra is always a variation on a theme: "Don't embarrass me," "Don't get yourself in trouble," "Don't make a scene." Talk about undermining affirmation! And Dad's always busy making pie-in-the-sky business deals, drinking to celebrate those deals, then drinking even more when the deals fall through because of all the drinking. He doesn't notice any of us, except for Edward, of course. He always has time for Edward, the crowned prince, the heir apparent, the creep!

I decorated our room with red and green crepe paper, bought a bottle of Seagrams 7 from the girls downstairs and opened the album. Figured Jess wouldn't mind if I broke it in. Thank God Jess has a record player. I've asked for a Zenith Circle of Sound stereo for Christmas, but I won't get it. Maggie says Dad's latest get-rich-quick scheme, something about oil filters for cars that clean your oil and make it last for years, collapsed, and money at home is predictably tight. "Ob-La-Di, Ob-La-Da." Life goes on. I love that song, because life does go on and money doesn't matter. I could live on practically nothing, because money doesn't rule the world, ideas do. I feel like I could spend my life in a room with books, chewing and digesting them. Idea-eating. I could open a restaurant and serve ideas.

Later

Jess is late. It's snowing. I wonder if it will be different at home now that I'm so different. Surely they'll see how much I've changed and they'll pay attention to what I have to say. I am so sick of being invisible.

Where can she be? I've been waiting forever. It's half past nine—I hope nothing happened.

I called her sorority, they told me she'd left. She's probably on her way.

Jess called. She's going out with that guy—Dean. He's in premed, whoop-dee-do. I told her it was okay but I lied, it's not okay. She's off with her rich frat boy and I'm here in this stupid dorm. I'm drinking the booze. Who cares? Things will be different next semester when I'm a Tri Delt, too. Maybe I'll call the girls downstairs and see if they'll drink with me. The Beatles are singing, "Happiness is a Warm Gun." Fuck you, Jess, and your groovy new boyfriend.

December 20

Jess didn't come home until just before hours. She tried to wake me, but I pretended to be asleep. This morning she brought me toast and juice in bed, trying to win back my good will. I ate the toast, although I wanted to kill the toast giver, who was telling me what a great time she had with Dean and how sophisticated and clever he is. She said that he's invited her to a big party in January, a toga party, and his roommate wants to take me. Well, he doesn't really want to take me, but he needs a date, so Jess and Dean want to fix us up. Jess told him I was cute and smart and sexy, so I guess I'll have to go and prove she's a liar! I'm on the bus, headed home for Christmas with a bad hangover and a feeling of doom. Before I left, I gave Jess the Beatles album and she said she loved it. She told me she had a special gift in mind for me, one she had to go to a special place to find. She promised it would be under my tree by Christmas.

December 29, 1968

Being home is like returning to a foreign land where you've once been poisoned by the food. Mother spends the days ordering Maggie and me around: "Fix your brother a sandwich, iron your brother's shirt, kiss your brother's ass!" I am the original Cinderella. Anyway, Mother is miserable and she wants us all to share it with her. Daddy has spent the whole time on a binge. At night he's loud and happy and full of himself, says he loves us and tells us we can do anything. The next day he's got the d.t.'s, is drinking milk, reading one of his right wing rags— "The blacks all have guns! They're going to revolt! Thank God we live in a poor neighborhood, maybe they'll spare us!"—and hardly says hello. I can't wait to get out of this fucking suburb and get back to Iowa! To sanity!

The only bright spot was the present I got from Jess. It's an army jacket, just like Mark Bates'. I love it so much and I wear it every day. Mother hates it, which makes me love it all the more.

Zoe marked her place with the rolling papers and closed the journal. She thought of her mother's family. Were her grandparents alive? She had an Aunt Maggie and an Uncle Edward. She wondered if they might look like her. They sounded as bizarre as her own family. But these people are my real family, Zoe thought, my blood relatives. Maggie had sounded cold. But Holly didn't. Through the pages of the journals her mother seemed full of life and full of pain, angst and anxiety. Zoe put on Holly's green army jacket and hugged it to her body. It had a strange, pungent odor. She dug into the pockets, pulled out a small bottle of patchouli oil and rubbed some on her wrist. Digging deeper she found a napkin from a place called Magoo's, a deposit slip from the Iowa State Bank and half a package of Juicy Fruit gum.

Popping a piece of stale gum, Zoe explored Jess's CD collection, then took out her own CD and put it in the player. She cranked up the volume and tried to bolster herself with "You Oughta Know," the Alanis Morissette song she couldn't stop playing. She wandered around Jess's apartment, then began looking for books. Joanne had always said you could tell a lot about a person from the books they read. In Jess's office Zoe found shelves filled with books on art, movies, fashion and advertising. Most of them looked new and unread. There were two shelves filled with paperback murder mysteries by women: Patricia Cornwell, Sue Grafton, Sara Paretsky. One half-filled shelf contained more well-worn paperbacks: *Woodstock Nation*; *Soul On Ice*; *Sisterhood Is Powerful*; *Our Bodies, Ourselves*; *The Future of an Illusion*; *Waiting for Godot*; *Nine Stories*. A Barbie lunch box served as their bookend. One wall was covered with awards: five Joey's, four Addy's, a Clio. The other featured a dozen photographs, mostly of Jess with celebrities. There was a photo of her with William Shatner signed personally to Jess, another of Tony Bennett and one of Bebe Neuwirth. The one of Jess with Andre Agassi wearing a cap with a sports drink label looked to be the most recent.

Zoe continued snooping. Within the office closet she found an alcove lined with shelves, stuffed to overflowing with old toys and board games. Most of the games had television themes like "Green Acres," "Dragnet," "Twilight Zone," but there were others, too, ones Zoe had never heard of: "Smog," "Pass Out," "Public Assistance."

She noticed one called, "What Shall I Be?" It was stuck between two other games and when she pulled it, the contents of all three came tumbling down. Boards, game pieces and cards flew everywhere.

"Oh, shit." Zoe scrambled out of the debris and began reassembling the games, gathering the playing boards and marrying them with the appropriate pieces. Then she heard a door open. "Shit. Shit!"

CHAPTER FIVE

Jess entered her front door laden with a large brown bag and her briefcase. She didn't see Zoe, so she turned down the blaring music and called out her name. Then she carried the bag to the kitchen and went searching. She found Zoe in her office, assembling board games.

"What are you doing in here?" Her voice was harsh.

"I fucked up. I can't do anything right. I opened this closet door and found this weird-sounding game, and when I started taking it down all these other games fell out. I'm sorry." Jess felt an urge to scold her, but Zoe seemed to be punishing herself, so Jess helped her complete the sets. They worked in silence until Zoe picked up the top from "What Shall I Be."

"Check this out. It's supposedly a career game for women, but look at your choices: model, nurse, flight attendant . . ."

"Stewardess," Jess corrected. "They weren't called flight attendants until later."

"Stewardess, actress, teacher, ballerina. Ballerina? Are they serious?"

"Unfortunately, I think so. Let me see the top." Jess looked at the side panel. "1966. Not that terribly long ago."

"This is a stupid game," Zoe said, reading the instructions.

"You pick these cards and they tell you what you'd be good at, or what you wouldn't." She picked up a card and read aloud. "'Your makeup is sloppy. Bad for Airline Hostess and Model.'"

Jess picked up another card. "'You are overweight. Bad for Airline Hostess, Ballet Dancer and Model.' Do they have anything positive to say?"

"Here's one," Zoe said. "'You are neat. Good for Airline Hostess, Teacher, Nurse and Model.'" Jess fitted the game board snugly on top.

"So where did you get all these?" Zoe asked.

"When I first moved to San Francisco I didn't know anyone, so I went to antique shows on weekends and started buying things that reminded me of home. It gave me something to do. Do you collect anything?"

"Bad karma."

Jess smiled and picked up the game. "Don't we all. Oh, I brought food home. Are you hungry?"

"Very."

"I brought some Thai food, vegetarian, no MSG. I doctor up the rice with garlic and herbs, so it'll take a minute."

"That sounds great."

"Come on, then. You can set the table while I cook."

Jess pulled out plates and a pan for the rice, then showed Zoe the silverware drawer. It was nearly 8:00. They'd be finished eating by 8:30. She could drop Zoe at her friends and get a few hours of work in before she was totally spent. She was about to suggest that they pack up the box when Zoe broke into her thoughts.

"Do you want me to read from one of Holly's journals while you cook?" Zoe asked, folding the second napkin. Jess said that would be fine, secretly glad for extra time to ponder her project. Zoe retrieved the journal and opened it to the spot marked by the rolling papers. While Jess tended the boiling rice, Holly's words stirred the air. And Jess began to remember.

January 28, 1969

The end of January already! Sorry I haven't written, but I've been busy and a lot has happened. We finished finals and I think I did well, especially on the Religion exam. But that isn't the most important thing I have to tell you. I ended up going to the toga party I was invited to by Jess's boyfriend's roommate, and it changed my life.

The party was the Saturday after finals. During that week, Jess—determined to enchant Dean—tried to figure out how to look like a Roman goddess. I watched from the sidelines as she took the white sheet she'd stolen from the maid and wrapped it seductively around her torso. She secured it with a cord and pins, then rearranged the folds, searching for the most flattering line.

"Holly, look at this. What do you think?" I was sitting on my bed staring at an algebra problem. She had the sheet wrapped around one shoulder.

"No cleavage," I said. "You've got to show cleavage."

"I don't want to look like a tramp."

"Lesson number one in catching a man," I said, "boobs. You've got them; you might as well flaunt them, Martin."

"Look at this, then." She tucked the sheet under both arms.

"Much better," I said. She looked in the mirror. Groaned. "This white washes me out."

"So dye it."

"Great idea, Holly. I'm going to have to buy a strapless bra." I suggested she go without one. "Never." She leaned into the mirror scrutinizing a pimple and I watched as she covered it with Clearasil. She started brushing her hair; I went back to my algebra problem. "Hol-ly?" I looked up. "What are you going to wear?" I told her I was going to steal a sheet, too. "Come here, put this on. Let's see how we can make it look."

"Are you trying to dress me up for the kill like you did with Randy? I said I'd date this guy, not sleep with him."

"This is going to be fun. Fun, remember fun? Come here." I donned the white sheet and Jess draped it around my shoulders and waist. I stood on my milk crate trying to see all of myself in the bureau mirror. I thought I looked like a pig on sticks; Jess said I looked great. She promised to do my makeup, and I told her I was thinking of cutting my hair.

"Don't you dare. It's long and blonde and guys love that."

"I was thinking about trying for a flip."

"I don't think you should."

"Why not? You can wear one."

"Do you want me to be honest with you?"

"Absolutely without hesitation don't even think about it, tell me the truth."

"Your hair's too straight."

"Oh." My visions of becoming the perfect Tri Delt melted like a Dali clock in a nuclear war. I made one last feeble attempt. "Are you sure?"

"Positive. But I think we can do something that will give you sparkle for the party. I think you should let me pierce your ears." Jess has pierced ears, and she'd pierced some of our dorm mates' ears, but I hadn't let her near me with her darning needle. I thought it was kind of low class, and my father considers it absolutely savage. She was persistent and finally convinced me that having pierced ears would solve most of my worldly problems, so I let her do it. That night we brought ice from the cafeteria, and one of our dorm mates who worked there got a raw potato. I drank an unknown number of shots of Seagrams pain medicine #7, while Jess numbed my ear with the ice. I howled from beginning to end, but don't remember feeling any pain.

The Saturday of the toga party my ears were infected, red and swollen, but Jess rescued me with a pair of large flat clip-on earrings. It hardly mattered. We were finally free. Free of algebra and rhetoric and Paul Tillich. Free of early morning classes and assignments and papers and sitting still. We were ready to party.

Jess had dyed her toga red, but the dye didn't take well and it turned a sour pink. She still looked great. I was in white, and Jess braided my hair and swept it off my face, saying it made me look like a goddess, although I didn't think so. She looked exquisite with her pink nail polish and dark hair and perfect gold earrings. She'd found a snake bracelet to go on her upper arm and a pair of brown lace-up sandals. She decided against the off-the-shoulder look, and there was no cleavage in sight. My toga, my sheet, looked a little better after we belted it into an empire waist, but I still thought all that material swamped me. Jess, of course, looked like she was born to wear sheets.

Our dates called from the lobby, and while we were putting on our coats, Jess said casually, "Holly, I want you to be yourself tonight."

"In this? I can't even find myself in here."

"There will be a lot of Tri Delts there."

"I see. I'll try not to embarrass you."

"That's not it. But you may want to watch how much you drink. For your own sake."

"You think I'm going to embarrass you in front of your sorority sisters," I said sarcastically. "Maybe I shouldn't go."

"I didn't mean it to sound like that. Fraternity guys can be real movers and those girls can be pretty catty. Just be careful. Okay?"

"I can take care of myself."

"You're right. Forget I said anything. Here, let me get this wisp." She took a falling lock of my hair and glued it back with her super hold hair spray. We took the elevator downstairs, and I couldn't believe my drop-dead gorgeous blind date. He was tall, with blonde hair and so pretty he could have been a model.

"He's too cute," I whispered to Jess on our way over to greet them.

"And nice, too," she said. I tripped on my toga walking over to them, but Jess caught me and I didn't fall.

"Damn it," I said.

"He didn't see it," Jess reassured me, but I knew she was lying. We were suddenly face to face with our escorts. "Holly, I'd like you to meet Dean Haines, and this is Jeffrey Dewey, your date. Jeffrey, Holly O'Neal."

"How do you do," I said, extending my hand.

"Hi," my date said, clasping my hand in his two. "You look very nice tonight." Very nice? What does he mean by that? I wondered. Is that down from great or up from horrible?

"And so do you," I replied. His toga was starched and folded perfectly at the seams. He looked like the archetypal Roman soldier, handsome and gallant. I suddenly wished I hadn't let Jess talk me into the empire waist. My breasts looked like they were wrapped in the Tao sign, they stuck out like two torpedoes aimed right at Jeffrey Dewey.

I don't remember what I said after that. I do remember that Jeffrey was very polite and very attractive, and I was very nervous. As we drove over the river to their fraternity, Jess sat in front with Dean, making clever conversation, and Jeffrey and I tried not to step on each other's lines, which were laced with long pauses.

When we got to their fraternity house—a big Tudor mansion across the river—the guys took our coats while Jess and I waited in the large foyer.

"Relax, Holly. He's not going to bite you."

"I need a drink."

"That shouldn't be too hard to find." We walked into a gargantuan living room. All the furniture had been pushed to the side, and in the center of the room stood three large aluminum garbage cans. The room was half-filled with half-naked couples in white sheets, looking like a Roman version of the KKK; some were drinking, others dancing. Jess stood out spectacularly in her pink toga.

"So this is what a toga party looks like."

"And this is the elixir of the gods," Jess said, grabbing a ladle off the side of a can and dipping it into the grape muck. She held it to my mouth and I took a swallow.

"Ulgh," I said, swallowing it.

"Grain alcohol," Jess wisely informed me.

"I know that. I didn't think it'd taste that bad."

"Let's try another," she said, dipping the ladle into the second can. "Maybe the mix in this one is better." She took a swallow, then held it up for me. I made a face. "This one isn't too bad," she said. I took a drink.

"It grows on you," I said.

"Puts hair on your chest."

"Just what I've always wanted."

"Would you ladies like some cups?" a voice from behind implored us. "Or maybe you want to stand at the trough all night?" We turned and there was my date, holding four Styrofoam cups. I felt my face redden, but Jess reclaimed our dignity.

"We were checking for nuances of flavor. We prefer the grape-grape to the grape. Thank you," she said, like a queen, as she took the cup. He poured us each a drink, then Dean came up and whisked Jess away to dance. Jeffrey and I stood nervously nursing our drinks in a stagnant silence. Finally, the god spoke.

"Would you like me to show you around?"

"That would be nice." Dumb!

He took me on a tour through the dining room, the kitchen,

the study areas and some of the dorm rooms. He prattled on about the history of the building: the dates it was remodeled, who owned it when, on and on and on like Jackie Kennedy at the White House. The alcohol was beginning to make my head dance and reminded me that I was there to have fun. Back in the living room The Doors' "Hello, I Love You" was playing on the stereo, and I got up my nerve and asked him to dance. He refused! I was humiliated and took a giant swallow of my grape muck.

"I hope you don't mind. I'm a very bad dancer."

"How do you know if you don't try?" He ignored this.

"Hey, I've got something I think you might like to see. Can you keep a secret?" I nodded. "Do you have a weak stomach?"

"Of course not."

He led me to the back of the frat house and up a narrow staircase. We entered a large room with a dozen bunk beds, at the end of which was a closet with a locked door. He felt for a key above the doorframe, found it and unlocked the door. Great, I thought, he's going to throw me on the floor, and no one will hear me scream. But there was a light on a string in the middle of the room, and when he pulled on it a bare bulb illuminated a small walk-in closet lined with shelves. On the shelves were jars and jars of different colored organic stuff in what I assumed was formaldehyde. I took a large gulp of my drink.

"Wow."

"Isn't it great?"

"What are they?"

"These are some things we've stolen from the University Hospital. You must never tell anyone you were here."

"What's this?" I asked, pointing to a gallon jar.

"That's a tumor, the size of a honeydew. Isn't it incredible?" I nodded. "It's the largest one I'd ever seen, I just had to have it." He sounded like he'd purchased a new sofa. "They took it off of a man's kidney. He must have been walking around with that for years. Can you imagine?" I took another drink. It looked gross, but the alcohol made it oddly fascinating.

"And this?"

"Oh, that's a female breast. With the underlying pectoral muscle. Breast cancer. And she was no flapper, either."

"So that's the, the . . ."

"Yes, that's the nipple."

I looked at the next jar. I wasn't about to be undone by a little dead human tissue. "I know what this is." I was looking at a turgid penis in a long thin jar that looked like it once contained imported olives.

"Good for you! That's actually my personal favorite."

Why was he showing me all this stuff? Penises and breasts and tumors? How did this match with the perfectly pressed toga? With the grand tour? "And how did you, ah, come by it?"

"That came off a cadaver we were using in anatomy class. I detached it myself." He sounded proud, like it was a deer he'd shot.

"I've always wanted a heart in a jar, myself."

"I'll try and get you one."

"Would you?" I asked sarcastically. And with a fake southern accent: "I'd be forever indebted to you, sir."

He bowed. "It'll be no trouble at all."

"I have to use the rest room." The room was beginning to feel airless, and I was getting dizzy. He locked the door behind us and showed me to the ladies room.

When I looked in the mirror and saw the alcoholic sparkle in my eyes—like I was having a private joke with myself—I knew I was high. I was dancing with myself in the mirror when Jess came in.

"Where have you been?"

"You wouldn't believe me if I told you."

"There are girls out there I want you to meet. Look at me. Are you high?"

"Not high enough. I want to dance, Jess!"

"Where's your date?"

"He doesn't dance. He's cute, but he doesn't dance. And I think he's got a psychological problem."

"Who doesn't."

"I mean really." She handed me her lipstick, and I applied it dutifully. "Anyway, he's not interested in me."

"How can you say that?" She powdered her nose.

"Just a feeling I have."

"Give the guy time, Holly. Let him get to know you."

I didn't think I could explain to her that getting to know me was the last thing this guy wanted to do, so I just handed her back her lipstick. "I want to dance, Jess."

"Come on, then. I'll find someone for you to dance with."

We went out to the living room, filled now with what seemed like hundreds of togas—togas wrapped in every conceivable fashion around every possible body part. Everything seemed loose and light and smooth; bodies moved in waves of white. People were laughing and dancing and staining their sheets with grape drink. Somebody was bobbing for the fruit floating on the top of the grape muck, and there were people lying on couches, feeding each other grapes and licking the juice off fingers and hands. It looked unbelievably sensuous and alive compared to the dark, organ-infested closet I'd visited. Jess got us drinks and I started swaying to the music. It was my favorite Bob Dylan song, "Like A Rolling Stone." My date, of course, was nowhere to be found. I decided to have fun in spite of him. I was high enough not to care much and not so high I didn't care at all. I felt, in other words, completely natural. A guy came up to me. I looked at him. He looked at me. Without a word, we started to dance. I was suddenly glad Jess had talked me into the empire waist. When the dance ended he grabbed my face and kissed me—on the lips and for a long time. Afterward I gave him a silly come-hither smile, then suddenly Jess came up and ushered me away.

"What do you think you're doing?" I demanded.

"Follow me."

"What?" I was annoyed. "This better be good." She ushered me into an empty library.

"Holly, listen to me. Stay away from that guy; he's dangerous."

"I'm dangerous, too."

"You don't understand. He's a mover. More importantly, he's the sorority president's boyfriend."

"So?"

"So if you have any desire to be a Tri Delt, you'll stay away from him."

"I danced with him. Besides, he came up to me."

"Judy was watching the whole thing."

"Then she must know her boyfriend's a tease."

"She tolerates little indiscretions. But not from a sister."

"I'm not a sister."

"But you want to be, don't you? You said you did. Tell me if you've changed your mind."

"Yes. No. I don't know. Do I have to decide right now?"

"Yes. I want us to be roommates next year. So tell me, do you want to be a Tri Delt, or should I quit going out on a limb for you? Do you want to stay together next year, or not?"

I envisioned myself next year, in a dorm room alone or with some dim-witted roommate, bored to tears and stripped of my soul. "Where do I sign up?"

"Come with me. There are some girls I want you to meet." She took me out and introduced me to a few of her sorority sisters. She even introduced me to Judy and to "Judy's boyfriend, Steve," emphasizing the word "boyfriend." Judy smiled, said hello, and asked me to come by the sorority sometime with Jess for study hours. Steve said hello, looked away and pretended the full-on-the-lips kiss was a fantasy. I hated him. I hated her.

In the meantime, the party had gone from sensuous to earthy. There were big puddles in front of the garbage cans, half-empty now. Hair that had been piled high on top of heads came tumbling down, and young men without underwear started to pay attention to the sensation of unrestrained genitals. The lights got lower and the togas got lower and the dancing got dirtier and couples started to drift off to corners, then to bedrooms. I still couldn't find my date. Not that I was looking. What was it about him? Jess and Dean danced and I watched them, while I smoked cigarettes and slurped grain alcohol. I started getting angry, but I couldn't remember the reason. I've been ditched by my date, I thought, maybe that's it. No, he was just cute, nothing more. I could live perfectly well without him and his room full of body parts. What was it?

I went to the rest room again and checked my face. On the edge, I thought. Watch yourself, Holly. "Oh, fuck you," I said to the image in the mirror. "I'll do what I want." I went back to the living room and sat in a corner eating grapes like they were potato chips. Finally, Jess came up and sat down next to me.

"Dean and I are going. Do you want a ride?"

"Are you going to ball him?"

"What do you care if I do?"

"Are you going to ball him? I just want to know."

"I haven't decided yet. What difference does it make?" I didn't tell her then, that I didn't so much care if she balled him; but if she did, she'd stay out all night, and I'd be left sitting alone in our room, dying of unexchanged anecdotes. Blue balls of the brain.

"It makes no difference," I said, stuffing three grapes in my mouth. "Do what you want. I'm staying."

"How will you get home?"

"I can take care of myself," I retorted.

"Fine. Take care of yourself," she snapped. And she was gone.

Go ahead, I thought. Just go. Leave me here alone. I ladled myself another drink. Just what you need, a voice inside me said. That's right, another voice shot back, this is exactly what you need. I drank it down in one swallow, and it almost came back. I swallowed hard a few times, making sure it stayed in place.

Then I got my brilliant idea. Where was that staircase?

I remembered that Jeffrey had taken me up a back staircase to a large bedroom and his exotic closet. It took me a while to find it, but I finally did and made my way up. I passed several rooms until I found the one he'd taken me through. Luckily, it was dark and quiet. I didn't turn on a light in case anyone came. When my eyes adjusted, I found a chair and stood on it while I ran my hand above the doorframe to the closet. I found the key and quietly opened the door. I closed the door behind me and turned on the light. There it was. I took the olive jar filled with the turgid organ and placed it carefully inside the front of my toga. I laughed, thinking about how shocked and delighted Jess would be when she saw it. I imagined it up on our shelf next to *Sexual Behavior in the Human Male*. Together, they'd make a real conversation piece. I'd just flipped off the light when I heard voices outside the door.

"No one's here. Come on."

"Are you sure?"

"Come here, gorgeous. Let me feed you a grape."

"And where is that grape?"

"Right down here. Feel it?"

It was Judy, the head honcho sorority sister, but I didn't recognize his voice. It didn't sound like her boyfriend, Steve. He was probably off kissing some other girl in some other bedroom. Damn it, what was I going to do now? Wait it out, I thought. I sat on the floor and listened to them groping.

"Oh, that feels so good." I was dying to know what he was doing. "Be careful where you put that, things could get serious."

"I want to put it all over you, over every inch of your—" She cut him off with what I surmised was a kiss. Curiosity overcame me, and I peeked through the keyhole and tried to see what they were doing, but it was too dark. I'd have to be content with sounds. I sat through the entire act, which wasn't long considering the state he was in. Afterward, she kept telling him how great he was, and cooing in his ear. It sounded to me like she wanted to keep going. Damn it, I thought, I better get out of here. Then they started talking again.

"Who was that chick I saw Steve dancing with?"

"A friend of one of our pledges."

"She was cute. I thought she was a Tri Delt."

"Never. She's definitely not Tri Delt material. She doesn't have the Tri Delt look."

The Tri Delt look, I thought. What's the Tri Delt look?

"Besides, I hear she's easy."

"The way she was dancing with him, I don't doubt it."

Easy? Who's easy? You bitch. You don't even know me. Who told you that? You're making it up! I couldn't stand it a second longer. I took a fold of my toga and wrapped it over my face, flung open the closet door and ran out of there as fast as my legs could carry me.

"What the hell—?"

"Who is that?" As I ran out the door the jar jostled between my breasts and its contents fell out onto the floor with a crash. The smell of formaldehyde perfumed the air as I whizzed past them.

Serves you right, bitch, I thought. Smell that for a while. I ran down the stairs and tried to remember what had happened to my coat. At the foot of the stairs I ran right into Steve himself: Mr. Cuckold. He was quite drunk and so was I, and I was quite mad; so I grabbed him and kissed him deeply, searching for the back of his throat with my tongue. At the same time I reached under his toga and grabbed his balls, and before he could grab me back I whispered in his ear, "Your girlfriend just balled a bunch of guys upstairs. They're standing in line." He looked at me like he hadn't quite heard me; but before he could say anything, I ran toward the front door and grabbed a man's coat hanging on a coat tree. Then I scanned the floor for my shoes. I could barely see through my fury so I donned a pair of big black rubber boots by the door, heavy men's boots. I escaped, throwing myself out the door and stomping down the steps as fast as I could.

I'd gone two blocks before I realized I was crying. The boots were hundreds of sizes too big and kept me from tearing off into a run. I hadn't even buttoned the coat, and by the time I did I was already freezing. The tears stung my cheeks when they fell, but I didn't care. I wasn't thinking, I was just moving. I hated that place, I hated those people, I hated everything about them.

And then, even though the boots held me back, I started running. The boots flopped on the densely packed snow. I was drunk and I was cold but I kept going, running with my head down against the cold. God, it was so cold. I could feel my ears start to sting and covered them with my hands. Goddamn it, everything was wrong! Wrong, wrong, wrong. I stumbled and fell, barely catching myself on my hands as I did. I lay on the ground and felt the cold snow against my cheek. Part of me wanted to stay there and freeze into the snow. Another part couldn't bear the indignity of it, so I dragged myself up.

I started walking again. It was before dawn on a Sunday

morning in a college town. There were no cars. And there wouldn't be any for a long time, and then only townies going to church. I'd have to walk all the way back to the dorm in the cold, across the Iowa River and up the hill to Burge Hall.

I cupped my ears again and put my head down into the collar of the coat that smelled of Canoe. God, how I hated life! No, it was the people in it. Get rid of the people and life would be just fine. Me and life and no people. What Tri Delt look? This was the worst night of my life. It should have been fun, and it was horrible. Why? What look? Think, Holly, think.

God, I felt so wrong. Now I'd never be a Tri Delt, and I'd never marry Jeffrey Dewey. There were two facts you could take to the bank. Judy would find out what I'd said about her and know it was me who tried to steal the penis in the jar. I laughed out loud when I thought of all those drunken Phi Psi's trying to sleep in a formaldehyde scented dorm room. Serves them all right, I thought. Serves him right.

What look? Not tall enough, not skinny enough? I'll show them, I'll never eat again. I felt the boot tops hit my legs in the shins and in the calves as I walked. Front, back, front, back, they slapped my legs as my feet slipped inside them. I took my hands from my ears to hike up the toga, which was slipping down around my ankles. I held it in place with my hands in the pockets of the oversized coat, cinching in the waist. Take an inventory, what's wrong? Hair: blonde, long, maybe too straight, but I could curl it. Face: okay, small, nothing out-sized, features not exquisite, but cute. Ears, infected, but that will go away. Skin, pink, there's no other way to describe it. Short, okay, I'll admit to short. Too fat, it's got to be that I'm too fat. I'll lose weight, which will make me look taller. I'll never eat again.

Suddenly a pang of real hunger roiled my stomach, and I realized I hadn't eaten a meal since the day before at lunch. On top of all that booze, I suddenly wanted food, real food and lots of it. I'll eat one more meal and then that's it, I vowed; it'll be my last. I'll show them all, I thought. I'll show them what perfection is. They'll see what a big mistake they've made. I'll show the Kappa Kappa Gammas and the Tri Delts and the Thetas. They'll all be beating down my door to get me to join their stupid sororities.

When I came to the footbridge across from the Union I started across it, then stopped halfway and looked out. Not one thing moved. Everything was frozen and seemed stuck in time. I felt my breath slow and simply watched. And in that moment I realized I didn't need anything except to be where I was, watching a cold winter morning be itself. And everything I needed I already had, because I was there in that morning and that was enough. And suddenly none of the night before mattered. I'm alive, I thought. "I'm alive," I said out loud. I pulled myself up to the ledge, leaned on my arms. "I'm alive, Goddamn it!"

I jumped down and tore across the bridge, punching the air and kicking my feet, letting my coat fly open and blow the folds of my toga. I headed up the hill, fast and furious, running not for speed, but for joy.

When I got to the block before our dorm, I slowed down. How am I going to explain this to Jess? I thought. I rehearsed my speech and when I got to our floor I almost hoped she wouldn't be there, so I wouldn't have to tell her yet. But she was there. I tried to be quiet, but she woke up and sat straight up like she always does, and I realized how much I'd miss her. I took a big breath.

"Holly, you're here. I've been so worried about you. I hardly slept."

I steeled myself against warming to her worry and stood in the doorway in the big coat and boots. "Jess, it's like this. I don't want to be in your sorority, I don't want to be in anybody's sorority. I hate those people. I hate the way they judge you. I hate the way there's a game I don't know how to play, and I don't want to learn how. And I don't care what they think of me, and I don't care what you think of me. Yes, I do, but not about this.

"I'm tired of trying to pretend that I like what I don't like, when even if I knew how to play and was good at it—which I'm just not—I don't care about it. There's got to be more than looking right and doing the right thing and knowing the right people and thinking the right thoughts. There has to be more than that, than what all those people at that party think.

"I've spent a lifetime trying to figure out how to make it work out for myself, to find out where I fit in, and I finally meet you and I think: Here's someone I can talk to, here's someone I can be myself around, here's someone who understands me and doesn't care that my hair doesn't curl just so—who even thinks it's kind of endearing—here's someone who could give two shits if I'm no good at algebra. Here's someone, most of all, who thinks, who really thinks, and who makes me think too, and who listens to what I have to say. I can talk to you, Jess, like I've never been able to talk to anybody else. But I'm telling you that if I have to, I'll give it all up because I can't, I won't, I won't and I can't be in anybody's sorority—because I don't belong there—I don't. I'd die there, trying to be what someone else wants me to be."

"Holly, you had one bad experience. It won't always be like that." I ignored her. I had to.

"I walked home and standing on the bridge over the river, I realized what it is. I want to be free. I'm alive and I have to be free or nothing else matters. I know I would die if I had to pledge, if I had to be under somebody's thumb. I won't have anyone telling me what to wear and who I can dance with, talk to, or sleep with. I've spent my whole life trying to get away from people with rules telling me what I can't and shouldn't do. I don't care if I never fit in anywhere, if I never belong anywhere, because I know I don't belong in that sorority. I'd rather stand and freeze to death on the banks of the Iowa River than live in a house full of girls I hated and had to work to get to like me. I won't do it. I won't put myself in a cage. Not for you, Jess. Not for anyone." Jess sat on her bed, stone still, not saying anything. "Say something. Say anything, just say it."

She looked at me puzzled, as though I was somebody she used to know a long time ago. "You don't want to be a Tri Delt?"

I wished she'd stop looking at me like that. "No. But if you want to be one, that's okay. I just can't. I'll still be your friend, but I won't be your sorority sister."

"What if I stay in?"

"I hope we'll stay friends. That's up to you."

"Of course we will. Nothing can keep us apart. We're best friends."

"We're practically the same person." I said it, but I didn't sound like I believed it anymore.

"That's right." Did she still believe it? I'd taken off the coat and boots and climbed into bed. I put my head on the pillow and my eyelids felt like they had boulders pressing on them.

"Hol-ly?"

"What?"

"Where are you going to live next year, if you don't pledge?"

"Jess, I don't want to think about it now."

"Will you live in a dorm again? Will you get another room-mate?"

"I don't know."

"But—"

"I don't know and I don't care. I'll be somewhere where nobody can tell me how to be."

Neither of us said a word after that, but I tossed in my bed for a long time. I was going to be free, and that meant I would be alone. Jess would join the sorority and I—what? Where would I go? At the river, all my questions seemed to have answers—cold, simple, pure. But as I listened to Jess's soft breathing in the bed next to mine, I wondered how any answer could ever be as pure as that sound.

CHAPTER SIX

Zoe turned the page of Holly's journal and began reading silently. Jess drained the rice, then turned back to the stove to reheat the vegetables. She remembered that morning and the way Holly strode about, high minded and full of purpose. Jess had wanted to join Holly in her conviction, or at least have a strong conviction of her own about who she was or who she should be. But as Holly proclaimed her freedom, Jess remembered thinking only one thing—she would never be a Tri Delt. She knew that if she activated and moved into the sorority house she would lose Holly, and that would be unbearable. Like two obsessive lovers, we were bound to each other, Jess thought. But that was a long time ago.

Jess served the food quickly, anxious for Zoe to eat and leave. She watched as Zoe chewed voraciously and saw Holly when she was pregnant. She remembered how sick Holly had been, how frightened they both were, and how hard they tried to hide the pregnancy from Holly's parents. Now your daughter's pregnant, Holly, what would you think of that? Jess stifled her harsh judgments and asked Zoe if she wanted more rice.

"So my mother never joined the sorority?" Jess shook her head no. "But you did?" Zoe asked, accepting the rice.

"I did, then I quit." Jess answered, reluctant to share more of the story.

"Why?"

"It was no longer cool," Jess said quickly. She took a bite of Thai noodles and thought about the real reason. When she arrived at the university she was determined to succeed, and according to her mother, that definitely meant joining a sorority. At first, she threw herself into pledge parties, mixers and sleepovers. But she was intrigued by Holly's honesty and intense questioning, and soon the Tri Delts and the activities at the sorority house seemed superficial and dull. The more parties Jess attended and the more sorority sisters she met, the more distant she felt. In the end, she never did form close friendships with other Tri Delts. She desperately needed Holly, to make her whole. And Holly seemed to understand that. Once Holly took a stand against the Greek system, Jess had to follow, to save herself. There was no way to explain that to Zoe without opening herself up to more questions.

"You quit because it wasn't cool?"

"The sorority chitchat was no match for my conversations with Holly."

"I think she only wanted to join because of you." Jess didn't answer. "So is that when you decided to become hippies?"

"'Decide' isn't the right word. It just sort of—I don't know, happened."

Zoe kept at it. "How did it happen? I've read a lot about that time. Was it a drug thing or was it political or what?"

"It was a combination of lots of things that are really hard to explain now."

"Try." Zoe was adamant.

Jess took a bite, chewed slowly then spoke. "Well, for Holly it was more of a personal awakening. She started reading books about Eastern religions and hanging out with some of the guys who had dropped out of fraternities. They were always discussing the meaning of life and the possibility of creating Utopia on earth. That was very big in the 60s," Jess said in a mocking tone, smiling at their naiveté. "Holly kept urging me to break the rules, be myself, do my own thing. Of course, I didn't have a clue what my thing was . . ." Jess stopped, sorry she'd started down this road.

"My mother turned into a hippie so she could do her own thing?" Zoe asked with a smirk as she pulled out a package of rolling papers from the back pages of the journal.

"It was as if someone had taken the bars off and set her free." And I wanted to be just like her, Jess thought, she seemed so free and authentic. Jess's mind wandered to an image of Holly during that spring. Holly had stopped shaving her legs and wearing a bra. She'd lost some baby fat, she looked great and guys were suddenly paying her a lot of attention. Jess remembered a night in their dorm room: Holly, in her hip-hugger bell-bottom jeans and peasant blouse, standing next to her at their sink. They were burning Jess's pledge book and singing a Tri Delt song. "We thought we were so radical," she said aloud.

"Being true to yourself, big deal. What's so radical about that?"

"Well, why do you wear a nose ring? Youthful folly? To shock the grown-ups? To rebel?"

"Yes."

Jess smiled. "Well, we were rebelling, too."

"Against what?"

"I was rebelling against my mother, who wanted me to fulfill her dreams. Celeste's plan for me was very simple," Jess noted. "Find a fraternity guy who was studying to be a doctor or lawyer, have a big wedding and join the country club. Becoming a Tri Delt was the first step, so quitting was a big disappointment to my mother." Jess took another bite, knowing it hadn't been that simple.

"What was my mother rebelling against?"

Jess's mind cast up a multitude of reasons, most of which she wouldn't tell Zoe. She made a safe choice. "Holly's parents didn't have high expectations for her. Even though she got some scholarship money, she had to take out loans to go to school. Of course, her parents had money set aside for her brother's education."

"So, it was really just about your own personal shit."

Jess was indignant. "Look, our friends were dying in a war nobody believed in, progressive leaders were being assassinated, America and Russia had nuclear bombs aimed at each other, cops were killing unarmed citizens and black people didn't have equal rights a hundred years after the Civil War. Every day something horrible seemed to happen. It felt like the apocalypse was just around the corner and we were powerless to fix it. So it's no surprise that so many of us decided to do a Timothy Leary and, 'Turn on, tune in, drop out.' Besides, there was this incredible surge of creativity in politics, art and music. And it all came from our generation."

"That's so genocentric." Zoe sounded condescending and self-righteous. Jess reminded herself to be polite, she only had a few more minutes with this apparition.

"Genocentric?"

"Your generation thinks everything begins and ends with it," Zoe said with disdain. "Frankly, the rest of us think it's time you got over yourselves."

Jess was about to object when Zoe pulled a photograph from the journal. It was of Holly and Jess dressed in full hippie regalia, flashing peace signs, standing together in a sea of people at an outdoor concert. Jess wore a long jean skirt with a tie-dyed halter top, large men's work boots, a leather headband, granny glasses and a silver peace sign on a leather rope. Holly was barefoot and wore low-slung navy and white striped hip-hugger bell-bottoms. On top was her white peasant blouse, laced with a dozen beaded necklaces. Her long blonde hair streamed out of her blue floppy hat. They looked innocent and young. Jess felt a wave of nostalgia and loss. "My, weren't you the fashion duo," Zoe chided.

"Don't be so smug," Jess shot back. "Your generation is starting to look a lot like ours with your flared pants and platform shoes. In fact, those pants you're wearing look like some I saw your mother in. How does that make you feel?"

"Very retro, okay?" She stared hard at the picture. "You guys looked totally stoned here. Did you and my mother do a lot of drugs?"

"We did a few drugs," Jess answered, then turned the conversation back to Zoe. "Do kids your age still smoke pot? What about Ecstasy? Isn't that what all you Gen Xers are doing these days?"

Zoe sat up and waved her fork at Jess. "First of all, I don't know any kids. Second of all, I'm sick of the way your generation of old hippies is always grouping people my age into this nebulous Gen X category, like we're all little slacker clones with too much time and money on our hands. We're individuals, and we don't all do anything or feel any one way. Some of us do drugs, but most of us don't. I'm not saying I haven't smoked pot because I have, but Ecstasy isn't de rigueur for someone my age."

"Well, pardon me. I'm afraid it's a marketing malady—always trying to define the target audience."

Zoe stood and carried her plate to the sink, sat back down, looked directly into Jess's eyes. "Tell me about your hippie days." The plea was emphatic, as if the answer were expected, owed.

"I'm sure there'll be plenty of those stories in your mother's journals." Jess ignored Zoe's disappointed look. "Let me help you pack your mother's things, then I'll drive you to your friends' house." She smiled insincerely and began putting the dishes in the dishwasher. She'd leave a message for Eric before they left, and hopefully he'd call his office before he went to bed. Maybe he'd even call her back.

Zoe ignored her directions and pretended to roll one of the papers into a joint. "Before I go, tell me about just one time you did drugs."

Jess grabbed the papers and stuck them back into the journal. "I don't think your mother, either one for that matter, would approve of that discussion."

"Was my mother still seeing Randy?"

"No."

"When did she break up with him?"

"We each broke up with our high school sweethearts the minute we put on love beads. Holly began seeing David Delaney."

Jess remembered the hours she and Holly spent hanging out with their new friends. Most of them lived off-campus in funky, run-down houses filled with incense and music. She remembered her false sense of independence. She remembered sleeping on acquaintance's couches and on mattresses on floors. She remembered sharing drugs and sleeping with men she barely knew, because it was "the friendly thing to do." She regretted the waste.

"Did Holly fall in love with David?"

"She spent a lot of time with him, but I don't think she was in love with him. They seemed more like pals who happened to have sex. Holly was much better about the free love thing than I was. I cheated at the hanging-out game and was always looking for a real boyfriend."

"Do you have a boyfriend now?"

"Do I have a boyfriend?" Jess laughed. It sounded so innocent. "I have Eric, I guess he's a boyfriend."

"Is he the guy in the tuxedo I saw you with in the photograph?"

"Yes."

"He's handsome."

"Well, looks can be deceiving." Jess looked at her watch and hoped Zoe would get the hint. After an uncomfortable silence, she did.

"I'll get my mother's things." Zoe followed Jess into the living room and moved toward the couch where Holly's journals were piled next to the armrest. She started to sit, then quickly stood up, turned and bolted for the bathroom. Poor kid, Jess thought. Poor Holly. She thought of Holly pregnant, alone and afraid. You only had me, Jess thought, and I was so little help.

A shiver ran through her. Had Holly written about the night Zoe was conceived? Jess remembered her promise to Holly, and hearing water running in the bathroom, she quickly flipped through the books until she found the one labeled August, 1969. As Zoe returned to the living room, Jess hastily slipped the book deep behind the sofa cushion. "Feel better?" Jess pulled the chenille throw over the seat cushion.

"Yes, but this is a drag. When does the throwing up part end?" Zoe sat down with a dejected huff.

"I think in your third month. I'm sure there are books you can read . . ." Jess tried to sound helpful.

"Forget it. I'm not planning that far ahead." Zoe picked up a stack of journals and started packing them neatly into the bottom of the box, too slowly, too carefully. Jess offered to help but Zoe refused, so Jess went to get her coat. When she returned, Zoe was standing at the parsons table re-examining her photographs.

"Tell me about Eric."

Jess joined her as Zoe picked up the picture of Eric and Jess at a dining table. She chose her words carefully. "We work together. He's an executive at my agency. I've known him for several years."

"Are you going to marry him?"

Jess took in a breath, then let it out with, "He's already married."

"Oh." Zoe's tone was judgmental. "Well, you look happy in this picture."

"We were all happy. That was taken at the Joey Awards last year and our agency won quite a few."

"What about his wife?"

"What about his wife."

"Does she know?"

"We're very discreet. I don't think so. I don't know, maybe she does and just doesn't . . ." Jess took the picture from Zoe and moved it to the back of the table.

Zoe immediately picked up another and showed it to Jess. It was a silver-framed photograph of a young woman in a wedding dress, Jess at her side. "When was this taken?"

"At my sister Kayla's wedding."

"Were you ever married? Do you have kids?" Zoe fired the questions. They caught Jess off guard.

"Yes. And no. I was married but Brad and I didn't have kids. I've been divorced for a long time." Jess quickly grabbed a shot of her ten women friends in front of a restaurant. They called themselves The Hepburn Club, Jess explained—a dinner club for women of any age, as long as they hadn't had children. The youngest was 30, the oldest 60.

"Why do you call it The Hepburn Club?"

"After Katherine Hepburn. She didn't have children and was successful and fulfilled." Jess thought of the women in her club, how unfulfilled most of them were. Successful, yes. And self-absorbed. Well, not all of them. Jess pointed out Leslie Rothstein. She was 54 and had recently left a high-powered job in a corporate law firm to become an advocate for patients fighting insurance companies. "Oh, and there's Anastasia." Jess pointed to the only African-American woman in the group. "I love her because she's so strange and impractical. She changed her name from Jasmine to Anastasia in 1970," Jess explained, "but now she calls herself Anesthesia because she can't remember anything."

"I changed my name, too," Zoe said. "When I found out Holly had died. Joanne named me Sarah, Sarah Elizabeth Ryerson. So totally boring, I've never felt like a Sarah. Zoe— that's what I want to be called from now on." How sweet, Jess thought. Now go away.

"Can I stay here?" Jess was shocked by the question and didn't answer. "Just for tonight? I promise not to bother you. You don't have to talk to me or anything. I'll sit and read. I promise not to interfere. I'll sleep on the couch."

"What about your friends?" Jess objected weakly.

"I'll go there first thing in the morning. They're not expecting me, anyway—I said I'd call them."

"You'll be out here all alone." Jess was sure she didn't want to leave Zoe snooping through more of her things.

"I can take care of myself."

"I don't think it would be a good idea. I have work to do. Lots of it."

"I'll leave first thing in the morning, I promise."

Zoe's defiance was beginning to wear on Jess, but she was suddenly too tired to care. "I guess it would be all right," Jess said, mentally ticking off the reasons why it was a bad idea. "I have a sleeper sofa in my office."

"Thank you. I know you have work to do, so I'll read. You go ahead and work."

Jess retreated to her bedroom and plucked a cigarette from the pack on the master bathroom floor. All but one candle had burned out. She used it for a light, then blew it out. She cleaned up the smaller pieces of broken glass and wondered why she felt so unsettled by Zoe's request to stay. Why hadn't she just said no?

"You're losing your edge, Jess Martin," she said to the image in the mirror. But that was old news. Except now, she thought, it's starting to show. She sighed and headed into to her office. Usually it was the only room in her house where she allowed herself to smoke, but she felt guilty that a pregnant Zoe would be sleeping there. She opened the windows and sat at her desk, pushing her day planner and a stack of bills out of the way. She went on-line and surfed the Net for companies with a similar profile to ProbTech. She pulled down menu after menu, but could barely concentrate.

After an hour and five cigarettes she considered calling Eric and asking for help. As always, she'd use their special communication system. She'd call his office and leave a message. Then she'd call his beeper and leave his office phone number. If he was home, he'd call his office, get her message, then call her. If he was in his car, he'd do the same. But what would she say to him now? I'm sorry, let me do it right? Or, you asshole, you got the demographics wrong and made me look like an amateur. No, whether it was telephone communications or work, Eric was in charge and he always had been. She vowed to handle this on her own.

Jess located a half-dozen more Web sites and took some notes. But soon her eyes grew tired and she couldn't focus, even with her glasses. She logged off and turned out the light. The day had been a waste, and now the night was a waste, too. Maybe a cup of coffee would perk me up, she thought, and she wandered out toward the kitchen.

CHAPTER SEVEN

Zoe sat in the living room engrossed in a journal. Seeing Jess, she leapt up and handed her a wooden box with a flip lid, the kind sold in seacoast beach stalls. Small shells were glued over its surface.

"I have some questions that maybe you can answer. What does 'give a damn' mean? Where's the Hogs Head Pub? There must be some reason she put all this stuff together."

Jess sat wearily in her overstuffed armchair, slipped off her shoes and studied the contents of the box. "I can't believe she saved this." She pulled out a black plastic ashtray with *Hogs Head Pub* imprinted on it; a package of matches from the Embers Lounge; a New York identification card for a women named Fran Epstein; half a dozen sea shells, sand attached; a pin that read "Give A Damn!" and a flamingo stir stick.

"Do you remember any of this? Why did she keep it this way?"

Zoe must believe that each object in Holly's box holds some special meaning, Jess thought. She's got to learn that not every saved object becomes a sacred one. Some become burdens. Jess's voice began monotonous and slow. "Holly and I went with some friends of hers to Florida for spring break freshman year." Zoe sat, waiting for more.

"Holly was in a group called 'Give a Damn.' They traveled to churches to sing and do anti-war skits. She and I drove with a group of six of them to Florida. Holly thought the vacation was exactly what we needed, a chance to relax on the beach, get a great tan and contemplate important ideas. She bought us each a felt hat to convince me to go. They're the ones you saw in the picture. She must have bought this box on the boardwalk."

"So 'Give a Damn' was a singing group? My mother sang?"

"A little."

"I can't carry a tune."

"Actually, neither could she."

"What did you do there? Did you have a good time?" Zoe leaned forward, eyes wide, elbows on her knees, chin perched on her hands.

Zoe's expectancy angered Jess. You don't get it, she wanted to say. Everything ended in tragedy. Why are you so determined to dredge this up?

Zoe sat, waiting. Jess took a deep breath and reluctantly set the story in motion. "I'd never been to Florida, but I'd heard stories and seen movies with Gidget and Moon Doggie at wild college parties. I thought that sounded exciting and romantic. Of course, we were both broke. I think I had around $75 for the whole week. Holly promised that would be enough. We'd eat one meal a day, she said, live the Spartan life. I imagined we'd meet rich guys who would treat us to expensive meals and put us up in a luxurious beach house." She paused. "It didn't happen that way."

"How did it happen?"

How did it happen? Jess thought. She remembered the trip in snippets, like old movies that skip frames during important scenes. She remembered some of what she packed: a new pink bikini for the beach and a very short jean skirt. She added two appropriately "important" books, *The Art of Loving* and a copy of *The Bhagavad-Gita*, and then what she actually did read, the latest edition of *Glamour* and her first copy of *Vogue*. She remembered that Holly's blue Samsonite was overflowing with books. She began to tell Zoe the story. She started with the facts.

Eight of us rented a cottage a block from the beach for $22 a night. There were two double beds, a fold-out couch and a roll-away cot about half the size of a twin bed. Because we were the youngest and poorest, Holly and I were stuck with the cot. We put a pillow at either end and slept with our feet in each other's face.

We spent the first three days sunning, smoking cigarettes and checking out guys, until we felt appropriately tan. This was before anyone believed in sunscreen and Holly's skin was a mess. She'd become so engrossed in a book, she'd forget to turn over. By mid-week she was red everywhere. I was a tanning pro, and worked my body around in well-timed intervals to guarantee an even glow.

The first three nights we partied with Holly's group and drank beer with guys from the cottages around us. The problem for Holly and me was that these were the kinds of guys we'd spent the last few months moving away from—frat boys or wanna-be frat boys who we were certain never had a deep thought and weren't capable of one. They got drunk and they got stupid. We got bored with their macho chatter and by Wednesday we were ready for a real adventure. I remember we paid to borrow IDs from two New York girls in a neighboring cottage.

"This doesn't sound anything like me," I protested, when Holly showed me mine. "It says I weigh 150 pounds. Let me see yours." I grabbed hers. The photos were of two dark haired girls.

"God, Jess, mine is worse! It says I'm five-seven. We'll get busted for sure. Maybe we should trade?"

"Maybe not. Look in the mirror." I told her my plan. "If I wear flat sandals and you wear your tallest platform sandals, you could look just about five-seven. If anybody asks, I'll say I've been on a diet. Nobody really cares, anyway. It's Florida. It's spring break. They want us to spend money in bars."

"That's another problem. I only have $25 to last me the rest of the week. How are we going to buy drinks?"

Sometimes Holly didn't get it. "We're not going to buy drinks. We're going to meet guys, Holly. Not frat guys, either. Real guys with real money who'll buy us drinks. Hopefully, they'll spring for dinner, too."

"And where are we going to meet these real guys? At the Daytona Beach Country Club or some place equally bourgeois, I suppose?"

"Don't go all snobby on me yet. I'll bet there are some bars that are mellow and cool at the same time. After all that beer, wouldn't you like a real drink for a change and a steak dinner if we're lucky? Surely there are a couple of okay guys out there who would love to treat two sexy coeds to a night on the town. And they probably aren't even Republicans."

"They better not be! Okay, I'm in, but only for the free food and booze. What are you wearing?" I wanted to look sexy, so I opted for my short jean skirt, sandals and a T-shirt I'd bought on the beach. It was a low cut ribbed cotton shirt with a beautiful orange and peach tie-dye design. I wore purple and turquoise beads and peace sign earrings to finish off the outfit. Holly wore her lowest hip-huggers, platform sandals, a white T-shirt and my silver peace sign on a long leather string. Holly insisted we wear our floppy felt hats. We looked good heading out into the warm Florida night: tan, young and ripe for trouble.

We stopped at the grocery store to check out the local paper for the hot spots. It was filled with ads for college bars, but the

Embers looked like the place where rich locals partied. I thought it was our best bet for free drinks and a free meal. Holly, of course, protested.

I tried to assuage her doubts. "First of all, it's part of a fancy restaurant. And see this picture, everyone looks sophisticated and rich. Besides, it's close, so we can walk there."

"I don't know, Jess, look at this guy. He's wearing a leisure suit. And this other guy is bald and he's wearing those god-awful white shoes."

"It's a picture, you can't tell about a place from a picture," I lied. "Come on. It's only four blocks from here. If we hate it, I promise we'll leave. But we're going to have to take off our hats when we go in." Holly was incensed, but I told her the bartender wouldn't think we were 21 if we wore our hats. I'd already come to be a little embarrassed about them; they weren't exactly fashionable.

Holly hated the Embers the minute we walked through the door. The walls were covered in red velvet wallpaper and lined with black leather booths. Tom Jones sang on the jukebox.

"God, Jess, we've wandered into hippie hell."

"I agree it's bad, but I bet they mix a strong drink. Let's sit at the bar, close to the door, so we can bolt if we have to." The bartender wore a bad toupee and a nylon shirt that glistened silver and blue when he moved.

"What can I get for you gorgeous ladies tonight?"

"We'll each have a vodka tonic." Thank God he didn't ask for IDs.

"I thought we weren't buying drinks tonight." Holly spoke so low I could hardly hear her over Tom Jones' crooning.

"Think of it as an investment. We buy this one and sip it slowly. Someone sees us and buys the next one. That's how it works."

"Here you are, ladies." He set two cocktails in front of us.

"Thank you so much. How much do we owe you?"

"First one's on the house. Kind of a thank-you for prettying up the place." He winked and patted my hand as Holly kicked me on the shin.

"That's very nice, thanks a lot." He smiled and headed to the other end of the bar.

"This is disgusting. He patted your hand. I can't believe you're making me sit here."

"Lighten up. We're drinking, aren't we? And for free, like I said. Try to act old." We threw our drinks down nervously. Not exactly sure how to act old, we started by lighting each other's Marlboros, then tried to strike a careless pose.

"Don't look now, but two real losers are headed our way," Holly said, chugging the rest of her drink. "If we bolt now we can get out of here with a crumb of self respect."

"Hello, ladies. Mind if we join you?" Two leisure-suited 40-somethings pinned us in before we could make our break. "I'm Bobby and this here's Henry Lee. Hey, Pete, get these two beauties another drink and put it on my tab."

"Make it a double, Pete," I said. "Hers, too." I figured we should at least get a good buzz if we were going to be tortured by such scintillating company.

"What are your names, ladies?"

"I'm Monique Chantecler and this is Veronica Chekhov," Holly purred in her best bullshit voice. Look out, I thought, Holly is ready to play!

"Monique. Is that French?" Bobby asked.

"Oui oui, my father was the famous Pierre Chantecler, poet, novelist and all around literary genius."

"Where are you girls—er, ladies from?" Henry Lee joined in.

"San Francisco—"

"Paris." We answered in unison.

"I'm from San Francisco and Monique, of course, is from Paris. We're on sabbatical. I'm an archeologist here to study sand formations along the Florida coast. Hol—I mean, Monique is a writer for a très très prestigious French literary magazine."

"My, my and so so young. You girls wouldn't be putting us on, would you?" Holly took the stage.

"I can't bee-leeve you think we'd lie about our work. And what do you boys do for a lee-vinque?" Holly's fake French accent cracked me up; it was all I could do to keep from laughing out loud. We gulped our drinks while Bobby droned on in great detail about the lucrative real estate business in Daytona Beach. Just as Henry Lee jumped in with his take on the future of the plumbing industry, Holly grabbed my wrist, glanced at my watched and shrieked, "Oh mon Dieu, Veronica, dear, we must go or we'll be late for our see-minar. Thank you gentlemen, so very much for the lee-bations. You too, Pete." We grabbed our purses and hats and dove for the door, tumbling out into the ocean breeze, gasping with laughter.

"God, you were great, Holly. Monique lives! And Veronica, what a terrific name! What made you think of Veronica?"

"Surely you've read Archie comics? You're the perfect Veronica, well, Veronica in training, anyway."

"Is that good?"

"Let me put it this way. Veronica always has great clothes, sexy long hair, a hot car and she dates the richest guy in town."

"Archie?"

"No, dummy, Reggie. Actually, I think his name was Reginald. Anyway, I say if the shoe fits, wear it. And speaking of shoes, mine are killing me and it's my turn to pick a bar. I vote for some place laid back, where I don't have to act old or tall. A place where we can wear our hats." Holly remembered the name of what sounded to her like a mellow place, the Hogs Head Pub. "It sounds like a down home normal kind of place where the local hippies hang out. With a name like Hogs Head we'll probably run into a bunch of misplaced Iowans and feel right at home." Holly removed her shoes and lit up a joint. We took off arm in arm, and skipped down the street singing our own bawdy version of a Tri Delt pledge song.

"You sang some old sorority song skipping down the street? How unbelievably uncool," Zoe said. "I read about some guy who was trying to get into a frat house and they made him sing the fraternity song 700 time before they'd let him go to sleep. It was like Chinese water torture only with music. I bet you still remember the song, don't you? Sing it," Zoe dared.

"Sorry to disappoint you. I'm afraid those brain cells are long gone. Besides Holly and I burned my Tri Delt song book 30 years ago."

"So you went to the Hogs Head . . ." Zoe picked up the ashtray and Jess continued.

"Yes, we went to the Hogs Head Pub and it was earthy all right, earthy, dark and filled with smoke. The walls and furniture were made of old barn wood and there were peanut shells all over the floor. The walls were covered with what looked like a bunch of junk from someone's long-dead relatives' attic—old buckets, muskets, saws, mirrors. There was even an old corset and a pair of long johns nailed to one wall. Holly thought it was quaint and laid back. I was reserving judgment until I could get a good look at the clientele. The band was playing a Steve Miller song somewhere in the background as we stumbled through the main room out a door into a beer garden. It was still dark, but my eyes were beginning to adjust. I could make out two or three tables of longhaired guys with a couple of typical earth mothers.

"You know the type, slightly overweight women with long flowing hair who smelled of patchouli oil and were very proud of their hairy legs and pits."

"No, I don't know the type," Zoe wrinkled her nose in disapproval.

"It must be a generational thing," Jess shot back.

"Clearly."

Holly found a table and sat down. She asked me why I was grimacing.

"Because I can barely see and my sandals are filled with peanut shells. Man, Holly, this place is filthy."

"Relax. It's not that dirty. Wow, the boo's so thick out here I'm getting a contact high."

"Contact high, bull. I'm totally stoned from that joint we just smoked. Where did you get that stuff? It's really strong."

"David gave it to me as a going away present. It's laced with a little THC so we're supposed to go easy on it."

"Now you tell me. What's THC?"

"Just really strong pot. Don't worry. My throat feels like sandpaper, I need a drink, fast."

"I hope we don't have to show our IDs. I'm too high to lie with credibility."

To our relief, the waitress brought us each a glass of Spanada wine and a basket of peanuts without asking to see any identification. I was glad that Holly was finally happy. And I was feeling more comfortable, too, although the THC affected my vision and everything had an odd glow around it. I didn't mind, though. In fact, it was pleasant sitting in a stoned blur, sipping wine, surrounded by strangers. After a while, the band stopped playing and someone turned on the jukebox. Janis Joplin began the first strains of "Get It While You Can." And then the two Adonises appeared.

"Excuse me, you girls look like you could use some company. Mind if we join you?" Standing next to our table were two of the most beautiful guys I'd ever seen. With the faint light from the bar behind them, one looked like Jesus Christ, the other could have been Matthew, Mark or Luke.

In my stoned state, they both looked gorgeous with their long flowing hair, full beards and perfectly tanned skin. I remember that Jesus wore a leather vest over his work shirt and tight, well-worn Levi's. His disciple wore a poncho and carried a pitcher of beer and two glasses. I was too stoned and awe stricken to talk, but Holly jumped in and invited the beautiful duo to sit. Hank, Jesus's real name, sat next to me and his friend, Jonathan, sat beside Holly.

Hank was the lead singer in the band and Jonathan played the bass guitar. I was in heaven! Even Holly seemed pleased with our sudden popularity. After we exchanged pleasantries, Hank asked if we'd like to slip out to their van for a few minutes to get a little buzz before they went back on stage. Holly quickly gave an enthusiastic "yes," then glanced over for my response. It rolled effortlessly off my tongue, "What are we waiting for?"

Hank put his arm around my waist as we made our way out through the crowd. When we reached the door he turned me around and planted a sweet kiss on my neck. I couldn't believe what was happening. We were with guys from the band, going out to their van to get high. I thought to myself, this is as good as it gets.

Jess stopped, took another sip of her wine and wondered at her false bravado.

"So what happened? You went to the van and what happened?" Zoe was eager.

"I'm not sure I should tell you any more."

"Oh, quit being such a prude; I'm not a child. Just tell me the fucking story."

"You know I don't have to tell you anything." Jess was annoyed by her attitude.

"Okay, please tell me the story."

"That's better. But first tell me, did Joanne and Paul ever do drugs?"

"What does that have to do with anything? No, they told me they didn't and they thought drugs were harmful. I got the lectures and made up my own mind. But I think my dad tried pot. I saw a picture of him when he was in graduate school. He had a full beard and wore a white flowing Indian thing. But he'd never admit it. So, go on. I want to hear the rest."

Jess took a breath and continued. "Well, we went to the van and it was a real love nest. It was carpeted from top to bottom with purple shag, and the windows were covered by paisley curtains."

"Yuk," Zoe said. "That's weird. Shag carpeting is so disgusting. Supposedly there are whole ecosystems that live in shag carpeting. I read this story where they did a study of shag carpets, and they found like 500 hundred species of—"

"Do you want to hear this, or not?"

"Sorry. Go on."

Jonathan put on an 8-track tape of Iron Butterfly's "In-A-Gadda-Da-Vida" and we sat down, Hank and I on a fakefur-covered mattress and Holly and Jonathan on two overstuffed pillows. Jonathan immediately lit a joint and Hank brought out a tiny vial filled with white powder. He poured the powder onto a large mirror with roses stenciled on each corner. I could feel my heart beating faster.

"You girls do much cocaine back in Iowa?"

"Sure—"

"No."

Our answers overlapped. Damn Holly, why did she always have to be so honest? I stuttered to cover our gaff. "I tried some once at a party, I don't think you were there, Holly."

"Really? When was that? You never told me you did coke; I'd remember if you did."

I glared back. "It was a while ago; I don't remember whether or not I told you," I lied. "It doesn't matter, anyway."

"Here, try this, it's really great shit." Hank handed me a short straw and the mirror, where he'd neatly arranged eight short lines of white powder.

"You first." I handed the mirror back to Hank and carefully studied his technique as he inhaled through each nostril. Then we each did our lines and sat back to groove to the music. I immediately felt a delicious rush roll through my body. My head seemed to be moving in slow motion from the pot, but my body was filled with energy. From a corner of the van I saw Holly talking to Jonathan at an amazing clip. She was more animated with him than I'd seen her since the night after the toga party.

My face was flushed and my body felt incredibly warm. Hank told me I was beautiful and pinned me against the mattress with a kiss. I'd never been kissed quite that way before, and it left me dizzy. Then things started moving too fast, and I was relieved when someone knocked on the door, interrupting our hot make-out session with the news that the break was over and the band was due back on stage.

"Did Holly make out with Jonathan?" Zoe asked

"Probably, but I wasn't really paying attention. Why?"

"Just wondering. So then what happened?"

Before we left the van, Hank poured out another line for each of us, then we headed back to the bar. Hank guided us to a table in front and kissed me once more before taking the stage. I couldn't believe how the evening was turning out. There we were, Holly and I, babes with the band! The waitress delivered a pitcher of Spanada, no charge, and as the music started I settled in, ready to be charmed by the gorgeous hunk on stage. I didn't drink any more, because I was already too high. I felt sexy, spacey and buzzed. I thought I was on top of the world.

But Holly wouldn't stop talking. The coke had turned her into a chattering monster. She was talking loud and fast about how smart and sensitive Jonathan was and how he'd read books by Watts and Hoffer and some other people I'd never heard of. Hank was singing a song I loved by Buffalo Springfield and I wanted to sit quietly and bask in his glory. But Holly kept up her serious talking jag.

"Why are you talking so loud?" I finally asked.

"I'm not talking that loud. I can't help it if I'm excited about the idea that insecurity could be a truly positive concept. I mean, excuse me if my talking is bothering you. I thought you'd care, but now I can see you're not interested. Well, that's too bad . . ."

The cocaine had awakened a side of Holly I'd never seen. The more she talked, the more I slouched down into my chair. I couldn't believe it. These two gorgeous men had picked us and were singing their hearts out in front of us, and all Holly could think about was some philosophical bullshit.

Finally, I interrupted her. "I'm going to the bathroom. Try to chill out while I'm gone." I escaped, making a sloppy beeline for the john, closed the stall door and dropped to the toilet. It was all turning to shit before my eyes. The combination of coke, wine and Holly's incessant talking had given me a killer headache, and I was dizzy from the THC. I hated the feeling and was angry with myself for getting too high. In the stall, I worked to find a balance. I sat in the bathroom for a long time trying to gather my wits.

When I got back to the table, Holly was watching the band and ignored me. She finished her wine in silence as the band sang its final encore. I was glad when Hank and Jonathan joined us again. They seemed anxious to leave and invited us back to the van for a joint. I looked to Holly who was already telling Jonathan yes.

Jess stopped abruptly, aware of Zoe's rapt attention.

"What happened? You went back to their van and then what happened?"

Jess took the night to its conclusion in her mind and lied. "You know, I can hardly remember. I know we smoked a joint and then I think the guys drove us home," Jess answered quickly. "The problem with doing drugs is that it's so hard to remember what you actually did while you were high. Aren't you getting tired? I'm beat. Let me show you where the bed linens are and where you can hang your things up if you like."

Jess led Zoe into her office and opened the hide-a-bed. She showed her where the towels and linens were and left her to change.

Jess wandered back into the living room and sat down in front of Holly's box. While she'd been telling Zoe about the trip, Zoe had neatly arranged most of the contents on the coffee table. They looked like some kind of peace offering. Jess picked up the Hogs Head Pub ashtray with its picture of a hog in sunglasses smoking a cigarette. She turned it over and over in her hand, remembering more of that night, how innocence quickly turned to darkness.

The four of them went to the van, their hormones raging, their passions exaggerated by the flush of cocaine. They drove to the beach, about a mile from the bar. Jess remembered that Jonathan put on a John Mayhall tape and fired up a joint. The four of them settled down on the mattress "to talk."

The talking lasted less than five minutes, then Hank began massaging her shoulders and kissing her neck, then her mouth. She peeked out of the corner of her eye while Hank was kissing her and saw Jonathan next to them on the mattress, putting the moves on Holly, who wasn't resisting. The necking quickly got hotter as Hank fumbled to unsnap Jess's bra. Jonathan already had Holly's pants unzipped. The last joint made it hard for Jess to keep her eyes open and focused, so she decided to try, for once, to let the night just happen.

In the middle of a long, deep kiss, Jess felt Hank pull his body slightly away from her, enough so that their lips strained to stay connected. As Jess tried to open her eyes, she felt another body pressing against hers, and strange, new lips took the place of Hank's. Jess's body stiffened. She forced her eyes open and was shocked to find that Jonathan had taken Hank's place. He was pressing her body into the mattress and working his hand under her skirt. She struggled against him.

Jonathan whispered, "Be cool," in Jess's ear. She quickly turned her head and saw Hank kissing Holly as he moved his hands under her T-shirt. Holly didn't seem to mind and was kissing Hank as deeply as she'd just finished kissing Jonathan.

Jonathan pulled Jess's head back down to the bed roughly and began kissing her again. Suddenly a wave of intense fear overcame her and she struggled harder to get away. But Jonathan had a grip on both her arms with one hand while his other worked its way between her legs until her underpants were around her knees. Another hand was moving under her shirt toward her left breast. Jonathan continued to press his lips on hers as she took inventory. She counted four, then five hands touching her body and when she reached to grab the hand on her right breast she realized it was Holly's.

Jess tried to scream out but Jonathan stopped her, pressing his lips harder against her mouth. She began to panic as she struggled against his hold, then she felt a sharp pain as a tooth gashed into her lip.

"Ouch, stop it, that hurts!" Jess pulled away with all her strength. She lost her bearings and fell on top of Hank and Holly as she tried to pull up her underpants. With one hand on Holly's breast, Hank reached out his free one and grabbed her butt moaning, "Oh baby, I want some of that next." Jess called out Holly's name as she tripped over a shoe and fell into the door. She grabbed the door handle to break her fall; it opened and she landed on the beach. The door slammed shut behind her.

It was eerily quiet outside the van; Jess could only hear the tide lapping the shore. She sat on the ground, her mouth swollen from the cut on her lip. Her leg was scraped by the fall and her beads were broken and scattered. She sat perfectly still as a wave of shame and guilt swept over her and a vague memory played in her head. She stared at her skinned shin and remembered other stifled screams, other uninvited hands touching, hurting. Then came the pain in her head, pounding until she thought her head would explode.

"Stop it, just stop it!" Jess screamed and pressed her fingers into her temples, hard, pushing the memories back into the darkness. She had no idea where she was, only that her head was splitting and Holly was somewhere having a hot time with two perverts. How could you do that to me? she thought. Then, as if on cue, Holly stepped out of the van.

"God, Jess, are you okay? Jess, say something."

Jess's swollen lip made it hard to form words. "Your boyfriend cut my lip, or was that my boyfriend? It's so hard to know who's who when you're in the middle of a fucking orgy," Jess growled. "But, hey, don't worry about me, I'll find my way home. You go back in and enjoy yourself. That's the kind of free experience you're always looking for."

"You're not going anywhere without me. God, you can be such a prude sometimes. Sit here for a second while I go back in and get our stuff. Man, you're a mess."

"Excuse me. I hope I haven't embarrassed you with my untidy appearance."

"Oh, shut up." Holly sounded like she was talking to a silly child. She disappeared back into the van. Jess tried to stand up, but lost her footing and fell back to the ground. She began to cry. When Holly came out with her shoes and purse, she was sobbing.

"How am I ever going to find a nice, successful guy if I keep doing this? And I keep doing this, going out with guys who do this, who think they can do this. I'll never get it, I'll just never get it."

"Here, Jess, put on your shoes and please stop crying. You'll find someone and I'm sure he'll be everything you ever dreamed of. But right now I think we should concentrate on finding our way back to the cottage. I think all we have to do is follow the shoreline. Don't cry anymore. Your mascara is running all over your face! Here, let me help you with your sandals."

Holly helped Jess to her feet and the two girls headed down the road, following the moon along the shoreline. The sound of the waves began to soothe Jess's bruised body and ego.

"I was going to ask them for a ride, but when I went in to get our stuff they were both passed out." Holly stopped. "Fuck."

"What's the matter?"

"Your hat's back there, isn't it? I'm going back for it."

"No way. We are not going back there." Holly promised it would just take a minute, but Jess was adamant. She didn't ever

want to see that hat again. Holly finally gave up and they walked
on. "I hope those guys get picked up for vagrancy and thrown in
jail. No, I hope they overdose and die. They're a couple of jerks."

"Geez, what's your problem. You didn't think they were so
bad earlier."

"Did anyone ask me if I wanted a million hands all over my
body? No. No, no, no. No one is supposed to touch me unless I
say they can. No one, not even you." Tears streamed down Jess's
cheeks as she marched ahead down the sandy shore.

"Jess, relax. I didn't mean to upset you." Holly ran to catch
up, but Jess kept up her speed. Holly was panting. "It's not like
anything was planned; it just happened. Nobody was out to hurt
anybody. I actually thought it was kind of interesting, you know,
not knowing for sure where one body ended and the next began."
Jess glared at her. "I kind of liked it; so sue me."

"Next time you want to have sex with a bunch of strangers,
leave me out of it."

"Fine. But one of these days you're going to realize that sex is
just sex, a natural part of life, not some ritual that has to be bound
up with eternal commitment."

Jess was indignant. "You make it sound about as romantic as
eating or farting. Maybe for you it's a natural process. I think it's
more than that."

"Did you really think we'd get romance from those two?"

Jess's head felt like Hank's van had landed on it. "I don't want
to talk about this anymore. Are you sure we're going in the right
direction?"

"More or less. Yes, I'm sure." They walked on the hard sand
in silence for a few minutes until Holly said quietly, "I'm sorry you
had a bad time."

"Let's just forget it." Holly lit a cigarette while Jess cupped her
hands around the match to break the wind. They shared it with-

out speaking and finally reached the cottage and safety.

Jess sat on the sofa, clutching the edges of the pillow and shivering. She remembered lying down head to toe on the little cot she shared with Holly, listening to Holly's breathing. She remembered that she tried to sleep, but couldn't get warm. No matter how many times she wrapped the blanket around her body, she couldn't shake the cold. The chill was everywhere, pressing in on her, like a lonely familiar ghost.

CHAPTER EIGHT

"Hello, earth to Jess." Jess looked up and saw Holly standing in front of her, telling her to wake up. But no, it wasn't Holly. It was Zoe, and this wasn't 1969. She was safe.

Zoe wore men's-style flannel pajamas covered with flying toasters and held a picture in her hands. It was of Holly and a stout woman with long dark hair and electric blue eyes. "Who's the woman in the picture with Holly?"

Still distracted, Jess smoothed out the pillow and returned it to the couch, taking the picture in her hands. "That's Kate. She was your mother's collaborator." Honest enough, Jess thought. "They wrote some great plays together."

"Where is she now? Do you have her phone number or her address?" Zoe made a move to grab a pen from her pack.

"I'm afraid you can't talk to Kate. She died a long time ago. In a car accident."

"So she's dead, too."

"I'm sorry. They were an incredible team, though, and your mother blossomed once she met Kate."

"Blossomed how?"

"As a writer. I went to the opening of one of their plays. That's when I took that picture. After Kate died, I begged Holly to move to San Francisco to live and work. But she wouldn't come."

"What kind of plays did she write?"

"Off beat, esoteric stuff. Nothing commercial."

Zoe carried the picture to the couch and set it on the coffee table in front of her. She asked Jess if she had a photograph of Holly's parents, and Jess promised she'd search through her pictures. Jess leaned back on the sofa, tired of talking and ready for sleep. Zoe made the opposite move, reaching toward the box for the Woodstock video. "So, you and my mother went to Woodstock?"

"No."

"I found a letter that said you were going. It's right here." As Zoe retrieved the letter from the pages of a journal and began reading aloud, Jess's mind churned, imagining how to lie her way out of the telling.

Dear Holly,

I'm sorry about Ellen and Bill. I definitely think you should get out of there. But to New York? I hardly have any money and if I go it'll be a stretch. I have about $150 squirreled away from tips that my mother doesn't know about. I had a fight with her today about Troy. She thinks I'm a tramp because I stay out late and she wants me to work more hours so I'll have more cash for school. (No, that's a ploy. She wants my life to be as dreary as hers.) I'm a fool to stay here. If you promise me it'll be cheap, I'll consider going. If you can lend me $40, I should be able to get there and back and buy a few meals, right? We can fly stand-by and it should cost next to nothing for food. But where the hell is Bethel, New York? Call me, I have a plan for how to lie to our parents. Woodstock Music Festival? Why not!

Love,

Jess

"Well? Zoe asked. "Did you go?"

"We went toward Woodstock. We never actually arrived there."

"When was Woodstock, anyway?

"I don't know," Jess lied. "Sometime in the summer." Zoe turned the video over and read the print on the sleeve. "It says here it was August 15, 16 and 17, 1969."

"Then I guess that's when it was. But we didn't go, so it doesn't matter."

"You said you went toward Woodstock. So tell me what happened."

"We ended up spending most of our time in airports, missing flights. It isn't very interesting. And it wasn't one of the finer moments of our friendship. Anyway, I'm tired."

"I want to hear about Woodstock. Then we can go to bed. Unless there's some reason you can't tell me about it?" Zoe stared directly at Jess. "I can always read about it in Holly's journal, but I'd rather hear it from you." Jess thought nervously about the hidden journal. "Come on, it can't be that bad. I've had un-fine moments with friends." Zoe was persistent.

Jess looked back at Zoe, so determined to hear the truth. Had she already read something? Either way, Jess didn't want to share the details of that trip. Feeling trapped, she shouted fire. "Ice cream!" she yelled out.

"What?"

"We need ice cream. What do you think? I have some Cookies and Cream. It's my personal favorite. I'll get us some." Jess jumped from her chair and hurried to the kitchen.

She soon returned with two large bowls of ice cream and sat on the couch next to Zoe, who was poring through journals and didn't look up. Jess set a dish in front of Zoe, then took a spoonful of hers and held it out, hoping her guest would do the same.

"Try the ice cream. You'll love it."

Zoe sat back and furrowed her brow. "Did you meet any men the weekend you were supposed to go to Woodstock?"

"We met lots of people. No one important." Jess swirled her ice cream, trying to make it soften. "Have some ice cream. It's delicious."

"Who did you meet?"

"I don't remember. It was a long and difficult journey," Jess said somberly.

Zoe didn't enjoy the irony. "Tell me what you do remember."

"I remember that Holly's mother had moved out of the house and left Holly to take care of her father." Zoe pushed her bowl aside. Jess wavered. If she began it, how would she end it? Maybe if she told every detail Zoe would get bored and stop asking questions. Zoe tucked her feet under the green chenille throw from Jess's sofa and settled back expectantly.

"Your grandparents were separated. I think Maggie was married and Edward was away at university summer school. Anyway, Mr. O'Neal was fired from his job selling tractor trailers and went on a long drinking binge Holly said she came in one day and he was on the phone, trying to get through to Queen Elizabeth. By the time her mother came home from her second job, he was blabbering incoherently. Ellen said she was sick of his drinking, packed her bags and moved out. Unfortunately, that left Holly alone to play nursemaid to him. She wanted out. Besides that, we were both working hard.

"Holly worked in a factory, packaging Hostess Suzy-Q's and doing summer tutoring. By day I was a carhop at the A&W, and at night I was a waitress at the country club. I didn't really want to go to Woodstock; I was making good tips and dating the golf pro. But I knew Holly was unhappy and thought it might be fun. We told our parents we were visiting each other, then I flew into

O'Hare and we took a plane to La Guardia. From New York we were supposed to catch another plane to Albany, then a bus to the festival. At least, that was the plan.

"Our plane was delayed leaving Chicago, and when we got to La Guardia airport in New York, our flight to Albany had left. So we waited for the next flight at the airport bar. We sat smoking cigarettes and sharing a whiskey sour I'd gotten with my new fake ID—" Jess stopped, wondering how to spin the story.

"So what happened? You're at the bar, and . . .?"

"There was one more flight to Albany. We went to the gate to catch it, but there was only one stand-by seat. So we sat near the gate with our Samsonites and our sleeping bags, watching the last flight leave without us."

"Bummer," Holly said. "What are we going to do now?" There was a flight leaving at seven the next morning, but we had no place to stay that night. Holly wanted to sleep in the airport. I told her there was no way I'd do that.

"Why not?"

"For starters, there's no bed."

"Where do you think we'll be sleeping when we get to Woodstock?"

"We're going to find someone who has a tent."

"We're going to ball some guys just so we can have a roof over our heads?"

"I didn't say anything about balling anyone. God, Holly, where did you think we'd sleep?"

"Under the stars."

"What if it rains?"

"If it rains, we'll get wet."

"I'm not getting wet. And I'm not sleeping in this chair. Why can't we get a hotel?"

"We can't afford to stay in a hotel in New York and expect to eat for the next two days." We sat for ten minutes, not speaking. Holly lit a cigarette, took off her sandals and crossed her bare feet at the ankles atop my suitcase. She pulled her blue felt hat down over her eyes. She still wore her hat everywhere. I'd bought a new gray hat to replace the red one I'd left in the van and—

"I thought you lost your red hat." Zoe was looking sharply at Jess. "That's what you said."

"I did lose it," Jess stammered.

"Well, did you lose it or did you leave it in the van?"

"I lost it in the van. What difference does it make?" Zoe didn't answer, just looked hard at Jess.

Jess sat, not wanting to tell any more.

"I'm sorry," Zoe said. I interrupted you. "I really want to hear about this. You were arguing about a hotel."

Jess nodded, reminded herself to be careful. She saw Holly with her hat covering her eyes, and began slowly. "I remember I spotted a phone and brought back the *Yellow Pages*, where I found an ad for the YWCA

Holly hated the idea. "The Y? Forget it. I can see it now. It'll be filled with old ladies, proselytizing to us in the hallways. They'll march us around like school girls and make us sing 'Onward Christian Soldiers.'"

"At least it'll be safe."

"I don't want that kind of safe."

"I do." I dragged her to the phone booth and as I was talking to the receptionist at the Y, I turned around and saw a security officer walking toward us. I took off my hat and tried to look like a straight girl pretending to be a hippie. I hissed to her, "Holly, take off your hat!" He stopped walking and just watched us. Did we look that weird? I put my hat behind my back. "All right," I said into the receiver, "we'll take two rooms."

"Two rooms," Holly said, "are you crazy? That will cost a fortune!"

I covered the receiver and whispered to her. "They won't let us stay in the same room. And take your hat off!"

"Fuck you."

I turned back to the phone. "Yes, we'll take the two rooms." Then I suddenly remembered the pot we'd stored in my socks in my suitcase. "Oh, shit." Holly looked at me, the woman on the other end asked if there was a problem. I wondered how I was going to explain the pot to this cop who wouldn't take his eyes off us.

I asked Holly one more time to take off her hat, but it was too late. He was coming toward us. He looked us up and down and when he got to my face, I flashed him my best Tri Delt smile, the one that said, "Me? Why, I wouldn't even take a drink, let alone a puff of marijuana."

I hung up the receiver and turned back around to hear him say, "Where are you girls going tonight?"

"We have a reservation at the YWCA," I said quickly.

"Come with me," he commanded, and I was sure he was going to bust us.

"What have we done?" Holly said in her worst defiant tone. Shut up, Holly, I thought. I wondered if mental telepathy might work, so I thought over and over, I have marijuana in my suitcase, Holly, be cool.

"I'm not sure you've done anything, but I'm going to find out." I imagined us behind bars, handcuffed together back to back. We'd spend the next ten years in jail and be released as old, gray-haired women, lacking any practical skills, spinsters for life.

He led us to a security office where we sat in two chairs opposite his desk. He took our IDs, scrutinized them, then made a phone call and read some numbers over the line. I sat stone still, but Holly fidgeted in her seat, mumbling under her breath about the ridiculousness of it all. After a long silence, he hung up and turned toward us.

"It looks like neither of you is missing or wanted."

"Of course not," Holly snapped. I stepped on her toe and when she cried out, he looked at her over the tops of his glasses.

"Does that mean we can go?" I asked, sweetly. He looked at us as though we might steal his ashtray. "We do have reservations," I said, "at the YWCA. We wouldn't want to lose the room."

"Don't you have any shoes?" he admonished Holly.

She lifted her foot to her face, taunting him. "Why, yes, I have two pairs."

"I suggest you put a pair on." She opened her mouth to argue with him, but I got my words out first.

"Of course. You're right—her feet were just swollen from the flight." Holly made a groaning noise and I stepped on her toe again.

He leaned forward and looked at us with narrowed eyes, then handed us our ID's. "Try to stay out of trouble. If I was your father I wouldn't let you out of the house like that. There ought to be a law."

His metal office door clanged shut behind us. "Asshole," Holly said. "There ought to be a law against assholes like him harassing innocent people." I didn't respond. "How dare he?" Holly complained. "He's probably one of those guys who goes to drive-ins and counts the used condoms, then proposes an ordinance to close them down for depraving the morals of the community. But he secretly gets off on it and jacks off—"

"Holly, shut up! You've obviously forgotten that the pot is in my suitcase!"

"The pot! Oh, shit!"

"We could have been busted. I'm not carrying the drugs anymore." We went to the ladies room and took the pot-stuffed socks out of my suitcase. I wanted to throw it down the toilet, but Holly said she'd spent ten dollars on it and refused. We put three joints in Holly's suitcase, then stuffed the rest into a rental locker along with our sleeping bags. I made her hold the key.

It was after 11 and we had to ride three buses to get to the Y. The last one dropped us off a few blocks away. There was hardly anyone on the streets, but there were lots of security bars on store windows.

As we turned the last corner, we saw two disheveled young guys standing outside the Y, smoking cigarettes. I stopped in my tracks. Holly wanted to know what was wrong and I pointed out the guys. "Come on," she said, "don't be a baby." We lumbered toward the stairs, and as we approached they threw their cigarettes down. The taller one stepped up to block our way.

"You girls from out of town?" I tried to step around him, but my suitcase hit his leg and fell over. He grabbed it and held it behind him.

"What's the matter, cat got your tongue?" The heavier man stepped in front of Holly.

"Get out of our way, we have a reservation here," Holly said.

"Fucking dykes," the heavier one said.

"My, you're a pretty one." The tall one glowered, then grabbed my arm.

"Give me my suitcase," I shouted, trying to step around him. He held me away with his arm. Holly tried to pass the guy who was blocking her, but he held out his leg and she tripped and fell. He grabbed her suitcase and ran down the street laughing, with Holly shouting after him. The guy who had my suitcase let go of my arm and ran off, too. Holly got up and started after them, but they turned a corner and I called her back.

We scrambled into the empty lobby and stood breathless and shaking. "We have to call the police," I panted. Holly agreed and we went to the pay phone. My hands were shaking as I got the number and dropped in the coins.

"Wait," Holly said. "If we call the police, they'll come here and ask why we're here. Plus, remember the three joints in my suitcase. Even if they don't bust us they'll call our parents, and we'll be in so much trouble. Besides, do you think we have a chance in a million of getting our stuff back?"

"We better have."

"Hang up the phone, Jess."

I did as she said, but dug for more change to call again. "This is fucked, Holly. I want my things back. I spent all summer working to buy those clothes, and I'm not about to let somebody get away with stealing them."

"They've already gotten away. What's in your backpack?" I had one change of clothes, my toiletries and money. "That should be plenty."

"It isn't." I finally called the police, despite her protests. They told me we'd have to come into the station and file a report. "Maybe this is a sign, Holly. Maybe we should go home."

Holly refused to consider it. We took a taxi to the police station where we filed a report and gave a description. No one seemed to care who we were or where we were headed, and we left, disillusioned. Holly wanted to go back to the Y, but I was too scared. So we took another taxi back to the airport and did just what I didn't want to do, we slept on uncomfortable airport chairs. Right before we went to sleep, I asked Holly if she wouldn't consider going home.

"You go home if you want. I'm going to Woodstock. I want to

be outdoors, listening to Jimi Hendrix and Joan Baez. It will mean defeat if we go home."

"Well, it better get better than this."

"Nowhere to go but up," Holly said. "You have to stop worrying, Jess. When we get there and everybody's on the same wavelength, it'll be groovy. You'll see."

"Stop. I have to pee," Zoe interrupted. "You know, you and my mother were nuts. You're lucky you didn't get killed." Zoe headed for the bathroom.

We were nuts all right, Jess thought, and careless and irresponsible. She went for more tea, but once in the kitchen, decided to switch back to wine. The cork slid easily out of the bottle and as she poured a full glass, Jess thought about those days with Holly. Alone we were two unstable chemicals; together we formed a dangerous combustible substance. Jess plugged the wine bottle as Zoe joined her in the kitchen, and Jess offered her a glass of bottled water.

"I think it's really odd that you don't know who my father is. I mean after hearing about how close you and my mother were and reading her journals, it seems like she definitely would have told you." Zoe looked straight at Jess.

Jess turned quickly, placing the wine bottle back on the counter. "Odd or not, she didn't." Jess turned back around, meeting Zoe's eyes. They stared at each other for a long, uncomfortable moment.

Zoe turned and moved into the living room, settling back on the sofa. "I don't think I'm anything like my mother, and I'm glad," she said.

"I think you'd be surprised. You've seen how much you look like her. And the way you came here, with such purpose. That was very much like something your mother would have done. Holly was passionate about the things she believed in and valued honesty more than anything. I think you feel the same way."

Zoe seemed unconvinced by Jess's big sister talk. "I want to hear what else happened on the way to Woodstock."

"I told you before, it isn't very interesting."

Zoe ignored her. "So you're at the airport in New York and you fall asleep."

Jess sighed. "All right."

The next morning we got the pot and sleeping bags from the locker, rushed to the gate and missed the first plane. We tried to get on one flight after another to Albany. There were hippies everywhere, and they must have heard about the festival because they were all flying to Albany, too. They also had more money than we did because they paid full fare, while we had to wait for stand-by seats. We sat all afternoon, until the last full plane departed.

"I'm miserable being poor," Holly said, sitting cross-legged in an airport chair. She started one of her slow pouts. I pulled my compact out of my backpack and patted some powder under my eyes. Holly made one of her rude comments about the stupidity of makeup, but I ignored her. "Maybe we could hitchhike to Woodstock."

"We'd get there and it'd be over. God, I look awful." I had big black circles under my eyes and a couple of new blackheads.

"Who's going to see you here?"

"That's not the point."

Holly offered me some potato chips from the bag she'd opened. We sat, mulling and eating. "What do you want to do?"

"I want to go home to Clear Lake."

"No!"

"I can't live like this. I'm hot and tired and I don't have clean underwear. I want to sleep in a real bed. So far this trip has been a bust. This is not my idea of fun."

"It isn't mine, either."

"Let's see if there's a flight back to Chicago."

"I'm not going back there." When Holly was stubborn, there was no room for discussion.

"I suppose you'd rather stay at the airport another night?"

"I want to go to Woodstock." Holly was determined, and I was too tired to argue again.

So we sat disunited, until I got a map and spread it across my lap. "Look how close Boston is on this map."

Holly pulled the map toward her and squinted. "It's the wrong direction, Jess."

"But if we fly to Boston, maybe we can catch a plane from there to Albany."

So we caught a stand-by flight to Boston. Of course, by the time we arrived, there were no seats on any flight to Albany. And Holly and I again sat disheartened in uncomfortable airport chairs.

"What do you suggest now?" Holly asked, lighting a Marlboro for herself, then one for me.

"It looks like Woodstock isn't in our karmic plan."

"Why doesn't anything we do ever work out?"

"We can't walk there."

"We could hitchhike."

I shot her a dirty look. "I want a bed and a shower."

"Should we try the Boston Y?"

"Absolutely not. I want to go somewhere where I can lie in the sun. Got any ideas?"

"Woodstock."

"Give it up, O'Neal, we aren't going to Woodstock."

"I can't." Holly took a puff on her cigarette and stood up. "Goddamn it, why are we so poor?"

"We're students, we're supposed to be poor. It's supposed to keep us out of trouble. Obviously, it's working," I sighed. "Where are we going to go?"

"I'll go anywhere as long as it isn't Chicago." Holly took the map and studied it. Then she pointed a nail-shorn finger at a spot on Cape Cod. "Provincetown. I want to go to Provincetown."

"That's pretty far."

"It's supposed to be great there. Tons of people, lots of hippie freaks. David's been there."

"How are we going to get there?"

"Hitch?"

"Aren't you getting tired of this story?" Jess asked Zoe. She was certainly tired of trying to stretch out every detail.

"Not really. I wish you'd get to the point, though."

"There is no point; it's all more of the same. It was one of those trips that never got off the ground. Nothing happened and we had a miserable time. End of story."

"Go on."

Jess sighed and began again.

I let Holly talk me into hitchhiking to Provincetown. With the rest of our pot stuffed into our packs and our sleeping bag rolls, we took a bus into Boston, got off and put out our thumbs. A cigar-smoking redneck in a pick-up truck gave us a ride as far as Hyannis. A cross dangled from his rear view mirror, and as we bounced in his cabin he droned on about Armageddon and judgment day, which he announced was just around the corner. He even gave us a date. I sat in the middle and got an earful, but Holly fell asleep with her head against the half open window. The driver came to an abrupt halt in Hyannis in front of a liquor store and encouraged us to repent our sins before it was too late. Holly and

I thanked him and tumbled out.

"You owe me for that, O'Neal," I told Holly, as I dug in my pack for some gum and pulled out an empty pack.

"I'll make it up to you, I promise."

"What now?"

"Now we have to find another ride or a place to stay."

I went inside and bought some gum. When I came out Holly was sitting on the ground beside a street lamp. I offered her a piece. Then I asked the looming question: "Where are we going to sleep?"

"On the beach?"

"Any other brilliant suggestions?"

"Too bad you didn't stay in the sorority. Maybe some of your sisters live here. God, I'm so tired."

I was too angry to answer her. It was dark, we were in the middle of nowhere, we didn't know anyone and we had no place to sleep.

Suddenly hope arrived, in the form of a 17-year-old boy. His name was Chris Gardner and his family had a summer house nearby. He had high cheekbones, perfect skin, brown shoulder-length hair. He was tall, wiry and wore blue jeans, but no shirt. He told us he'd wanted to go to Woodstock, too, but his parents had forbidden it.

He was an only child of wealthy parents and his biggest fear was that he'd grow up to be a carbon copy of his father, marry a girl with money from Connecticut, and live a dreary, ordinary life among the rich and well-bred society of his parents. I thought it sounded like a wonderful life, but he told us we were the lucky ones because we were free spirits, out on our own, with nobody telling us what to do or who to be. He made our lives sound thrilling, just when we'd begun to feel like scruffy failures who couldn't even find their way to Woodstock. We had no money, no place to sleep, and he envied us.

I watched his soft hands as he talked. They were hands that would never carry a tray of hamburgers to a car full of noisy teenagers or punch a clock in a factory. And still, we felt sorry for him. Nobody expected anything of Holly or me, except to stay out of trouble and marry above our station. We didn't know where we were going to sleep that night. Chris Gardner knew where his grandchildren would sleep. I imagined a portrait gallery of ancestors staring at him as he descended the grand staircase in his winter home in Litchfield, Connecticut. But for him, among all that tradition, there was no room to discover who he was. We offered him our deepest sympathies and told him we wished he could come away with us to a free, adventurous life. But for all our sympathies for Chris, it getting late and we still didn't have a place to stay.

"Why don't you stay at my house?"

"We couldn't do that," Holly answered quickly. "What would your parents say?"

"They'll be asleep. I'll tell them in the morning." I looked at Holly, my eyes pleading. "There's a day bed in the living room. You can sleep there."

"You won't get into trouble?"

"I don't care if I do."

We crept into the Gardner's house. Chris turned on the light in the foyer, illuminating a wall with portraits of three Kennedys— John, Bobby and Ted. It reminded me of the Catholic families in Clear Lake with their Trinity of Father, Son and Holy Ghost. Chris directed us to an alcove enclosing a small day bed. We thanked him, climbed into it and lay in the darkness. The air was quiet and still and smelled old and aristocratic. We were a world away from our Midwestern lives and decided it felt just as oppressive to us as it must have to Chris.

"So neither of you slept with Chris Gardner?" Zoe interrupted.

"He was a nice boy who tried to give us a place to stay." Zoe looked disappointed, which annoyed Jess. "We didn't sleep with every guy we met, if that's the impression you've gotten. Besides, we didn't even spend the night there." Jess was sorry she'd admitted that to Zoe and vowed to cut the story short.

"Tell me what happened." It sounded more order than request.

Jess began slowly. "We tried to go to sleep, but it wasn't long before we heard angry voices upstairs. Chris came down and told us his parents didn't want us in the house. He walked us outside, apologized to us, then said good-bye.

"We walked back toward the liquor store. I was pissed and tired, and Holly was cranky by this time, too. We stood under the bright streetlights and tried to decide whether to head back to Boston, go home or go on to Provincetown."

Jess stopped, remembering the rest of the trip.

"Well?" Zoe asked.

"All I remember is that I blew up at Holly. I was exhausted, I'd had it with her and I let her know it." Jess stopped, started again. "We fought. Then we . . . hitchhiked back to Boston and flew home. After that, we barely spoke to each other."

"So you got a ride back to Boston." Zoe was too persistent.

"We found a ride back to the airport, yes. And we didn't speak to each other the entire way." Jess took a sip of wine and ended the tale. "That's the story. I told you it wasn't interesting. We flew back to Chicago; Holly went home. I flew on to Sioux City and took a bus home. I wish there was more," Jess lied.

"So you're telling me you didn't meet any guys there."

"No," Jess said, glad she'd buried the notebook. She could rest now.

Zoe stood up and grabbed the framed picture of Holly and Jess off the table. She walked around the couch, then around again. "Are you looking for something?" Jess asked.

"I want to know who my father is. The more I think about it the less I understand. My mother opens my file, even sends me a letter telling me she wants to meet me, but she conveniently forgets to include my father's name. Then she dies. I would never do that. It's cruel." Zoe turned her tirade toward Jess as she paced around the room. "You know, I find it really hard to believe that you have no idea who my father is."

"I don't." Jess tried to regain control.

"How could you not know? You were always together. You told each other everything."

"We did not, and you're going to have to accept that. I've told you what I know. I'm worn out. I need some sleep." Jess said good night and left Zoe in the living room. She wanted the security of her bedroom, even in its disarray. She wanted what she couldn't have, sharp angles and no dust.

CHAPTER NINE

Jess hurriedly performed her nightly ritual with toothpaste and moisturizer. She tried to fold the bedspread and sheet into a neat triangle, then slid into bed, turned out the light and curled her knees to her stomach under the covers. She tried not to think about Zoe and her questions. I want my life back, she thought, I want her out of here.

Jess's head swirled with memories. She opened her eyes and stared hard at the door. You could have made her last days so complete, Jess thought bitterly. Holly wasn't important to you until now, when you need her. She closed her eyes but kept seeing herself and Holly, all alone by the liquor store in Hyannis. She sat up, lit a cigarette and remembered the real story of that frightful trip.

Holly went inside the store and emerged with two Tabs. Then she asked to see the map again and Jess, too tired to care, handed it to her. Holly pointed out that West Dennis was only a short distance from Hyannis. Didn't Jess have an uncle in West Dennis? Jess nodded reluctantly, and Holly berated her for not mentioning it before.

"Maybe he'd take us to Provincetown." Jess shook her head.

She didn't want to ask her uncle for anything.

"Why not, is he a bum or something?"

"He's not a bum," Jess told Holly. "But he and my parents are on the outs. He got them to invest in his company, which was supposed to make them a fortune so they could send Kayla and me to college. They ended up losing all their savings when the company went bankrupt. My uncle was the company president and my dad suspected he was less than honest about the whole deal. I haven't seen him in seven years. My dad would kill me if he knew I contacted him."

"Don't tell him."

"He'd find out. My uncle and my mother write. Besides, my uncle has money and my dad doesn't. I think his ex-wife got him into some great business deals."

"All the better. He's divorced and rich. Let's go."

"It's too far. We'd have to hitch again."

"We have to hitch back to Boston, anyway! All we want is a ride. Hey, maybe he'd let us spend the night."

"No!" Jess's voice was strained.

"What's your problem? Your uncle lives nearby, we're stranded and you won't call him. That's just great." They didn't speak for ten minutes, until Holly broke the silence. "Go ahead, go home. But first, give me your uncle's address and I'll look him up. Maybe he'll let me stay." Jess protested that she didn't have it. "I'm sure they have a phone book in West Dennis. Look, if you don't want to go, that's okay by me. Just don't rain on my good time." Holly kept pressing and finally, Jess gave in.

They hitched a ride with a couple in a Buick, who dropped them off at a West Dennis coffee shop. Jess found her uncle's address in the phone book and they walked five blocks to a Cape Cod style house. There was a light on inside and, as they started toward the door, Jess felt sick to her stomach. Holly rang the bell.

"This is a beautiful house. I wouldn't mind living here. How old did you say your uncle was?"

"Late thirties. Maybe even 40."

Uncle Jack opened his door in a blue silk robe and leather slippers with a drink in his hand. Jess saw the surprise in his face, which quickly turned into a big grin.

"Jess Martin! How great to see you! Come on in!"

He reached out to give Jess a hug, but she resisted and turned to introduce Holly. As Holly said hello, Jess noticed the gold link bracelet her uncle wore on his wrist and the gold chain with an Italian fertility charm that hung around his neck. His thick, brown hair was bleached blonde and he looked older than Jess remembered. But he was still handsome.

Uncle Jack turned off the television and picked up pages from the newspaper spread out on two overstuffed chairs. He told them to sit and asked them what brought them to his neck of the woods.

"We've been trying to get to the Woodstock Music Festival," Holly said. "Near Albany, New York, if you can believe that."

"You're a long way from Albany."

"We ran into a little trouble. Now we're just trying to get to Provincetown."

"What do your parents think about all this traveling, Jess?" His voice sounded daring and Jess tried to match his tone.

"They don't know we're here," she answered.

"And we hope you won't tell them," Holly interrupted.

"So you're trying to put me on the spot, hey, Jess?" Jack teased, slowly taking a sip of his drink. "Don't worry. I can keep a secret. Say, I'm forgetting myself. Can I offer you a drink?"

Holly asked for a Tab, Jess wanted a glass of water. When he swept out of the room, Jess picked up a photo from a bookshelf. It was of her uncle and a redheaded woman in party hats, toasting each other at a New Year's Eve party.

Holly noticed the book-filled shelves lining the walls. "My God, Jess, look at all these books! There must be thousands of them."

Uncle Jack returned with their drinks, and Holly asked about his books. Jess sipped her water and listened as Uncle Jack told Holly that his ex-wife collected first editions, and that she'd started him on the obsession. "One of her few good qualities," he said, winking at Jess.

There it is, Jess thought, that obnoxious wink, that easy familiarity.

"Truth is, I haven't read many of these books. I'm more of a collector than a reader," he told Holly.

Jess wondered whether he'd read any of them. He'd flunked out of college and the only thing Jess ever remembered him reading was *Playboy*. She didn't join their discussion but sat still, determined not to be taken in by his pseudo-charm.

Finally, Jess yawned and Uncle Jack insisted the girls spend the night. Holly thanked him profusely for his hospitality; Jess just nodded and gathered up her backpack. He showed them to his spare bedroom suite in the attic of his house. Too tired to shower, they passed out on the twin beds.

The next afternoon Uncle Jack knocked on their door. He entered, and Jess and Holly woke from a deep slumber as he opened the attic windows and let the ocean breeze blow in. Jess sat bolt upright, trying to get her bearings.

"Day's a wastin', girls!"

"What time is it?" Jess asked.

"2:00. You were so tired last night, I didn't have the heart to wake you this morning. Now I'm afraid you're too late to make the afternoon bus to Boston. You can stay over tonight and I'll drive you to the station in the morning." Holly protested, saying she still wanted to go to Provincetown, but Uncle Jack said he was responsible for seeing they got home safely and that was that. "Hurry and get dressed; I have big plans for the rest of your day." With that, he was out the door.

After he left, Holly hopped out of bed and told Jess that she had to admit she was glad to be staying in the same place for more than one night. Jess answered her with a grunt, and went quickly to bathe.

After they dressed, Uncle Jack ushered them into his Cadillac convertible to take them to his girlfriend Shelley's house for the afternoon. He was in a jovial mood and joked with Holly, who seemed to enjoy his sense of humor. The more he tried to joke with Jess, the more she withdrew, disturbed by his too-familiar manner. He took what he called the scenic route and pointed out houses where people with old east coast money lived.

"Are we talking Mayflower old money or turn-of-the-century old money?" Holly quipped.

Uncle Jack laughed, then explained the difference between old money and new money. "My ex, Geraldine, was definitely old money. Her grandfather made his fortune in steel. Most of the new money people have made their money in real estate or the stock market. The old money people look down on the new money folks, which I've never understood. If you ask me, money is money." He turned down a street lined with beautiful old houses and continued talking. "Then there are folks like Shelley who have mixed it up a bit. Her first husband was old money, but her last husband—who passed away a couple of years ago—came from Texas. Oil was his game and that's considered new money out here."

"So what are you and Shelley, since you both married money?" Holly asked.

"Very, very lucky." Jack laughed and tugged Holly's hat down over her eyes.

Jess sat staring out the back seat window, impressed by the grand houses along the way and thinking about what her Uncle had said. She wished she were old money; it sounded so substantial, so dignified. But then she decided she'd settle for old money or new money, anything but what she was: Midwest—no money.

Uncle Jack turned into the driveway of a beautiful Mediterranean style house. "Welcome to Paradise, it's a long way from Iowa." Shelley opened the door and greeted Uncle Jack with a big kiss and immediately hugged both the girls, tittering about how sweet they looked and how nice for Jack that they could visit. Jess was suspicious of her enthusiasm, and sized her up.

Shelley had large breasts and skinny, bird-like legs. She was overly tan and her dyed red hair was teased into a smooth dome shape. Noticing her outfit—white mules and tight sand-colored capri pants with a fuchsia blouse—Jess decided Shelley was definitely new money and exactly the kind of woman who would be attracted to Uncle Jack.

"Oh, Jack we have to take them to the party tonight. Ginny and Sam will get such a kick out of having cute girls spice up their party." Shelley fussed with Uncle Jack's collar as he explained about the party they'd been invited to.

Holly was quick to decline. "Thank you, but we only have the clothes in our backpacks and there's nothing party-worthy there, trust me."

Shelley wouldn't take no for an answer. "Don't worry, honey, it's a Hawaiian theme party and it won't take me more than a couple of hours to whip up dresses for you." Jack explained that Shelley had designed costumes for the local theatre troop before she met her last husband. Shelley quickly measured the girls, then gave them towels and sent them out to the pool.

Trees and dozens of potted plants surrounded the heart-shaped pool. Holly and Jess found a patch of sunshine and spread their towels on lawn chairs. Jess had barely spoken since they arrived at Shelley's, but Holly kept up a constant chatter about Jess's uncle, his books, his house and their good fortune to have a place to stay. Jess closed her eyes against Holly's voice and tried to relax. Finally, she dozed, but was soon awakened by the Rolling Stones' "Honky Tonk Woman," coming from the far wing of the house. When she looked up she saw Holly, reading. Beyond her, Will Block, Shelley's 21-year-old stepson, tan and wearing red trunks and thongs, walked toward them. Jess couldn't see his eyes through his sunglasses, but did notice that his wavy hair was tousled and that he stood nearly six feet tall. He introduced himself and after a few minutes of small talk pulled a joint from his pocket, inviting them to share it. When Will told them he was a philosophy major at Yale, Holly was suddenly interested, and they began discussing Plato, Nietzsche and Kant. Jess wished she had a transistor radio to drown out their intellectual posturing.

When Will found out Holly had been on a swim team, too, he challenged her to a race. He let Holly win, and Jess, jealous of their connection and tired of being left out, gathered up her things. As she passed the two cavorting in the water, she asked Will if he was going to the party. He said he had other plans, but that he might stop by later with some friends.

After Shelley gave them a preliminary dress fitting, Uncle Jack took the girls back to his house to get ready. Jess applied makeup while Holly combed her hair and complained about going to a dull party filled with old people where they wouldn't know a soul. Secretly glad to be going, Jess let her rant. She had begun to imagine herself summering on the Cape, living a privileged life far from cornfields and small-town minds. But she'd need to meet someone who could make that a reality. Maybe he'd be there tonight.

Uncle Jack picked up Shelley and the two returned with the girls' dresses. Jess's was a colorful print sheath with spaghetti straps. She liked the print, but her cleavage showed and she tried pinning back the straps, which only helped a little. Holly's was a scooped neck, floor-length flowered dress that she said she hated. "When in Rome, Holly," Jess told her. Holly grumbled and picked up her hat.

As the girls descended the stairs, Uncle Jack wolf whistled; Shelley applauded. Uncle Jack asked Holly if the blue felt hat she was wearing was attached to her head permanently. Holly informed him she wasn't going anywhere without her hat. He laughed and said the hat looked charming on her, then rolled his eyes at Jess.

When they arrived on the steps of a huge beach house, the front door flew open and a large woman with a deep tan and a big straw hat appeared. She wore a strapless muumuu imprinted with big purple flowers. She looked to be in her mid-forties, but the skin on her chest looked ancient. Before either of her invited guests could speak, she pulled Jack and Shelley to her bosom saying, "Jack, Shelley, darlings, I'm so glad you could make it." She rocked them until she saw Jess and Holly. "And you brought children! How cute!"

"Ginny, these are the girls I called you about. This is my niece, Jess Martin, and this is her friend, Holly O'Neal."

"Of course. There I go forgetting myself again. You'll have to excuse me, I'm just a native girl who can't remember her manners. Wait till you see my hula this year, Jack! Come on in, girls, and welcome to Governor's Manor. That's what we call it, but it's not quite right. It's so quaint here, don't you think?" She didn't wait for an answer but moved on, yelling over her shoulder: "Well, get the girls a drink for God's sake, and where's Sammy? Sammy? Come over here, honey, and meet our guests."

The girls were whooshed through the house and out the back door onto a large patio that ran the width of the house. The patio was bordered with poles strung together with wire. Hundreds of lanterns hung from the wire, burning candles and casting a romantic glow. There was a kidney-shaped pool, white wicker furniture and tables with fresh flowers. The middle-aged guests were dressed in colorful draped material; Holly complained that it looked like an adult toga party.

Then their host appeared. Sammy was skinny, fiftyish and balding, in white shorts and a Hawaiian shirt. He called a caterer over and asked the girls what they wanted to drink. Jess requested a vodka tonic, Holly a rum and coke.

"Are you sure the girls should be drinking, Jack?" Shelley asked, and Holly and Jess gave her a hard stare.

"Of course, they're with me," Jack winked. The caterer went to make the drinks and Sammy introduced the girls to the guests around the patio, then went off to greet new arrivals.

Once they got their cocktails, Shelley and Jack started making conversation with couples they knew, and Jess was glad to be left alone. Holly could only complain about the bronzed, diamond studded, middle-aged guests.

"This is stupid. I can't believe we're at this party."

"Are you determined to be miserable?" Jess secretly wished Holly would take off her hat since it looked so out of place. Guests kept pouring onto the patio, and Jess hoped to find someone at the party who wasn't too old.

"Look at these people. They look like they've been coming here every summer for the past hundred years. They all have the same tan and that same attitude. What is it?"

"Money," Jess answered. Holly agreed. To Jess, the other guests' lives seemed complete and linear, like Chris's. Jess wondered what it might feel like to be so sure of your place in life. She envied it.

"I don't want their money, but I'd love to have this view,"

Holly said. They looked out, taking in the breathtaking ocean that rimmed the horizon.

"The money buys the view," Jess reminded her. A caterer lit more candles around the pool as the sun set; the lanterns burned bright. More caterers brought out trays of fresh fruit, and the girls amused themselves trying to figure out which couples were together. But no one paid them any attention.

They decided to get another drink and went to the kitchen, where women were bustling about, preparing hors d'oeuvres. The bar was off the kitchen, and Holly asked the bartender for a double for each of them, then they wandered back out to watch the adults party. They stood near the pool. Holly gulped her drink and talked about how out of place she felt. Jess sipped hers and wished Holly would try to fit in. The hostess borrowed a guitar from one of the guys in the band, and sang a folk song about rich folks hating poor folks and white folks hating black folks. The rest of the guests joined in, and Jess wasn't sure if they were joking or if they meant the words. There were no black folks there and no poor folks, except for Holly and Jess.

"I hate these people," Holly proclaimed and downed the rest of her drink. "And I hate being here."

"So leave. I'm tired of hearing about it," Jess shot back.

"Fine." With that, Holly turned and headed back toward the kitchen. It was then that Jess noticed Will standing by the pool with three other boys.

Jess shot out of bed, memories flooding her mind. She went to her closet door and stood on her vanity chair to reach the top shelf. She pulled down several boxes and brought them to her bed. She opened the first box labeled "College," and began flipping through photographs.

There was a picture of Holly and her dressed in their matching sweater and skirt outfits, another was a landscape of their dorm room filled with clothes, stolen street signs, empty liquor bottles and posters. There was a picture of Holly's psychedelic mobile hanging from the ceiling light, one of Jess's makeup collection on the bureau, another of the milk crate Holly used as a stool. Jess thumbed through more photos until she found the stack from that trip, banded together.

First was a photo of Holly hitchhiking with her backpack and her thumb out. The next was of Jess in a pair of white, fringed cut-offs and striped cotton T-shirt, sitting in an airport chair, giving the peace sign, a campy forlorn look on her face. There was a picture of Chris Gardner in front of the liquor store and one of Holly at Shelley's pool in a red and white bikini, a book over her chest. Next was a long shot of Jess and Holly in their Hawaiian dresses before the party, then one of Jess with Uncle Jack and Shelley. The last was a photograph taken from a distance; it was of Jess talking to Will and his three friends at the party.

"Oh, my God," Jess said aloud. "Zoe's father."

Just then, Zoe knocked on Jess's door. Without thinking, Jess ran to the bathroom, ripped up the picture, threw it into the bowl, and flushed the toilet.

"Jess! Jess!"

"Just a second." As the picture started to disappear down the bowl, Jess stuck her hand in and tried to fish it out. Then, remembering her promise to Holly, she stopped herself.

CHAPTER TEN

Zoe called Jess's name again. Jess shoved the box of photographs under her bed skirt, then opened the door. Zoe stood with a stack of journals in her arms.

"There's nothing here about your trip to Woodstock. Wouldn't she have written about that? If she did, why didn't she include that journal? I don't understand."

"Are you sure you've looked through all of them?"

"I've checked the date. There isn't one. Why wouldn't she have sent it?"

"I don't know." Jess was breathing heavily. It's my fault, she thought, all of this is my fault.

"How could you not know? You were always together."

"I told you before, we didn't share everything."

"I've done the math. I was born April 17th, eight months after Woodstock."

"Gestation is nine months."

"Gestation is 40 weeks. Anyway, I was a month early." Jess looked at Zoe suspiciously. Jess had been led into a trap. "Joanne told me. That puts the date of conception at the time you and my mother didn't go to Woodstock." Zoe looked victorious.

"I've never been very good at math," Jess said, meekly.

"Well she slept with someone. And there's got to be some way I can find out who." Jess glowered and Zoe softened slightly. "She never told you anything about my father?"

"No," Jess said sadly, because she was lying and because the truth was awful and because she'd promised never to tell it. "She never told me. Maybe no one can give you the answer you came for."

Zoe looked at the floor but wouldn't let it be. She started in again, insistently. "Why wouldn't she put his name on my birth certificate? And even if she wanted to keep it a secret for some reason, why wouldn't she have told you? This isn't fair. It isn't right."

"I'm sorry, Zoe." Jess tried to sound calm, mature. "Maybe there are some questions that can never be answered."

"That is such bullshit! Maybe she didn't even know. I'll bet that's it. I'll bet she had no idea who got her pregnant. If you guys hadn't been so cheap and fucked so many different guys, maybe I'd have a fighting chance to find my father. Free love, free sex, do your own thing, it's all a bunch of fucking crap!"

Jess grabbed Zoe's arm and wheeled her around until they were face to face. Zoe's cheeks were red and her eyes shot daggers, like a tigress ready to pounce. Jess began talking slowly, enunciating her words. "Don't you say that about her."

"I'll say whatever I fucking—"

Jess tightened her grip. "You will not say that about her here."

"I just want to know why she wouldn't even—"

"Stop it! If you're angry with your mother because of who you think she might have been, or because she gave you up, or she didn't provide you with every bit of information you think you're entitled to, we'll stop here." Zoe tried to pull away from Jess's grasp, but she held firm. "Holly wasn't a saint. She was far from perfect, but she was an incredibly strong woman and I've never been closer to anyone in my life. I will not listen to you degrade her."

Jess let go of Zoe's arm, surprised at her own words, because they rang true, and the force of that made her unsteady. She softened. "You came to my door. You told me you wanted to find out about your mother, and I said I'd tell you about her. But that's not really why you're here, is it?"

"Of course, that's partly why I came. But my mother is dead. Maybe my father isn't. I want to find him."

"I don't know who he is."

"I don't believe you."

"I don't care."

"That's obvious," Zoe said, under her breath.

"No, goddamn it, I don't. But here." Jess marched out of her bedroom and over to the sofa. She reached between the cushions and retrieved the journal. "Since you're so intent on knowing the truth, read this," she said, and shoved Holly's journal at Zoe. "Find out for yourself. But do me a favor. Don't ask me any more questions." Jess left Zoe and rushed to her bedroom. She closed the door and stood behind it. Fine, you little bitch, she thought. You asked for it. Just leave me out of it.

Jess forced herself back into bed and curled into a ball, feeling guilty that she'd given Zoe the journal, hoping the night wouldn't be a long one. She put her fingers on her temples and pressed hard, trying to push the memories away, but there was no relief. All she could see were the two girls in their party dresses, plummeting toward the end of that horrible night.

Jess remembered watching Holly head into the house for a drink. Tired of hearing her complain, Jess was happy to be alone. She joined Will and his friends by the pool, anxious to connect with someone her age, anyone who wasn't Holly. Jess remembered sitting poolside, while the lanterns cast a magical bouncing light on the water. All four of the boys were handsome, despite their talk of drug adventures, and Jess flirted shamelessly with them.

She laughed at every joke and splashed water around the pool so she could show off her long tan legs.

Will was the best looking, but to Jess, he was too pretentious and intellectual. There were three others. Two were from Boston and went to school with Will. They reminded Jess of the frat boys back home; they had blonde good looks, but were boastful and immature. The third, Tyler, had dark brown hair, was built like a body builder and seemed more worldly. He even looked older than the other boys. Jess remembered being impressed when he said he summered with his parents next door to the party hosts.

Tyler suggested they all go down to the beach and Will told Jess to get her "cute" friend to join them. Jess agreed reluctantly. She thought Tyler was the most engaging, that maybe she'd have a chance with him if Holly would spend some time with the other boys. She swept through the house searching for Holly until she heard someone talking about a girl who had locked herself in the bathroom. Of course it was Holly, writing furiously in her journal. Jess practically had to pry her out.

As Jess dragged a sullen Holly through the house, Holly insisted on stopping at the bar for another double rum and coke before they made their way to the beach. The guys started a small driftwood fire and they sat together, smoking a joint and making jokes. Holly got higher and louder, telling stories about pompous professors and loser classes. Jess was glad when Tyler offered to show her his father's yacht.

They walked past his pool and the outdoor bar, where Tyler got her a drink. Then they made their way down the dock to his father's boat. He unlocked the cabin, all the while teasing Jess about being from Iowa.

It was dark and musty inside the cabin. Tyler told a snide joke about how the Iowa officials had to put AstroTurf on the football field to keep the cheerleaders from eating the grass. Jess didn't laugh and asked him to turn on the lights. Tyler said it was more romantic in the dark. Then he grabbed her.

He kissed her roughly and when she tried to push away, he grabbed her hands. He was strong and held her hands hard by her sides, kissing her chest, licking the skin between her breasts. She felt her skin dimple with goose bumps, contradicting her fears. He kissed her neck and started to talk.

"Come on, now. Just a kiss." She relented, afraid to deny him. After a soft, slow kiss, he poked his tongue deep into her throat, then pulled back and purred through his lips. "There now, that's better, isn't it?" Her body began to respond and she found her arms around his shoulders.

He put his hand under her dress and began to massage her thigh, moving up as he squeezed. He found the top of her underpants and started to pull them down. She protested and reached around to pull them up. This didn't feel right and she wanted him to stop. But he had no intention of stopping. He quickly grabbed her arms again and turned her completely around. She lost her balance as he pushed her forward over the back of a sofa, her arms pinned in front of her body. He held her roughly with one hand while he undid the zipper on his shorts. "Stop it," she heard herself say. "Please, stop it."

"What's the matter?" he sneered. "I thought this is how they like it, down on the farm." He leaned in, pushing up against her bare buttocks and began to force his way. He prodded and pushed and Jess cried out as he entered her. When she reached behind to push him off, he grabbed her arms and twisted them behind her back. Every time she moved, he twisted them higher on her back until all she could do was cry out in pain, begging for him to stop. Finally, with all her strength she pushed her body backward, sending him onto his backside. She pulled her panties up and ran, hearing his drunken laughter as she stepped onto the dock. Then she heard him begin to moo. Too scared to cry, she crossed back to the beach fire, but Holly was gone.

Jess heard laughter coming from the house. Panting and near tears, she stumbled as she ran toward the house, past some party-goers and right into her uncle. He was just drunk enough and the shadows were dark enough that he didn't notice the fear in her face.

"I'm going to find Shelley, then we gotta call it a night." He stumbled toward the house.

At that moment, Jess saw Holly running up from the beach, flushed and angry. "Where have you been all this time?" she demanded. "Why did you leave me there?"

"I went for a drink," Jess answered harshly, still wincing with pain. She had been violated in the most horrible way and her emotions were so raw she could hardly control the shaking. And there was Holly standing before her, looking self-righteous and angry because Jess hadn't taken care of her. She felt ready to explode. She wanted to slap Holly, yell at her for being so selfish. But all she could do was stand and shake and imagine screaming, Why did you let this happen to me? Jess stood, fighting back tears of humiliation.

As the girls glared at each other, Uncle Jack and Shelley appeared and told them it was time to leave. Holly and Jess didn't speak on the ride home, and the next day they slept until Uncle Jack knocked on their door. He drove them to the bus station and they sat silently on the ride to the airport, each blaming the other for the misery of her fractured being.

Jess's temples pounded with pain. Shivering, she rose and took four aspirin, left the light on and crawled deep under her covers to hide from her memories. The problems of her present life were overwhelming her. She didn't have the will to do battle with ones from her past. She held her head in her hands and hoped for morning.

In the next room, Zoe lay between the fresh sheets in Holly's army jacket, devoured the notebook and wept. Unable to sleep, she rose and went to Jess's bedroom door, started to knock, then remembered what Jess had said. She went to the living room, sat on the sofa and flipped through every journal, page by page.

CHAPTER ELEVEN

Jess woke with a start. She was sweating, anxious. About what? A dream. They were on a yacht, she and Eric and Uncle Jack. The two men were working on a project, a big business deal, and she was typing. But all the keys on the typewriter had been moved around and no matter how fast she moved her fingers, she couldn't type a coherent sentence. They were standing over her, hurling insults.

Jess pulled a pillow over her head to smother the anxiety and drown out the pulse of a solid base guitar coming from next door. Or was it coming from inside her apartment? She pulled the pillow from her head. It was coming from her office. Then she remembered Zoe, in her guest room. Jess let out her breath, pulled the pillow back over her head and covered her face. She held it tightly, until she was desperate for air. She held it longer, until she couldn't stand it another second. Finally she gasped for breath and threw the pillow across the room. "My kingdom for a hand gun," she muttered as she climbed out of bed and headed for her bathroom.

As she brushed her teeth, her mind was a jumble of should-haves, must-dos and who-cares. She should try to reach Eric. And say what? Sorry I failed. She'd need coffee for that conversation, and a cigarette. She should send Zoe on her way as quickly as possible so she could get some work done. She should go to the office; she should get on the Internet again and find a fresh hook for the wayward ProbTech campaign. Something hot, young. Who am I kidding? Jess thought as she surveyed her face in the mirror. What I really should do is call the headhunter who keeps hounding me. But before I do anything, I need a shower. That was the one thing she was absolutely certain about. Not a warm gentle bath, a brutal shower. The sting of hot water would pummel her back to life.

She showered quickly then dressed in jeans, an oversized blue sweater and black boots. After applying her makeup, she entered the hallway where she heard the voice of Country Joe McDonald through her closed office door. "And it's one, two, three, what're we fighting for / Don't ask me I don't give a damn, next stop is Viet Nam . . ." She smiled, remembering Holly bellowing the tune, practicing for her troupe. She never could carry a tune, but she certainly was enthusiastic. The song ended and the Woodstock crowd cheered.

Jess made her way to the kitchen. Spotting the debris on her living room floor, she saw Holly's journals strewn everywhere, her blue felt hat next to them, and regretted the previous evening's confrontation. She retrieved the hat and wondered how Zoe had reacted to the truth in Holly's diary. I'll know soon enough, Jess thought, as she made her way to the kitchen to put water on for coffee. Maybe she should soften the edge with a breakfast peace offering. A good breakfast, Jess thought, and then on your way. If she took Zoe to her friends within the hour, she could get to the office, locate the ProbTech file and get started on the new campaign before 11:00. Pancakes, eggs, toast, and orange juice. The perfect send-off.

Jess finally found her griddle hiding in her oven with other pots she stored there. It had seemed like a good use of space since she never baked. She found a pancake recipe and followed it perfectly, afraid any misstep would result in chaos.

After she buttered the griddle she stood with spatula in hand, ready to turn the pancakes. Staring at the bubbling orbs, a sharp memory came to her. She saw her Uncle Jack flipping pancakes in her mother's kitchen while her mother giggled at a joke and at his prowess with a spatula. He always appeared when her father was out of town on a sales trip. Uncle Jack slept on the couch in their den and her mother adored him. He was handsome, jovial and quick, and he came with a boatload of jokes and empty pockets which Jess's mother filled. Celeste loved her baby brother. Jess had loved him, too.

Jess liked the way her uncle teased her and she loved taking attention away from her mother, who resented it. Uncle Jack was a worthy opponent in board games and taught Jess how to swim, do back flips and play underwater games. He was so different from her father. "Different in the worst way," Jess said aloud. Her vision was disrupted by the sight of black smoke rising from the pan, followed by the smell of burning pancakes. She heard Zoe enter the living room.

"Shit! This just sucks." Zoe's voice was sharp, frustrated. Turning off the gas and releasing the pan from the hot burner, Jess looked around the corner. Zoe, still in her pajamas, angrily closed a journal, then tossed it onto the mound on the floor.

"Is there a problem?" Jess asked, not wanting to know the answer.

"Oh no, no problem. It's just that, according to Holly's journals, I don't exist."

"What do you mean?"

"Here's the journal from the summer when I was conceived and as you can see, half the pages have been torn from the end of it. The next journal begins when Holly came to visit you in the spring of 1970, after she gave me away. There's not a word about my father, about being pregnant or about my birth. I guess she couldn't wait to erase the whole dirty little episode from her life. Or did you tear the pages out or hide another diary?" Zoe continued digging through the journals as Jess grabbed the one from August 1969. She opened it and was relieved by the missing pages. She'd been saved from having to tell any more. She closed the book and set it on the coffee table.

"You have everything she sent to me."

"It isn't enough."

"Can't you understand how it might have been for her? I'd think in your condition you'd have a little more sympathy." Zoe shot Jess a hateful glance. "There was so much we had to deal with, and she was so sick for the first three months."

"She just wanted to forget about me."

Jess talked fast, trying to say the right thing. "She didn't want to forget about you. She thought about you all the time. When she went to the home to wait for you to be born, she wrote me lots of letters about her experiences."

"Where are they?" Zoe interrupted, jumping up from the floor.

"I'm afraid I don't have them. When I left Los Angeles, I threw out almost everything from my past."

"Perfect," Zoe scowled.

"But Holly did think about you, and I don't know why she tore those pages out—"

"Because that's when she got pregnant and she didn't want me to know who my father is." Jess ignored the comment and tried to change the subject. "Look, I'm fixing breakfast. Pancakes. And I can make some—"

"I'm not hungry." Zoe headed back toward Jess's office, then reeled around and came back. "You lied to me. You said you went home after spending that night in Hyannis, but you didn't. You went to your uncle's house. Why didn't you tell me that? And you went to a party there. Why didn't you tell me about that, either?"

"I—"

"And my mother was gay, wasn't she? Kate wasn't just her collaborator, she was her lover." Zoe's face was red, her voice harsh. Jess nodded. "And when were you going to share that bit of information with me, or did you decide I was too immature to handle having a dyke for a mother?" Zoe stared hard at Jess.

"No, I . . . yes, Holly was gay and, yes, Kate was her lover. They had a wonderful relationship." Jess spoke slowly, trying to regain control. "I should have told you. I'm sorry. It wasn't because I didn't think you could handle it."

"At least she left that part in her journal. I guess it's easier to admit to being kissed by a girl at a party than to admit that you had a baby out of wedlock."

Jess looked toward the journals and memorabilia scattered over the floor. "Look, Zoe, this isn't easy for me either. You walk in here demanding answers to all kinds of questions and somehow I'm supposed to know exactly what to tell you. I don't."

Zoe glared at her, turned and headed toward the bathroom. She turned back. "You could start with the truth. When are you going to stop lying to me? When is everybody going to stop lying to me!" Zoe stormed out and Jess heard the bathroom door slam and the water begin to run.

Jess went back into the kitchen, confused and weary. She threw the pancake mix down the sink and rinsed the bowl. She should have told Zoe the truth about Kate. Oh, well, another fuck-up. A few more and I might get used to living in emotional squalor, Jess mused. She poured a cup of coffee, then returned to the living room and sat, fatigued by Zoe's anger and blame. She stared out the window until a question formed in her mind. What girl had kissed Holly at the party? Holly never mentioned that she'd met anyone there. Jess picked up the journal from the coffee table. Paging backward, she began reading.

August 17, 1969

Jess is taking a beauty bath and I'm lounging atop a beautiful bedspread in her uncle's attic bedroom suite. We've been saved! We finally have a clean, dry place to sleep. Her Uncle Jack is cool; his living room is lined with first editions. He's very well off and summers in this 100 year-old house. He's taking us to this Hawaiian theme party that his friends have every year.

Jess got out of her bath; she's putting on makeup and curling her hair like she plans to meet Mr. Right tonight. I'm sunburned and the side of my face is puffy and red. Not likely I'll meet anyone; but I did have an interesting conversation with Will today— "Uncle Jack's" wacky girlfriend's stepson. He said he might be at the party tonight. Anyway, I'd rather stay here and read, but Uncle Jack won't let me. Hopefully there will be plenty to drink. He just came in with our outfits for the evening—Shelley made them for us. More later. Aloha!

Later

An awful thing just happened—I feel so weird. A girl just kissed me. A real kiss with meaning, and I let her. I took a bottle of rum from the bar and locked myself in this bathroom. Does this mean I'm queer? I wish I'd never come to this party. I can't be queer. It was so weird.

Jess and I were at the bar by the kitchen and some women were going in and out, preparing the food. This tall girl, with long straight black hair and brown eyes looked at me and smiled. I smiled back.

Jess and I went back to the pool and sat for the longest time on lounge chairs watching the people at the party mill around.

Everyone else seemed comfortable, like they belonged, but I felt like a fake. I hated being there. I watched two people, obviously not married to each other, trade flatteries a few feet from me. Why is everything always about sex? Everyone was flirting and there was that feeling in the air that sex was on everyone's mind. But it was different here than at school, more desperate, as if the stakes were higher.

Anyway, the hostess came out and started singing an awful song on a guitar. Jess spotted a group of guys our age, including Will, son of Shelley. It was then that I knew I'd lost her. I didn't want to talk to Will. He's interesting but too full of himself, so I went inside for another drink and watched Jess from the kitchen. She was batting her eyes and talking to all four of those guys like they were the most interesting people she'd ever met. It makes me sick to watch how flirtatious she can get. I'm sure she thinks they think she's groovy.

I got bored and since the house was empty, I went to the den and sat watching the news, happy to be numbed by the rum and the current events, so factual and straightforward, so far removed from me. There was a feature on the Woodstock Festival and everyone there looked free and untainted. I sat there wondering what in the hell I was doing at a stranger's house in West Dennis, at a party filled with people who hated poor folks and black folks and had probably never seen either in their entire lily-white lives. I wanted to escape from there, to run out the front door, stick my thumb out and never look back, when a voice behind me said: "With a hat like that, you should be at the festival."

I turned around, and standing behind me was the girl I'd seen before, staring at me with her deep brown eyes. "Actually, I was supposed to be there." We watched thousands of kids listening to music in front of the giant sound stage.

"I wanted to go, too, but I had to work this party for my mother."

"I'm sorry." She bent over and rested her arms on the back of the sofa. She seemed so confident.

"Mom runs a catering business and summer's her busy time. This is an annual event for the Olsons, their wild Hawaiian party. Mother caters it every year."

"Would you like some rum and coke?" I offered her my glass.

"No, thanks, I don't drink. But I have some pot if you want to share a joint."

"Great." She led me upstairs into a bathroom off a far bedroom.

"Are you sure no one will come up here?" She assured me that no one used that part of the house and locked the door behind us. We sat, me on the toilet, she on the bathtub, and she took out a joint and lit it. We took turns standing at the window, blowing the smoke into the dark, and we talked. She goes to a small liberal arts college out here somewhere. She's on scholarship and wants to study archaeology. She said she likes finding hidden, buried things that no one in recorded history has seen before. She asked me what I wanted to do. I told her I didn't know, that I liked to read and that was about it. I went over to the window and took a hit, then looked out at the ocean.

"What kind of a career can you have reading?"

I pressed the pot into my lungs and as I exhaled out the window, I realized I had no answer. "I don't know, maybe I'll be a librarian."

"A librarian?"

"Wrong choice?"

"Stuck in a dusty old building with books all your life?"

"It has to beat being stuck in a pit scraping dirt away from bones."

"You have a point."

She came over to me. We finished the joint and leaned out the window, side by side. The pot gave me a mellow buzz and I asked her if she thought the people at the party were as weird as I did. As we watched them dancing and laughing below us, she told me who was with whom, who had been with whom, and who she thought was going to be with whom eventually. Then we looked at the night sky and named as many constellations as we could. Suddenly it didn't matter what all those people below us were doing.

"Sometimes, don't you just want to jump out of your skin?" I asked her.

"Why?"

"Because it's such a nuisance. I mean, all this eating and sleeping—it's such a lot of trouble. If you were free of your body you could float anywhere, unbounded. You'd never be too cold or too hot, or too empty or too full, or too sad or too confused, or —"

"Or hopeful, or happy, or in love, or in lust—"

And with that she took my head in both her hands and faced me squarely toward her, and the world went into slow motion. She's going to kiss me, I thought. I watched her face as she brought it close to mine and I saw her lips part slightly as she turned her head a little to one side. And when our lips were just about to meet, she pulled me toward her and our lips did meet, and she was kissing me. I didn't resist, I just kept thinking: I'm being kissed by a girl.

But the kiss was sweet and I found myself kissing her back, and I felt my hat fall off my head, and I thought, I have to get my hat. Then I forgot about the hat and a minute must have passed, ten minutes must have passed and we were still kissing, until finally something way back and from very far down came racing up to the front of my consciousness and screamed: No, no, no!

I wrested my face from hers and stood there looking at her. She looked back at me, puzzled, then turned her head to one side in a question. I stood shaking like a spinning top before it falls and said, "I have to go." I grabbed my bag, ran out and locked myself in this downstairs bathroom. What will Jess think? I wonder if it shows. Oh, no. Someone's knocking at the door—have to go.

The final pages were gone and with them the story of what happened the rest of that night. Jess closed the book and laid it on the counter. "So that's what happened," she whispered softly. "You must have been so confused."

Chapter Twelve

Zoe entered the living room, interrupting Jess's thoughts. Despite the chopped off hair and the facial rings, she looked radiant in her long flowered wrap-around skirt, pale blue T-shirt, heavy Dr. Marten sandals and Holly's love beads. Jess watched her, mesmerized by her youthful beauty.

Zoe strode over to the couch, sat down and started in again. "I just want you to know that when you've been lied to all your life you can't bear even one more lie. I mean, I have two birth certificates. One has Joanne and Paul's names on it. It's like they thought they could make it up as they went along and I'd never know."

Jess was surprised at how little it took for her to be angry with this imitation Holly. "Wait a minute. Where's the big lie, Zoe? Your mother gave you up for adoption, which your folks told you, right? When did they tell you?"

"When I was four."

"It seems to me that everyone has actually been quite honest with you."

When Zoe responded, she spoke softly, resigned. "I don't expect you to understand, just accept that it's very important that people tell me the whole truth and not just a little part of it. I'm tired of people editing the truth. It's been that way my entire life and it's wrong. People who aren't adopted don't understand. There's a hole in me where other people have knowledge. You know where you came from and where your parents' parents came from. You have a history. I don't. I just hoped you'd be honest with me and not try to protect me or my mother, who's dead, so it no longer matters. You were my only chance to know her . . ."

Jess was quiet. I'm sorry, Holly, she thought. She turned to Zoe. "I'm sorry." Silence again.

"My real birth certificate says: Father—unidentified. Why do you think she didn't want anyone to know? I mean, when she tried to contact me and opened my file, you'd think she'd have put all the pieces of the puzzle together. It seems cruel to leave out one of the most important parts. Do you think you could help me find my father?"

Jess felt a pang of regret. "I'm sorry. We were good friends, but like I said, we didn't share that."

"Who was Will?"

"Will was my uncle's girlfriend's stepson. He brought some friends to the party, as you read."

"Did Holly meet him?"

"She met him at my uncle's girlfriend's house before we went to the party."

"And the rest of those guys?"

"I flirted with them. Holly watched me. You read the rest."

"She didn't meet them?"

"No. It was just me." More lies to hide the truth.

"Did she write you any letters after that trip? Did she tell you she might have been seeing someone late that summer? Did she go back to Iowa City before school?"

"I don't have any letters." The truth.

"Was David Delaney my father?"

"I'm sure it wasn't David." Another truth. "Zoe, please stop asking. The one thing I don't know is who your father is." One last half-truth. After an uncomfortable silence, Jess said, "I saw you in the nursery at the hospital. If you'd like, I can tell you about Holly's pregnancy and how you looked when you were born."

Zoe's lips pursed. "I guess that will have to do."

"Okay." Jess searched her memory. "Well, school started a few weeks after we returned from our failed trip. I'd gotten a part time job at Seiferts, selling clothes, so I arrived a week early to go through training. Holly and I had made arrangements to live in the same rooming house—my room was in the attic and Holly's was on the first floor at the back of the house, next to the kitchen. Holly got jobs as a waitress at the Pizza Palace and at a bookstore. We had full class loads and no classes together. So the truth is, that semester we rarely saw each other."

"Did you miss each other?" Zoe asked.

"Yes, but we were both stubborn. We'd said some really mean things to each other before we left Boston, and the chill continued until early November. I remember when we finally made up, the night I first learned about you. I was studying for a mid-term when Holly knocked at my door. I opened it and she burst in, tears streaming down her face. Like the way you came in."

"I wasn't crying."

"No. But I've never heard anybody knock with such vigor. Anyway, Holly came in and said, 'Jess, I think I'm pregnant.' I sat with her on my bed and asked her when she last had her period."

"When was it?" Zoe was wide-eyed, ready to pounce.

"She couldn't remember," Jess said, relieved to be telling the truth. "She said she thought she was getting a period in September, but it was very light."

"What part of September?"

"I'm not going to play this game, Zoe. And besides, I don't think she knew. Do you want me to tell you this or not?" Zoe was silent.

I asked Holly if she was sure she was pregnant. She said she was pretty sure, that she'd been throwing up for weeks. She was petrified. I told her the first thing we needed to do was to go to the doctor to make sure.

"You'll go with me?" she asked, looking like a lost child.

"Of course I'll go with you."

"But I was so mean to you. How can you stand me?" She was crying again. I got out the phone book and told her I'd been mean to her, too, and that I was willing to bury the hatchet if she was. "Consider it buried."

"Now what was that doctor's name where we got the birth control pills? And why weren't you taking them?"

"They made me gain weight, so I stopped. The joke's on me now, isn't it?" she said.

"Didn't you ask her who my father was?" Zoe asked.

Jess worded her answer carefully. "Of course I asked her. I asked her that night."

"And . . .?" Zoe was sitting on the edge of the couch.

"She said she couldn't tell me. She said he didn't matter and she made me promise never to ask her again." Jess took a sip of coffee. "I never asked her again."

Zoe started to say something, then ran her fingers over the love beads. "Well, all right, tell me the rest."

The next day Holly wore the gold band we'd used to get birth control pills and we saw the doctor. She was pregnant. He gave her vitamins and told her to make an appointment on the way out. Of course we didn't. Holly was in shock. I remember her asking me over and over on the way home, "What am I going to do, Jess?

I can't have a baby." I had no answers for her. I asked her if she would consider an abortion, but from the start, Holly didn't want that. Besides, they weren't legal, and I had no idea who would perform an illegal one. Holly was just scared and confused. We sat together in her room and commiserated.

"You know, sometimes they use coat hangers," Holly said. "I read this story about a woman who got an abortion in an alley from some guy who wasn't even a doctor."

"Why is it that every abortion seems to be performed in an alley?"

"Anyway, he did it with a coat hanger, then left her there to bleed to death. Someone found her, but now she can't have kids." Holly was lying on the bed, her shirt pulled up, surveying her rounded stomach. "I can't do that. There's a baby in here." I was relieved that she wouldn't have an abortion because it seemed so dangerous. I was afraid, too; I'd heard the same stories she had. I told her the only other option was to have the baby and give it away.

"Or have it and raise it myself," she reminded me.

"Yeah, right," I said. "Let's see, between the two of us we have maybe $100. You have no car, no real job, no education, no husband prospects. And I don't see you raising a kid alone."

"All right, all right, I get your point." Holly lay back with a huge sigh and pulled the blanket up under her chin. "What am I going to do? I can't have a baby. Make it disappear." She began to cry softly. I crawled into bed next to her and she put her head on my shoulder.

"I don't know how to make it go away. I think we have to make a plan so that you can stay here and have it. Maybe we can find a nice couple to adopt it."

Holly looked up at me. "Have the baby and give it away. That's it! And I know the perfect couple. Niles and Annie!"

They were hippie friends of ours who actually were married. I thought that was a great idea.

"Did they try to adopt me?" Zoe interrupted.

Jess shook her head no. "Our plan was full of holes. We didn't know there were legalities involved with adoption. We thought Holly could have the baby and just give it to them. Believe me, you're much better off not having Niles and Annie as parents."

"Don't be so sure of that."

"Trust me. I don't know Joanne and Paul, but they're better parents than Niles and Annie would have been. You may think your parents are uptight, but they also look stable. Besides, Niles and Annie were divorced within a year after you were born."

At the time, Niles and Annie were our only married friends. We'd met them through Mark Bates, who seemed to know everybody in the counterculture. They were both 20 and had been married six months. We'd gone to their wedding in May; they held it outdoors at the reservoir near Iowa City. I thought Annie was the most beautiful bride I'd ever seen with her long flowing hair braided with ribbons and flowers. She wore a white cotton Indian dress with embroidered flowers and no shoes. Niles wore his favorite blue jeans with a tuxedo jacket from the thrift store. He was shoeless, too. We weren't sure if the guy who married them was a real minister, but I do remember that he read from *The Prophet*. Niles and Annie read poems they'd written, then we all sang Peter, Paul and Mary's "Wedding Song" and they were married. Even Holly thought it was wonderfully romantic.

The week before Thanksgiving we went to Niles and Annie's house and told them our story. Niles thought adoption was a great idea. He said he wanted lots of kids, so why not start right away. Annie said she had to think about it; it was a big responsibility. But the next day she called and said she thought it was a groovy way to have a baby without having to get fat. So the plan was in place. Holly and I felt like we could relax a bit, until we realized that we'd have to go to our respective homes for two full weeks during Christmas break. We'd talked our parents into letting us stay in Iowa City during Thanksgiving break, but they were adamant that we come home for Christmas.

We spent the next three weeks helping Niles and Annie make plans. Niles built a cradle, Annie knitted a baby sweater and Holly said she was happy for the first time in months. It was all so sweet and naive, like playing house. Of course, we didn't know that what we were planning was not only illegal but impractical. We hadn't even considered how we'd pay the hospital bills. Reality hit when December 20th rolled around, and Holly had to take the bus to Chicago for Christmas break.

"Thank goodness you're not throwing up any more. That would have been a dead giveaway," I told Holly as we packed our bags.

"I'm starting to really show, though. What if my mother wants to go shopping or something?"

"When was the last time you went shopping with your mother?"

"You're right; Ellen doesn't shop, and if by some miracle she wants to, she'll ask favorite daughter Maggie, not me." I told her to stay in her room as much as possible and to only come out for meals. And I told her to call me every day for moral support. "I wish I could go home with you," Holly said, folding and refolding her army jacket into her Samsonite. Then she put it on and lay on her bed.

"Are you kidding!" I laughed. "Celeste has pregnancy radar. She'd have you bundled up and off to church to confess your sins before you could open your suitcase. Better you visit your mother.

In this situation, Ellen's total disinterest in your life will be a godsend."

"We sprung for a cab to the bus station and I hugged Holly so tightly I thought I could actually feel you."

Jess stopped talking, suddenly aware of the connection she felt with Zoe. Zoe looked down and Jess went on.

"Before putting her on the bus, I took off the silver peace symbol I wore on a leather rope and put it around her neck. We hugged again and as I watched her board the bus, I had the feeling I was sending her off to her execution. In a way, I was.

"It went pretty well the first few days. We talked on the phone every day and Holly did what I suggested and spent most of her time in her room. But when she called me on Christmas Eve, her brother listened in on the second phone and went directly to Ellen with the news that Holly was pregnant. All hell broke loose at the O'Neal house, and by New Year's day Holly was on her way to a home for unwed mothers in Minnesota."

"Just like that, they stuck her away in some home? That's barbaric! Like something out of Dickens. I can't believe her parents would do that to her." Zoe was shocked. "These days they have day care for babies in the high schools so the mothers can finish their studies."

"Back then there was a lot of shame surrounding illegitimacy. And frankly, I think the pendulum has swung too far in the other direction. Don't you think having a day care center in a high school sends the wrong message to the rest of the students in the school? Like, 'Hey it's okay to have irresponsible sex because we're here to help. You won't even miss a class.' I think a little shame wouldn't hurt."

"Oh, look who's talking about the shame of irresponsible sex."

"I'm only saying that most teenagers aren't equipped to be full-time mothers. And I know so many women—mature, responsible, well-off women—who can't have children of their own and want desperately to adopt."

"Like Joanne?"

"Yes, like Joanne. It seems like a good solution for everyone involved."

"Except for the kid, who spends the rest of her life looking for her mother and wondering why she didn't want her. Better to have an abortion and get it over with than sentence a child to that kind of hell."

"Wait a minute," Jess said. "Are you telling me you would rather not have been born?"

"Well, no, but—"

"Listen to me!" Jess could feel the anger growing. But when she heard the strident tone in her own voice, she softened. "Once Holly made the decision to have you she began to love you. When she was at the home she said she never wanted to give birth, that she wanted to keep you inside of her forever. She said that was the only way she could think of to keep you truly safe. She talked to you all the time. She knew you'd be a girl and she called you Zoe from the beginning."

Zoe stroked the love beads. "What was it like in the home? Did you ever visit her there?"

"The inmates, that's what Holly called them, weren't allowed visitors, except for family. But we wrote every week. We talked on the phone when we could, but the nuns were strict about phone privileges. Holly's folks had put my name on a list of people who weren't allowed to call Holly, so I had to wait until she called me. Our plan was that, a few days before you were due, I'd go to Minneapolis to be with her. But I got a frightened call from her in April. Her water broke and she was scared because you weren't supposed to come for a month. I hopped a bus to Minneapolis and went to the hospital where you were born. At least there it was possible to get in to see her."

"Did she have natural childbirth? Did she get to hold me when I was born? Who was there with her?" Zoe barraged Jess with questions.

"She was all alone. No one but medical staff was allowed in the delivery room; this was before the days of labor coaches. Even natural childbirth was a radical concept. Holly wanted to give birth without drugs but they paid no attention to her and gave her what they called a saddle block. When I arrived, you were already born and in an incubator."

"Did she hold me?" Zoe's voice was softer now.

"The policy at this particular home was no contact with the birth mother. So no, she never got to hold you. She wasn't even supposed to see you, but she did. We sneaked out of her room that night and went to the nursery, which was on a different floor. You were so amazing! A perfectly formed, tiny little baby, all small and red. You lay there in a little diaper under some lamps to keep the jaundice away. Holly couldn't take her eyes off you and just kept repeating, 'That's my baby, that's my beautiful baby girl.' I don't know how long we stood there, but at some point a nurse came and told us to leave because we were unauthorized visitors. Before we left Holly held her palm up to the glass of the nursery and said, 'I'll always love you, Zoe. You'll always be with me. I will never forget you.'"

Zoe's lip trembled, then she started to cry. Jess reached out awkwardly and pushed a strand of Zoe's hair from her face. "She loved you, Zoe. She really did."

Zoe sat, sobbing quietly. When she spoke, the words came out in a tumult of sounds. "When I was little, I wrote her letters. I told her about my life, what I looked like, who my friends were. I asked her over and over why she left me. I wanted to know her. I wanted her to know me. And now it's too late. It's too late."

"I know," Jess said. "I know." Zoe moaned and threw herself at Jess, who could only grip her wailing body.

Jess remembered the morning the nurse shooed Holly and her away from the nursery window where Zoe lay sleeping. Back in Holly's hospital bed, Holly had collapsed in Jess's arms. She kept sobbing that she'd made a big mistake, she shouldn't have given her baby away, no one could take care of her baby like she could. And what was she supposed to do with all this milk? She ached to feed her baby and her breasts ached from their fullness.

Jess said nothing. She could only hold Holly while she cried about her baby. And now she held Holly's child, crying for her mother. Jess looked about her living room, strewn with items from her own youth, then down at Zoe in her arms. There was nothing left to say.

Just as suddenly as she lunged at Jess, Zoe pulled away. She wiped her eyes, then thanked Jess. Jess's heart sank when she saw the sorrow in Zoe's eyes. What have we done to you? she thought. Was it really the best solution? Zoe was saying something about finally having some answers and thanking Jess for her time. Jess nodded without hearing the words.

"And I guess you'd like your living room back. I'll pack up my mother's box. You did say I could keep it?"

Jess nodded and stood on unsteady feet, while Zoe began gathering the journals. Jess turned to get her coat, then turned back. She felt a pang of sadness as she watched Zoe place each item into the box. She didn't want Zoe to take Holly's things. Holly had given them to her and she'd never been able to go through them. "Why don't you leave these things for now and we'll go out for breakfast. Are you hungry?"

"Not right now, but I might be by the time we go someplace."

"Is there anywhere in San Francisco you haven't seen? The Wharf, North Beach, the Marina?"

"Haight-Ashbury. I've always wanted to go there." Zoe continued placing things into the box.

"We'll have breakfast somewhere in the Haight. Afterwards, I have to stop by my office; then we'll come back, pack up the box and I'll take you to your friends. Sound like a plan?"

"Sounds fine," Zoe said, as she stood. Jess went to get her purse and when she came back, Zoe was stuffing a couple of Holly's journals into her backpack. "I want to wash the tears off my face before we go." Zoe headed for the bathroom and closed the door.

Jess sat back down in front of the collection of mementos still lining her coffee table. A picture of Holly had fallen to the floor. Jess picked it up and looked hard at the bright young face mugging for the camera. "Okay, I kept the promise," she whispered. Jess thought back to that night in November, decades earlier. The night Holly had come to her room, pregnant, frantic. She remembered how Holly had just kept crying and saying it was her fault, all her fault. The friends made a pact never to tell anyone what had happened. Jess tucked the photo into the stack of books. She felt a chill. "So many secrets," she muttered.

"Are you talking to yourself?" Zoe was standing next to the couch, freshly scrubbed and ready to go.

"Let's get out of here!" Jess exclaimed too loudly, and jumped to her feet.

Chapter thirteen

The women climbed into Jess's BMW and as Jess turned right out of the parking garage, Zoe retrieved a San Francisco street map from her backpack. Paul had taught her how to read maps when she was just six, she explained. If you ever find yourself in a strange place, he'd told her, buy a map and you'll know how to negotiate your way out. She located Haight and Ashbury streets and asked Jess if she needed directions.

"I know the way. But be prepared. The Haight isn't anything like people imagine."

"I know that," Zoe said, with the assurance of an expert. "I had a friend who lived there. I just want to see it for myself."

Jess headed across Market, where a police car blocked her way. A hundred demonstrators carrying placards protesting Chevron's plan for offshore drilling marched and shouted slogans. "Damn it, I should have known. Greenpeace is in town."

"I have a friend who's a member." The infamous Annabelle, Jess thought. "Do you have a problem with Greenpeace?" Zoe asked.

"I think you can make your point without shoving it down people's throats."

"You sound like Paul," Zoe shot back. They're just demonstrating, they aren't holding a gun to your head. Haven't you ever protested anything?"

"A long time ago."

"I have. Lots of times. I went to a demonstration against animal testing. I even volunteered to help with an oil spill. My friend's really radical, too—"

"Annabelle?"

"Another friend, Megan. She went with a group from PETA to a mink farm and released some of the animals."

"You mean stole them?"

"I mean they let them go."

"Do you think that's right?"

"Sure, why not?"

"If people want to raise minks and other people want to wear dead ones, don't you think that's their decision? What happened to freedom of choice?"

"The animal didn't have a choice. Besides, those people don't know how horrible living conditions are for the minks, and if they did, they'd stop wearing fur. PETA just tries to raise awareness."

"I think you can raise awareness without ripping coats off people's backs."

"I didn't say I ever did that."

"Would you?"

"Maybe. Anyway, I'd never buy one either, okay? Or eat any meat, especially foie gras. They force-feed those ducks you know, until they get so fat they can't even walk. It's the cruelest thing, just so rich people can have paté at their parties. I mean what gives them the right . . ."

Zoe droned on and Jess stopped listening. She was watching the earnest, purposeful demonstrators pass by. Jess suddenly had a strong visceral memory of sitting under a bridge in the rain. Holly was next to her crying. She could taste the stale damp cigarette they traded back and forth. Mostly she remembered the feeling that night, the night she realized that everything had been lost.

She turned to Zoe and almost said the words, "Do you remember that night?" but caught herself. Zoe wasn't Holly, even though the resemblance gave Jess goose bumps. Zoe had been an infant in May of 1970.

"... I mean, I wear leather shoes, but lots of people think that if you're really concerned about animals you should be concerned about all animals and not just the cute ones. I've seen people carrying signs against wearing fur; but they're wearing leather shoes and leather belts to hold their jeans up. But then, a lot of people don't wear any leather, they wear vinyl that looks like leather. So maybe that's what I saw."

Who are you? Jess wondered, as the young woman, so similar in coloring and intensity to her lost friend, carried on about issues that for Jess had long ago been supplanted with the need to survive and the drive to succeed. Jess nodded but didn't speak. Zoe finally stopped talking and they sat in silence as the demonstrators passed. Jess made a stab at conversation.

"I will say they're very well organized."

"That's the way it is. You choose a route, get a permit, then a police escort."

"A police escort for demonstrations, what a novel idea."

"Where have you been the past ten years?"

"Earning a living, smart ass. May I remind you that when we demonstrated, it was against the government and the police, so to actually have a police escort seems sort of ironic to me."

Zoe continued to sermonize on the demonstrations she'd participated in. Jess nodded, but stopped listening. She was trying to reconstruct that time, so many years ago. Then it came back to her, anti-war demonstrations and Michael.

It was early spring; he was talking politics. She remembered

Michael's intensity as he told her about his plans to change the world, romancing her with tales from the anti-war movement. The campus was a hive of unrest that spring and Michael was one of the leaders of SDS.

Jess met him when he talked her into posting rally notices in the Union bowling alley where she'd gotten a new job. Curious, she went to the rally, and after Michael's rousing speech, she brought him to her bed. Michael was thin, with straight dark hair that hung over brown eyes. He was smart, observant, argumentative and never sat still. Jess didn't always understand his politics or his anger against the establishment, but she found his passion very seductive. Too many people had suffered under the capitalist system he told her, and it had to be destroyed, "by any means necessary." Jess loved his grand gestures and his fiery speeches. But more than once she had wished he'd stop talking and just make love to her.

Jess was a good listener, even when she didn't agree, and Michael loved the attention. He took her to meetings so she could help with the business of the revolution, which usually meant fetching sodas and sandwiches for the guys who were plotting the rebellion. Still, Jess was convinced that by leafleting and protesting she could help end the war in Viet Nam. She also held out hope that the system could be changed from inside, without violence. But she kept those opinions to herself and never contradicted Michael. She couldn't win an argument with him anyway.

"Was my mother political?" Jess turned, looked oddly at Zoe, and was brought back to the present.

"Holly steered clear of political parties. I think she voted Libertarian when she did vote. I know she was for McGovern against Nixon. At least, that's what she told me."

"Didn't you believe her?"

"We agreed not to talk about politics after 1970."

"Why?"

"Well, she wasn't in school and I'd joined SDS—"

"I've read about that," Zoe interrupted. "Students for a Democratic Society. It was a group of students who organized on college campuses and were big advocates for change. A lot of them were Marxist-Leninists who believed that the state ought to be overthrown by violent means. Others believed the state should be overthrown, too, but they hated violence. Then there were the peaceniks, of course. They may have protested to be part of the party, but mostly they just wanted to get stoned and be left alone. After the war, SDS splintered off, and each of those groups had its own agenda: there was the Revolutionary Communist Party, Line of March, the Weathermen . . ." Jess marveled at the way Zoe spit this out, like a child reciting state capitals.

"How do you know all this?"

"I took a modern U.S. history course. Since all this was happening around the time I was born and since I didn't know who my parents were, I've become sort of an expert." Zoe continued on, giving her textbook interpretation of the times.

As Jess watched the demonstrators pass, she remembered embracing Holly the morning she stepped off the bus in Iowa City. She recalled that Holly looked waif-like, fragile. Her usually ruddy cheeks were almost sallow, her healthy glow was gone.

Holly had stayed in Maywood after leaving the home for unwed mothers. Her parents had kept Holly's pregnancy a secret and lied to their friends about where she'd been, but Ellen still berated her for bringing shame to the family's good name. After a week she grew tired of Holly's sulking silence and gave her bus fare to Iowa City.

Holly arrived the day after the Kent State catastrophe, when four students were killed by the Ohio National Guard. Student governments and SDS groups all over the country were holding meetings and calling for protests, and the University of Iowa had a large SDS membership. In Iowa City the local police and the Iowa National Guard were everywhere, so the entire student body was on edge. Jess wore a black arm band in solidarity and couldn't wait to tell Holly about her relationship with Michael and her involvement in the anti-war movement. She wanted Holly to feel as committed as she did.

But when Holly got off the bus, she was more interested in going to the Union to look up David and Mark. Jess hadn't the heart to tell her that the fraternity and sorority types had taken over the Pit, and their friends had scattered to off-campus coffeehouses and bars. And that she rarely saw them any more.

Jess walked with Holly down the steep hill toward the Union, talking nonstop about all she'd learned about politics and power. Holly nodded without answering while Jess made ever-grander statements, all borrowed from Michael's speeches and the movement propaganda. But when Jess started to preach about the freedom that was certain to ensue when money was abolished and people bartered for goods, Holly burst out laughing. She wanted to know what kind of exchange you'd make for a chicken, who would raise and butcher it and what they'd get in trade. Jess stopped talking and quickly lost her confidence, her rhetoric diminished under Holly's practical scrutiny. They walked the rest of the way in silence.

When they reached the bottom of the hill, they saw that SDS was having a pig roast in the open field next to the Union to protest the Kent State killings. Holly was delighted by the spectacle and the women sat on the grass, watching a hundred people sing, play Frisbee and dance in the soft warm spring air. It might have been a scene from the previous spring, except for the pig on the spit and the people wearing arm bands and leafleting.

As they watched the action, David and Mark appeared and greeted them warmly. They asked Holly where she'd been; she lied and said she'd taken the semester off to earn money. Jess noticed that David's hair was halfway down his back now and tied in a ponytail; Mark had grown a blonde mustache. Their clothes seemed even scruffier than before. Jess sadly realized that their lives hadn't changed; they were still into getting stoned and hanging out. Mark admitted that he was now "underground" dodging the draft. David had recently returned from Des Moines where he'd been sent for a physical. He told the draft board he was gay, then found a sympathetic psychiatrist in Iowa City who wrote a letter vouching for his homosexuality. He was waiting to hear whether or not the draft board believed him. If they didn't and he was drafted, he planned to go to Canada. When Jess asked if they were going to the rally that night, they said they couldn't afford to risk arrest. Instead, they were planning to party and invited the girls. Holly enthusiastically agreed to go.

Mark and David left to score some pot and Jess realized how estranged she was from her old friends. Michael and the movement had become all-consuming; she couldn't remember the last time she'd gone to a party just to have fun. There was never any laughing with Michael and his comrades, the situation was too serious—there was always work to be done, critical causes to champion and changes to be made. Jess was sure Holly would join in if she could only hear about it firsthand.

After some pleading, Jess convinced Holly to attend the SDS meeting that afternoon. Michael was in charge of the heated discussion held in a professor's crowded basement. They were planning the evening rally and everyone disagreed about everything, from the order of the speakers to whether to have an open microphone. Some advocated violence, others opposed it. And like too many other meetings, it quickly turned into a showcase for competing intellects and a battle of egos. After three hours they finally agreed, that in the interest of free speech, anyone who wanted could take the floor for five minutes. The rally would be billed as a protest against the Kent State killings and the war in Viet Nam, but any topic would be acceptable: the war, civil rights, getting ROTC off campus, even tuition increases.

When the meeting was over, Jess and Holly walked outside into the bright afternoon sunlight of the professor's tree-lined yard. Holly had a look of disgust and was about to comment when Michael approached, bursting with revolutionary fervor. He kissed them both and invited them to join him and the others at the Mill before the evening rally. Holly declined, saying she wanted to browse the bookstore, but Jess was swept up in Michael's glow and his urgency won her over again. Jess watched Holly walk away and had the smug sense that Holly, with her books and her overwrought thoughts, was hopelessly out of touch with the times. Jess felt sorry for her.

That evening hundreds of boisterous students gathered in the grassy field before the steps of the Old Capitol building; someone had painted the letters ROTC in black on each of its four pillars. When Michael stood at the microphone and spoke about the lives that were being lost in Viet Nam on both sides, the crowd grew solemn. Moved by his words, Jess knew that if Holly could only hear Michael, she'd understand that a human life should be worth more than politics, than ideology, than countries, and that's why the movement was right. Energized, she ran the block to David and Mark's.

When Jess arrived, she saw a room full of hippies listening to music, drinking wine and smoking pot. She only recognized Firm Guy and Bullet, who were arguing about whether meditation was an opiate of the people or a path to enlightenment. She found David, Mark and Holly on the fire escape smoking a joint. They sat looking out with a full view of the Old Capitol's grounds, bordered by Clinton Street with its local stores and bars. Jess saw that protestors crowded the entire grassy area and were beginning to spill onto the sidewalk.

When Jess stepped outside, she couldn't hear the speeches, only the shouts and chants. Mark offered her a toke on the joint. She declined and began her monologue, as a stoned David and Mark listened halfheartedly. She told them she was ready to risk her future for theirs, but they weren't willing to do the same. She said they were blind to the lies and corruption of a society that had ignored them and that was gunning down students like animals. Mark finally answered that while he agreed that the world was absurd, protesting wouldn't change a thing. Holly sat in silence, which only made Jess talk faster and louder.

Jess argued that if they weren't part of the solution, they were part of the problem, then pleaded with Holly to join her at the rally. Holly answered that she didn't like crowds. Jess told her that wasn't a good enough reason; she could stand on the edge of the crowd and at least hear the speeches.

"I listened to those people at that meeting. I'm not against students holding a rally, but I think advocating violence is obscene. We don't share heroes, Jess. Mine are Gandhi and Martin Luther King, Jr., not Che Guevara, Fidel Castro and Karl Marx." Then Holly landed the brutal blow, suggesting that Jess's newfound ideals had more to do with love than with politics.

Jess shot back dramatically, "We can't let the government get away with killing us."

"They've already gotten away with it," Holly responded. "And I hate what they're doing in my name."

"Then do something. Let them know they can't go around

killing people: Vietnamese, Cambodians, U.S. citizens!" After listening to dozens of Michael's speeches, she could recite all the arguments.

"I'll write a letter."

"What effect is that going to have?"

"What effect is standing around singing, 'Give peace a chance' going to have?"

"Do you want your brother sent to Viet Nam to get killed?"

"Hey," Holly said, "maybe that wouldn't be a bad idea."

Mark chimed in. "We're old enough to die for our country, but not old enough to vote the fuckers who are putting on this war out of office. What power do we have?"

Just then police cars pulled up to the streets that separated the college buildings from the town. They watched as the crowd noticed their arrival and began chanting, "Down with the pigs, down with the pigs." Someone in the crowd started oinking, and the whole crowd joined in.

"I'm going," Jess said.

"To be an idiot," Holly protested.

"To exercise my rights. There's more to life than flower power and Panama Red. Go ahead, stay stoned, be mindless. You don't care about anyone but yourselves, none of you care." Some of the crowd began moving toward the police cars. A wall of Iowa National Guardsmen stood in the background in full riot gear, complete with guns, billy clubs and gas masks.

Holly saw them and stood up. "All right, I'll go with you."

"Don't bother. We don't share heroes, remember?" Jess climbed quickly back through the window, ran down the stairs and outside. Holly was at her heels. Then the shouting demonstrators moved off the green, toward them and the retail stores across the street. As the protestors neared Iowa Book and Supply, someone at the microphone accused the bookstore of overcharging for books and taking an obscene profit. He encouraged the demonstrators to burn the store to the ground.

Holly and Jess were suddenly surrounded by protestors. Police sirens filled the air and more Iowa City squad cars appeared at either end of Clinton Street. They stopped, blocking off the exits from both sides, preventing traffic from moving but giving the students open access to the street itself. The protestors moved closer around Holly and Jess, cutting them off from the way they'd come.

"Jess, we've got to get out of here."

"No, I want to stay."

"Let's try to get back. Please."

"What, are you scared?"

"No, but—yes." They watched as someone hurled the first rock at the bookstore window, breaking it. Then another and another. The angry mob compressed itself onto Clinton Street, then gas-masked National Guardsmen moved in on it, making the crowd even tighter and forcing Holly and Jess closer to the bookstore.

"Jess, let's get out of here before we get hurt."

"We've got to show them that they can't do here what they did at Kent State." Jess started to move off into the crowd and Holly grabbed her arm.

"What right do these students have to break windows?" Holly asked.

"It's the only power we have, don't you see? They'll never change unless we act."

"Just tell me what the owners of Iowa Book and Supply have to do with Kent State? With Viet Nam?" She shouted to be heard over the screams of demonstrators clashing with police.

"They're all part of the imperialist complex, don't you see?"

"No."

"They raise us up to be good little citizens, teaching us what they want us to know out of textbooks that Iowa Book and Supply sells, how to be good little consumers and keep people in Third World countries in chains, while we enjoy the fruits of their cheap labor. And then we kill them when they don't have the kind of government we want them to have. It's disgusting. They don't want us to know the real truth—" Jess ranted.

"What are you talking about? You get this shit from Michael—you don't know what you're saying."

Jess ignored her and harangued on. "They tell us the Vietnamese are gooks, that because they're our enemy they're bad people—when all they really want is the same thing we want, peace—"

Holly grabbed her arm again. "And this is how you get peace? Throwing rocks through windows?" Holly screamed.

The group was now chanting, "Hey, hey, ho, ho, Western civ has got to go."

"We've got to show those fuckers in Washington that they can't kill people in Viet Nam or in Ohio." Jess pulled her arm out of Holly's grip.

"Throwing rocks isn't going to change anything!" Holly looked small in the middle of the madness.

"Just you watch. It will." After all the bookstore windows were broken, the students who were throwing rocks pushed toward Seiferts clothing store next door. Jess watched in horror and fascination as the mob moved like a mindless amoeba. Holly grabbed Jess by both arms and shook her shoulders. "Leave me alone!" Jess yelled, pulling away. "I'm going with them."

Suddenly Michael emerged from the crowd in his red headband and torn T-shirt, sweating and excited. When he saw Jess, he handed her a rock. "Do it, Jess, throw it through Seiferts' window. Smash the capitalist pigs." He shouted at her as she stood, vacillating.

"Is Seiferts part of the problem, too, Jess?" Holly shouted. The crowd moved and they were forced to move with it.

"Come on, Jess, the pigs are coming. Throw it," Michael screamed. The crowd pressed in; people were shouting and pushing.

"No," Holly yelled. "You worked there! What the hell do people who sell clothes have to do with telling lies? With Kent State? With the Viet Nam War? What gives you the right to break windows? Tell me! What right?" Holly tried to grab the rock from Jess's hands, but Jess yanked it back. She held it high over her head.

"You just don't get it, O'Neal, do you?"

"Why don't you fucking explain it to me. In real words, your words, not a bunch of rhetoric some hotheaded boyfriend put in your mouth."

Police sirens drowned out their voices as someone grabbed Jess's arm and twisted it behind her back; the rock fell to the ground. "You're under arrest." It was an Iowa City policeman. Jess looked around for Michael, but he'd disappeared.

"Leave her alone. She wasn't going to throw it," Holly shouted.

"Shut up. You're under arrest, too." As the crowd surged forward the policeman pushed the girls into a waiting paddy wagon filled with other demonstrators. Holly seethed, staring at Jess as they stood in the crowded wagon. Jess was afraid. Suddenly, everything was too real.

At the jail the girls were fingerprinted, their photographs taken, and they were put into a cell. They sat together, while their cell mates talked and sang protest songs. To Jess, they sounded powerless and she wished they'd stop. Holly sat stone-faced and silent, and Jess could only sit in silence herself. After an hour, a new group of students was brought in. To make room for them, the group Holly and Jess were in was released. As they left, Jess saw Michael in line waiting to be fingerprinted.

"We torched the Old Armory building, Jess—burned the fucking thing to the ground. Five people were sent to the hospital. It was great." Michael was beaming, his eyes wild with power.

"That building doesn't even belong to the military. It's used for graduate student offices," Holly said.

"It was used by the pigs in World War II," Michael said. Holly shook her head. "It's symbolic," Michael chided her. "Besides, the worse, the better. Right, Jess?" He winked at Jess and she smiled weakly. The girls were ushered outside.

"'The worse, the better.' What does that mean, Jess? What did he mean by that?" It was dark and had begun to drizzle. Jess and Holly walked side by side, heads down. Jess felt sick, but Holly kept asking her what Michael had meant.

"He means that the more students get their heads cracked by the police, the more press we'll get. And with more publicity, more people will be outraged, then radicalized. They'll become revolutionaries and join the armed struggle against the pigs and what they stand for." Jess recited the words like a child reciting a poem, memorized without ever understanding its meaning. Her voice had begun strong but lost energy as she thought about the meaning of the words she was saying.

"What do the pigs stand for?"

"Oppression." Her voice was a whisper.

"No. What Michael wants is oppression. 'By any means necessary.' Now I get it. These people don't care about the truth, they don't care that people suffer. They just want power. Jess, this is fucked, don't you see?" Jess pressed into her temples, suddenly so confused her head ached. Deep inside she feared Holly was right, but she couldn't admit it, not now. They walked on in silence and were near a bridge over a small creek when a thunderbolt struck a nearby tree and it began to pour. As they ran under the bridge for cover, Holly fell on a piece of broken sidewalk. The cement ripped her jeans and drew blood from her thigh.

They sat under the bridge, shivering and wet. Holly lit a cigarette. She paid no attention to the blood, turned away from Jess, leaned against a wooden support beam and sobbed silently. Jess watched her. Finally, she asked what was the matter. Between sobs, Holly choked out her words. Why had she brought a baby into this world when everybody in it was hating and killing each other. She was sorry she had the baby, sorry for the baby who was somewhere crying for her; she couldn't comfort her, and even if she could, it would be a ruse. There was no comfort in this horrible, sorry world. Holly huddled over her own knees, rocking, crying.

And Jess couldn't comfort Holly. Her own chest felt like something heavy was pressing into it, and she couldn't speak. She only had vague fleeting thoughts. That everything was breaking down. That there was no truth. That there were no values worth holding, because nothing that anyone did mattered. Like the gash in Holly's leg, the truth of the universe had become clear: there was no Band-Aid for suffering and there would never be. She could offer Holly no comfort; she could only watch her cry. Jess was certain they felt the same hopelessness; but she knew that if she tried to reach out to Holly, she couldn't contain her own suffering and they would both drown. All Jess could do was huddle with her under a bridge and share a stale cigarette.

The traffic began moving, jolting Jess out of her reverie. She looked over at Zoe, reading from a journal. As Jess turned onto a side street toward the Haight, she felt an overwhelming sense of grief.

In the end, it had all seemed so futile. After school ended, after all the speeches and protests and meetings and flyers, the war wasn't over for two more years. Then the world went on. Jess thought about her generation. They were educated; they became teachers and parents and lawyers.

What did they tell their children? she wondered. That it was a glorious time to be alive? That everything we fought for was noble and good? Did they perpetuate that lie? Or did they tell the truth about the sick underbelly of the times, the loss of values, the twisted logic, the pathetic grab for power on all sides? Does anyone remember that all the maps had been destroyed?

Still, Jess yearned to believe in the future, in hope. But it was her own future she didn't believe in any longer. That was the bitter truth, the one she kept at bay. And the feeling, like the one under the bridge, that everything was already lost.

CHAPTER FOURTEEN

Jess turned the corner and found a parking spot at the intersection of Haight and Ashbury in front of a head shop. She shut off the car and tried to breathe away the heaviness in her heart and make sense of the scene before her: the dirty street filled with teenagers buying and selling drugs, older street people begging for money, stray dogs and cats, resale stores, pizza stands and shops offering 60s paraphernalia in a 90s package. She hadn't been down the street in years, and seeing it now she felt sad and a little guilty. Such a waste of good human life.

"Are you all right?"

"Welcome to Haight-Ashbury," Jess grimaced. "Where you can buy used records, bongs, blue jeans and pretend things never change." The women plugged the meter and strolled among the Bohemian residents, runaways and tourists. The more Jess saw the sadder she became, but Zoe seemed oblivious to the filth and enthusiastically dragged Jess into shop after shop. Jess had to admit that if trade is the measure of success, the stores were doing a booming business. Zoe seemed like a teenager at a mall. She found a rayon print dress at a used clothing store and Jess bought her a purple knit hat to match. At a tattoo parlor Zoe bought some fake tattoos, one spelling "Mother" in the shape of a heart, which she gave to Jess.

For herself, she found a barbed wire tattoo that she planned to wrap around her upper arm. At one head shop Zoe explained how to get high using a whipped cream dispenser. At another, Jess couldn't help but marvel at the variety of bongs available for power pot smoking.

Jess tried to catch Zoe's enthusiasm, but she couldn't ignore the lost souls filling the street. One young woman in ancient and unwashed hippie clothes sat holding three kittens and begging for spare change. Two guys, one barefoot and in need of a shower, stood on a corner and exchanged money and drugs. A man and woman, both stoned, argued loudly while a crowd gathered around them. It was painful for Jess to see the children of people her age so lost and alienated, the tragic legacy of the sixties drug scene. She told herself that most were just going through a phase and would somehow find their way out. Like I did, thought Jess. Then she remembered what it took for her to finally give up drugs, and she shuddered.

Zoe was too fascinated by the stores to be aware of Jess's mood. She found a magnetic nose ring in the next head shop, like the real one she wore. She insisted on buying it for Jess, who put it on her upper ear instead of her nose. At a used record store Zoe bought a Rage Against the Machine CD for Annabelle and a Neil Diamond record for Joanne as a joke. Up and down the street they traveled, Zoe leading the way. Finally Zoe's enthusiasm won Jess over, and her mood brightened.

Halfway up the second side of Haight, Zoe began feeling queasy, so they stopped in a coffee shop for a snack. When they were seated in a wooden booth by the window, Jess put the nose ring on her right nostril and examined herself in her compact mirror.

"No, it doesn't work. Absolutely not on this nose. I think I'll wear it on my ear, if that's okay with you." Zoe warned Jess that she was behaving a lot like Joanne, and if she wasn't careful she'd soon be shopping at Talbots. While Zoe ordered toast and tea from the large waitress with thick strands of blonde unkempt hair,

Jess tried not to stare.

"I can't believe that hair," Jess said, when the waitress sauntered away. "It looks like she hasn't combed it for weeks."

Zoe looked at her with mock chagrin. "She's wearing dreads. You could have that look if you wanted."

"I thought dreads were a political statement. Besides, I don't think my hair would do that."

"Sure it would, it's easy. You get a dread perm and then each time you wash your hair you twist it from the roots."

Jess tried to imagine herself pitching clients with her hair in dreadlocks, and what her perfectly buttoned-downed married boyfriend might say. She felt a wave of anxiety settle into a small knot as she checked her watch. Already 11:00. The waitress brought Zoe her toast, and Jess tried to concentrate on what Zoe was saying. Something about a friend named Hugh from Minnesota, a straight-A high school student who became enamored of the 60s and talked his parents into letting him transfer from St. Olaf to Berkeley. Before long he had dropped out and began living on the streets. His parents kept sending him money, thinking he'd find his way back to them. Instead of helping, their support made it easier for him to buy drugs and stay high. The Sunday before Thanksgiving, the San Francisco police found him dead of a meth amphetamine overdose in an alley off Haight Street.

"I'm so sorry."

"So was I. He was my best friend in high school, the first guy I slept with. I really needed to come here. I wanted to see where he lived. And where he died." Jess asked Zoe whether she did any drugs now, and was relieved when the answer came back negative. "But sometimes Adam and I go to this bar—well, we used to go—where they serve cosmopolitans and play retro disco, Donna Summer and Gloria Gaynor. Lots of people there do Ecstasy."

"So you dance?"

"I love to, but Adam's more the outdoor type. Mostly what we do—did—is camping and hiking. I don't know what I'll do now." Jess nodded, reluctant to start that conversation again. "And what about you, Jess? Do you do any drugs?" Jess was glad she didn't have to lie.

"Sounds like you guys did enough drugs in college to last a lifetime! What other drugs did you do? Besides, let's see, pot, coke, THC . . .?"

"Have you heard of the *PDR*?"

"What's that?"

"*Physicians Desk Reference*?"

"Right—the one that lists all the drugs."

"Well, start at A and go to Z." Zoe looked shocked. "That's a joke, Zoe." Jess punched her arm playfully. "We never saw drugs as a moral issue, it was all about rebellion and fun. And the fact that drugs were illegal just made them more enticing. It depresses me now, thinking about where drugs have led so many of us." Jess shook her head and took a sip of tea. "I can't believe some of the risks we took. The one time we did a drug deal, even though it was for someone else, we didn't even—"

"You sold drugs?"

"Wait a minute. We weren't pushers, if that's what you mean." Zoe looked at her quizzically. "We didn't make any money, anyway. Well, $50, maybe. It was a crazy idea of Holly's. We only did it once. I'm sure Holly wrote about it. It was in the summer of '70, see if you brought that one." When Zoe found the entry, the women began reading silently together.

Friday, June 5, 1970

Jess and I are on a plane to New Mexico—to get rich! Jess is reading *Glamour* magazine, so I'll tell you the story of my grand scheme.

A week ago Wednesday I came careening up the stairs into our room—well, it's become our room, it used to be Jess's at the rooming house. I nearly knocked Jess down as she was coming out our door. Anyway, the conversation went something like this:

"Jess, close the door, I've got the answer to our prayers! I have a plan! A business plan!"

"You? This I have to hear." She was clearly skeptical.

"Shut up or I won't tell you." I looked under our beds to make sure no one was hiding there. "Turn on the stereo so no one can hear us."

"Is this illegal?"

"I have a way of getting us out of this hell hole of a rooming house next year. Forever! We are going to make so much money, we'll be able to buy a goddamn house, the Taj Mahal, the president's mansion!" She looked at me even more skeptically. "What are your plans for the summer, Jess?"

"I'm going home to waitress at the country club—"

"No, you're not."

"I'm not?"

"How would you like to take a weekend trip to a sunny warm spot, cultivate your tan and make a shitload of money?"

"Who's going to pay me to cultivate this tan?"

"You and I are going into the transportation business!"

"You found us jobs as travel agents?"

"No, listen. David and Mark are going to that meditation conference in California next week."

"So?" She sat on her bed and started filing her nails.

"So, they also have a little business to take care of in Albuquerque, if you know what I mean, and they can't—"

"Drugs."

"Well, yes, drugs. But—"

"You want us to do a drug deal for David and Mark?"

"Not exactly. God, Jess, will you listen to me for one second? We aren't going to actually do the deal. All we're going to do is transport the stuff back from New Mexico, after David's friend Craig scores the pot. I love it! I'm in transportation—the family business. Won't Ellen and Bill be proud?"

"I don't like the sound of this."

I ignored her. "We'll dress up like Monique one and two, the perfect Young Republican roommates, and no one will suspect a thing." Jess didn't look thrilled with my brilliant plan.

"We could get busted."

"We could die of poverty. Starvation. Boredom in this rooming house where we can hear Gloria snoring through one wall and Beth balling her boyfriend through the other!" She shifted on her bed. She lit a cigarette.

"How much can we make?"

"We get five percent of the profits."

"How much is that?"

"I didn't ask, but thousands. Look, all we have to do is carry the stuff back on a bus. David and Mark will pick us up on their way back from reaching nirvana. What could be simpler?"

"God, Holly, I don't know. It's one thing to deliver a little pot around town or put MDA into capsules, but to transport the stuff? I heard about a guy who's been in a Mexican jail for three years and isn't even allowed visitors. My mother would kill me if she couldn't come to jail and rag at me for being there."

"I can't believe you're afraid of a few kilos of marijuana. It's not like we're buying the stuff—that's the dangerous part, that's when people get busted. You want out of this damn rooming house, I know you do. We can get our own apartment. Come on! Think of it as the spring vacation for our souls we didn't get this year. We need this."

"All we have to do is carry it back?"

"I promise. I can't live on what I make at the Pizza Palace and I can't go home. I'll die there." Jess thought while I used all my psychic power to sway her.

"All right. I'm game."

I jumped on the bed and fell backward, kicking my heels. "You'll see, we're going to be rich, rich, rich! I'm going to get us out of this prison. Some day you're going to thank me for this."

She put out her cigarette and shook her head doubtfully at my enthusiasm. "I hope you're right."

When we boarded the plane we looked like typical freaks, with our long, wild hair, beads, vests and blue jeans. But inside our Samsonites we're each carrying the exotic costume of a well-bred sorority sister, replete with white gloves, just in case. I imagine us changing into our disguises in a phone booth in New Mexico, emerging as Monique le Grand and Monique le Grand Deux.

June 6, 4 A.M.

I'm sitting on a Greyhound next to Jess, who's curled up asleep against the window seat, her head on my backpack. We're headed north toward Denver. What a day, what a night!

When we landed in Albuquerque, Craig picked us up and brought us to a friend's house—a Mormon student he'd met on campus. Craig is so skinny his jeans were falling off his nonexistent ass, and he kept hiking his pants up behind him. He has brown hair down to the middle of his back, tied in a ponytail, which he plays with when he isn't hiking up his pants, an altogether unappetizing picture. When he dropped us off and left to meet his contact, Jess and I snooped around.

"Did you ever meet a Mormon?" Jess was looking at a picture of five very healthy looking guys who could have been brothers.

"No, but I saw some in that movie about the locusts." I picked up a large group photo from the mantel. The men all wore suits, the women blue dresses and odd caps. "Look, a clan."

"Maybe they're like the Catholics and aren't supposed to practice birth control."

"No, I think they're polygamous." Just then a beautiful guy who couldn't have been more than 18 walked in. He had short brown hair and dark playful eyes. Or did he just look gorgeous, I wondered, compared to Craig. He told us his name was Darl. "You must be Craig's friends, come to carry the boo back to Iowa." He said he wasn't a narc and not to worry. I asked him if the photograph was of his family. He picked it up, named all the people in it, then he brought out the largest bong I'd ever seen and we smoked some pot—after he turned the family photo face down. Then Darl went to class, and Jess and I sat in the living room, listening to music. This was going to be easy.

A while later Craig came back, pulling on his pants, bummed. His contact's shipment from Mexico hadn't arrived and the phone numbers Craig had for other dealers were a bust. There had been a big drug raid earlier in the week—just our luck—and most of the dealers had gone into hiding. To further bum us, Craig told us he had to split to Iowa that night, as planned. We didn't have a return ticket, because we were scheduled to take the bus to Denver.

"Does this mean you're going to strand us here?" Jess asked, sounding her edgiest.

"Mark knew I had to be back tonight. Here are his contacts." He handed me the papers with the phone numbers.

"Just what are we supposed to do with them?" Jess demanded.

"Give them a try in a day or two if you want. Whatever."

"What do you mean, whatever? We're here to carry the stuff back, not to buy it."

"It's okay, Jess, we don't have to buy anything. Relax." I hate it when she gets shrill. "It isn't Craig's fault."

"Is it your fault then? Do you want me to yell at you? Why didn't we know this before we came down here?"

"It's just one of those things. Be cool."

"Be cool? So this whole trip is a bust and we won't make a dime."

"We have a day before we have to meet David and Mark in Denver. We'll explore Albuquerque. Get some sun."

"I could be back home earning money at the country club. Now we're stuck here without a cent. Why did we come here before we knew the deal was done?"

"Look," Craig interrupted us, "here's the money the guys gave me to score. There's fifteen hundred dollars. Take it." I'd never seen that much cash before. I took the money and gave it to Jess to stuff into her bra, since I of course, refuse to wear one anymore.

After Craig left, I suggested we put on our bathing suits and sit in the back yard, to catch the afternoon rays. I knew the sun always cheered Jess up. We sat baking and I hoped I could convince her to relax and enjoy our mini-vacation. She took out the cash from inside her bikini top and I watched as she counted it. Then she cut it and gave me half, and we sat thumbing through it.

"Think of what we could do with all this money."

"We could buy a car and travel all over the country for a year."

"We could each buy $750 worth of clothes. We could buy a leather jacket with a real fur collar," Jess fantasized

"We could buy a Harley Davidson. If we pooled it."

"Jewelry. Diamonds."

"Steak every night for a year." My mouth was watering.

"I thought you swore off meat?"

"But a really good steak with lots of fat in it, sounds great right now."

"We could fly to San Francisco."

"Hell, we could fly to Paris!" Then we looked at each other

and said simultaneously, "It's not our money." I handed it back to her and she stuffed it out of sight. We decided that we'd spend some of it anyway, a hundred or so, for our trouble. After all, we had a day to kill, a place to rest and sunshine.

Later we walked to campus and watched the students. Nearby was a string of small shops where we found an interesting little bakery and tea shop with pine walls and lots of hanging plants in the windows. We went in, sat down at a booth and ordered some sassafras tea from the waitress. A few minutes later the proprietress of the shop, a longhaired earth mother, came up with a large glass jar of green-colored tea.

"I thought you girls might like this instead."

"What kind is it?"

"Marijuana."

"Great." She poured us each a cup, then sat down and talked to us. She's a large woman and wore a purple housedress that covered everything except her enormous cleavage. She told us her name was Rosalind but now she only answers to Roz. She's from New Orleans, and has jet-black hair down to her waist, which she wears in a barrette clipped at the base of her neck. She came to Albuquerque in the early 60s to go to school. She fell in love, got pregnant, got married, dropped out. She put her husband through school, then medical school—after which, of course, he dumped her. She stayed on in Albuquerque to raise her daughter and a year ago she'd saved enough money to open her shop. Now she bakes pastries for local restaurants and sells coffee and tea retail. She talked to us about how things have changed from the mid-60s to now, from the peace and love movement to the separation and hate themes of today.

"Hell, who's together now? The blacks have their own thang, the women are getting their own thang, the men have always had their own thang, and pretty soon everybody's going to have their

own little corner and nobody's gonna be talkin' to nobody. I tell
you thangs have changed forever and they've gotten ugly. U-g-l-y."

"I don't know about that," Jess said. "I still think people are
trying to get together. I think people want to live—"

"'In-A-Gadda-Da-Vida.'" She said this with great disdain, lit
up a small cigar and blew the smoke away from us.

"What?"

"'In-A-Gadda-Da-Vida.' That's when the shit hit the fan," she
said, picking a piece of tobacco from her teeth.

"What do you mean?"

"Iron Butterfly. "Ball." 1969. When I heard that, I knew it was
over. The death of music. I even held a little funeral. Lit a candle,
said a prayer, sang a hymn, a good hymn. 'In-A-Gadda-Da-Vida.'
I tell you, it's a tragedy, a real tragedy." She stopped and her
breasts heaved with a deep breath, as if everything bad that had
ever happened to her could be pinned to that one song. She
looked away and I watched as she recomposed herself. "Say, here
I'm shooting my mouth off, and I haven't asked what y'all are up
to." The tea was beginning to have a dizzying effect and she
seemed so harmless and so trustworthy that I let her in on our little dilemma. I told her our contact couldn't score, so we were on
our way back to Iowa via Denver.

"Why didn't you say so? Y'all need some pot, you've come to
the right place. I have a source for you. How much money do you
have?"

"Fifteen hundred dollars." Jess glared at me, and I knew it
was time for a powwow. Roz must have sensed it too and suggested we think about it and come back if we were interested in her
source. She told us the pot would cost $100 a kilo. Jess and I went
out into the hot New Mexico sun.

"Why did you tell her everything?"

"I didn't, exactly. Anyway it's no big deal. She can help us."

"I don't want people knowing why we're here."

"Why are you so damned uptight?"

"I don't want to get busted."

"We won't."

"Can you promise me that? Well, can you?" I didn't answer. "We're only supposed to carry it back. 'The transportation business,' remember?"

"But wouldn't it be cool if we scored! Showed those guys we don't need them, that we can do it all ourselves. Transportation— and sales! A full-service company. Ha! And think of all the money we'd make! Jess, we'd get Craig's cut, too!"

"You think so?"

"Of course!" I could see the money wheels turning in her mind. We walked along in the heat until finally she spoke.

"If we buy fifteen kilos, that's five more than what the guys are expecting to buy. We could have five kilos of pot for ourselves."

"How much is that if we sell it?"

"God, Holly, I don't know, do you have a pen?" I dug in my bag and pulled out a pen and an old deposit slip. We sat on the curb and Jess began her calculations.

"Well?"

"Well, just a second. I'm not a math major." She figured while I lit two cigarettes and handed her one. She finally looked up, took a puff, and said, "We could probably make maybe $500 apiece. Besides what little the guys are giving us. Wow. But we came here to carry it, not to buy it."

"What's the difference, really? Once we buy it, Jess, it's all the same. And this Roz, she seems cool, don't you think?"

"She's a little too earthy for my taste. I mean, she's got to be over 30 and her tits are falling out of the top of her dress!"

"So she's not a fashion plate. Does that automatically disqualify her as a trustworthy human being?"

"No . . ."

"It does in your book. Well, I think she's cool because she's not afraid to dress however she wants and say exactly what she thinks."

"Even if it's wrong. The death of music. I mean really."

"Well, she's kind of right. Do you like "In-A-Gadda-Da-Vida?'"

"No, but—"

"There."

"One song doesn't mean the death of music."

"It's part of a trend."

"There's something about her I don't trust."

"What?"

"It's just a feeling I have."

"Then I'll do it myself," I said.

"Do what?"

"I'll make the deal by myself—you don't even have to be there. Stay with the Mormons and when the deal's done, I'll meet you at the bus station."

"You mean it?"

"Abso-fucking-lutely." I don't know where I got the chutzpah to say that. Maybe it was the hot sun or the frustration I felt at Jess for being so damned concerned about appearances. Hell, if she was worried about how someone dressed, what in the hell was she doing hanging around me?

"How about this?" Jess offered. "You buy it and I'll carry it back on the bus."

"It's a deal." We went back to the shop and told Roz. She made a phone call and set up the deal for later, then invited us to her house for a home-cooked meal. She gave us her address and while she closed up the shop, we headed back to Darl's to get ready.

"I'm still not sure about her."

"What do you think she's going to do?"

"I don't like the fact that she's going to let you take her car and buy the drugs. She could be setting us up."

"She's helping us. God, sometimes you are so paranoid."

"Now, tell me the plan again."

I felt competent, in charge. For once I had the plan, and Jess was following me. "I score the pot, drop it in a locker at the bus station, then come and get you at Roz's. Roz drives us both back to the station, I give you the key to the locker, you take out the trunk, and check it as your luggage. Just like in the movies. It's simple."

"It doesn't sound simple. Why doesn't she drive you to get the pot?"

"Will you quit it? You're driving me crazy with all these details. Besides, why should she put herself in jeopardy? I mean, Christ, she's letting us drive her car!"

We walked back to Darl's house to get our things. Roz had instructed us to buy a footlocker, some towels and some powdered detergent. She told us to line the bottom of the locker with the towels and detergent so the narc dogs at the bus station—if there were any—would be thrown off by the scent. Darl drove us to a Ben Franklin five and dime, where I called David from a pay phone. I'd been instructed to call the meditation conference only in case of an emergency, but I thought he and Mark should know what a brave and dangerous thing we were doing and on their behalf. When David came to the phone he sounded far away and very, very stoned.

"Craig left us."

"Holly?"

"Craig left us and we have the money and we found a source, and if you want, we'll buy it. It's $100 a brick." He took a long time to answer. "David. David, are you there?"

"I'm here. Go ahead."

"Go ahead and what?"

"If you think it's a good deal, go ahead and buy it. Break one or two open and check them out—you'll be able to buy 15 kilos at that price. Did Craig leave you his scale?"

"What scale?" Now David sounded like he was coming back to earth.

"You have to weigh the pot. And don't use their scales, they're probably rigged."

"Where am I going to get a scale?"

"Can't you buy one?"

"I guess so."

"Buy one and bring it back with you. I'll see you tomorrow. Do you remember the bus you're taking?"

"The one that leaves here at midnight." We said good-bye and I hung up. Suddenly, I'd wished he'd told me not to do it, that it was too dangerous and he was going to come to New Mexico, do the deal himself, and rescue me. Not only was he not going to rescue me, he was tossing me to the fates and wanted me to buy a scale. I was at the point of no return.

While Darl waited outside, Jess and I went into the Ben Franklin store and bought a footlocker, but only after we argued over colors. She convinced me no self-respecting sorority girl would be seen with an army green trunk so we bought the metallic blue one. We found the detergent and towels, then looked at scales. They had a postal scale and a bathroom scale, but no scale for measuring kilos, so we bought the regulation bathroom scale. Darl dropped us off at Roz's house and we said good-bye to him.

Roz greeted us at the door with a garland of flowers in her hair and gave each of us a big earth-mother hug. Her house was a paradise, cozy yet bright, and I wanted to move in immediately. Everything was wood and plants, incense and candles burned. She opened a bottle of French wine and served a vegetarian dinner, some kind of wheat dish and fresh salad made with all natural ingredients. She was proud to tell us that there were no preservatives in anything she ate, that all the herbs she used came from her garden. She told us stories about the "old" days when she was in college, and I remember thinking that I'd like her to be my mother, or big sister, anything. Jess seemed to be enjoying herself, too, and we even told Roz about trying to get to Woodstock, but neither of us mentioned the Hawaiian party.

Roz suggested that we take a walk up the street to buy some ice cream, but Jess was too full and wanted to stay and listen to music, so Roz and I went to the Dairy Queen. We ate our cones as we strolled back to her house and she asked me if I wanted to see her garden. We walked around to the back and she pointed out different plants and flowers she had growing there. I told her how I loved seeing things grow when I was a girl, that I always had a garden and loved digging in the dirt. She was sitting on a bench and I was sitting at her feet, looking at some exotic herb, when she said, in her low throaty voice, "Darlin', you sure are a sweet young thang." The tone of her voice was too familiar, and I quickly placed stones around the walls of my psyche. I turned away from her and asked her the name of an herb.

"So. Do ya call yourself a free spirit?"

"Of course." My answer was cold, heartless.

"I don't." I suddenly hated the way she said "I" as though it were "Ah."

"Why not?" I asked, as if I didn't care to hear the answer.

"Darlin', I've been around this sun 33 times. I know when a person is bullshittin' themselves."

"I'm not bullshitting anyone." I was getting angry. Roz brought her feet up to the bench, resting her bulk on her side and placing her chin in her hand.

"You and your girlfriend pretty close?"

"Best friends." Fuck you.

"That all?" She sounded so stupid and so direct I wanted her to disappear.

"Of course that's all." I felt my knees getting numb from kneeling on the ground, but I couldn't exactly stand up or switch positions because I couldn't let her see my face. I stared hard at the herb, trying to remember its name and not the feeling I was trying hard to push away. I wanted this conversation to end.

"Well, all I know is that bein' different ain't never been a crime."

"I know that!" All of a sudden a wave of revulsion came over me. Who was this woman who claimed to see something in me? How dare she say I was different! I stared harder at the herb. Then the revulsion turned in on me. "I've got to go." I shot up and ran into the house. I went straight into the bathroom, locked the door, looked in the mirror. There it was on my face, the look everyone could see, the knowledge everyone knew. I scrubbed my face with a washcloth until it hurt, then rinsed it 40 times. Jess knocked on the door.

"Holly, we've got to go. I put your sorority outfit behind the door. Do you see it?"

"Yes."

"Hey, let me in, will you?"

"No."

"Come on. I have to pee."

"No!"

"Okay, okay. Just hurry." I got dressed in the blue pleated skirt and white blouse that Jess had brought for me, then pulled my hair back and braided it. When I came out, Jess whistled at me and I shot her a dirty look. In the living room, I found a half-smoked joint in an ashtray. I lit it and smoked hit after hit until it was gone. It must have been laced with something awful because when Jess came out of the bathroom, I was so stoned I couldn't keep a thought in my head. I stood up and tried not to sway.

"You better get going, Holly."

Roz walked in with a bag of food. "Yes, y'all better head over to P.J.'s house if you want to score your pot in time. I've wrapped up some food for you girls to take on the bus. I put in some special brownies, too, made with my own blend of cocoa and grass. You'll dig them."

Roz went to get her car keys and I hated her, but I couldn't remember why. One thought, just one thought at a time. Where was I going? Oh, yes. The drugs. I turned to Jess. "You have to come with me."

"No way."

"But—"

"No. You said you'd score it. I'm carrying it on the bus. That's the plan."

"Jess, just this once, we have to change the plan . . ." I could hardly mouth the words.

"No, the plan stays."

"I can't do it."

"What do you mean you can't do it?"

"I can't go by myself."

"Then we aren't doing it."

"Okay." I sat back down on the couch. My head was spinning and my tongue was thick.

"You did this on purpose, didn't you?"

"Did what?" In my stupor I couldn't imagine what she was talking about.

"You waited until the last minute to tell me you were too scared to go by yourself, so that I'd knuckle under and go with you. Well, I'm not going." She sat with her arms crossed over her chest in a white shift with a brown and white checked jacket over it, looking the perfect coed.

"I am not scared." I stood and grabbed my backpack. "I'll go by myself, I'll do it myself." Roz returned with the keys and I headed toward the door. I was about to exit when Jess called me.

"I'm coming with you."

"Don't come if you're going to be mad at me." We went out the door with Roz's directions, and both headed for the passenger seat.

"I'm not driving."

"Jess, I can't drive."

"Why not?"

"I'm too high."

"You didn't drink that much."

"I smoked some pot—there was something in it. Please, please drive." She got behind the wheel and without a word, started off. I put my head against the window and let the hot breeze blow on my face. I started a low even moan. Then she started in on me.

"I can't believe you'd do this to me. You promised you'd do this part! I said I'd carry the stuff back and here I am driving you to buy this shit."

"I'm sorry, I'm sorry. So let's not go. Turn back. Forget it."

"You never follow a plan, that's your problem. You're so god-damned blasé about everything—you let shit happen and never think about the consequences. And you never once think of how what you do affects other people."

I was getting dizzier by the second. "Jess, shut up. Please, just shut up."

"No. You could ruin everything for me, I hope you know that. Look at you."

"I'm sorry, okay? I'm sorry, but how was I to know there was something in that pot?"

"That's not the point."

"Yes, it is. Ohhh." My head hurt and I could hardly hold it up.

We pulled up to a small ranch-style house with several cars parked out front and Jess turned off the car. We walked up, rang the doorbell. A guy in blue jeans and a red bandanna appeared, looked at us in our sorority finest, carrying a blue metallic trunk and white bathroom scale, and asked if he could help us, through a smirk.

"We're here to score some pot." Jess said it like she was a southern preacher backed by the authority of God himself. I could tell she was faking, she was just as scared as I was. He showed us into a room where two other guys stood around a dining table under a bright overhead bulb that cast a stark light. I saw guns in one corner, leaned against the wall. Other guys—I was too scared to count how many—stood in the periphery, talking in hushed tones, as if funeral services were about to begin. Our funerals, I thought.

Jess and I and our scale and trunk were ushered down the basement stairs and into a little room, filled with kilos of marijuana. Nondescript guys, who looked like they could have all worked the road crew for Grand Funk, quickly passed us our 15 kilos which Jess dutifully weighed on our bathroom scale. I stood with my knees knocking, not speaking. They all weighed right, some even over 2.2 pounds. I was petrified and thrilled at the same time. We were pulling it off. We went back upstairs and Jess paid the money to the guys standing around the table, while another guy helped me load the locker into the car.

It took no more than ten minutes but it felt like two years. I was panting when we finally got into the car, and we drove off without saying a word. We were a few blocks away and beginning to thrill to the success of our escapade, so I lit up two victory cigarettes.

I was handing her one when I looked behind us. "Oh, fuck. Oh, fuck."

"What?"

"Cops." A patrol car was behind us and although his lights weren't on, I knew he was following us.

"Just be cool, maybe he'll go away." We pretended to ignore him and drove on toward the bus station.

I talked between my teeth, hardly moving my lips, as if he could read them in the rear view mirror. "What are we going to do? What if we get to the station and he's still behind us? What do we do then?"

"Holly, be cool."

"Okay, okay." We drove on, and then it happened. He put on his lights and had us pull over.

"That's it, my life is over," Jess said.

"It's all my fault," I moaned. The policeman came to the window and Jess smiled at him like she was having her homecoming queen picture taken. He shined his flashlight right into my eyes and I squinted. I hoped he couldn't hear the sounds my stomach was making.

"Going a little fast there, weren't you, girls? Just where are you headed in such a hurry?"

"I'm dropping my friend over at the bus station."

"Tell me," said the cop, "where are you going?"

"Denver—"

"Iowa—"

"Iowa by way of Denver," Jess said.

"Seems like kind of a circuitous route." He shined the light into my eyes again. Jess took a deep breath and started explaining.

"You see, Officer, it's this way. This is my sorority sister, Holly O'Neal. Delta Delta Delta. As you can see, she's terribly upset. She can hardly talk. I'm dropping her off at the bus station headed for Denver because her fiancé, David Delaney, is meeting her at the Denver bus station tomorrow afternoon. He's been in Viet Nam and he's headed back to Iowa, where he's from. He's a farm boy she met at the university's Young Americans For Freedom Club. She's beside herself as you can see, she's worried, she's scared, she's—oh, my God, Officer. David, well, he had his—he had his left leg amputated in Viet Nam—he fell on a Viet Cong mine—it blew his leg right off. He's just getting out of the hospital in California and he'll be on that bus, the bus that Holly wants to catch up with in Denver, if she can get there in time. Holly wanted to surprise him when he gets to Denver and if we don't get there soon, she'll miss her bus, and it'll be four days before she sees him back in Iowa. Oh, Officer, it's just terrible what she's been through, because you see, now David might not be able to have children. And on his last leave well, I know she probably shouldn't have, she should have saved herself, it was a mistake, or maybe it wasn't because now Holly's pregnant and she wants to keep this baby, David's baby. She wants the baby to have a name, too, so please, Officer, understand that we're not bad girls, we really aren't, we want to do the right thing, we really do, want to do, the right thing." She sat, with her head bowed, waiting, folding and unfolding her hands.

He stood there dumbfounded, as I tried to shed tears for effect and worked not to laugh. I put my forefinger in my mouth, bit down hard on it and a loud snort came out of me. Jess started to shake and tears came down her perfect sorority sister cheeks.

"Girls, girls, don't cry, I can't stand to see a lady cry." He pulled out a handkerchief and handed it to Jess who handed it to me.

"I'm—sorry—" Jess choked between fake sobs, "We don't mean to burden you with this, but, but, well . . ."

"There, there, now when does the bus leave?"

"In about 15 minutes and we might not make it."

"You girls follow me and I'll see that you get there in time."

Jess's sobs stopped suddenly. "What do you mean?"

"I'm giving you an escort."

"An escort?"

"To the bus station. Now put that puppy in gear and we'll see that this young princess meets her prince charming with time to spare."

"Oh, thank you. Officer, thank you!" He climbed into his squad car, turned on his flashers and siren and sped off, his two charges and their trunk load of marijuana following close behind. Jess and I tried not to squeal.

"Jess Martin, you are a genius. You saved our lives! You're a genius! And a real sister. I'm going to see that you're elected sorority president. Greek Week Queen! Most likely to succeed."

"Just remember this, O'Neal."

"An unwed mother never forgets a kindness."

We arrived at the bus station with sirens blasting and lights flashing. The officer took the trunk and carried it into the station for me, while I bought my ticket and watched as the trunk left a trail of soap flakes on the station floor. Jess drove back to Roz's. They came back a few minutes later with time to spare, so Jess and I sat with our feet on our blue metallic footlocker, eating chips and reveling in our good fortune. When we first boarded, she made me sit in a different row, but we crossed the Colorado state line, and now we're sitting together. Jess is still asleep. This is one for the books!

Jess chuckled as Zoe marked the place and closed the book. She remembered the incident for the first time since it happened and marveled at their daring.

"Wow, you guys were so lucky. Did you end up making a bunch of money?"

"Hell, no. After a cramped ten-hour car ride with David and Mark, we got back to Iowa City and they weighed the pot. It had dried out and lost half its weight. Apparently, wetting down the bricks before they're weighed is the oldest trick in the book. Of course, no one told us that. Anyway, our grand scheme for $500 apiece turned into a measly $50 and a few dime bags worth of pot. I was angry at Holly for wasting my time when I could have been earning decent money waiting tables in Clear Lake. And by that time I had rent due and couldn't get out of my Iowa City lease. My mother expected me to earn a lot in the summer for the following school year, and Holly and I both owed the university money."

Jess paid the check and scrutinized the waitress's dreads as she strolled away. She was suddenly impatient. "Let's get out of here. I need to stop by my office on our way home."

They got back into the car and Jess headed for downtown San Francisco. They drove in silence with the windows open, enjoying the warm fall day, until Jess mused, "You know, you have so much Holly and I were always scrambling for money. But I will say we were resourceful. We always made big plans, anyway."

"Hey, I work in the lab at school," Zoe retorted.

"I bet you never set foot in a corn field or a corn canning plant or in a bakery factory like the one where your mother packaged Suzy-Q's."

"Oh, tell me how you walked to school in the pouring rain and snow. How many miles was it? And you never complained and you were barefoot, right? Wait, let me get my violin out."

Jess laughed. "All I'm saying is that Holly and I were always broke, especially that summer. We were ready to do almost anything for money."

"Anything?" Zoe asked.

"That same summer, after our failed drug trip, we got jobs modeling, if you can believe that."

"Wow! I can't imagine Holly as a model." Zoe shook her head.

"She couldn't either. It began with a job in a health club and escalated from there."

"You have to tell me. It sounds delicious."

"It was just another scheme, one where we actually did make some money, though. Here's my office. Do you want to wait in the car or come up?"

"I want to see where all this sex, excuse me, I mean all this lifestyle advertising, is created." Zoe grinned at Jess, who chuckled.

When she locked her car, Jess noticed that there were only five cars in the lot. One was Harper's Jeep Cherokee, parked in the next row.

As they rode the elevator to the 22nd floor, Zoe chattered on about a man she'd read about who had been caught in an elevator in a San Francisco office building during the 1989 earthquake and lost his arm and both legs. Jess smiled. She was beginning to enjoy Zoe's disaster stories.

The elevator doors opened onto an empty reception area. There were half a dozen message slips in Jess's mail slot. As she glanced through them, Zoe wandered into the conference room and marveled at the panoramic view. Jess joined her and showed her to the antique telescope poised in the corner. While Zoe looked through it, Jess pointed out Alcatraz, Angel Island and the Bay Bridge. Dozens of sailboats dotted the indigo water and they watched two ferries' wakes crisscrossing as they made their way across the bay. "Wow, I'd never get any work done if I had this view."

"You get used to it. Come on." Jess directed Zoe through the locked door with her pass card and they moved on to the executive suites. Jess was surprised at how quiet the office seemed. Even on a Saturday the office was usually buzzing with activity. She looked at her watch. It would pick up, the creative types were just getting out of bed after a hot night at the clubs.

Zoe followed Jess into her office. The ProbTech file was on her desk. Jess picked it up and flipped through it, unsure of what she was looking for. Then she remembered the storyboards. She'd need them to revise the campaign. "Wait here for a minute. I have to pick up something from the graphics files. I'll be right back." Zoe nodded, sat down at Jess's desk and began thumbing through a copy of *Advertising Age*.

Jess hoped she could locate the boards quickly. Despite the Zoe distraction, she was smarting from the failed pitch and needed a day to assemble a plan before she talked to anyone. The graphics department was next to the creative area where Harper and Dennis worked. As Jess rounded the corner she heard Harper on the phone in her cubicle. Jess stopped short when she heard Harper laugh, then exclaim, "Don't worry, Eric. I'm all over this. I took both ProbTech files, copied everything and went over the info all morning. I bet I know more about this client than you do. Oh, really?" Her voice was seductive, throaty. "Yes, I heard it was awful, but we can fix it. I'll work all day tomorrow and by Monday I'll have a new campaign that will knock your socks off. Hey, thanks for giving me the chance to show my stuff. The shoot? Oh, yeah, it's still on. The crew call is at 4:00 this afternoon. The talent is scheduled to be on the beach at 5:00 and the whole thing should be wrapped by 6:30 . . . a drink sounds great . . . right, to celebrate. Eight at the Cliff House is perfect. I already have some ideas to run by you for the new campaign . . ."

Jess had heard enough and ran back through the glass doors, forgetting the storyboards. Her stomach was clenched so tightly she could barely breathe. She ran to Eric's office, located the ProbTech file in his file drawer, grabbed it and ran back toward her office. She stopped short and leaned against the wall trying to remember exactly what she'd heard. Harper had copied the files at Eric's request. Had he asked her to work on the account?

Jess bit her lip. Maybe she'd misunderstood. Maybe they were talking about another account. No, she was sure Harper had said ProbTech. Jess felt the heat rise in her face. So Harper was to be his rising star, his new protégé. Well, they can both go straight to hell, Jess thought. Fear mixed with anger as she tried to think clearly. I'll go confront Harper. Or maybe I'll call Eric and ask him why the drink at the Cliff House. Maybe it really was innocent. No, everything with Eric was calculated. He's hot for Harper. The thought made her sick. "You bastard," Jess muttered, as she marched into her office, startling Zoe.

She swirled about in Jess's office chair, pointed to an article in the magazine and began pontificating about something she'd read. When she saw Jess's flushed face she stopped. "Hey, what's up?"

"You know what? I don't feel like working today."

"Really?"

"What do you say we get out of here? Have you ever been to Sausalito? Would you like to go? We can drive over there and I can show you where your mother wanted to live when we vacationed here once. What do you say? How about it? Would you like to see it?" She spoke too loud, too fast.

"I haven't been, but I've heard it's beautiful." Zoe stood up, stretched and laid the magazine on the desk.

"I feel like driving. Let's go to Sausalito!" Jess fought the feelings of hurt and betrayal that had quickly overshadowed her anger. She needed to think, to make a plan and a drive would be just the thing. Then she remembered. "But your friends, they're expecting you."

"No, it's cool," Zoe answered quickly. "They're actually friends of a friend and we didn't have a plan. I can go later this afternoon." Jess felt like hugging Zoe, but instead picked up the file, flipped off the light and closed her door.

Jess peeled out of the parking garage, hitting the bumper guard. After a few minutes of heavy swearing, she got out and examined the fender damage. It might have to be replaced, but Jess didn't care. They made sure the turn signals worked and started through traffic toward the bridge. After a few minutes of silence, Zoe asked Jess if everything was all right.

"It's work and Eric and it's too complicated to explain." Jess pulled out her cell phone and turned it off, then began zooming in and out of traffic, intent on moving forward. Zoe fastened her seat belt tighter and held on.

CHAPTER FIFTEEN

They drove in silence toward the tollbooth as Jess played out a dozen scenarios in her mind. They all ended badly and she finally decided to table any plans to confront Eric or Harper until she'd calmed down. There was too much at stake.

She paid the toll and looked over at Zoe, gazing out across the bay. Zoe turned to face Jess, tucked her sandaled feet under her and asked, "What were you telling me before we stopped at your office, something about my mother modeling? I just can't picture my mother as a model."

"Well, it wasn't modeling in the conventional sense. And she really hated every minute of it." Jess adjusted her mirror and headed across the bridge. She was happy to steer her mind away from her troubles, and poured herself into the storytelling.

It was early June, we had no money and we each had to pay the university what we owed before they'd let us back into school. We were desperate to find work so we answered an ad and got jobs as exercise assistants at Elaine Powers Studio for $5 an hour. We had to record every woman's weight and measurements: bust, waist, hips, thighs. They told us to hold the tape measure loosely when we measured the women the first time. When we re-measured them three weeks later, we were supposed to pull the tape measure like a vise grip so they'd think the program was really burning off the inches. That way, they'd sign on for another series. Holly, of course, was appalled by the dishonesty. I was just uncomfortable being that physically close to women I didn't know.

We also had to show the women how to use the exercise machines. Members started each exercise session standing with their butts inside these wide canvas belts that jiggled, supposedly to loosen the fat. Then we instructed them to move to a large rolling drum covered with wooden rollers, like small rolling pins. They were supposed to sit up against the rollers to loosen more fat. After that, we told them to go to the rowing machines, treadmills or bicycles to actually burn off the fat. But hardly anyone ever took the final step. They'd just grab the latest fashion magazine and park themselves at the belts or rollers until the session was over.

That was fine with Holly and me. While the women rolled and shook their fat, Holly and I spent most of our time on the bicycles, burning off the pizzas we'd eaten that spring. That's where we met Bridget. She was a go-go dancer and bartender at the Gaslight Lounge, a bar on the Coralville Strip just outside of Iowa City. Bridget was in her thirties and had long, bleached blonde hair and a great body with big pointy boobs that Holly said were definitely fake. Her face was rugged and lined from cigarettes and too much sun, but she exercised almost every day to keep her body in top shape, and she kept us entertained with stories of the bikers, frat boys and businessmen who came into the bar. She was always inviting us to stop by for free drinks, and one night we took her up on her offer.

The smoke-filled Gaslight Lounge was so different from the college bars we usually went to, it felt like stepping into a time warp. In one corner was a gaslight fireplace, Charlie Pride's voice crooned on the jukebox, the walls were covered with red velour wallpaper and the carpet was a thick red shag. It reminded us of the Embers in Florida, and Holly wanted to leave right away.

"Hey, you good lookin' chicks, get your butts over here." It was Bridget from behind the bar in a tight, shiny red dress. "I was beginning to think you were too stuck up to party with the real folks in this town."

We climbed onto bar stools and ordered seven and sevens, trying not to look too out of place. There were no other women in the bar, just guys in work clothes and a few suits. When Bridget went to change clothes for her act, a tall man in a gray suit sat down next to me. He had thinning hair and a mustache and told us his name was Joe Taylor. He asked us if we were models. I knew Holly was rolling her eyes behind me, but I was intrigued.

"I'm Jess Martin and this is Holly O'Neal." I turned to Holly who smiled with her lips closed and nodded, but I went on. "And we're not models. Well, I guess we're kind of models." Holly kicked me under the bar. "Not really. Actually, we're students."

"Well, I work with models all the time, and you two could definitely model." He stirred his drink.

"Really?" I bounced my hair back from my face, giving him my best Cheryl Tiegs smile. "What do you do?"

"I'm a promoter."

"What exactly do you promote?" Holly chimed in cynically.

"I put conventions and rock shows together, that kind of thing."

"That sounds interesting." I turned my body toward him, shutting off his view of Holly. "Mr. Taylor, is it?"

"Call me Joe. It's a good job, keeps me on the road most of the time. Say, I have a job coming up this weekend that you girls might be interested in. But you're probably busy with school."

"Actually, school's over for the year. A modeling job?" I tried to contain my excitement as Holly cleared her throat and reminded me that we had a job. I glared at her. "We're not that busy." I turned back to Joe as Bridget took the stage dressed in a tiny white halter top, tight, white hot pants and white fringed go-go boots.

"It's in Des Moines," Joe continued, "at the fair grounds. It's a farm implement dealer show and I need girls to work the Monsanto booth. I hired four girls from a modeling agency, but two of them canceled on me a couple of hours ago." Someone turned the music up several decibels and Aretha Franklin belted out "Respect," as Bridget started bumping and grinding on the platform stage. Joe excused himself to make a phone call and Holly railed at me.

"I'm sure this guy's a pimp, and you're ready to sign us up as his new 'girls.' God, Jess, if I'm going to be a hooker, I'm doing it on my own terms and I sure as hell don't want some guy pimping for me."

"He's not a pimp. Why do you always have to think the absolute worst of every guy in a suit? He's a nice guy, a business-man. You heard him. He's a promoter and he hires models." I opened my purse and put more blush on my cheeks.

"It sounds shady, so leave me out of it."

"Let's at least listen to what he has to say. We're not exactly rolling in dough from Elaine's," I snapped, sensing that my big chance at a modeling career was about to slip away. "Can't you be a little open minded, just this once? I won't do it without you." She agreed to listen, but made no promises. When Joe came back, the music was lower and Bridget was swooning in her high white boots as Al Green sang "I'm So in Love with You." Joe bought us a drink and I took the initiative.

"Okay Joe, tell us what we'd have to do in the—whose booth is it again?"

"Monsanto, it's a chemical company—"

"They make pesticides that poison our food," Holly interrupted him.

Joe smiled and continued in a patronizing voice. "Well, Holly, that's not exactly true. They manufacture herbicides and insecticides that keep bad pests and weeds from destroying the food we do eat. The models in the booth hand out literature to dealers who stop by, and every couple of hours they give a little presentation that describes the products Monsanto sells. It's an easy job. I have an RV that the girls stay in and I pay them $75 a day for three days." He sensed Holly's resistance. "And I have a lady friend I stay with." I turned to Holly. Together we'd make over $400 for the weekend. I waited as Holly took a long sip of her drink.

Finally, she answered. "I guess we could do it."

Yes! Thank you, Holly! I turned to Joe. He gave me his card and told us to call him the next day so he could get our sizes for costumes.

"What costumes?" Holly shot back.

"I think they're blazers with the Monsanto logo on them." He told us he'd pick us up at 5:30 Friday morning. The other girls lived in Des Moines, and we'd meet them at the booth at 8:00. Holly protested the early hour. She had no ambition when it meant losing a minute of sleep. Joe told Holly to think of it as a big slumber party. He told us to call the next day and tell his secretary our sizes and where to pick us up. He shook our hands and headed out the door.

"$75 a day! That's incredible. I told you he was a nice guy."

"I still don't trust him. But for $75, I guess I can stand around a booth and smile at a bunch of farmers. I'm not going to sell any disgusting chemicals though. They can't make me do that. I'll just stand there mute and hand out brochures." We left and waved to Bridget, but she didn't notice us. She was sweating to Aretha again, lost in a world of respect.

It was cool and cloudy on Friday morning when Joe's big tan

Winnebago pulled up in front of our rooming house. I was still pulling rollers out of my hair as we climbed inside. It was the first time I'd curled it in nearly two years, and the brush rollers were twisted and wound around wads of hair. Joe was too cheerful for Holly's taste, but he offered us coffee and cigarettes as we headed to Interstate 80 for the two-hour drive to Des Moines. After an hour, he suggested we go in the back and try on our costumes.

Holly opened the big white box with her name on it and shot me a death stare. She held up a pair of bright green hot pants, tall green boots, a top covered with strands of yellow spaghetti-like material and a cap with several yellow plums bursting from its crown. My costume was a chartreuse mini dress covered with fluffy green leaves. It had puffy sleeves and a low cut back. It also had green boots to match and a cap that was covered with what looked like a dozen antennae with green balls on the ends.

"You're awfully quiet back there. Don't they fit?"

"We haven't actually tried them on yet, Joe. I thought you said something about blazers. These look more like clown suits." I held up the hat, shaking my head in disbelief.

"The client had this brainstorm a couple of days ago and wants the models to dress as weeds and insects. Holly, you're a ragweed and Jess, you're a milkweed. Do you see the script in the bottom of the box? After you try on your costumes, you need to practice your parts for the skit."

"Nobody said anything about a skit." Holly was starting to panic. "I'm going to kill you for this," she hissed.

"I thought we only had to hand out brochures and stuff. This looks like some kind of show. It says here I'm supposed to say, 'Hi, I'm Monica Milkweed and I'm ever so nasty when I grow in your beans.' I don't think I can do this, Joe," I continued, trying to keep my voice steady. "You see, this isn't really what we had in mind. I thought this would be more of a real modeling job, you know, where we'd get to stand around and look nice."

Joe didn't sound cheery any more. "This isn't New York, it's Iowa; this is what Iowa models do. Ask the other girls how many fashion shows they've modeled for. Probably none. Trade shows, conventions, that's what modeling is about in the Midwest. Besides, it's too late to back out now. Just learn your lines and have fun and remember, I'm paying you pretty good money." He turned the radio up and left Holly and me to our costumes.

Holly pulled the hot pants over her underpants, then slid the green boots on and tied the halter top. I shimmied into the tiny green dress, donned the green boots and hat and finally turned to face Holly. She was pouting.

"Maybe this won't be so bad. I brought some pot. We can stay stoned and before we know it, it'll be Sunday night and we'll each be $225 richer." I was trying hard to be positive.

"There's not enough pot in Colombia to make me get up in front of a bunch of farmers dressed like a fucking weed!" Holly pulled her hat on.

"It doesn't look that bad." I fought hard to keep from laughing.

"Sure, laugh at me! Let's put your little hat on shall we, Monica Milkweed?" Holly put my hat on my head. "There, now don't you look just like a *Vogue* cover girl."

"I don't think Verushka started this way." We fell laughing onto the small couches facing each other.

"You girls okay?"

"Just groovy," Holly yelled back. We climbed back into our jeans, then she threatened me. "You owe me, and if you ever tell anyone I dressed up as a weed and paraded around in a tent for a bunch of horny farmers, I'll kill you."

Zoe burst out laughing and Jess joined in.

"So, did you do the skit?"

"Oh, yes. And it was the longest weekend of our lives."

It was cold for summer and we had to sleep in the RV with Jody and Trisha, two "real" models from the John Robert Powers modeling agency in Des Moines. They were pert and overly optimistic about their careers and Holly hated them. They played insects. Trisha was a rootworm and wore a white tube costume that rose a foot over her head but barely covered her butt. Her face stuck out of a hole in the side of the tube. Jody was a corn bore. Her costume was a dark brown shell and a body suit with six legs attached to it. It rained the entire weekend, it was damp and cold inside the tent, and after each performance, we had to stay and "work the crowd" as Joe called it. Holly caught a cold the first night and never stopped complaining.

At 5:00 Sunday, Joe came with a handful of cash, and we headed back to Iowa City in his RV. Holly slept, but I sat with Joe and quizzed him about the promotion business. He dropped us off at the rooming house and told us he'd give us a call when he had more work. Holly said 'over my dead body,' and that was the end of our modeling careers.

Jess and Zoe exited the Golden Gate Bridge and entered Sausalito. Jess drove Zoe around the town, explaining to her how Holly had wanted to live there after they graduated. "Back then there were more book stores per capita in Sausalito than anywhere else in the world. That was all Holly needed to hear to fall in love with the place. When we visited after graduation, she talked to an older hippie couple who owned a houseboat and she decided that would be the ideal way to live. Now the bookstores have been replaced by boutiques and only wealthy people live here."

As they made their way back through town, Zoe asked to stop. It was just after noon, the saltines and water Jess had packed were gone, so she stopped for lunch. Houlihan's was on the pier, so Jess requested a table overlooking the water. When they were seated Zoe admired the view, then looked on the menu for a vegetarian dish.

Chapter Sixteen

As Jess stared at the menu, thoughts of Eric and Harper working late nights on a new ProbTech campaign suddenly crowded her mind. Her stomach knotted again and she looked around for the waitress, anxious for a drink. When the she finally appeared, Jess ordered a glass of chardonnay, Zoe a bottle of mineral water. The windows were open and a crisp ocean breeze blew in. When the drinks arrived the women ordered lunch, then sat and looked out at the expanse of water.

"You have a great life, Jess. You're successful, you're beautiful, and most important, you're free."

"Thank you, but looks can be deceiving. Remember?"

"Well, from the outside, you look great."

"You haven't seen me at work. My job is exhausting. I have to stay tuned to what's hip and young and happening. And it's doubly exhausting because I have Harper and the rest of the up-and-comers nipping at my heels."

"Harper?"

"The senior copywriter who's after my job. And my boyfriend."

"The married man? Eric?" Jess nodded and flashed on the conversation she'd overheard.

"Everyone deserves someone just for them." Jess nodded without believing Zoe's platitude. "Aren't there any single men you're interested in?"

"No. Well, there was someone." Jess had met Dan Fiori while he was doing restoration work on a nearby home. He was a history buff who always had a friendly dalmation with him. "And he doesn't look bad in a tool belt, either." Zoe's rapt attention brought Jess back to earth. "Forget it," she said. "He's at least five years older than I am. Maybe more."

"What's five years? My philosophy is that you can always trust a guy with a dog. Adam has a dog, and—"

"And you aren't exactly trusting him these days, are you?"

"But at least when a guy has a dog you know he doesn't mind a little pet hair. If he can put up with pet hair and doggy kisses you know he has to be forgiving, so he can't be all bad."

Zoe's logic seemed so simple. Eric hated dogs. He and Rosemary had two exotic cats that were always being whisked off to the veterinarian.

"Have you gone out with him?"

"We went for coffee the day he finished the restoration. After that, I ran into him in the neighborhood park and we talked for a few minutes. But what was I supposed to do, ask for his business card? And what was I supposed to tell him? 'I'm somebody's mistress, but I'm available?' I've even driven by the park, hoping he'll be there. He never is. Anyway, I can't imagine what he'd see in me. He's so mellow and I'm such a stress machine." Jess thought of Dan, so unlike her type. He was rumpled and always looked like he needed a haircut. But he seems so decent, she thought. Too decent for me.

"The neighbor whose house he worked on told me he's an ex-cop. Apparently his wife left him and his two daughters for her doctor. Once he became a single parent, he decided being a beat patrolman was too risky, so he quit his job to raise his daughters. He started doing construction work, developed a taste for restoration, and now he has a small word-of-mouth business. His girls are in college."

"So he's perfect for you. That's one thing about Adam. He's mellow to a fault. Which drove me crazy, sometimes. His friends and his brother and sisters take advantage of him. There was always some friend dropping by who needed to borrow some money or a place to stay. I can't tell you how many mornings there was someone sleeping on his couch. I won't miss that. Sometimes I wished he wasn't such a great guy—to everyone else. I wished he didn't need anybody else. Do you think that's selfish?"

"I think you know what you need. But I'm not sure if it's selfishness or just self-interest. My boss created a new position for an assistant creative director and I have to decide who gets promoted. Whoever it is will be one step below me, in line for my job if I were to leave. I'm torn between choosing someone who's good so it actually makes my life easier, or choosing someone who isn't so I'll look great by comparison. Unfortunately, the best person for the job is Harper. She's in her twenties, she has great organizational skills, she's creative and she's a much better writer than I am."

"Does she have as many awards?"

"She will," Jess said, as she thought—thanks to Eric.

"How soon do you have to decide?"

Jess took a second swallow of wine and saw that the glass was half-empty. She told herself to slow down, then took another large swallow. "If I were unselfish I'd have already given it to her. Hell, I don't know what I'm doing any longer. Holly always knew what was important, even early on. I never did. I was too busy following impossible dreams." Zoe took a long sip of her water and listened intently. "When Holly was diagnosed with breast cancer for the first time, we spent lots of time together. But when her treatment ended and things got back to normal for both of us, we didn't talk as much and I lost track of her again. I was busy making my climb up the agency ladder. So I don't even have memories of her from some of those last years. It was only after it was too late—I'm sorry I missed those years with her. After Kate died, Holly and I were always going to take a trip together, but I could never get away." Jess sat quietly for a moment and imagined Eric sharing a drink with Harper. "Maybe the smartest thing I can do is to let Eric go."

"You said it."

"It's just that once you've created the life that you thought you wanted, you look at it and it's not what you want at all, and then you worry that this is all there'll ever be. Work isn't everything, but that's what I've made it." Jess stopped, then thought of her predicament. "You can't open a can of worms without making some kind of a mess. I've made a mess of it and I'm going to have to clean it up. I'm sorry, I'm meandering." Jess drained the last sip of wine.

The waitress returned with their lunch, a salad for Jess, a vegetable sandwich for Zoe. When the waitress asked if she wanted another glass of wine, Jess hesitated, then nodded yes. She wondered what Zoe would think of that. She knew what Holly would say. Fortunately, Zoe was more interested in hearing about her mother than in counting Jess's drinks.

"So after you modeled, what did you do? Did you and Holly ever work for Joe again?"

"Joe never called. But I came up with another scheme to make money. I decided that Holly and I were going to be Playboy bunnies."

"No way! Not with those outfits! And what's the deal with Hugh Hefner? Why is he always in his pajamas? He's the grossest old man! I bet he can't even get it up without Viagra."

"May I remind you that bunnies made a lot of money. Or so we'd heard."

"But the whole idea was to titillate men, right? And wasn't that about as un-feminist as you could get?" Zoe seemed shocked, but there was playfulness in her voice.

"This was before the women's movement. Besides, we were going for the money. Maybe I shouldn't tell you this," Jess teased.

"Oh no, you're telling me. Talk, now!" Zoe held up a knife and pointed it Jess's way.

"Okay, but promise me you'll keep an open mind. And put down your weapon."

"I'm all bunny ears."

"It was still early summer and I'd borrowed my mother's Malibu so Holly and I could drive to Lake Geneva, Wisconsin, this beautiful resort area. You grew up in Minnesota, you know how pretty the upper Midwest can be."

Zoe nodded, then took a bite of her sandwich.

"Lots of wealthy people lived there and that's where the Playboy Club was. My cousin Philip was my father's nephew. He was working as a waiter at a country club in Lake Geneva with some friends from college. He'd convinced my mother that Geneva was a respectable place that catered to the best people. He said I could make tons of money waiting tables and if I came up he was sure he could find me a job. My mother reluctantly agreed. I didn't tell anybody I had another plan. And all I told Holly was that we would work as waitresses. We were driving northeast toward Wisconsin, enjoying the ride, when she spoke up."

"Tell me again why I'm driving to Lake Geneva with you instead of signing up for the night shift at the factory?" Holly unrolled the window and let the wind whip her hair. She looked tan and healthy in her faded jeans, T-shirt and Dr. Scholl's sandals. She was braless, as usual. "And what time is our interview tomorrow and where are we staying tonight?"

"God, Holly, I told you this once. You never listen to me anymore."

"Sure I do. When I think you have something to say worth listening to." She poked me in the ribs and laughed out loud.

"Fuck you."

"Fuck you and slow down, the speed limit's 75." She slipped her sandals off, lounged back in the seat and stuck her feet out the window.

"I know what the speed limit is and I'm going 84. They don't pull you over unless you're going 10 miles over."

"Who told you that?"

"I don't know, somebody. Anyway, I'm only telling you this once more. We're staying with my cousin and his roommate, Kip. Oh, and Philip said they're having a party tonight. I didn't tell you that part.'"

"Far out! Go on." Holly took a drag off her Marlboro and fiddled with the side mirror with her bare foot.

"We have an interview tomorrow morning with a Miss Winslow at the Playboy Club for a dining room waitress job that pays something like $100 a day."

"That's the part I remember, $100 a day. How can that be? There must be something weird about this job. You're sure we don't have to dress up as weeds or bunnies or anything equally weird?"

"You know everything I know." Actually, that wasn't true. I turned up the radio and checked the rear view mirror. The truth was that we would have to wear costumes, bunny costumes.

Holly knew about the Playboy Club from her father's friends

who were members. She wasn't wild about the idea of working there, but the money was too good to turn down. Plus, I promised her that we'd have a great summer, lounging around the lake all day, partying with my cousin and his friends at night and making a ton of money. I'd lied to her about the costumes, but Holly had a great little body and once we started making money, I thought she wouldn't mind. I could already picture myself in a teal satin bunny suit and cute little ears.

My cousin met us in the driveway of his big Victorian apartment house. He was 23 and looked tan and handsome with his sun-bleached hair and madras shirt.

"God, you look great!" I gave him a big hug, then we followed him into his living room.

"You two are going to be a hit tomorrow. They'll beg you to work for them. Are you hungry? I know you're thirsty. Kip made a pitcher of margarita's to celebrate your arrival. Kip, come out here and say hello to my cousin and her friend." Kip popped his head around the kitchen door and waved. He was a shorter version of Philip, but with a blonde goatee. "He's so shy," Philip said, "Where are those drinks, dear? We're dying of thirst out here." He chatted on happily. "You girls need to get dolled up if you're going to party with us at our 'Mad Dogs in High Heels' party tonight. Here's your invitation." He showed us a brightly colored drawing of two dogs wearing false eyelashes and lipstick with spike heels, howling at the moon. "It starts at 10. I do hope you brought something sexy to wear?"

Holly and I looked at each other and frowned. The parties we usually went to were casual affairs, where jean shorts and T-shirts were the dress code. Holly unzipped her bag and dug around. She pulled out a slightly wrinkled, but suitable, purple T-shirt mini dress with a Day-Glo Picasso pattern painted on it. Philip added a long scarf that matched perfectly. I had a new pair of slinky, black rayon hip-huggers, and Kip loaned me a red sequined crop top he'd worn at Halloween to go with them. Thrilled with our ensembles, we headed off to Philip's room to change.

"Are Philip and Kip together?" Holly was putting on make-up, something she hadn't done since freshman year.

"It's not like they're a couple or anything. They're gay, but they're just friends."

For a while, I'd suspected my cousin was gay, and he'd admitted it to me the year before. Still, I was surprised to see how comfortable he seemed and I wasn't sure how I felt about that. It didn't offend me, but it did make me sad because I'd always imagined him with a wife and lots of kids, the same way I imagined myself. I wasn't ready to talk to Holly about it. "I think sandals, what do you think?" I modeled my pair of black platforms.

"You haven't asked me for fashion advice since forever. Yeah, they look fine. But, back to Kip and Philip. I'm sure they're lovers."

"So now you're an authority on gay relationships? I'd know if Philip had a boyfriend, and what's this lover shit, anyway? He and Kip go to NIU together, they have classes together, and they hang out together, just like we do. They're friends."

"Like us."

"Like us except that we're not gay. Not all gay people who hang around together are doing it, you know."

Holly slipped into her dress. "Would it bug you if they were lovers, I mean if Kip really was Philip's boyfriend?"

I was becoming more uncomfortable with the conversation, but wasn't sure why I felt so defensive. "I don't know. I like Kip, but it's hard to think of my cousin with a lover, I mean with someone I know. I don't think he's that serious about all this, anyway."

"So what you're saying is, it's okay if he's gay as long as he's not seriously gay, as long as he comes to his senses at some point."

Holly was starting to sound smug and I hated her for it.

"That's not what I said and you know it. You always do that."

"Do what?"

"Pick on me like that. You take a side and quiz me, especially when you know I haven't thought it out yet. I get so tired of it."

"And you haven't thought it out yet, how you feel about your cousin being gay. Admit it."

"Oh, so now you're a shrink and you think you can tell me what I'm thinking and how I feel about my own cousin? Well, I think you're full of shit." I grabbed my brush and turned to the mirror. "And how do you think you'd feel if your brother were gay?"

"I don't know." She paused. "I don't think it would bother me, but it's hard to imagine my straight-arrow brother gay, he's so macho and such a womanizer."

"I think it might bother you more than you know. I don't really appreciate you taking jabs at me like you're so together all the time about everything." My anger was turning to hurt and Holly could tell.

"I'm sorry, sometimes you're such an easy target. It's just that deep down inside, I know you're still hoping for the husband, kids and the house with the white picket fence. I think you want that for your cousin, too, and not with a cute blonde guy named Kip. Tell the truth," she teased, "you're still harboring hope that you'll turn out right someday, you know, the way you and Celeste planned it back in junior high, with the long white wedding dress and the rich husband?"

"Drop it, okay! Besides, if that's what I'm looking for, I sure as hell wouldn't be hanging around with you, would I? At least I still go out with guys. You're fucking celibate. I guess that's so you can sit back and judge everybody else without feeling like a hypocrite." We were treading on dangerous ground and we both felt it.

"Fuck you. I go out with guys. David and I went camping at the reservoir just last week."

"I forgot about David. Sweet, safe, David. You treat him like a little brother." Two could play this game.

"Shut up about David. You don't know anything about our relationship."

Thank God Philip and Kip interrupted at that moment. "Are we fighting? A little lover's quarrel?" Philip cajoled.

"We're not fighting and we're not lovers." I stormed out of the bedroom and poured myself a tall margarita.

Philip and Kip put two huge plywood dogs in red dresses, rhinestone collars and pumps, outside on the lawn. By 10:30 every room was filled with beautiful young guys, unfortunately all gay and not the least bit interested in either Holly or me. Holly and I danced with Philip and Kip and their friends, but we never danced together. We both drank too much, and when the party was over we passed out in the spare bedroom.

"When did my mother know she was gay?" Zoe interrupted.

Jess considered the question. "I honestly don't know. We never talked about that. She didn't tell me she was in love with Kate until they'd been together for years. She rarely talked about guys, so she probably knew something was different. But, honestly, I don't remember anyone being openly gay then. Philip and Kip were straight at work. And I didn't know any women who admitted being gay. I'm sure they existed, but gay people weren't in the popular consciousness like they are today. So I'm not sure when Holly knew. Maybe you can find the answer in one of her journals."

"You're right. Go on. I interrupted."

The next morning Philip entered our room at 8:00 singing his own version of "Did You Ever Have To Make Up Your Mind," and carrying a tray of coffee and croissants.

My head was throbbing so hard I couldn't focus. "Damn, Philip, who wound you up? Go back to bed."

"Sorry, little cousin. If you want to be presentable for your interview in an hour and a half, you'd best be climbing into the shower immediately. You, too, short stuff." He nudged Holly, who moaned, then turned and covered her head with a pillow.

"They can have their job, I don't want it. Just let me sleep."

Philip was relentless and started bouncing on the bed until we were so nauseous we had to get up. I looked at Holly. The make-up she'd applied so carefully the night before was all over her face, and her eyes had dark mascara circles under them.

She groaned. "God, Jess. If I look half as bad as you do, we're in big trouble."

"You do," I assured her. "Let's get to work. I'll puke first."

Holly laughed. "Just puke quietly, my head is killing me."

We stumbled around, trying our best to shape up. Kip and Philip cheered us on. By 8:45 we looked fairly presentable in brightly colored sundresses with sandals.

"We're supposed to bring a swimsuit," I told Holly, fishing mine out of my suitcase.

"Why?"

"Maybe we get to go for a swim after the interview. Just bring it. I'm ready, how about you?"

"Ready as I'll ever be." Holly took a final sip of coffee, then held her stomach. "Man, am I hung over." I felt awful, too. It had been a long time since I'd had that much to drink. "Quick, let's go while I can still stand up." Holly grabbed her suit and we headed out the door.

We followed Philip's directions and after a few wrong turns drove up a wide, tree-lined driveway to a large white building with

the Playboy emblem above the door. A man in a uniform offered
to park our car and another man directed us down the stairs to
Miss Winslow's office. Along the hallway walls were dozens of pictures of famous people posed next to Playboy bunnies at the club:
Tony Bennett, Frank Sinatra, Joe Namath, Englebert
Humperdink, Telly Savalas. Even with a killer hangover, I was
impressed.

The door to Miss Winslow's office was open, so we walked in
and sat down on two puffy chairs facing a sophisticated glass desk-
top. The room was a pale melon color with floor-to-ceiling mirrors
on two sides. A picture on the credenza behind the desk showed
a black haired woman in a turquoise caftan smiling next to Hugh
Hefner.

"Up, up, up! Let me get a good look at the two of you. Turn
around, stomachs in, chins out. Up, up. There, that's better." A
petite, raven-haired woman of indeterminate age marched into the
room, her voice startling us into compliance. She wore a blinding
red suit with a fitted jacket, a short tight skirt and three-inch spike
heels sporting red pompons on the toes. Her lipstick matched her
suit and her skin was tanned to perfection. Even though I was
nearly a foot taller, I was instantly diminished in her presence, feeling as gangly and awkward as a pre-pubescent. I stood up so
quickly my head swooned, and I would have tipped over if Holly
hadn't put her hand on my arm to steady me.

"We want to be Playboy bunnies, do we? Lots of girls do, but
few make the grade." Holly began a slow glare at me while Miss
Winslow went on. "We have the highest standards here at Lake
Geneva, and we only hire girls with high standards as well. Sit, sit,
sit. I assume you brought resumes." We hadn't. It wouldn't have
mattered, we were clearly out of our league.

"No resumes? You'll have to fill out applications then. Stop
and talk to Margo when we're finished. You do have waitress

experience, of course."

"Of course," I managed to squeak out, clearing my throat to sound more convincing. "We have extensive experience. My name is Jess Martin and I worked last spring as a waitress at one of the most exclusive country clubs in Iowa." Holly turned and started to open her mouth, but I continued before she could blow it. "This is Holly O'Neal and she's worked as a waitress, too." Holly nodded.

"Good. Now then, let's get down to business. I want you both to go through this door and change into your swimsuits and heels. Ask Margo, the attendant at the desk, to weigh and measure you before you return to my office. Right through here and be quick as bunnies, I have appointments waiting." She showed us to a door in the back of her office that opened into a large locker room.

When the door closed behind us, Holly grabbed my arm. "Tell me this is a nightmare and I'll be waking up soon! Waitress? Bullshit! You want us to be goddamn Playboy bunnies! Jesus, Jess, I can't believe you set me up like this. I'm not going to do it "

"I think it would be fun. And it's our chance to make great money." Holly started to say something when five of the most beautiful women I'd ever seen strode through the dressing room in full bunny regalia. They were tall, tan, with boobs pushed up into little shelves, satin ears, cute little collars around their necks and shapely giraffe-like legs. Holly backed up so fast to let them pass that she stumbled over a dressing table and landed with a thump in a chair.

"They must be 28 at least. They're gorgeous," I whispered, in awe.

"Yeah, if you like the overly primped, overly made-up type. Let's get out of here."

"This won't be so bad, Holly." I pulled my bikini bottoms up and adjusted my straps. "It'll just take a few minutes."

"A few minutes in a torture chamber is an eternity. I'm not going back there."

"Let's at least see what she has to say, then we'll go to the beach before we leave."

"I don't care what she says, I am not going to be a Playboy bunny. And we don't need this humiliation, Jess."

I resorted to begging. I told Holly she didn't have to be a bunny, but that I really wanted the job and I couldn't face going back to Miss Winslow's office by myself. I got her to agree to put on her suit and come with me.

"You owe me, Martin, big time and no kidding," Holly said, as Margo weighed and measured us. Margo wrote the numbers down, slipped them in an envelope and instructed us to give it to Miss Winslow, which we did when we returned to her office. Neither of us had heels, so Miss Winslow called Margo and had her bring two pairs. While we waited for the shoes, Miss Winslow gave us some insight into life at the bunny hutch.

"Meals and rent are covered and my bunnies all live together like one big happy family in the dormitory. Bunnies earn $2.00 an hour and get to keep all their tips. There is no, I repeat no, fraternizing with any club members. If a bunny is caught talking to a member outside of work, she'll be suspended. If a bunny gains weight or gets sunburned she's not allowed to suit up and doesn't get paid until I say she's fit to go back to work. Any questions?" Miss Winslow's red lips moved so fast I felt dizzy. "Any questions?" she repeated, louder.

"Ah, no, well, none that I can think of now," I said. Holly grunted.

"All right then, let's stand up and show me what you've got. Jess, you first. Slip on the heels, walk across the room, pick up the tray on my desk, take the glass off it and serve it to me. You are familiar with the bunny dip?" I nodded; Holly groaned. "Okay, go."

She made it sound like a relay race, so I thought I'd better hurry. I donned the shoes, shot up and wobbled across the room, catching my balance halfway to her desk. I could feel the left side of my bikini bottom slipping up over my cheek, but fought the urge to pull it down. When I reached Miss Winslow's desk, I put my hand on my hip like I'd seen Playboy bunnies do, picked up the tray and walked to the side of her desk, where I deposited the empty martini glass with a little dip that nearly cost me my balance. I smiled broadly, tucked the tray under my arm, walked around the front of her desk and set the tray there. With my other arm outstretched I walked slowly away from her, standing as tall as I could, chest out, butt tight, head high.

"Very nice. Jess, is it?"

"Yes."

"Have we ever walked in high heels before?" She asked with a hint of sarcasm.

"I wear them all the time." The truth was I hadn't worn heels since I quit the Tri Delts.

"I see. Now it's your turn, Molly."

"Holly."

"Right, Holly. Get up and show me your stuff."

Holly shot me a harsh look, stood up and sashayed across the room with her rear end swaying back and forth like it had its own motor, hip slung far to the right, arms akimbo. She looked like a tart in a comedy show.

"A little less bump and grind, hon'. We're ladies, remember?" Miss Winslow wrote something in her book as Holly stopped in front of her desk, picked the glass off the tray, reached across the desk and leaned over and plopped it in front of her. "Very well, now walk back to your chair, slowly, fluidly. How tall are we, dear?"

"Five three and a half and still growing," Holly replied.

"Were we on the swim team in high school?"

"I don't know about you, but I won first place at state doing the butterfly."

"That explains the strong shoulders. Okay, girls. If you'll stand next to each other I'll snap a Polaroid for the file. There, that's fine. Smile." She took our picture and thanked us for making the trip. "As I said, you'll have to fill out applications on your way out so I can check your references. You're both lovely girls, but as you know not everyone has what it takes to become a Playboy bunny. Thank you again and I'll be in touch. Step back through here and change. Margo will show you the door." She shuffled us out and when the door was closed behind us, Holly began a slow fume.

"The nerve of that bitch. Was I on the swim team! God, I could have killed her. This was such a waste of time, I can't believe it. What a joke. Why would anyone ever want to be a Playboy bunny?" I changed in silence, more depressed than angry. "Say something, Jess. Surely you don't want this piece-of-crap job?" Holly took hold of my arm and turned me around. "Why aren't you pissed?"

"I am pissed, okay? It was humiliating and I'm sorry we came. Isn't that what you want me to say?" I slammed the locker door shut, grabbed my suit and purse, and headed for Margo's desk. Holly followed me out and Margo handed us the applications. We took them and stood outside waiting for the car.

"I know you wanted to do this, but it would have killed our souls, don't you see?" I nodded. "Besides, neither one of us can walk in high heels, we'd be spilling drinks all over the place." I laughed at the thought of Holly in heels and handed her the car keys. We spent the drive to Chicago laughing about Miss Winslow and yelling at drivers to "show us your stuff." I mimicked her voice and kept calling Holly "Molly," then Holly folded our applications into a pair of bunny ears and we took turns wearing them all the way to Chicago.

Zoe laughed. "I can't believe you wanted to be a Playboy bunny. Like, seriously."

Jess felt she had to defend herself. "The whole idea of the Playboy Club was different then. It was more sophisticated and less blatantly sexist."

"How is a woman dressed up like a bunny not totally sexist?"

"Of course you're right. But somehow back then it didn't seem so pathetic. Lots of girls wanted those jobs; it was a great way to make money."

"Sure, like Hooters."

"Not like Hooters. Back then the Playboy Club was upscale, more of a gentlemen's club than the clubs you see everywhere today with nude girls and lap dancing. And remember, this was before pornography was all about full crotch shots. Before *Hustler* magazine changed everything."

"Downright wholesome, hey?"

Jess smiled. "There's nothing wrong with sex. That's what your mother always said."

"You're right. I'm being generationally critical. Sorry. But do you think if you were my age today, you'd get a job at Hooters?"

"God, I hope not." Jess shuddered, glad those days were long past. Zoe finished her sandwich and asked Jess if she wanted to take a walk down by the water. Jess declined and ordered tea. She watched as Zoe bounded down the pier, then remembered more about the drive home from Lake Geneva.

She remembered how strongly Holly protested the idea of the

Playboy Club. She kept telling Jess how dishonest it was, that it was all tease and tempt. Holly carried on about how plastic the rest of the world was and how she and Jess were better than any Playboy bunny because they were beautiful inside and it had nothing to do with their height or the size of their boobs.

Jess knew Holly was right. In theory. But that day in Lake Geneva she wanted men to desire her and want her in a place like the Playboy Club, where they couldn't have her. A place where they could only look, Jess thought. Where they couldn't hurt her or be mean to her, where they even had to pay her for being so nice and sexy. A place where at the end of the night she could go back to a bunny hutch, safe, pretty and unsullied.

Back then, Holly didn't understand. But later she did, Jess thought. After she watched my soul shatter into a million tiny pieces. After she helped pick up those pieces. Jess was suddenly chilled and pulled her coat over her sweater. She watched Zoe at the water's edge staring across the bay. The girl was growing on her. She was glad she'd taken the afternoon off, even though she knew she'd pay dearly for it.

It had been a long time since Jess had spent time with a woman who wasn't overwhelmed by her work, overstressed by her relationships, or over indulged by her therapist. Except for a few friends, Jess had to admit that she was tired of the people she knew. Zoe made her feel young and fresh, as though life still held possibilities. "Dream that it is," she whispered, "it's a fine feeling."

Zoe came up the stairs and plopped back into her chair. She'd seen a group of sea lions playing in the water and began telling Jess about sea lion mating habits, something she'd learned in class. As they walked to the car, Jess listened, enchanted by the energy in her voice, but paying little attention to the words.

CHAPTER SEVENTEEN

The afternoon sun was bright and warm, and Zoe begged Jess to put the top down before they drove back across the Golden Gate Bridge. *What a perfect comment on my life,* Jess thought. *I have a convertible I never use.* So she agreed enthusiastically and soon they were driving with the wind blowing their hair.

As they cruised toward the bridge, Jess turned the radio to KFOG and they listened to Sheryl Crow sing "Run Baby Run." Zoe pulled out a battered green spiral notebook with June August 1970 in large script letters across its front, and began reading silently. Jess found herself humming and tapping her fingers against the steering wheel. It was strange to feel calm when everything around her was in turmoil. Like being in the eye of the tornado, Jess guessed. She looked over at Zoe, engrossed in her reading and admitted that she felt lucky to be sharing the day with her. Lucky and sad because Holly wasn't there with them, telling her stories in person.

"Do you remember Archie?" Zoe asked, turning a page.

"Archie who?" Jess searched her memory.

"Some rich guy who lived in Chicago."

"Archie, Archie. I don't remember anyone named Archie."

"Well he sounds like a real loser. Listen to this." Zoe read the story aloud as Jess drove across the bridge, dodging the patterns of sunlight and shadow that splashed across the road.

June 28, 1970 3 P.M.
"Bridge Over Troubled Water." Jess is harmonizing to the Simon and Garfunkel song on the radio. We're on I-80 headed toward the western suburbs. I drove most of the way, but we just stopped for gas and changed drivers. The windows are open and the wind is blowing my hair and stinging my cheeks, but it feels glorious. It's a perfect summer day and we're speeding to Chicago to look for work there—after our fiasco at the Playboy Club. The song just ended.

We came from Philip and Kip's. They're roommates and I loved them both. They're silly and flirty. They don't act like the men I know, like they have all the power and I'm there to sweep up. With them, life seems like one big party. I wish I could be like that.

Jess says she needs a job where she can clear at least $200 a week after expenses. She just asked me for the bunny ears and I put them on her head.

"Do they help you think?" I teased her. "We still have time to go back and get you some real ones."

"Didn't you hear Miss Winslow? 'Not everyone is bunny material.' I think we fall into that category."

"I bet the bunny mother would have plucked you right up if you hadn't been with me."

"One mother is enough."

"One mother is too much." I lit a Marlboro and offered Jess a puff. I explained to her that when we get to Archie's house, if she wants him, she can have him.

Archie Barrett Junior is a rich man's son. Archibald Senior and my dad sometimes do business together—mostly they imbibe together. Mother thinks Archie Senior stole some of Dad's business ideas. Anyway, Archie Senior is away on an extended holiday looking for the next Mrs. Barrett, and Archie Junior is sponging off his father as usual, living in the Riverside mansion. There's a coach house above the garage and Archie offered us the place for the summer. The only minor problem is that deep down inside I know that Archie Junior has other habitation plans.

"Is this guy a real dog?"

"Actually he's kind of cute, in his own way. He's big and burly, with thick, dark hair and lots of charm. Best of all, he's got money. You'll love him."

"Twirl on it, O'Neal."

"You haven't said that to me in years. Is that a term of endearment?" Jess laughed. "I'm serious. Please, do me a favor and be nice to him."

Jess checked her reflection in the rear view mirror. "We'll see."

3:30 A.M.

I'm sitting on a plaid recliner and can barely see to write. I can't believe Jess Martin She's so fucking contradictory, there's no way to figure her out. And Archie, what a fat-cat loser he is. This is all so bizarre—I have to get it out.

We pulled into the Barrett's circular drive around 5:00, tired and hungry. I considered it a good sign when Jess freshened her face as we drove up. Archie Junior came out to greet us and he looked good. He had a little color in his face and though he's a little overweight, he's still a pretty powerful presence. Must be in the genes. He's 28, and I could see Jess's approving look when I introduced her. I didn't tell her that Archie is no mental giant.

Archie brought us here, to the coach house, which was the maid's quarters until the third Mrs. Barrett died young and tragically and Archie Senior stopped entertaining. The space is cramped and the ceilings are vaulted so Jess can hardly stand up. When we arrived, there were boxes piled in one corner—Archie told us he'd taken the liberty to outfit us with a few essentials. Jess and I opened dishes, silverware, toasters and mixers, all new, all for us. I could see that Archie Junior was dollaring his way into a liaison, trying to buy both of us. We oohed appropriately, as much as we could over domestic accouterments. Archie told us he'd made dinner reservations for the three of us at Adolph's and left us to get ready. I feigned excitement, but when he left I told Jess I wasn't eager to go.

"Why not?" Jess asked. She turned on a hand mixer and demonstrated for me as if she were an appliance model on "Queen For A Day."

"It's a pricey, stuffy supper club on Rush Street with Italian waiters who come to your table and sing to you. I've picked up my dad and Archie Senior there more than once. It's an old men's club—big steaks and lots of scotch." I started rummaging through the clothes we'd stuffed helter-skelter into our suitcases.

"What should I wear?" Jess asked.

"Dress up for Archie. He'll like that."

"What does he like?"

"My guess is he favors the sleazy over the sophisticated. Wear heels, those slinky black bells you wore to Philip's party—and this." I pulled out a revealing mesh top of hers.

"What are you going to wear?"

"Jeans." I pulled out a faded pair and held them up.

"You can't wear jeans!"

"Why not?"

"Holly, please, don't wear jeans." I put my hands on my hips and made a line with my lips. "For me."

"Okay, but I want you to know what a sacrifice this is." I made her pick out my outfit; she chose black hip-hugger bells and a silky white shirt. I made a face but put them on, while Jess stood at the bureau mirror and checked her profile in the mesh top. "So, do you like him?"

"He's kind of cute."

"He's not too beefy for you?"

"It looks good on him." Jess put on earrings and turned to me. "Why do I get the feeling I'm being set up?"

"Because you are?"

We finished dressing and in full makeup, met Archie outside. We squashed ourselves into his white Corvette and Archie pulled out as many different kinds of pills as his father had kinds of booze. Jess took Valium and I took a hit of speed. We barreled down the Eisenhower and when we arrived at Adolph's, they gave us the table at the top of the stairs overlooking the dining room, the one reserved for visiting dignitaries. I couldn't help but think that we were getting the royal treatment because of Archie's dad, not Archie. He didn't seem to care.

Jess did her best to charm Mr. Money, and he seemed interested in her, so I thought I was off the hook. After dinner we decided to bar hop and downstairs from Gino's Pizza, I spotted one that looked interesting.

"I want to go in there."

"No, you don't."

"Yes, I do."

"That's a fag bar. Let's go." It sounded like a command, so I stood my ground.

"I'm going there."

"I can't let you, Holly." Now he sounded like a fireman trying to prevent me from running into a burning building.

"You can't stop me."

"Trust me, you don't want to go there."

"Why not?" I was just high enough to demand an explanation.

"Well, I'm not going," Archie said.

That's because you're chicken, I thought. "I'll go myself," I said. "I'll meet up with you later." Archie looked at Jess, who shrugged her shoulders and smiled.

"Suit yourself," he said. "We'll be at Mother's, it's a bar on Division—"

"I know where it is. I'll meet you in an hour." They took off and I waited a few minutes, then walked down the stairs to a place called Punchinello's.

At the door I was carded by a gray-haired gentleman, and I could tell by the look on his face that we both wondered what the hell I was doing there. I walked into the bar and saw a piano surrounded by middle-aged men singing old show tunes. I was one of three women in the place. The other two were middle-aged, very large and very drunk, sitting on either side of the piano player, singing loudly and horribly out of tune. I stood to one side and watched the easy familiarity of the men with one another and listened to their banter with the bartender. I closed my eyes and tried to imagine them all as women, then as a mixture of men and women, and wondered what made them sound so different. Some of them called each other by women's names. There seemed to be quite a few "Dorothys" there. They told funny sex jokes, no innuendo was left untouched. The atmosphere sizzled with sex, but it was playful, like the guys at Philip and Kip's party. There was something intriguing about the men's casual attitude. It was that there was no shame in it. But I felt shame, watching them. Shame for whom, I wondered, for them? For myself?

Someone startled me from behind and asked if I wanted a cocktail. "Oh, no. Thank you," I said and bolted for the door and out into the street, to the strains of "Somewhere Over the Rainbow."

I walked up and down Rush Street watching the action. There

were drunken conventioneers, suburban husbands on the prowl, and young men and women drinking in the noise and the rhythm of the street. They all seemed to be looking for sex. What a ridiculous place this world is, I thought. I tasted something sour in my mouth and blamed it on the scotches I'd consumed in lieu of dinner. I kept walking, watching the easy couplings, the frantic gestures, the manic, come-hither looks, the desperation in the faces, saying, "Please somebody, please." I witnessed the laughter covering the pleading, concealing the deep human need. What a sad world this is, I thought, and here I am another sad seed in it.

Keep walking, I told myself. Don't stop putting one foot in front of another, don't let anyone stop you, don't come to a place where there's someone across from you asking you questions you can't answer, asking for answers you don't have because there is no simple honest answer. I found myself in front of Mother's and was glad to be there.

I joined Jess and Archie and we danced, the three of us together underneath the colored lights. The beat was loud and welcome and it felt good to be a part of something unconnected, a threesome—spare the intimacy. Let me lose myself in this group, I thought, this pulsating unconnected group of human flesh, brain severed from body, bumping, grinding, pulsing, an amoeba, undifferentiated, undefined.

Driving back in Archie's Corvette—I made sure Jess sat next to him—they laughed and joked while I sat absorbed in my own confusion. Back at Archie's he insisted we come into the house for a nightcap, and I was too high to say no, so we went in and he fixed us each a highball. Jess was as drunk as I was but maintaining her cool, something I can never do when I've had that much alcohol.

We sat in the living room, which is the size of a small ballroom, in front of Archie's deceased stepmother's oil portrait above the mantle. Archie produced a vial of cocaine, spread it out on a mirror and offered it to Jess and me. We each did a line. Archie talked on and on about who he knew in the record business, how often he went to Vail and how he'd take us there next winter. I was feeling jittery and nervous, but Jess kept Archie engaged, chattering about nothing. I wanted to get up and go outside, but I was stuck listening to them because I couldn't bear the thought of being alone. Archie was sitting on the couch and Jess was next to him. I watched from an armchair as they shared another line.

Archie suggested we go up and look at his father's portrait in the master bedroom, so we climbed the big circular staircase, past the seven bedrooms—each with its own bath—and entered the huge master suite. The three of us jumped on the bed and made fun of Archie Senior's portrait. Archie sat between Jess and me and it wasn't long before he started tickling Jess, then me, and we were giggling and rolling around the bed.

Of course, the mood quickly changed, as you can imagine when a high 28-year-old man is in bed with two equally high "free spirits." Archie was on his knees facing us, trying to find our ticklish spots, when suddenly he lunged at me and pressed his face into mine until he found my mouth. He planted a thick wet kiss there, then pried open my mouth with his tongue. I opened wider to get air, he went deeper and I gasped. He pulled his tongue out, then went to my throat and started the kind of hard teethy suck that's sure to cause a bruise. Out of the corner of my eye I saw Jess start to squirm away. He reached out a hand, grabbed her wrist and held her fast to the bed.

"Let me go," her voice was far away and small. He pulled on her arm hard and she yelped. "Let me go, let me go."

"What's the matter? We're all friendly here."

"No . . ." Jess tried to get away from him.

"Let her go," I said. "Just let her go." He did and she fell back, then picked herself up and darted from the room. Without a word he turned toward me, reached under my shirt and squeezed my breasts like they were exercise grips. He kissed me hard and I kissed him back, harder. With our lips locked in a battle of tongues, he grabbed the top of my pants, unzipped my bell-bottoms and struggled to slide them off. He spread my legs and went after my crotch like a slave at a Roman banquet. I can play this your way, I thought. I grabbed hold of his arms, pulled myself to his face, gave him a deep-tongued kiss then pushed him onto his back. As quickly as I could, I yanked my face away from his, straddled his thighs and unzipped his pants. After I pulled them down to his knees, I bent over and nibbled the tip of his cock, now straining out of the top of his underwear.

Zoe was reading fast and loud, letting out shriek after shriek. Jess could feel herself blushing as she listened. "I can't believe I'm reading this about my mother!" Zoe said, laughing. She continued reading between hoots.

Archie let out a yelp, followed by, "Oh, Mother Mary."
Without stopping to ask what he meant, I stripped off his jockeys and sucked him like his was the last morsel of flesh on the face of the earth. I tugged on his balls, put my hand around his cock and gave him a strong, deep suck. He groaned when he came in my mouth. It was over in seconds.

"Oh, shit," he said, and I knew he was as sorry he'd come as I was glad. And then, "Oh, baby, you are really something." He looked down at me and smiled in that gooney post-coital way.

"I know," I sighed, without smiling. I stayed there between his legs and watched him close his eyes. Really something, I thought. Once I was sure he was asleep, I left him lying there, sat on the chaise lounge and lit a cigarette with Archie Senior's hooded eyes following me. I winked at the portrait. "Sorry, Archie. In the marriage bed, no less." I turned and looked at Archie Junior snoring softly, perfectly satisfied.

It's so uncomplicated, this thing with men. What most men want is an erotic whore in bed, one who knows instinctively how to effect the perfect balance between aggression and surrender. I can tell where a particular man's balance is within minutes of foreplay. Like every good whore, I know how to make a man feel as though there are no limits to the lengths I'll go to please him. Before the baby, a lot of guys believed I was the hottest thing they ever took to bed. But that wasn't me.

It isn't that I don't take pleasure from the experience. I always enjoy the sex, except of course when it's as one-sided as what I delivered to Archie Junior. But I always leave part of myself out, a part that witnesses, watches. I don't bring that part to any of the beds I've been in. Because it isn't in those beds. It's not in any bed. But then there was that kiss in West Dennis and the earth mother in Albuquerque. Forget it. For-get it.

Anyway, when I came back here, Jess was in bed, but she wasn't asleep.

"How was he?" she asked. I couldn't tell by the tone of her voice if she was making light of it or if she was genuinely upset.

"I've been gone five minutes, that should tell you plenty."

"Asshole."

"Who?"

"You."

"What did I do?"

"You balled him."

I couldn't understand her logic. "I didn't ball him. I gave him a blow job. It took ten seconds. He's out of our hair for a while. You should be thanking me." She sat up, then got up and started pacing.

"Thanking you? I thought you wanted to set me up with him. I thought you didn't want him."

"I don't want him. But the way he was acting, I thought I'd better pacify him."

"Is that what you call what happened?"

"Come on. You didn't really want him, did you?" She stopped, mid-pace and looked at me skeptically. "He's sleazy. His daddy has money, that's his only redeeming virtue. Don't you agree?" She was silent for a minute.

"I'm not staying here one more night."

"Fine, we'll leave tomorrow."

Jess climbed back into bed and I listened as her breathing slowed. "You're not mad at me are you?" she asked.

"Why should I be mad at you?" But I am mad at Jess. So much for doing a friend a favor.

CHAPTER EIGHTEEN

Jess turned onto Lombard Street as Zoe finished reading the entry. Her mind was flooded with memories.

Zoe turned a page, then shrieked. "This is incredible! Now I know where those matches are from. Pandora's Box! Whoa, baby!"

"Pandora's Box, that I remember. But I don't think your mother would tell you that story. Don't read it, find something nice and sweet to read to me instead. Surely there's something in there that isn't X-rated."

"Oh, I'm reading it all right and I'm reading it out loud. Do you think your sensitive ears can stand it?" Zoe teased.

"I can hear Holly's ashes turning over now." Jess said grinning, as Zoe settled back in the seat and began again.

July 6, 1970

The best laid plans of mice and girls. Everything's gone to hell. I'm at home, bummed and broke. Jess went back to Iowa to work in the country club and I start tutoring and waiting tables tomorrow. I'm sleeping on the porch for the summer because Mother turned my bedroom into a den. She said it was my problem, since I said I wasn't coming home. All my stuff is in the basement. I make journeys up and down dank stairs late at night. At least I have my own space. I want to tell you what happened on the way to the O'Neal prison.

Jess and I got up the morning after the disastrous night with Archie Junior and neither of us said a word about what happened. We packed up our things and I wrote Archie a note telling him we wouldn't be back, that we were staying with a friend in the city. We headed downtown, picked up a *Reader* and sat in Grant Park, eating donuts and looking through the want ads. Jess pulled up her shorts and applied lotion while I read aloud.

"'Waitresses wanted.' I don't want to be a waitress. Do you?"

"Depends on how much money we can make," Jess said.

"I've been waitressing on and off since I was sixteen. I want out of the food transportation business. I want something interesting."

"Like what? Stuffing Suzy-Q's? Buying drugs?"

"Detasseling corn. That would be fun," I teased.

"You aren't hick enough."

"Here's one for a receptionist. Doesn't pay."

"Gee, too bad. I had my heart set on spending my summer in a stuffy office building with a bunch of suits."

"Listen to this. 'Attractive girls wanted. One hundred dollars or more per day. Massage.' How about that? A hundred dollars a day and we'd only have to work two days a week. We could spend the rest of our time at the beach. Or cooking for Archie Junior. Let's do it!"

"Holly, we don't know how to give massages."

"There can't be anything to it."

"But dirty, smelly bodies, all oiled up, yuk. And why do you have to be attractive to give a massage?"

I pondered this. "If you had a choice of some hairy dirty old man, or a young tall blonde Swede to be your masseur, which would you pick? Let's at least call about it." We went to a pay phone and I dialed the number. When the woman who answered heard how old we were, she wanted us to come in right away. We walked to the near north location above a pizza parlor and rang the bell for the second floor. "Look," I said to Jess, "'Pandora's Box.' Weird name."

"This is creepy."

"It's above a pizza place. How bad could it be? If we don't get jobs here we can always come downstairs and waitress." We were buzzed in and walked to the second floor. We entered a small hallway and peered over a high desk. A young, hip-looking woman rose to greet us.

"Hi, my name's Sharon," she said, extending her hand. "You must be the girls who called?"

"I'm Holly O'Neal and this is my friend Jess Martin." I felt Jess's elbow in my back.

"Hi. Let me show you around. Like the ad said, you can make at least a hundred dollars a day here; it's really up to you. The girls work either the day or night shift, and right now I have both open. I'm very proud that in seven months we haven't had one case of venereal disease. Isn't that great?" I nodded and Jess jabbed me, hard.

"We insist on the use of condoms, but what you do in your room is your business. This is a massage parlor and we have many important clients here, who must remain anonymous. The house takes 60 percent of the fee and you keep the rest. You also keep any and all tips. Any questions?" Jess and I were dumb struck. "No questions?"

"Uh, not right now," I said.

"Good, let me show you around." She led us through double doors and into a large parlor decorated like an old movie set. It was a shabby room with heavy molding, thick burgundy carpeting, two large marble fireplaces and a bar off to one side. The curtains were a heavy purple velvet and blocked out the sunlight. There were about six girls standing around. They looked older than Jess and I, and most of them were dressed in skimpy outfits.

A gray-haired man was talking with two of the girls at the bar. One of them had on a sheer orange robe, with only the skimpiest panties on underneath it. The man was openly staring at her breasts, while he shared a joke with the second one, who was lighting his cigarette. Sharon led us through a long hallway with small rooms on either side. In each room was a little brown armless couch and the ugliest ivy wallpaper I'd ever seen. Sharon demonstrated how the couches folded down into a bed.

One room had an ironing board and a television set. "This is for the girls to come and relax. We think it's important for the girls to have a room of their own, no men allowed. Each girl is assigned one parlor room during her shift, and as I said, what you do in there is your business. But we expect you to use protection. We're very proud of our health record."

"I can tell," I said, and wondered if she could hear the mocking tone in my voice. "I like the wallpaper."

"Oh, thanks, The girls helped pick it out."

Yeah, I thought, because they spend so much time staring up at it.

Sharon led us out to the front desk and Jess followed close behind me. "Don't you have any questions?"

"Yes, when can we start?" Jess stepped on the backs of my ankles. "Ow! That is, if we decide to take the job."

"You can start tonight if you like. But I'd like you to fill out these applications first."

"Applications?" Jess looked petrified.

"Just a formality." She looked at Jess. "You can do it later if you want. I'll tell you what. Why don't you girls think about it and call me later if you decide you want to apply." I thanked her and we walked out. Actually, Jess ran out and I could hardly keep up with her.

"Wait. Wait up!" She turned toward me as I ran alongside her.

"What the hell were we doing in there? Do you know what kind of a place that was?"

"It was a massage parlor, like she told us—"

"It's a whore house!"

"Come on, she said we could do whatever we wanted in those rooms."

"Did you see the way those couches folded down, we wouldn't be giving massages on those."

"I don't know, you're giving a massage, your hand slips and pretty soon you're jacking some guy off. What's the big deal?"

"What's the big deal? The big deal is that it's prostitution and it's against the law!"

I struggled to keep pace with her. "Since when have we ever done or not done something because it was illegal!"

"You can't think this is okay, Holly! You just can't." She stopped and turned toward me again. "Do you think this is okay? Would you want to do it?"

I thought for a minute before I answered. "I don't think it's wrong, if that's what you're asking. I mean, my God Jess, what's the difference if we dress up like bunnies for the Playboy Club and strut around in front of a bunch of guys who are thinking about what they'd like to be doing to us, which is exactly the same thing we would be doing if we took this job, but in this case we'd actually be giving some old fart a little real pleasure? Do you think that's wrong?" She started walking again and I could tell she was having a hard time with my logic. She put her fingers to her temples and pressed hard like she does when something bothers her.

"It's not like I think it's wrong. It's just gross, that's all."

"It's just sex. Sex isn't gross, it's just sex."

"How can you be so casual about it?" Jess sounded disgusted, as though I'd asked her if I could drown her cat for a science experiment.

"What's the worse that can happen? We might get VD? Seven months without one case. Aren't you impressed?"

"You've got to be joking. I can't believe you'd even think about doing something so disgusting—"

"It's a lot less disgusting than putting on a bunny costume and parading like a cock tease in front of a bunch of letches—look, but keep your dirty little hands off. That is what is disgusting. Not sucking some guy's cock. Not giving him a hand job and calling it a massage. At least that's honest—a fair trade. None of that false mystery, that ridiculous cat and mouse, that here-I-am-but-don't-you-dare-touch-me bullshit! That's what's disgusting."

"But to do it for money?"

"For the same money—no, for even more money than you'd put between your boobs stuffed into a bunny costume. Why can't you see that it's the same thing, only this way—this massage parlor—is more honest."

"I don't want honesty."

"What do you want?"

"I want, I want, I don't want to think about this any more." She pressed hard on her temples again and I knew it was time to stop.

"Okay, I'm sorry. We won't take the job. I didn't really want to do it, anyway." Jess was breathing hard and I knew I'd upset her.

"But you might have, if I would?"

"I doubt it," I said. "I don't think I have the balls to do it by myself—I mean ovaries. No, I'm sure I wouldn't." She seemed relieved. We walked on, found a delicatessen on Grand Avenue and ordered pastrami sandwiches and fries. After I'd finished mine and started in on her fries, I couldn't resist a few more jabs. "Say, Jess."

"What?" she asked, slapping my hand away from her plate.

"Just think. If we took that job in the massage parlor, I bet we'd learn some incredible tricks from those other girls."

"Like how not to marry a man?"

"Oh, no." I snuck around the side of her plate, slid a fry off and had it in my mouth before she could react. "Like how to do things to a man only hookers do."

"So, you admit that it's hooking we'd be doing? You're going to get fat if you keep eating like that."

I ignored her. "We prefer to call it a massage parlor. Improves the circulation. Brings blood to the—extremities."

She laughed. Finally. "You want to do it and I'm holding you back. You could have a whole new career, Holly." She folded her napkin and put it under her plate. "But I did love the clothes. I'm dying to have an orange see-through robe like the one that blonde had on. Do you think we could go back and ask her where she got it?"

"I have a better idea: Let's take the job and you can dress up like a Playboy bunny. You could specialize in it—you'd have a corner on the market. Jess Martin at Pandora's Box now appearing nightly in her bunny ears. They'd be standing in line for a massage from you—I bet you wouldn't have to work all through graduate school."

"I'm not going to graduate school. But I can see you at Pandora's—you'd insist on standing stark naked, so they'd know exactly what they'd be getting: 'Here, I am, take it or leave it, if you don't like it, fuck you.'"

"No," I said, sucking down the last of my Tab, "I've never admitted this to anyone, but it's been the dream of my life to dress up like an ear of corn and open my silks to a man dressed as an insect. I'm searching the world for a man like that, and I'm desperate. I'm at the end of my stalk. Won't you please help me find him?" I held my knife up to my throat in mock suicide, and she laughed in her light, free, Jess way, and everything was right between us again.

CHAPTER NINETEEN

Reluctant to have the afternoon end, Jess had taken a circuitous route home. She'd wanted to continue driving until every story had ended happily. The women were still smiling when Jess pulled into her garage and the door rumbled shut behind them. She shut off her car and they gathered up their packages and went inside.

Zoe dropped her sweater on the chair, then headed quickly to the bathroom. Jess hung up her coat and sat down, surprisingly relaxed. The afternoon had been an unexpected but welcome diversion and she'd succeeded in pushing thoughts of presentations, ad campaigns, Eric and Harper out of her mind.

"That was so much fun." Zoe sat down next to Jess and yawned.

"I've worn you out! Maybe you should lie down for a little while." Jess stood up and Zoe yawned again.

"This pregnancy thing is weird, one minute I'm barfing, the next I'm totally jazzed, then I'm asleep on my feet. What is it, around 4:00? Maybe I do need a rest." Zoe picked up one of Holly's journals and moved toward Jess's office. She stopped and turned toward Jess. "Thank you for telling me the stories, and for listening to me." She looked down at the floor, then turned. "Anyway, thanks and wake me up when it's time to go, okay?"

"Okay." The door closed and Jess was alone. She moved toward the stereo, flipped through her CDs and chose an old favorite, Joni Mitchell's "Ladies of the Canyon." The late afternoon sun streamed through the blinds as Jess went into the kitchen. She hadn't made her usual Saturday trip to the grocer, so the Diet Pepsi stash was depleted. She spotted the basket of lemons on the counter, a gift from a neighbor. She'd make lemonade. How hard could that be? As she squeezed lemon after lemon she tried to hold on to the pleasant afternoon, to keep her mind away from the feelings of betrayal that kept intruding through the familiar lyrics. She'd squeezed nearly a dozen lemons into the glass pitcher when the sound of the doorbell shattered her calm.

Jess checked her watch quickly, moved to the door and looked through the viewer. It was Eric. The knot in her stomach returned and she felt a tightening in her throat. She stepped back, took a deep breath, glanced into the mirror by the door, then turned the lock.

"Eric. I wasn't expecting you." She opened the door and he moved quickly past her.

"What do you mean you weren't expecting me? I told you last night and in several voice messages today I'd come by." Jess glanced at the phone, surprised that she'd forgotten all about messages. It was usually the first thing she did when she came in. "Where have you been all day? I figured you'd be hard at work. I must have called 20 times. Haven't you checked your messages? Why didn't you have your cell on?" Eric filled the room with questions as he removed his leather jacket and laid it carefully on the back of the couch. His blonde hair was tousled but otherwise he was impeccably dressed in khakis, polo shirt and top-siders. "And what's all this junk? Looks like you raided a flea market."

He picked up the blue floppy hat, photos, love beads and tossed them carelessly from the chair to the coffee table, then sat down. As world's collided in the middle of her living room, Jess ran to rescue

Holly's treasures.

"I took a few hours off, drove to Sausalito." She hated the guilty feeling that crept like a shadow across the room. She knew Eric was thinking that she didn't deserve an afternoon off, not after the mess she'd made of his top account. "I needed a few hours to myself. It was a tough week," she finished, her voice small and meek. As she spoke, she gathered more of the souvenirs and stacked them protectively on the corner of the coffee table.

"You do look a little burned out. I think what you really need is a jump-start from me. Come here." He grabbed her arm and pulled her close. "You smell like lemons." He tucked a loose strand of her hair back into the barrette and kissed her deeply, with a sense of ownership.

Not this time, she thought, remembering the conversation she'd overheard outside Harper's office. She pulled away with a quick smile. "What I need is something to drink. I'm making lemonade. Want a glass? I only have to add the sugar." She moved toward the kitchen and Eric followed.

"Lemonade. How Midwestern. Sure, I'll have a glass, if you spike it with something." As she measured the sugar, Eric moved behind her, reaching his arms around her waist, moving his hands over her breasts. His touch was intense, greedy, and Jess didn't like the way it made her feel. She pulled away, went to the cupboard across the room and grabbed a bottle of vodka. "Here, make yourself a drink."

"For someone who should have been missing me for a week, you're not very friendly. What's up?" Eric took the bottle and sulked as he poured a strong shot of vodka into his glass.

At that moment Zoe rounded the corner into the kitchen, bumping squarely into him. "Oops! Excuse me. I didn't realize we had company," she said with a yawn. "Sorry, I was just about to take a nap. You must be Eric."

"And you would be . . .?" Eric, unsettled by the intrusion, set the bottle on the counter.

"Zoe. I'm here for a glass of water."

"How about some lemonade. I just made it. It's not bad."

"Cool." Zoe poured a glass and turned to leave. "Just pretend you never saw me. I'm not even here."

The door to the office closed loudly and an uncomfortable silence filled the kitchen. Jess poured herself some lemonade slowly, keeping her eyes on the glass and away from Eric's glare.

He shook his glass and the ice made a clinking sound like he was quieting a crowd to make a speech. "When were you going to tell me about your guest? Who is she? Is she spending the night?"

Jess turned to the refrigerator, trying to sound nonchalant. "The daughter of a friend, and I was going to tell you. She came last night. It wasn't planned; she just appeared."

"I guess that puts an end to our plans for the evening, doesn't it." His tone was sarcastic.

"I didn't realize we had plans for the evening," Jess replied, suddenly angry. "You said you'd try to stop by. That isn't exactly a plan, is it?" She put the lemons in the disposal, then turned to face Eric. "Besides, I know what that means. You stop by, we have sex, you leave and I spend the rest of Saturday night alone, working. As usual." Her tone surprised them both. She'd never complained before. She always made certain he didn't feel any pressure. But she was tired of pretending it didn't bother her to be last in his life, and today she wanted to tell the truth.

"Whoa, where is this coming from? I thought we both understood how things are. That is, until Josie's out of school." He sounded genuinely surprised. "I thought you were okay with this."

"Well, I'm not." Jess felt her resolve weaken.

He was silent for a moment, then spoke. "I'm sorry you feel

that way, because I'd hoped to stay here with you tonight—all night. Josie's at a slumber party and Rosemary has a bad cold, so I'm sleeping in the guest room. She takes that cold medicine and is out till morning. She'd never miss me." He paused, took a final sip of his drink, looked at Jess. "But I guess that's not going to happen now. I suppose I should be going so you and your little friend can enjoy your evening." He set the glass down on the counter.

Jess felt an old fear. He was going to leave. She'd made him angry and she was going to lose him. She forced herself to think. He had to be lying about staying all night, didn't he? He'd only spent the night twice in their three years together. And what about meeting Harper for a drink? She'd heard them make plans. Had she been mistaken?

Eric went for his coat and Jess followed, trying to figure out what was happening, trying to decide what to say, how to fix it. Work, that was the answer. She blurted out, "Tomorrow I'll work all day on a new campaign strategy for ProbTech. I can't believe we were so far off target, but I can fix it. I'll have it on your desk first thing Monday."

Eric turned, half-smiled. "Why don't you hold off for a bit? You know how fast things change with those guys. I'll give them a call Monday and sort things out." His voice was condescending, cold, when he added the final insult. "Besides you are looking tired. Take some time off. You'll feel better."

Jess felt a wave of nausea, hearing not Eric's words, but Brad's, words from years ago: "You're so burned out, I can't believe you're the same person I married. Why don't you fix yourself up? You look terrible."

Eric kept talking, saying something about his trip to Hong Kong and jet lag, but Jess only heard the sound of her own heart breaking. Finally, he opened the door and before she could gather her wits, he kissed her on the forehead and was gone.

To Harper, Jess thought. To his younger, brighter protégé, his new project. She stood looking at the closed door for a long time, then turned to the mirror. Her weary face stared back at her—the dark circles under her eyes, the sprinkles of gray all mocked her. He was right. She was tired. Old and tired.

For too many years she'd kept up the dance, working late and weekends. She'd given up any semblance of a personal life for this, to be betrayed by her married lover. She continued to stare into the mirror, watching the tears well up in the corners of her eyes. Suddenly she saw Zoe's reflection behind her. Jess turned quickly, brushing her hand across her face, diverting her eyes. "Zoe! You're not resting!"

Zoe looked puzzled. "I did a little. Did Eric leave? I'm sorry. You should have told him I was going. Call him and I'll take a cab so you two can have the rest of the evening together."

"No, please, I couldn't bear it if you left. Please, stay here tonight." The words poured out of her, unedited and pitiful. Jess turned away, fighting back more tears.

"Are you crying?" Zoe turned Jess back around. "What happened? What did he do to you?"

"He just left. That's all. They all leave, eventually. He's on his way to a rendezvous with Harper. I shouldn't be surprised."

"You're kidding, right? I mean it's bad enough that he's cheating on his wife, but now he's cheating on you, too? I'm sorry, that didn't come out right. What happened?" Zoe went to the couch and patted the seat next to her for Jess to sit down.

"It's too complicated and sordid for your young ears. What I need is a drink."

"Let me fix you something. Do you want wine?"

"I don't think so."

"Lemonade?"

"Okay. But put a shot of vodka in it. It's on the counter. Better make it two shots." Jess wiped her eyes and sat down.

Zoe ran off to fix her drink, then yelled from the kitchen, "Just so you know, I was hoping you'd ask me to stay. Those friends I told you about—they're really Adam's friends. I hardly know them. It would be weird if I showed up on their doorstep, with us being broken up and all. So yes, I'd love to stay. I like it here with you. I don't want to leave."

Jess heard the sound of the ice machine and soon Zoe was back, drinks in hand. She sat down next to Jess. "Okay, so where were we? Oh, yes. Men suck." They each took a long sip and stared out the window as the afternoon light began to fade.

CHAPTER TWENTY

Jess suggested they move outside while it was still warm, before the fog rolled in. She opened the glass doors to her redwood deck and dusted off the wicker lounge chairs. Zoe followed and they stretched out, facing the bay. They watched cargo ships in the distance as they moved toward the pier. Jess took two large swallows of lemonade, then set her glass down, shutting her eyes against the afternoon light, against the distance in Eric's eyes.

"Do you want to talk about Eric? I'm a good listener." Zoe sounded almost sweet

"I wouldn't know where to start." Zoe was silent. "First of all, he lied to me. But I shouldn't be surprised, I bought the lie a long time ago." It's sordid and ugly and I've let myself be used, she thought.

"He's a total jerk. All men are."

"No, I'm a fool for believing it would be different with me. I don't know what I wanted, but it isn't this."

"So, why don't you end it?" The question was simple, direct.

"He may have beat me to it."

"You deserve better than a married man."

"There's more to it than that, Zoe." Jess was suddenly annoyed by Zoe's naïve confidence. "This is also about my job, my life. He could ruin my career. He just took me off one of his biggest accounts. Damn, I wish I'd taken better notes."

"He couldn't be responsible for all those awards in your office."

"He gave me the opportunity to earn them. I'd be stuck with second tier accounts if it weren't for Eric." Thinking about what might happen to her without Eric made her heart sink. What the hell am I going to do now? she wondered. And then the familiar voice asked its usual questions: What did you do wrong? What did you do to make him leave you? "Nothing," she said aloud.

"Nothing what?"

"Just my inner voice, telling me I've fucked up again. Anyway, Eric's looking for his next challenge. I suppose that's just who he is, who he's always been. Well, I can still make the grade. But Harper . . ."

"What about her?"

"He's seeing her for a drink tonight. I think he's giving her my account."

"What a serious asshole." Zoe kicked her shoe across the deck. "Did you ask him?" Jess shook her head no. "Why not?"

"If you ask, you have to be prepared to hear the truth. If you hear the truth, you have to act." They pondered Jess's words. "Anyway, I'm burned out on the subject of relationships. Especially my relationships. My relationship."

"Me, too," Zoe chimed in. "It's like Annabelle always says: 'Men. You can't live with 'em and you can't kill 'em.' It's a cruel joke, how different men and women are. God created us to be attracted to each other, but he made us so different we can hardly stand each other."

"Isn't that the truth," Jess sighed. "It's only a good thing from nature's point of view. Sometimes I think if we were rational about it, people would just stop procreating." They sat in silence for a minute.

"So, you think I should have this baby?" Jess choked on her drink, wondering where that conclusion had come from. "Sorry, that's just where my mind goes whenever it has a moment of silence. Go figure!" The women laughed.

"I don't know what you should do," Jess said. "Do you think of what's growing inside you as a real little person? I mean, can you imagine the baby? What do you want? And are you sure you don't want to talk this over with Adam?"

"No! Besides, he'd probably want to get married and then he'd think everything was perfectly fine."

"Would getting married be so bad?" Jess questioned.

"You're kidding, right? Marriage is a big enough deal, but add a baby to the mix and it's beyond comprehension. I read about this woman, she had four babies in four years, then she just exploded! She poisoned every one of her kids, then blew her husband's head off." Zoe's rash over-dramatizing made Jess laugh.

"I don't think you're the murdering type."

"Probably not, but I could see me flipping out. You and I both know I'll be the one who will end up doing everything if I have this kid. Isn't that what women do? Sacrifice for 18 years and then their kids leave without a word of thanks? In the meantime, you've had these kids with some supposedly great guy, and when you're a little older he leaves you for someone younger."

Jess didn't know how to respond to these too-often truths. "Do you think Adam is that kind of guy?"

"You never know." Zoe took a sip of lemonade and pursed her lips. "My father is."

"Paul?" Jess wanted to hear more.

"Yes. Steady, practical, Paul. A hypocrite. He had an affair. And I was the one who found out about it."

"That must have been hard."

Zoe sat up and turned to Jess. "I was washing his car one Sunday, the summer after I turned 14. I went to pop the trunk in the glove compartment to vacuum it. He keeps his fishing gear there and it gets totally pitted. Anyway, in the glove box I found a letter from a woman named Patricia. She told him she loved him. She called him "Pauly" and talked about how they'd spend their honeymoon in Mexico after the divorce."

"Oh, my. But he didn't leave your mother."

"Not for long. I kept the letter for a week, I was so mad at my dad. One day he yelled at me about staying out too late—or something equally stupid—and I lost it. I brought out the letter and read it in front of them. It was cruel, I know, I thought Joanne was going to die. But I was so mad at him."

"I bet. What happened?" Jess asked.

"They had a terrible fight. My mother even threw their wedding picture at him. Self-controlled Joanne actually threw something. My father said he'd never promised this woman a wedding, and that made my mother even angrier. He said it started as an innocent flirtation, but then the woman got serious. He'd been trying to break it off, but she threatened to tell his family. Mother was hysterical and got my father to admit that he'd been fucking her. He moved out for four months and Joanne started divorce proceedings. She'd cry all day and watch old movies all night. It was awful. I felt terrible."

Jess sat up and set her drink on the glass table. "But they never divorced, so they must have worked things out."

"They didn't work anything out. My dad had a heart attack. Not a big heart attack, but enough of one to freak everybody out. So right away my mother took him back! Can you believe it? Anyway, I was so angry at her and so miserable at home, I stopped studying. I skipped school, started smoking pot—I even tried cigarettes. When my quarter grades came my mother sent me directly into therapy. My whole family was in therapy for a while, well, Mother, Dad and me. Scott never had any problems. He was too busy being perfect. Anyway, I don't have the best view of marriage."

"But why were you mad at Joanne?" Jess was puzzled. "She stayed with him, didn't she?"

"Some people find that admirable. Look at Hillary Clinton. The press canonized her for sticking with Bill. Sometimes staying is the hardest and most honorable thing to do." Jess wasn't sure she believed what she was saying, but it sounded like what Zoe needed to hear.

"Well, *St. Joanne* fits her now. I think she loves playing the martyr. Of course my dad was thoroughly humiliated. He must have shrunk two inches. Ever since then Joanne's been on a self-improvement kick and has my dad completely under her thumb. Now she's going to become a therapist herself—child psychology. As if she ever had a clue what her children were thinking. But none of that matters because now I know my real mother. Well, from her journals and from you. If you think about it, I probably know more about my mother than most of my friends do about theirs."

"Let's go back to Adam for a second. Do you think he's like your dad?"

"Who knows? He's already cheated on me. If he cheated while we were married, I'd divorce him in a nanosecond. I mean, doesn't it make you wonder about Eric and his wife? He sounds like the kind of guy no one could trust. What must their relationship be like?"

"I try not to think about it," Jess admitted sheepishly. "Is Adam serious about the woman he's with now?"

"Who knows?" Zoe stood up and leaned over the railing, breathing deep. "I don't know. He's called me a bunch of times. I suppose if I told him about the baby he'd want to get married. But I don't want him that way. Anyway, it's my baby, my body and my decision." She picked a bud off an impatiens plant. "I just keep thinking about what it would have been like if Holly had raised me."

"Banish the thought, Zoe. You are a thousand times better off with the parents you have. As much as I loved Holly, she was not prepared to be a mother at 20."

"Maybe not. But it still seems so unfair."

"It is unfair. It's grossly unfair. Welcome to life." Jess said this without rancor. "It seems to me your parents have tried to make things good for you. They've given you what Holly would never have been able to. It seems like whatever you were interested in, your parents supported you. You went to summer camp and had vacations, right? And they're still paying for your education."

Zoe looked away, then she shot angrily back. "So, as long as they give you money, it's okay?"

"Well, turn it around. Because they've supported you, does that mean they don't love you? The last time I looked, most parents are thrilled to be able to afford to send their kids to college. And your mother stayed with her errant husband. Some would call that loyalty, not selling out. If he had remorse, anyway, and it seems he did. So you didn't get everything you wanted, everything you thought you deserved. Well, guess what—no one does. I know it's been hard for you. You might think your parents have sold out or that they have corny values, but you are lucky to have them. They're not the perfect couple, and they made different choices than you would make. But before you go judging their failings, try to see it from their point of view."

"Geez, sounds like I hit a nerve. I only know that I don't want a loveless marriage, or a loveless relationship." Zoe turned and looked squarely at Jess. "I'd rather die first."

As Zoe continued pulling buds off the plant, Jess said nothing and they sat in silence. Zoe clearly wasn't ready to hear what Jess had to say, so she leaned back and turned to watch the first touch of fog gathering above the water. Jess was amazed at how credible she'd sounded, how mature and strong-minded. When did I develop such a convincing shtick and why don't I apply it to my own life? She thought of Eric, then shook her head to erase his face from her mind. "Do you love Adam?"

Zoe paused. "Yes. Definitely, yes. But that's what I'm afraid of, don't you see? Okay, it's true, I freaked out. He was pressuring me to give up my apartment and move in with him. I mean we practically lived together anyway; most of my things were at his house. He said that since we'd known each other eight years and still loved each other, it was time to make a commitment. I freaked. I told him I needed more space, not less. So we broke up and when he ran into an old girlfriend one thing led to another, and he cheated on me. Well, he didn't exactly cheat, we had broken up. But, God, couldn't he have at least waited until I got all my stuff out? That was almost a month ago. Now he's seeing her pretty regularly, I think. Well, actually I don't know." She sat back down, then continued.

"They say people who are adopted push other people away before they can be pushed away themselves. How do I know I wouldn't do that to this baby? I understand what my mother meant when she said she wanted to keep the baby inside her. I want that, too. Then the baby would just stay with me, where it could always be safe. I wouldn't have to make any decisions. I wouldn't have any regrets."

"One thing I can assure you is that, no matter what you do, you'll have regrets. There is an answer for you, and it'll be the right one. But no matter what you choose, you'll always wonder where the opposite path would have taken you."

"So, you think I should have this baby?"

"How far along are you?"

"Nine weeks. But I knew I was pregnant after a couple of weeks. I felt different. I took a home pregnancy test the day I missed my period. I wanted to know right away so there would be plenty of time to have an abortion."

"So you've considered that?"

"Annabelle and I called the clinic and made an appointment. They ask you to attend a counseling session before they'll schedule one. It freaked me out. I mean, I'm completely pro-choice and I have friends who have had abortions; a few have had more than one. But when the counselor asked if I'd talked it over with Adam and I hadn't, I started thinking more about my real mother and father and why they made the choice they did."

"That was very mature of you. It's an enormous decision and you're right, you have a little time to make the right choice for you and your life."

Zoe laughed. "You sound like the counselor, Jess."

"Well, it is an important decision, that's why they call it your right to choose. It's not a choice to take lightly."

Zoe was quiet for a minute, then asked, "Did you ever have an abortion?"

CHAPTER TWENTY-ONE

Jess was tempted to lie. But there were some things she didn't need to lie about. Holly's daughter was on an honest search and she deserved to know this truth.

Jess took a breath. "Yes. I had an abortion."

"Do you regret it? I'm sorry, that didn't come out right. I mean, who was the father? Were you in love with him?"

"I thought I loved him, but he didn't love me. And sometimes I do regret that I don't have a child now. He would have been a little younger than you But at the time, it was the right thing to do."

"How old were you?"

"Twenty. It was before abortions were legal."

"Who was the father?"

"His name was Nate Hamilton. And he was black, which made things even more complicated."

"Tell me about it. I mean if you're okay with that. If you don't want to, I'll understand."

"Are you ready for a long, involved story?" Zoe nodded. "Let me get you some more lemonade first."

Jess went into the kitchen, poured two glasses and opened some pretzels. She stood for a moment, looking out the window at the fog as it eased its way through the trees, silently embracing the hills above the bay. It was late afternoon, approaching twilight, that melancholy time of day that always reminded Jess of all that she would never be. So many paths are closed forever, she thought.

She walked to the doorway of the deck where Zoe sat, leaning back on the lounge chair, her eyes closed, her left arm resting on top of her head. She wondered what Zoe was thinking, but didn't ask. Instead, she set down the glasses and bowl of pretzels. Zoe opened her eyes, looked into Jess's and smiled. The look was intimate, natural, and Jess couldn't remember the last time someone had looked at her that way. Warmed by it, she sat down and slowly began her story.

It was fall, 1970. I was a junior English major with a journalism minor, and I'd just landed a paying job as a part-time reporter for the *Daily Iowan*. I was a novice, so I spent most of my time writing about sorority exchanges and various committee meetings, all very mundane. Much of what I wrote got bumped because there were always more exciting things happening on campus.

But one day I got a break. Anyway, I thought it was a break. Raymond, my editor, sent me to the Afro House to talk to Nate Hamilton and James Rogers about their boycott. I knew I'd only gotten the story because no one else was around when the call came, but I didn't care.

"The Afro House? Me? Okay, sure!" I told him. "Do I need to take a photographer with me or, no, I guess that's a little premature. I'll go over there, dig around and see what I come up with. Hey, thanks, Raymond. Thanks for the story." I grabbed my notebook and coat and bolted for the door.

I called Holly and asked her to meet me at the Union in an hour. I had just enough time to stop at the library and review some back issues of the *Daily Iowan* to catch up on what had been happening with the black student movement over the past several weeks.

When I arrived, Holly was waiting for me. She looked great and particularly healthy in a cranberry sweater, long jean skirt, and work boots. Her hair hung down her back in a long thick braid. I asked her if she'd lost weight.

"No, but I've been eating better, you know, natural foods without preservatives," she said as she lit a Marlboro and blew a puff of smoke over her shoulder. It was late September, and we'd only seen each other three or four times since school started. I'd rented a studio apartment at the new Mayflower apartment highrise. It was too sterile and bourgeois for Holly's taste, so she'd moved into a one-room apartment overlooking the river.

"How about you?" She asked. "How's your Lois Lane gig going?" I told her I'd just been handed my first real assignment and asked her what she was doing for the next hour. "Just studying. And later I have to develop some film for my photography class. Why?"

"Come with me to the Afro House. You have your camera, right?" Holly nodded. "Take some pictures for my story. My editor will be so impressed if I come back with a story and pictures. I'm sure they'll even pay you for the photographs."

"You think they might publish one of my photographs?" Holly pulled her Nikon out of her bag. "I have both lenses and a couple of different kinds of film. What will I be shooting?"

"I don't know. You're the photographer, you decide. I'm meeting with two black football players—they represent the players who are boycotting the team."

"No shit! Boycotting the Hawkeyes? In this town that's treason."

I filled Holly in about what I'd read. It felt great to know more about an issue than she did. "The boycotting players have come up with demands for the coaching staff and the athletic department because they say that black players are treated differently than white ones. The worst thing I read is that when a black player gets hurt, the trainers put ice on the injury for a few minutes and then send him right back into the game. But when a white guy gets hurt, he's sent to the locker room to see the doctors, and they almost always keep him out for the game."

"Maybe the black players are better than the white ones. In my high school, without the black players, we'd never have won a game."

"But it's wrong, don't you agree?"

"I don't know, Jess, it sounds like an awfully big generalization. How can you prove something like that?"

"It's right here." I showed Holly copies of the articles I'd read. "But that's not the only thing," I went on. "The players are also angry because the university isn't actively recruiting black students unless they're jocks. We bring them here so we can use them to play ball and bring money into the school. That sounds like slavery to me." I folded up the articles emphatically and checked my watch.

"I thought slavery was when you held people as prisoners and made them do your bidding. What they're doing isn't right, but I don't think it's slavery. I mean, these guys are getting an education, after all."

As usual, I thought Holly was being too particular and was blind to the bigger picture. "Look," I said, "just come with me and you can hear it for yourself." She agreed, and we headed to the white frame house on Church Street that had recently been transformed into the Afro-American Cultural Center. I had my press card in hand as we climbed the stairs and crossed the wide porch. Through the screen door we heard voices above loud Temptations music.

"Should I knock?" I turned and asked Holly.

"This is your gig, not mine." I did, and a heavy-set black woman appeared at the door. Her Afro was picked out into a huge circle around her head, and she was wearing a long orange and brown robe-like dress over a turtle neck sweater.

"Yes?" She looked us up and down without smiling.

"Hello . . . I . . . we're from the *Daily Iowan*. We have an appointment to interview Nate Hamilton and James Rogers."

She told us to wait and left us standing on the porch. She walked down a hall, out of sight, but we heard her voice. "Nate, Jimbo, there are a couple of white sisters here to see you." She let the word "white" roll out of her mouth with a nasty twang and we heard people laugh.

"She certainly wasn't very friendly," Holly commented as she adjusted her camera strap.

"Why should she be? We're the oppressors."

"I'm not oppressing anyone," Holly shot back.

"Not you personally, dummy, white people in general."

Two large, beautiful black men appeared at the door and invited us in. Holly and I sat with them around a big wooden table in a room that was once a dining room but had been converted into a workroom. Flyers and books were stacked everywhere. Posters on the walls quoted Eldridge Cleaver and Malcolm X. I moved copies of *Soul On Ice* and *Soledad Brother* off a chair and sat down.

While I took notes, Nate and James explained their grievances. They said the university wasn't putting enough money toward recruiting black students. The black population at the university represented less than eight percent of the total university population, and half of those black students were involved in football, basketball or track. As the two men talked, Holly moved around the room with her camera, looking very official as she snapped dozens of photographs.

James, or Jimbo as the woman had called him, was a huge guy who wore sunglasses and acted like any moment he might explode. He quoted people I'd never heard of: Bobby Seale, Angela Davis. He spoke in a rolling voice, like Martin Luther King, Jr., and pounded on the table to drive home his points. Jimbo said the university was a microcosm of white society, with white supremacists in power, and those white supremacists used the black man for their own financial gain and then cast him aside.

Nate was quieter, calmer. His voice was soft, yet firm. He wasn't as big as Jimbo, but he was better looking. He had warm, dark brown eyes, and he looked right at me when he talked; he even smiled occasionally. He kept bringing the conversation back to the actual demands the boycotting team members had presented to the athletic department. I felt he knew that was the story the paper would cover and he seemed anxious to help me get his message across. Jimbo seemed more interested in spouting platitudes and trying to shock the naive honky girls.

I couldn't take my eyes off Nate Hamilton and by the time the interview was over, I was smitten. He seemed to sense it and helped me gather up my papers, touching my arm as he led us to the front door. Holly was still snapping pictures, oblivious to the sparks of attraction between Nate and me. As we said our goodbyes, Nate pulled my notebook toward him and wrote down his phone number. "In case you have more questions about the boycott," he explained with a glimmer in his eyes.

"God, was that guy gorgeous or what?" I practically skipped down the stairs as Holly rewound her film and we headed back to the Union.

"Which guy?"

"You can't be serious? Nate, the strong, gentle, beautiful guy.

Certainly not Jimbo. What a righteous asshole!"

"He's sure well-read though, I mean, he quoted nearly every black leader I've heard of."

"Nate didn't have to quote anyone. Did you see? He gave me his phone number." I showed her where he'd written it. "Do you think that means he wants me to call him?"

"Well, if memory serves me, that's pretty much what he said. "'In case you have more questions about the boycott.'"

"That's what he said, but is that what he meant? I think he wants to see me."

"Of course you think that. Look Jess, when do you want these pictures? I need to get going." Holly was suddenly impatient. It was 2:30 and I had to write the story and submit it by 7:00. We agreed to meet at the library at our usual spot—second floor in the back by the windows—at 6:30.

It was 6:30 before I knew it, and I'd rewritten my story twice, trying to focus on what Nate said without leaving James completely out. I had no time for fine-tuning and still had to pick up Holly's photos. I couldn't be late, so I ran as fast as I could up the library stairs to our table in the back. Holly was there, surrounded by her usual stacks of books.

"Where are they?" I was winded.

"Hi to you too. Sit down and I'll show you."

"No time. I have to get back." I grabbed the envelope and turned to leave.

"Aren't you even going to look at them?"

"I'm sure they're great. Look, I have to run or I'll miss the deadline. I'll call you. Thanks." I bolted back to the *Daily Iowan* and rushed into the editor's office at 7:01.

"You're a minute late, Martin," Raymond said impatiently. "What have you got?"

"Here's my story, and I've got some great photos to go with it."

I handed him the envelope, beaming proudly as I caught my breath.

"Aren't we the eager beaver. I thought all the staff photographers were tied up this afternoon." He opened the clasp on the envelope.

"They were. But I have some resources of my own." I tried not to sound smug as he opened the envelope.

"What the hell are these?" My stomach knotted as he flipped through the stack of black and white photos with a scowl on his face. "This is a bunch of crap. We can't use these." He threw the stack onto the desk.

There must have been 15 prints. Some looked like close-ups of fabrics, the curtains or the back of a chair. There was a close-up of an ear double exposed over the cover of *Soul On Ice*, a fish-eye shot of Jimbo's mouth and an out-of-focus shot of a hand on the table. I gathered up the photos as quickly as I could, mumbling my apologies.

"This is a newspaper, Martin, not an art gallery. From now on use a staff photographer or no photographer. Got it? We've got deadlines here and we can't afford to screw around." He motioned me toward the door and I left, humiliated.

Damn you Holly, I thought. Of all the times to get arty on me. At least you could have taken one shot of Nate and James in a normal pose. I was angry about being humiliated in front of my editor, but I was even angrier because I'd hoped she'd taken a good picture of Nate that I could keep.

Zoe suddenly jumped up, ran into the living room and grabbed the photographs from the box. "Wait, that's what these are," she exclaimed, holding them for Jess to see. "Look, that's the picture of Jimbo's mouth." She laughed, fell back on her chair and Jess joined her as they sifted through the pictures together.

Chuckling, Jess handed the pictures back to Zoe. "She was a

very good photographer. She was especially good at portraits and landscapes. I have a photo in my office that she took of the Golden Gate Bridge that's absolutely stunning. Would you like to have it?"

"No, thanks," Zoe said. "I prefer these." She had a twinkle in her eye that made Jess's heart ache for Holly. "Okay, so you were really hot for Nate. Then what happened?" Jess continued, and for a few minutes lost herself in the story, forgetting how it ended.

Later that night I was at home trying to study, but I couldn't get Nate out of my mind. I ran my fingers across his phone number, wondering what it would feel like to be kissed by a black man. I opened the envelope and browsed through the photos, stopping on a pair of eyes. Those were Nate's, I was sure of it. I spotted my notebook on the floor and without giving it another thought, dialed his number. A woman answered. Sounding as official as I could I asked for Nate, and she called him to the phone.

"Hi, Nate. This is Jess Martin, we met this afternoon. I'm the reporter with the *DI*."

"I know who you are. What's happenin', pretty lady?" His voice was warm and relaxed and for the next half hour we flirted over the phone. We talked about the boycott, classes and school. He told me he lived in a house with four other guys. I was relieved to discover that the woman who answered the phone was a roommate's girlfriend. When I told him I lived alone at the Mayflower apartments, he warmed up even more.

"Maybe I should stop by tomorrow evening and give you an exclusive interview. What do you think?" He sounded so sexy I squirmed, winding and unwinding the phone cord around my arm. We made a date for the next night and I spent the rest of the evening cleaning up the mess that came with working and going to school. Before I went to bed I couldn't resist calling Holly to tell her my good news. But first I told her that the editor hated the photographs and that she'd made me look like a fool.

"The man's got no imagination. Is that my problem?" Holly sometimes got belligerent when she'd fucked up and I told her so. But I also told her I forgave her because I had just landed an exclusive interview with Nate Hamilton. "What kind of exclusive interview? I thought you turned your story in tonight." Holly sounded confused. She'd been sleeping when I called and wasn't responding with the enthusiasm I'd wanted.

"It was bullshit, a ploy. We pretended to have business to take care of, but in reality he wants to see me."

"So you're not going to interview him?"

"Christ, Holly, no. We were flirting, you remember flirting? It's what we used to do, before."

"Before what?"

"Before we started hanging out and sleeping with guys. I can't explain it—either you get it or you don't." I was sorry I'd called.

"Just be careful, you don't know anything about this guy."

"I know enough. He plays fullback for the Hawkeyes, he's from Chicago, he's 21 and he's big and strong and gorgeous."

"And he's black."

"So what?"

"Nothing, except that—never mind. I hope you have a great night. Can I go back to bed now?" She yawned.

I hung up and thought about what Holly had said. The fact that Nate was black didn't make any difference to me, I told myself. But deep down, I knew it wasn't true. I loved the fact that he was black. I turned out the light and climbed into bed, feeling more alive than I had in months.

The next evening I dressed carefully in a low-cut black ribbed sweater that showed my cleavage. I tucked it into my tightest jeans and belted them with a wide men's belt I'd found at the army-surplus store. I put on beaded earrings that hung nearly to my shoulders and a black leather choker with my astrological sign dangling from it. To finish the look, I pulled a bit of my long hair to the side and braided two thin strands of orange and blue leather through it, leaving the leather ends to fall loosely. Very exotic, I thought, surveying my look. How could Nate resist me?

I dimmed the lights and lit the three new candles I'd inserted into Mateus and Lancers bottles. I tuned the radio to the campus station that played jazz in the evenings. Around the room I'd arranged several copies of the *Daily Iowan* folded with my stories on top. That day, I'd begun reading the *Autobiography of Malcolm X*, so I laid it on the coffee table near the couch. I brought out some chips and poured them into a basket, then opened the bottle of Mateus Holly had brought me when I moved into the Mayflower. When the doorbell rang, I quickly surveyed the room. Too obvious, I decided, so I blew out the candles and turned up the lights. I opened the door and was rewarded by Nate's warm, dark eyes as he smiled the widest, whitest smile I'd ever seen and he kissed me on the cheek.

"How you doin'? You look great. You know, my friend Kirby lives on the third floor. I'll have to introduce you."

"Great. Come on in. It's not fancy, but it's home. Can I get you a glass of wine? I'm having one."

"That'd be cool." He moved across the room gracefully, not like a man who weighed over 200 pounds and regularly crushed even bigger men on the football field. "You have a fine view from here. Man, check it out! You can see from the Pentacrest to the stadium."

"It's wonderful with the lights down. There are some binoculars there." The perfect excuse, I thought, as I dimmed the lights again and re-lit two candles on my way to the couch with the wine.

"How did you get so lucky? Kirb's crib has a view overlooking the heating ducts." I explained that I'd signed up to move into the Mayflower before they completed construction. I'd wanted to live alone and have some privacy.

"Shall we toast?" I said, handing him his wine.

"To you and your privacy." He lifted his glass.

"To you and your boycott." We sat on the couch sipping our wine until Nate asked if I got high. He pulled a joint from his pocket, lit it and passed it to me. I took a very controlled hit to make sure I didn't get too stoned. Nate took a long hit, then snuffed the roach and began to tell me about the latest developments with the boycott.

I had a hard time concentrating. He smelled of spicy aftershave and looked incredibly sexy in his black turtleneck and well-worn jeans. He had a woven leather band around his wrist. I tried to notice everything about him as I worked to listen to his words. I kept watching his face, marveling at the dark, rich color of his skin and how the candlelight reflected in his warm, brown eyes. Everything about him was exquisite.

We talked and laughed for an hour before he made his first move. He set his glass on the table and leaned toward me. Gently brushing the hair from my face, he held my chin in his hand and raised my face to his. His lips were soft and so big they covered my mouth. He kissed me slowly, tenderly. His strong arms surrounded me and as he pulled me closer and began to kiss me more forcefully, I let out a muffled moan. It was too much. My entire body was on fire with a desire I'd never felt before and it scared me. I pulled back, expecting a struggle, like so many other times, when the man I was with was too aroused to take no for an answer. But Nate immediately loosened his arms, pulling back to look me squarely in the eyes.

"You're some kisser," I managed to say, as I pulled farther away and reached for my wine.

"Takes one to know one," he said smiling. As he picked up his glass, my eyes tried not to stare at the bulge in his jeans.

I took a sip and told myself to stay in the moment and trust my instincts. I set my glass down, reached for his hand and turned it over in my palm, noticing how the dark brown hand revealed a lighter palm. I was mesmerized. "You have a very long life line, do you know that?" I traced the line coyly with my finger.

"I do now." He took my hand in his and began kissing each finger. I could feel the warmth return with each kiss, but as he put his arms around me, I pulled back again. I turned my head quickly and buried it in his shoulder so he couldn't see the tears filling my eyes. Damn it! I thought. What is wrong with you, Jess! Why can't you just go with it?

As if he knew exactly what I needed, Nate lifted my head and looked into my eyes. He said the words I'd been waiting to hear from every man I'd slept with, words I'd never heard: "Jess, nothing will happen here if you don't want it to. I'm very attracted to you and I'd love to make love to you. But it has to be something you want too, or it's no good, no good at all."

And so we made love.

"Wow. That's beautiful." It was Zoe, pulling Jess into the present.

"It was." Jess knew that was all she was willing to tell Zoe about that night.

"I love this story; but can it wait a minute? All this lemonade is going right through me." Jess was happy for the moments alone. She took the photograph of Nate's eyes and held it, remembering one of the sexiest nights of her life. Nate had told her he could wait. But suddenly she couldn't wait another minute to be close to that gentle man.

She remembered putting her finger on his lips to hush him

then kissing him deeply, passionately, like she'd never kissed anyone before.

Her lips parted as his tongue reached in and moved slowly, warmly, around hers. As they kissed he moved over her, until they were lying side by side on the couch. Jess was breathing hard as he reached under her sweater and unsnapped her bra. Then he pulled her sweater up and his full, soft lips surrounded each nipple, sending warm tremors pulsing through her body.

When the sensation became too much to bear, Jess grabbed his sweater and he helped her pull it over his head. She remembered the golden glow of his hard, rolling muscles, glistening with the heat of his passion in the candlelight. Moving her mouth to that special curve where his arm and shoulder met, Jess traveled toward his neck. Then she kissed his chest over kinky patches of hair, leaving warm, wet places. She'd never seen or kissed anyone so beautiful and strong as Nate Hamilton.

She kissed him hard on his lips as he unfastened her belt and pulled back the buttons of her jeans. And then his hand was between her legs where the heat raged. She closed her eyes, held her breath as he reached inside her. She felt her legs fall open wider, eager for his caress. Her hips raised to meet each stroke. Jess was wild to have him inside her. As he pulled away to undo his jeans, his erection pushed through his shorts, black, hard and hungry.

He moved over her, gentle but strong, and Jess felt his cock rush toward the heat. Like a wave, he rolled into her deeper and deeper, taking her breath away again and again, until suddenly her whole body exploded with a long, quaking shudder, a sensation of pleasure she'd never felt before. Nate pushed harder and raised himself onto his arms. He threw his head back and let out a loud moan as every inch of his body tensed, then released.

Jess remembered lying together afterward, very still. No words seemed necessary. She lay with her head on Nate's chest, his fingers gently stroking her hair. She wanted to savor that moment, stretch it into a lifetime. But Nate broke the silence when he asked to spend the night. "I couldn't bear it if you left," she whispered back. But by the sound of his steady breathing, she knew that Nate was nearly asleep. They moved to her bed and Nate was soon snoring softly. Jess lay awake an hour after that, reveling in her first orgasm with the beautiful black god.

CHAPTER TWENTY-TWO

Zoe hurried back from the bathroom and sat on the edge of the lounge chair. "Okay, where were we?" Hoping Zoe wouldn't notice her flushed face, Jess asked if she was getting hungry for dinner. "I'd like to hear the rest of this story first. Unless you've changed your mind?"

"Where was I?" Jess asked, feigning ignorance.

"Making love to Nate Hamilton is where I left you. I don't know where you went from there."

Jess laughed. "Oh, yes." She cleared her throat and went on.

For the next few weeks I saw Nate almost every night. He always came to my apartment, he was always late and we always made love. He wasn't anything like the hippie guys I slept with, strung out or nervous or stoned. He had a lot of experience and taught me things about sex I never knew. I was completely enamored.

But Nate's falling out with the Hawkeyes became more contentious, and the coach finally gave the boycotting players an ultimatum: shut up and put up with things as they were or be kicked off the team. The players ignored the ultimatum and kept holding rallies, writing letters and missing practice. Finally, the coach ousted all 16 boycotting players.

The Des Moines Register published an editorial against the coach. Then several professors backed the players and spoke out in support of their demands, saying that diversity was long overdue. The local television station aired a feature about the players and editorials called for the coach to reinstate them.

In the end, the coach took the coward's way out. He asked team members to either vote the players back in or dismiss them. The team voted nine of the players back and dismissed the other seven. Nate was one of the seven kicked off the team for good.

After that, Nate and I spent more time together talking about how he'd cope second semester when he lost his scholarship or whether he'd ever be able to graduate from Iowa. Then there was the draft. The Viet Nam War was raging and Nate's lottery number was low. I suggested that we hold a fund-raiser to cash in on the sympathy so many people had expressed, and hopefully to bring in enough money to help the seven players pay their tuition and stay in school.

At first I felt privileged to spend time with Nate, honored that he wanted to discuss his problems with me and thrilled that he chose my bed to unwind in. But it bothered me that he never made a plan with me, let alone a date, and never took me out. He usually called around 10:00, then he'd come over to talk, get high, listen to music and make love. I told myself Nate needed me; and I was hoping to endear myself to him by helping him through his crisis so unselfishly. One night, after I'd waited by the phone for two days, I decided I needed a break, so I drove to Solon to see Holly.

She'd turned 21 in the spring and got a job bartending in Solon, a little farmer's town outside of Iowa City. The bar was called The Barn and Holly loved it because all the local farmers drank there. Except she hated working Saturday nights, when the owner hired strippers and all the frat boys came.

The Barn was a low, square building. Along one wall was a big oak bar with a mirror over it. The wood floors were worn, and there were barn-wood walls, a pool table, a jukebox and a makeshift stage for the Saturday night go-go dancers.

That night, the bar was empty except for a couple of farmers in feed caps playing pool, and an older couple sitting at the bar. Holly sat reading on a stool by the cash register. Her eyes lit up when she saw me and I was surprised at how glad I was to see her, too.

It was strange, not living with Holly. I found myself cutting out articles and jotting down notes so I'd remember things to tell her. Every day I'd see or hear something and think of telling Holly, or I'd laugh, imagining how she'd respond to a pontificating professor. I missed her; she'd been my sounding board. Seeing her that night, I felt whole again.

"It's about time you came to see me!" She laid her book down on the counter. "You look bummed. Let me fix you something special." She grabbed a bottle of vodka from the back bar.

"Great! Make sure it's strong and tastes good. This is some classy place!"

"Feels like heaven to me! Here, taste. It's called a kamikaze. You're supposed to shoot it down, but I put it on ice because I know you like to sip your drinks." I took a little sip, then a gulp. Holly lit two cigarettes and handed me one. I felt instantly at home. "So, have you joined the Black Panthers yet?"

I laughed and stirred my drink feebly with the straw. "No. I really like Nate, though. He's not like anyone I've ever been with. I mean, he's only a year older but he's so much more mature."

"He didn't grow up in Clear Lake or even Maywood, that's for sure. If he's from south side Chicago, he probably does seem older. Kids grow up fast there; they have to. I read that he was one of the seven players kicked off the team for good. Bummer."

"Don't I know it, that's all I've heard about for weeks. But it is a big deal. He'll lose his scholarship and have to go to work now." I felt I needed to defend him.

"Oh, like you and I have been doing for the last three years. Poor Nate." Holly's sarcasm made me more defensive.

"Well, it's harder for a black guy. Iowa City is a prejudiced town. Besides, he'll get drafted if he leaves school. He could die, you know."

Holly changed the subject. "So, you two have been going out a lot, I take it."

"He comes over a lot. The sex is great and I'm learning about what it's like to be black and discriminated against all the time." I wanted to tell her how unappreciated I felt, but I couldn't bear to admit it out loud.

"But it bothers you that he never takes you anywhere, right? That he doesn't want to be seen with you in public." Holly took a long drag off her cigarette and looked me directly in the eyes.

"That's not it! I don't need to be wined and dined. I'm glad to be there for him." I threw back the rest of my drink and handed the glass to Holly, who immediately poured me another. "Okay, it bugs me a little. I mean, who's being discriminated against? I'm not ashamed to be seen with him, but apparently he's afraid of pissing off the black brothers and sisters by showing up in public with me. It sucks. But I really do love—like him."

"You deserve better."

"Right." We sat for a minute, smoking. I waited while Holly poured two more beers for the couple at the end of the bar and made change so the farmers could continue their pool game. "So how's your love life?"

"I've sworn off sex."

"Come on."

"Really. After seeing girls dancing for dollars here, I don't ever want to have sex again. I have a new friend, though. His name is Floyd. I met him here."

"Floyd, what kind of a name is Floyd?"

"It's a great name and he's a great guy."

"Are you sleeping with him?"

Holly laughed. "No. We're just friends. But good friends."

"Is he in school?" Holly laughed again.

"No, he's out of school. He lives up here . . . owns some land."

"Cool. Hey, what are you guys doing next Saturday night?"

"Don't know, why?"

"Nate and I and some guys from the Mayflower are having a benefit for the players who were dropped from the team, to help them pay their tuition next semester. We're having it in the party room and a lot of important people will be there. You have to come, there's even going to be a band."

"I'll try. Hey, maybe we should hold a fund-raiser and see if we can get some rich people to donate money for our tuition!" She laughed and I laughed too, thinking of how absurd the idea sounded. "You're not putting up money for this, are you?" Holly asked warily.

"A little," I lied. In reality, I'd paid a $100 deposit to reserve the room and promised Nate I'd provide food for the night. Nate and his buddies said they'd furnish the beer and wine and get the band. All totaled, the fund-raiser was going to cost me quite a sum of money.

"Jess, I hate to say it, but I think this guy is using you."

"Of course you'd think that, but he isn't. He really cares about me."

"Where is he tonight?"

"I don't know . . . but it's 10:30. Close up and let's go back into town. I'll leave my car at the Mayflower and you can pick me up on your bike—but you have to promise not to drive fast." Holly had bought a used Suzuki motorcycle to get back and forth to work; she'd told me she got a speeding ticket almost every week.

"Okay, but first you have to tell me where we're going. And why."

"I want to cruise over by the Afro House and see if Nate's car is there."

"Jess, that's so junior high. Blow him off and we'll go to Little Bills. We haven't been there in ages and I'm in the mood for some rockin' music. I need to forget about being down on the farm for a while."

I agreed, on the condition that we'd drive by the Afro House first. Holly cleared beer glasses off the bar and said good night to the customers as they left.

A half hour later I was perched on a fence, behind a tree in the yard next to the Afro House. We'd spotted Nate's yellow and black Cutlass parked halfway down the block and I made Holly stop. It wasn't enough that I knew where he was; I wanted to know who he was with. Holly waited in the street on her bike, poised for a fast getaway.

Loud music blared from the windows and the house was packed with people. Unfortunately, as I was getting ready to climb the tree for a birds-eye view into the house, Nate and a tall black woman stepped onto the front porch. He lit a joint. I was so close I could smell the smoke, but the music made it impossible to hear what they were saying. I prayed that Holly would stay put and not blow my cover until they returned to the party.

The fact that I couldn't hear them wasn't important, since they spent the time between tokes kissing and giggling. I heard him call her Amy and I wanted to scream when he pulled her close for a long kiss. The nerve of that guy! I lost my grip and slipped forward, letting out a squeak as I righted myself.

"Who's here? Hey, who's out there!" Nate collected himself

long enough to look up and at my tree. "Go back inside and tell Lawrence to come here." Before she left, Amy turned to Nate and planted a big kiss on his lips. It was the break I needed. I bolted from the tree to the street and jumped onto Holly's bike.

"Asshole," I screeched as Holly maneuvered her bike up the hill. "He sleeps with me nine of the last 15 nights, then has the nerve to make out with someone else. You should have seen them, his hands were all over her." I screamed over the sound of the motor as we cruised down Iowa Avenue. We pulled into the alley behind Little Bills and locked up the bike.

"I had a feeling this thing would backfire and you'd get hurt," Holly said. I flashed my fake I.D. as Holly paid the $2 cover for us and we took a seat at the crowded bar. "Two kamikazes."

"What do you mean 'this thing?'"

"This fascination with Nate and his black struggle. It leaves you vulnerable. If you want my opinion."

"This is not a black and white thing, Holly. It's a cheating guy thing."

"You said yourself you hadn't made any sort of commitment to each other. So he made out with another girl. He didn't lie to you about it, did he?"

"No, but it still hurts." I took a big gulp of my drink and immediately felt better. "Dance with me. I'm just drunk enough and it'll shock all the loser guys in here." Holly protested, but I dragged her onto the half-full dance floor. I started wiggling and bouncing around the floor with great bravado, trying hard to shake the sadness and confusion from my head. Holly kept her movements smaller at first, trying to be inconspicuous. But after a few more kamikazes she began to dance with a vengeance, too.

An hour later, sweaty and feeling dizzy from the alcohol, I motioned toward the door and Holly nodded. We stumbled into the alley, laughing together like we hadn't in months. We laughed all the way to the Mayflower, cruising by the Afro House once more and yelling "Black Power" as we passed.

Of course, the next night Nate charmed me back. I didn't mention Amy, and he certainly didn't. The day after that I called Holly and told her the party was still on and asked her to come and bring Floyd.

That Saturday I rushed home from the paper at 4:00, an hour later than I'd planned. When I walked into the Mayflower party room, nothing had been done, no tables or chairs set up, no posters hung. Nate's friends, Kirby and Derrick, who lived at the Mayflower, were lounging on the two couches, watching football.

"Hey baby, how you doin'?" Kirby called out.

"Okay. What's going on? Has the food been delivered?" I tried to control the anger in my voice.

"Oh yeah, they brought it in a couple hours ago. It's in the fridge. Me and Derrick were just takin' a little break from the action. You just tell us what needs to be done and we'll do it."

"Where's Nate? Has he been here? Did the beer come?"

"The beer came, but we haven't seen Nate. Look at that brother run, that man runs like a fuckin' gazelle." Kirby and Derrick turned their attention back to the game and I panicked. I scurried around, put the cold cuts on trays and set up the napkins, plates and glasses. When the game ended, Kirby helped me with the tables and chairs, and Derrick hung posters around the room.

The band came at 6:30, but there was still no sign of Nate. Once the bouncer came to stand at the door and card people, I left Kirby in charge while I dashed upstairs to change. People would start arriving at 7:30 and I needed to look great. I'd gone to the import store and bought a dashiki, which hung loose and made me look more like an ethnic earth mother than I liked. Still, it seemed appropriate—a solidarity gesture for the cause.

Primped and polished in my Afro best, I went downstairs at

7:15 to make certain everything was ready. I was sure Nate would be there, taking charge. When I learned that no one had seen him, I began a slow boil and grabbed a beer. I dimmed the lights, lit the candles on each table and stood back to survey my work. It looked great. Fuck Nate if he couldn't show up to help with his own damn party! I'd organized a great party and I vowed to enjoy it. Several professors, people from the athletic department and some administrators had promised to come, so I planned to play the gracious hostess. I was sure I'd meet influential people who'd notice how sophisticated and together I was. I don't need Nate Hamilton and his righteous bullshit, I told myself. With new resolve, I brought the food out and took my position by the door.

Half an hour later I was still standing there, second beer in hand, waiting for my guests. It was almost 8:00, only two people had arrived, and I didn't know them. Since the band was only paid to play for two hours, I didn't want them to start until more people came, so it was deathly quiet. Finally, at 8:15, seven black players showed up with girls, and I nodded to the guitar player to begin. By 8:30 there were 20 people at the party, players, administrators and some students who lived at the Mayflower. The cover charge was $10, but so far we hadn't made enough to pay for the beer and the band, let alone put seven guys through college.

By 9:00 the room was almost full and Nate finally showed up with three guys and four girls; Amy was one of the girls. Nate left her and walked over to me. Smiling, he put his arm around my waist and whispered, "Nice job," into my ear.

"Where have you been? I thought you were going to help set up?" I tried my best not to sound like a shrew.

"I'm sorry, babe. Didn't I tell you? I had an interview for a part-time job at the athletic department. It went great and one of the guys in charge wanted to talk to me about the boycott afterwards. It's a cool job, I have a good chance at it."

He went on about his interview, but I'd stopped listening. Something else had caught my eye. It was Holly standing next to the bar, with an old bald guy who had to be 80 years old. They were both wearing overalls and looked like something out of "Green Acres." Holly had her hair in two long braids and was wearing her big brown work boots.

"Excuse me, Nate." I brushed past him and headed across the room, where Holly and her companion were sipping beer and chatting with one of the sociology professors.

"Jess, hi!" She looked at me with what I thought was an odd, defiant look.

"Can I talk to you for a minute?" She followed me into the hall. "Who is that guy and why are you dressed like a farmer? This isn't a hoe down."

"That's Floyd and what's wrong with the way I'm dressed? This is how I dress, okay? If it's not ethnic enough for your new friends, fuck 'em." She was slurring her words and I knew she'd been drinking.

"You're drunk, too? Jesus, Holly, I need you for moral support and you show up like this?"

"You need me, do you! I thought this was a party and we were invited guests. I didn't realize I was only here to lend you moral support."

"You know what I mean. You are a guest, but Nate just got here and he came with Amy and now you're here with that man who's old enough to be your grandfather. This is a joke, right?" The night was turning to shit before my eyes.

"How liberated of you, Jess. Floyd is a joke, but Nate isn't. That is so like you. You haven't met him and you've totally dismissed him, just because he's older. What does that say about your highfalutin ideals about discrimination? You're such a hypocrite."

Sometimes when Holly got drunk, she made too much sense.

She kept talking louder, gesturing with one hand and spilling beer with the other. I saw my journalism professor and his wife walk through the door, so I grabbed Holly's arm and dragged her into the rest room.

"I don't know what your problem is, but I can't deal with it tonight. I'm sure Floyd's a very nice man, but I expected him to be younger. You knew I'd be shocked, didn't you? There were plenty of times when you could have told me he was old. You kept it a secret on purpose."

"Like you'd have heard anything I had to say. It's all 'Nate this and Nate that!'" Holly threw the rest of her beer down the sink. "Nice dress, Jess. Where did you get it, the Afro Exchange?"

"Fuck you. There are a lot of important people out there and I'm trying really hard to—damn, I don't know what the fuck I'm doing." I leaned up against the sink, suddenly so confused I couldn't think anymore. "But you came here looking like you just finished plowing the north 40. There are candles on the tables, it's suppose to be an elegant party and I wish you'd worn something nice. So sue me."

"I didn't mean to embarrass you. This is what I'm into now, and I refuse to put on an act to impress some bleeding hearts." She adjusted the strap on her overalls and turned to face me. "This is supposed to be a party, so why are we standing in the bathroom? I'm going out to dance with Floyd."

"Fine, have a great time." I held the door as she sauntered out, then followed behind her.

Holly grabbed Floyd and they hit the dance floor. Amy and Nate were glued together in a sensual dance of their own. I ducked into the kitchen where Kirby was getting more ice.

"Hey, lady! This is one great party. We've raised almost $400."

"Terrific. $100 is mine to pay for all this food." I was tired of being used and ready to take it out on anybody. Kirby was an easy target.

"That's cool. You shouldn't be footing the bill, especially since I see Nate is hanging with the sisters and not with you. That's a damn shame." I took a long slow sip of beer, trying to hold back tears.

"You deserve better, sweet thing. I bet you got lots of passion tucked away behind that pretty face." He moved toward me and put his arms around my waist. I struggled to move away, surprised and angered by his advance. "Come on baby, you know you're lonely for some black lovin'. Let Kirby make you feel better." He pressed himself into me and I could feel him hard against my leg. His lips were rough and he smelled of liquor.

"Stop it, you asshole!" I kicked my knee toward his bulging pants and rushed out the door, leaving him gasping for air. The room was filled with people laughing and smiling. Floyd and Holly were kicking up their heels on the dance floor; Nate was standing with his arm around Amy's waist in the center of a crowd, laughing with his friends.

I threw my beer in the trash as I rushed past the bar and slipped up the elevator to my apartment. Slamming the door, I threw myself onto the couch and cried hard, moaning over my pitiful life. My best friend was a mean-spirited brat, the man I loved pimped me in front of a room full of important people, and his best friend hit on me in the kitchen.

"What a horrible night. Did you and Nate break up after that?" Zoe grabbed a handful of pretzels.

"It was definitely over. Nate called a few more times and wanted to come over, but I was too upset. As usual, I'd imagined our relationship to be more than it was. After that, I found out I was pregnant."

"Did you tell him?"

"I was too humiliated to tell anyone except Holly. There was no 'considering options' for me. I wanted it over as quickly as possible. But abortions weren't legal. At one point Holly had me swallow some concoction with cloves, caster oil and vodka that was supposed to induce a miscarriage. Two hours later, I was vomiting uncontrollably, but there was no sign of a miscarriage. Then she told me about someone she'd met at the home for unwed mothers who knew a doctor in Chicago who . . . well, we got his name and she took me there."

"What was it like? I mean, you don't have to tell me if you don't want to. But I'd like to know if you're willing to talk about it."

"It wasn't exactly a clinic and it was nothing like it is now, in legal clinics."

"I'd still like to know about it."

Jess took a gulp of air and began.

Holly drove the Malibu and we traveled east on I-80 toward Chicago. It was a Friday morning. I had a million questions and wanted more details about the abortion, or the "Big A," as we'd started calling it. "Tell me again how you know about this doctor? And how do we know that the police won't bust in and haul us off to jail?"

"When you put it that way, we don't. It is illegal, so you're not going to get the AMA seal of approval or anything. But I think this doctor, his name is Dr. Niland by the way, is a real doctor. I told you he's black, right?"

"I believe you left that detail out. It seems appropriate, though." I thought of Nate and wondered what he'd think if he knew what I was about to do.

"His office is in a poor part of the city. Actually, it's south of the Loop and it's pretty much in the ghetto. But, I'm sure everything will be okay."

Right, I thought. I'm going to a doctor in the ghetto to have an illegal abortion and Holly is sure everything will be okay. "Maybe I should rethink this, Holly. Maybe I should look at some other alternatives. Maybe if I told Nate, he'd want to take responsibility. Maybe we could get married."

"Jess, that's a truly stupid idea. Nate is not husband material. And you don't really love him. He was a guy you balled and unfortunately the timing was bad. It's ludicrous to think about marrying him."

"Maybe it wouldn't be so bad. He's a nice guy and the baby would be beautiful, you have to admit."

"You could never handle it. Besides, I've been reading this book called *The Feminine Mystique*. If you got married you'd become like all the other women who try to find fulfillment as wives and mothers, only to lead desperate, empty lives because they have no real sense of who they are."

"Oh, really?" I felt nauseous again and had to wrap my arms around my stomach to keep from barfing.

"This book is great, it talks about how fucked the feminine roles are, how they're the main barriers keeping women from realizing their complete human potential. Trust me, you don't want to join the ranks of the desperate and empty by marrying some guy and having his baby. According to Betty Friedan, you'll never achieve a higher level of self-realization if you settle for being just somebody's wife and the mother of his screaming kid. Will it make you sick if I smoke?"

"Yes, but everything makes me sick, so go ahead. Just roll down the window so most of it goes outside. What is that book called again? *The Feminine Mystery*?"

"Mystique, *The Feminine Mystique*. Friedan says there's this retro 50s plot to keep women at home having babies. This mystique of feminine fulfillment is what we're all supposed to aspire to. You know, the happy, pretty housewife who is totally satisfied to care for her husband, her children and her home. She's been taught to pity the poor neurotic, unfeminine, unhappy women who want to be poets or physicists or presidents. It's all a crock of shit."

"That's pretty far out."

"You know, Jess, you have other options besides marriage."

"I'm a little old for a stint in the home for unwed mothers, don't you think?"

"You could have the baby and not get married."

"I'm having a little déjà vu here, Holly. You remember not that long ago, when the shoe was on the other foot and we were contemplating single motherhood? Do the words 'no money, no job, no education' spark a memory? I can't raise a baby by myself."

Holly took a long drag off her Marlboro. "We could raise the baby together. You and me."

"You're kidding, right?"

"I think it could work. It's not too late to change your mind."

"I can't believe you're telling me this. What about all that stuff about the female mystique?"

"Feminine mystique."

"Whatever. Didn't you just get through telling me how having children stunted women's growth? How I'll never be self-realized if I have a kid? And now you're telling me you think I should have this baby and we should raise it together?" I didn't understand why Holly couldn't see the contradiction. "This is not what I need to hear right now. I feel guilty enough. Besides, you were the one who arranged this. So let's not talk about anything as stupid as raising a baby together. I have to go to the bathroom. Can we stop?"

"There's a rest stop up the road. I'll call Dr. Niland again to make sure he doesn't ditch out before we get there. Give me your change." I emptied my purse as Holly drove on in silence.

We stopped and when I got back in the car, I left my jeans unbuttoned and slouched low in my seat. I was suddenly very tired, not so much sleepy as weary of all this talk about mystiques, self-realization, marriage and raising babies. Of course, I didn't want to get married, especially to someone who didn't love me. And I certainly wasn't ready to be anyone's mother. But I had this gnawing feeling that what I was about to do was absolutely, unequivocally wrong.

I felt trapped and betrayed by my body. Part of me wanted to be punished for being so bad and careless. That was the part that thought I should get married and have the baby. I figured that would be the punishment I deserved for my terrible mistake. The other, more reasonable side wanted this to be finished as soon as possible so I could get back to my life. And now Holly had her own absurd idea. What a mess.

Holly came back with good news—the doctor would be waiting. We were still two hours away, so I decided to try to save my energy and sleep for a while. I dozed fitfully while Holly searched for songs she liked on the radio.

"Jess wake up. We're here." Holly nudged me gently. It was late afternoon and we were parked in front of an old, run-down grocery store. I looked down the street and saw that most of the buildings were abandoned and there was broken glass everywhere. Someone had spray painted slogans in bright green on the walls of the building, "Black and Proud," "Kill the White Oppressor." I felt weak and small.

"Holly, I'm going to be sick." I opened the car door and threw up in the gutter. Holly leaned over the seat and held on to my arm, then pulled me back inside and wiped the sweat off my face with her scarf.

"I'm so sorry this happened to you, Jess. But you don't have to go through with it. We can figure out some other way—"

"Stop it. I already blew it, okay? If I go home, I'm dead. If I go inside, I'm dead. You know as well as I do that you and I cannot raise a baby. So please, I don't want to hear any more of your plans." I was fighting back tears. "I wish I could be sure this guy knows what he's doing. Do you think he does?"

"He's a doctor, I'm sure he does. He told me it only takes a little while and that he'll do something called a D and C." She said he explained it to her on the phone and he seemed very nice. "You have to decide Jess. Whatever you decide, I'm with you 100 percent. But if you don't want to go through with it, I'll drive away from here right now."

Holly was holding my hand as she talked. I took a deep breath and made my decision. "Let's go. You carry the money." It was going to cost $300; we'd both worked overtime to come up with it. "Are you sure this is the right address? This doesn't look like any doctor's office I've ever been in."

"He said it's upstairs, the door is supposed to be next to the grocery store. Here it is." Holly pointed to a door with a dirty glass windowpane. Stenciled on the window were the words "Dr. Abraham Niland, Chiropractor."

"God, Holly, this guy's not even a real doctor. I can't believe it, a chiropractor above a grocery store. My legs are going numb and I'm going to be sick again." I gagged twice, then Holly opened the door and we started up the grimy wooden staircase. Newspapers and other debris were scattered everywhere. Holly was in front and with each step the panic grew. It felt like I was living someone else's life or watching a bad soap opera scene. But at least on "Guiding Light" the handsome hero boyfriend always burst through the door and carried the heroine off to a life of marital bliss. I turned to look down the narrow stairway for any sign of rescue, but the door below was closed tight. Holly pushed the buzzer at the top of the stairs, outside another door that was also stenciled with Dr. Niland's name. After what seemed like hours, a tall, older black man with graying hair opened the door.

"Hi, we called earlier. That is . . . I called about my friend who, well . . ." Holly was nervous, but at least she could talk. My throat was dry and tight and I couldn't make a sound. I just stood, shivering.

"Yes, of course. You've had a long drive, haven't you? Come in where it's warm. I'm Dr. Niland." His voice was smooth and friendly and he smiled as he led us into a small waiting room. It smelled musty, like old magazines, and the air was dry and hot. The walls were covered with ancient flowered wallpaper that reminded me of my grandmother's house. An old fashioned radiator gurgled and banged as we sat down in two faded easy chairs. A large, old television set, topped with rabbit ears wrapped in aluminum foil, sat in one corner of the room. A calendar on the wall hadn't been changed since April.

Dr. Niland brought us each a cup of water, then sat down in a straight-backed wooden chair before us. He wore a blue doctor shirt that made him look vaguely official. His dark brown eyes looked tired and sad, and I thought they matched the room. The late afternoon sun streamed through the window magnifying the years of dust that hung in the air.

"I don't know your names and that's fine if you don't want to tell me. But I am here to help you."

"I'm Holly and this is my friend, Jess." Holly spoke up, her voice cracking slightly.

"I'm the one who . . . who needs your help." My hands clutched the plastic cup like it was a final sacrament.

"Well, Jess, you and I need to talk. Have you had a pregnancy test?" I nodded yes. He asked several more questions—the date of my last period, whether I was taking any medication, if I was allergic to anything—all questions a regular doctor might ask. I began to relax a bit. "Are there any questions you'd like to ask me about the procedure?"

I wasn't sure what to ask, or even if I wanted to know anything. He seemed to sense my discomfort, so he began to talk in a low, fatherly voice about the procedure. I listened without comprehending much. I think, at that point, I didn't want to know the details. Why bother with details, I thought, when I've already begun the downward spiral into the abyss. There was no stopping now.

"Holly, I hope you don't mind waiting here while Jess and I go to the next room. I'll turn on the television and there are some magazines for you to read. And don't worry about your friend; everything is going to be fine. I'll take good care of her."

As Dr. Niland moved toward the television, Holly shot a wary look my way and whispered, "Are you sure? We can still leave. Do you want me to go in with you?" The TV crackled loudly and we both jumped.

"No. He seems nice. I'm glad you're here." I squeezed her hand, then followed Dr. Niland.

He closed the door behind us and motioned for me to sit on an examining table. Its vinyl cover was torn at the corners and there wasn't any sanitary paper over the top. The room was small, just large enough for the table, a work stand and a cabinet. The dirty green walls looked like they hadn't seen new paint in decades, and the panes in the only window had been painted the same pitiful shade.

Dr. Niland appeared with a syringe filled with something to help me relax. He asked me to bare my hip, which I did quickly, too frightened to object. The shot hurt and Dr. Niland apologized, saying I'd feel better in a few minutes. He held out a gown and told me to take off my pants and make myself comfortable on the table, then he disappeared through a door at the side of the room. I undressed quickly, keeping my socks on, then lay back on the table and covered myself with the sheet. In the next room I could hear the theme music for "I Dream of Jeannie."

The "procedure." It was such a sanitary sounding word, without a shred of emotion or meaning. How convenient, I thought. I felt the drug easing its way into my system and began to relax. It reminded me of the few times I'd flown, the sudden calm I felt when the plane lifted off the ground, when all responsibility was taken out of my hands and my life was out of my control.

Lying on that table in the middle of a Chicago ghetto, listening to the TV in the other room while a strange doctor prepared for the procedure, I felt oddly relieved. It wasn't so much because the pregnancy was about to end, but because the deciding was over. Someone else was in control.

The next thing I remember was Dr. Niland's tired black face looking down at me. He held my hand and asked if I was ready. I nodded, then fought back tears of gratitude as I thanked him for being so nice to me. He smiled, then gently placed my legs in the stirrups and disappeared at the end of the table.

Most of the rest was a blur, but there was one disturbing moment. The doctor was talking to me in a low, patient voice, explaining each step as he proceeded with the dilation. Suddenly, the door to the waiting room opened. I heard Holly, in a child-like voice, say, "Don't let him do it, Jess. Please, don't let him take our baby." Dr. Niland hurried Holly out of the room before I realized what had happened. A few minutes later he came back, patted my arm and promised me that everything was going fine, that I shouldn't worry. I was past worrying.

When it was over, Dr. Niland wrote down precise instructions while I sat on the side of the table trying to clear my head and regain my composure. He left and I stood on wobbly colt legs, steadying myself to keep from falling as I dressed. When I was ready, he helped me into the room where Holly was waiting. He went over the notes with her and gave her two small envelopes, one with some painkillers and the other with antibiotics. He also gave her his card and wrote his home phone number on the back, so we could call him if I had heavy bleeding or a high fever. In return, Holly gave him the envelope with $300 in small, wrinkled bills. He seemed a little embarrassed as he tucked the envelope into his pocket. He didn't count it.

As we moved toward the door, I was overwhelmed with a sense of gratitude. I turned around and thanked him. Before I closed the door, I thanked him again. He nodded and told me to take care of myself and to stay out of trouble.

Holly and I didn't talk until we had driven a few miles down the dirty city street. It was Holly who broke the silence. "How do you feel?"

"Empty and tired."

"Did it hurt much?"

"I wanted it to hurt more so I'd feel like I was really being punished. I deserved worse for getting myself into such a stupid mess. That doctor was so nice to me; he was the nicest doctor I've ever had. I didn't deserve to be treated that nice." The words tumbled out in an angry jumble and I started to sob.

"I'm glad he was nice to you." Holly was uncomfortable and dug through her pockets until she came up with some dry Kleenex. "Here, go ahead and cry, you'll feel better." I blew my nose, then cried most of the way back to Iowa City. We hardly talked, and never said a word about her outburst.

Zoe sat quietly, absorbing the story. "My mother wanted you

to keep the baby."

"She said she did."

"Do you think that's because she was sorry she gave me away?"

Jess had never thought about that. It had seemed so absurd at the time, and later Jess had only wanted to forget the experience. Now, with Zoe there, it made sense. "You're probably right. I think my abortion brought up a lot of feelings for Holly about the pain of giving you up."

"Having that abortion must have been horrible for you."

"I don't think I could go through it again."

"I think Holly would want me to have this baby."

"Do you think you should base your decision on what you think someone else would want?"

"No. I wouldn't have a baby because Adam wanted me to, so it doesn't make sense to have a baby because I think my dead mother would want me to. You can't do things to please someone else."

Jess felt a huge responsibility to help Zoe think clearly. But the burden of Zoe's need and the sadness of her own story left her feeling empty. "If you can learn that, you'll be ahead of me. Back then, I was making bad choices on every front. I imagined Nate to be someone he wasn't and myself to be someone I wasn't. It never would have worked. And I could never do what Holly did, go through a pregnancy, see my baby and then give it away. It would have been too painful. Even though having the abortion was the right thing to do, it changed me. I was demoralized, I was angry. It took a long time to forgive myself."

"But you did?"

"Yes. But your choices change you and you always have regrets. Although the more careful you are about your choices, the fewer regrets you'll have. After the abortion, I couldn't face my regrets, so I threw myself into my work at the paper. I'd take any story, I didn't care. As long as I was asking other people questions about their lives, I didn't have to think about my own. I did what I do best, throw myself at things and try not to think about the past."

"I guess it's a little late for me to do that."

"What you might want to do if you want my opinion, and I'm not sure you do, is to project past this crisis as much as you can. Take all the directions in your mind, play them out, see yourself in every scenario, so you have a broad perspective."

After a few moments of silence, Zoe asked Jess if she and Holly ever talked about the abortion. Jess thought back. "Holly and I pulled away from each other after that. She moved out to Floyd's farm and kind of went into hiding. We didn't see each other for almost a year. No, I guess we never did talk about the abortion again." Jess sighed, then continued. "You know, Zoe, I think having you then giving you up changed Holly in a deep and profound way. In fact, I don't remember your mother ever having a boyfriend again after she had you."

"That's because she was in love with you." Zoe said it softly, but matter-of-factly.

"Oh, no. We were just good friends. And we drifted apart." The thought was unsettling, and Jess was suddenly cold. The sky was finally dark and Jess suggested they go indoors. As they walked back through the sliding doors, Jess took a last look at the bay. The hills were only visible in silhouette against the sky.

CHAPTER TWENTY-THREE

Jess closed the door to the deck, trying to push the chill away. She flipped the switch on the lamp next to the couch and loaded CDs into the player. Zoe took the glasses and pretzels to the kitchen, talking all the while about a friend who turned gay after she found out her boyfriend was having an affair with her sister. Jess listened, not hearing the words but only the sound of Zoe's voice. It had the same tone as Holly's, increasing in intensity as she told her story. She watched Zoe gesture, opening, closing and turning her hands to expand every point, just like Holly. Jess felt the wave of sadness settle in her chest. It was a familiar sadness that brought with it a devastating feeling of loss. You're going to leave me, too, just like your mother did, she thought. Tomorrow you'll walk out my door and take Holly with you. I'll never see you again. Zoe finished her story and laughed, then looked to Jess for a response. There was no response, no way to describe how she felt. Only a diversion would do.

"Are you hungry? There's a great Japanese restaurant in the neighborhood."

"Will you let me cook for you?"

"I'm sure I don't have a thing in the kitchen."

"I'm used to throwing things together. You should see some

of the concoctions I've made for Adam. All I ask is that you talk to me while I cook."

Jess followed Zoe into the kitchen, happy to be distracted. She felt emotionally drained, and vulnerable in the place that only held darkness. She'd made many decisions without conceiving of the toll they would take later on, the regret, the sense of loss. She watched Zoe search through her cabinets, full of the youthful exuberance she once felt. You will make terrible mistakes, too, she thought. No matter what.

Zoe pulled out cans and asked rapid-fire questions. She found a jar of spiced red peppers, a can of white asparagus, a package of rice, a can of stewed tomatoes, some frozen pita bread, capers, a potato, an onion. She reached into the refrigerator and pulled out a carton of eggs. "Are these fresh?"

"I made pancakes with them this morning; what's the expiration date?"

"I can't make it out. I'm sure they're fine. Smell this, do you think it's still good?" Zoe held up a small round object from the bottom of the fridge.

"I'm sure it isn't, and I don't want to smell it to find out."

"Do you remember when you bought these?" Zoe held up a package of pre-peeled carrots and a couple of stalks of celery.

Jess shrugged. "Are you sure you want to do this? Why don't we just order out?"

"Let's not waste the money, I'll probably just throw it up anyway."

While Zoe chopped vegetables and opened cans, she asked Jess about her and Holly's last year at school. Jess searched her memory. She told Zoe that she lived at the Mayflower through her senior year, dove into her work at the *Daily Iowan* and didn't see Holly, until the first semester of that year when they had a class together.

"What kind of class?" Zoe asked, running water into a stockpot.

"Greek drama. I remember getting out of my car the first day of class and seeing Holly. It was early fall and I felt like I was finally getting my life together. I parked in the lot behind the English building and was surprised to see Holly get out of a green '54 Chevy. I can still remember what she wore. Funny how one's memory holds on to the most unimportant details, isn't it?" Jess got up and poured a glass of wine. "She had on long blue overalls, brown work boots and a red flannel shirt under an old farmer's jacket. Her hair had grown even longer. It was almost to her knees and she wore it in a braid down her back. I called to her, and that's when we realized we were headed for the same class. She said she was still living on the farm with Floyd and didn't get into town much anymore except for classes." Zoe poured herself a glass of soda water and while she cooked, Jess's mind opened again, spilling out memories.

Two of the plays we were assigned were *Electra* and *Lysistrata*, and after that first class Holly and I walked uptown to buy them. We talked about sharing a drink, but I had to rush off. Kurt Vonnegut was in town to give a talk, and I wanted to see if I could land an interview.

Holly and I always sat next to each other in class, but we didn't share our personal lives. In the late fall we read *Lysistrata*, and the teaching assistant had us pair up and enact a scene. I played Kleonike and Holly was Lysistrata. On the day we performed I brought costumes—long flowing robes with gold trim—and we entertained our classmates with a campy rendition of Lysistrata giving the oath that Kleonike repeats. They vow to abstain from sex until their husbands get so sex starved they agree to end their warring. For a moment it felt like old times, and again we talked about going out for a drink. But I was on deadline and had a story to deliver, so I took a rain check. I rarely saw Holly outside of class.

"Do you ever use your dining room?" Zoe interrupted, and Jess wondered if she'd even been listening.

"Not much. On holidays, of course," Jess said. In truth, she hadn't entered it for two years.

"How about if we eat in there tonight? I'll even set the table."

"Sounds great." Zoe continued chopping and finding odd things to put in what appeared to be a vegetable stew. There were black beans, rice, all sorts of vegetables, spices that made Jess sneeze.

"So, you never spent time together?"

"Not until the following May. The *Daily Iowan* was covering the opening of the Iowa City Women's Center and I begged my editor for the story. I was determined to see my byline under that story and on the front page, and he finally relented. The morning of the center's grand opening, the staff photographer and I were there. The center was in an old wood frame house near campus. Women were everywhere, preparing for the opening party that night; setting up tables, stacking flyers and putting the finishing touches on the paint. The photographer took pictures while I interviewed the organizers. As the head of the center—I think her name was Dawn—described the services the center would provide for women, I took detailed notes."

The center offered yoga classes, rape counseling, birth control counseling and small group sessions in political activism. But according to Dawn, one of the most important services was abortion counseling. Iowa didn't offer legal abortions, and the best the Women's Center could do was to help set up abortions for women in more liberal states like New York and California. Iowa's failure to legalize abortion frustrated and angered the women at the center more than any other issue. A poster on the door read "Get your laws off my body."

I bought a button with the feminist power sign on it and wore it when I handed in my story. "The time is now," I wrote, "for women to unite, to get in touch with their power and take charge of their bodies. We've been subservient and powerless for too long. It is time to rise up and liberate ourselves. Sisterhood is powerful and the revolution has begun!"

I thought my article was inspired. I proclaimed spring 1972 as the beginning of the Iowa women's revolution. My editor thought it was a little too inspired and definitely too long. He insisted I cut 300 words. I argued that every word was essential, but he was the editor, so I made the cuts.

When I finished editing, I ran home to change for the opening. I ended up being late for the ribbon cutting because I couldn't figure out what to wear. I wanted to look androgynous, but everything I owned was either too sexy or too pedestrian. Finally, I settled on a faded work shirt over a white T-shirt—no bra, Levi's button-fly jeans, only slightly belled, and my brand-new work boots, which I felt compelled to rub with potting soil and scuff with a wire brush. I wore a little mascara, a bit of blush and fluffed my hair so it looked uncombed. In the new environmentally-safe cloth bag I'd bought that afternoon, I stuffed a partially read copy of *Sisterhood Is Powerful* and a copy of *Our Bodies, Ourselves*.

When I arrived, the house was filled with women of all ages, dressed in everything from skirts and blouses to granny dresses and overalls. But I did notice that there were no black women there. The Women's Center was only a block from the Afro House, but our respective searches for equality and liberation had definitely separated us. After surveying the crowd, I got a glass of punch from the kitchen and headed for a table where several volunteers with clipboards were signing women up for activities at the center.

"Well, imagine meeting you here, sister!"

I shrieked. It was Holly. "I should have known you'd be here! Hell, you were spouting ideas from *The Feminine Mystique* before most of these girls, I mean women, could read."

"You mean *The Female Mystery*," she joked.

I swatted her with a flyer. Then I couldn't resist and gave her a big hug. She hugged me back, harder. "What's going on with you?" I noticed she'd cut her hair into a blunt cut around her shoulders and wore a black shirt tucked into her jeans.

She told me she'd moved out of Floyd's farmhouse and into Black's Gaslight Village. Black's Gaslight was a group of mismatched rundown buildings on a hilltop, lit at night with eerie gas lights. The owner, Mr. Black, was a very old man with very young children. He owned the complex of apartments, most of which looked like he'd built himself. Everyone around town knew about Black's, and it had a waiting list because only the hippest people from the counterculture lived there. I was suddenly jealous.

Holly and I wandered into the living room where four couches circled the room. It was filled with women and a sense of camaraderie, which gave us both permission to open up.

"So what are you doing?" she asked. "Are you seeing anyone?"

"No! And I want to keep it that way. I've been studying my ass off and practically living at the *DI*. All that keeps me going is the thought of getting out of this podunk town and finding a real job that pays real money."

"I'm with you, there!" Holly raised her glass of punch and tapped mine. We drank to the future and spent the next hour catching up and listening to speeches and appeals for money.

Before leaving, we signed up for activities. I chose abortion counseling, and Holly signed up to be a birth control counselor.

To work as counselors we had to attend a day-long workshop called "Body and Soul Work for Women," the following Saturday. Holly and I were excited about doing good works for the cause, and we arrived at the center for the workshop early Saturday morning, carrying the required paraphernalia. The list of items read like a weird scavenger hunt—a sack lunch, a dish for a potluck dinner, a rug, a flashlight and a pillow. The workshop was run by a group of women from San Francisco called the Feminist Gynecological Self Help Clinic. Some of them looked smart and liberated with their wire-rimmed glasses and bushy long hair. I was put off, though, by their equally bushy legs and armpits, and by other women in the group who looked like men with their crew cuts, work shirts and men's shoes.

The lectures in the morning were interesting but one-sided. Two tall women with buzz haircuts talked about the atrocities women were subjected to, by men, in the name of "modern" medicine. They talked about unnecessary hysterectomies and drugged childbirth. They preached about the benefits of natural childbirth, without stirrups, drugs or an episiotomy. They condemned birth control methods that endangered women's lives by altering our chemical makeup or forcing us to put foreign bodies into our uterus. They urged women to stop using tampons and use something called the menstrual sponge instead, a reusable, environmentally safe product—the thought of which made me nauseous.

Another woman with long black hair and a pencil-thin body blasted the advertising world. She ranted that all advertising misleads, manipulates and preys on women's insecurities—insecurities created by advertising—so that we allow ourselves to be exploited. She said the sexist use of women in advertising perpetuates the stereotype that we're weak, decorative, sex objects who can be persuaded to buy known carcinogens, like douches and external genital sprays, so that we'll feel attractive to men. She held up a deodorant ad and a cosmetic ad that she said tried to make women feel inadequate or ugly because they didn't have the right look. At the end of her presentation, she proclaimed body odor natural and beautiful, and damned antiperspirant spray as another weapon to subvert our self-esteem.

"Wow!" Zoe had stopped stirring and was staring as Jess talked. "That is so radical!"

"See what we went through so that you could have the right not to wear deodorant!" Jess joked. "Let's see a little respect, missy."

"I got your respect right here, lady!" Zoe tossed a piece of bread into the air and caught it in her mouth. Jess applauded. "Finish the story. I have some serious cooking to do."

"Okay, where was I?"

"Somewhere between douches and deodorants."

"Right. I remember there were speeches all morning. One heavyset woman, Robin, lectured us on the politics of sex and how women should take charge of their own orgasms. She told us to be wary of men who said that clitoral orgasms were inferior to vaginal ones."

Zoe laughed. "No shit! An orgasm's an orgasm if you ask me."

"Her point exactly. But then she started talking about the os—the amazing and wonderful os! The os, as you well know, hip, modern girl that you are, is the opening at the center of the cervix. According to Robin, the os held the secret to all that was good and feminist. 'The os represents the gateway, the center of a woman's sexual power.'"

After three hours of rhetoric, I was on feminist overload and so hungry I felt faint. Deciding the os would have to wait, I grabbed a sandwich from my pack, slipped out of the living room and headed for the backyard. It wasn't long before Holly joined me.

"So what did you think?" I asked tentatively, not sure what her response would be.

"I think if you cut through all the generalities and overblown posturing, there's a lot of truth to what they're saying." Since Holly had eaten her sandwich mid-morning, she held out her hand and waited until I tore my sandwich in half so she could share.

"I guess. But they all seem so angry. Why do you think that is?"

"Maybe they've all had terrible relationships with guys," Holly answered.

"In that case, they'd have to hold the damn thing in the football stadium." Holly laughed and I took a bite of my sandwich, afraid to tell her what I really thought. I swallowed, then decided to risk it. "Or maybe—now don't get pissed at me, Holly, for saying this—but none of those women is exactly a raving beauty. Maybe they never had dates, so this is their way of getting back at men."

Holly disagreed, of course. "What's the matter," she quipped, "you don't like crew cuts on overweight women?" I laughed. "I don't think any of the women who spoke seemed like they ever gave a shit about men in the first place. That's part of the whole feminist agenda, not needing a man in your life to be whole."

"So that's what I have to do to be whole, sleep with women?"

"Don't worry, Jess, you could never be a dyke; you require too much makeup. But I respect what these women are trying to do—change the world for women. I think everyone should just be who they are."

I thought for a moment, chewing slowly. "I can agree with that. I'm tired of trying to figure out what men want and even more tired of trying to figure out what I want in a man. But I don't hate them, I'd just like a rest from them. Hey, how about all that advertising stuff! I felt like a traitor, having just sent out 15 query letters to advertising agencies from New York to San Francisco!"

"You're kidding?" Holly seemed shocked. "You really want a job in advertising?"

"Don't tell me you were buying that bullshit about advertising being misleading and manipulative?"

"Well, think about it, Jess. Maybe misleading is a little strong, but advertising by its very nature is manipulative." Holly took another bite of her half sandwich.

"I prefer to think of it as enlightening. Good advertising provides a service by pointing out the benefits of a product so people have the information they need to make an educated decision about what to buy."

"That sounds like a quote right out of your Marketing 101 textbook. Let's just agree that there's good advertising and bad advertising and hopefully you'll only write good advertising, okay?" Holly folded up the napkin and tossed it at me.

"Okay." I didn't agree so much as I didn't want to argue with Holly, not on a sunny spring day, not after feeling close to her again. "Hey, what about this os thing? Do you know what they're talking about?" I lit two cigarettes and handed one to Holly.

"I think the os is at the bottom of your uterus, you know, where the uterus fits into the vagina. God, it seems strange to be talking about all this, using all these correct clinical words."

"I know. I much prefer more familiar words like 'bush,' 'box' and 'beaver' to describe my most intimate parts." We laughed.

"And don't forget 'snatch,' my personal favorite," Holly joked. We saw women begin to stream out of the center. They were breaking for lunch which meant we wouldn't have to be back until 1:00. "Hey," Holly said. "My motorcycle's in front, let's go lie by the river for an hour. Unless you'd rather stay here and debate the finer points of clitoral orgasms with some of the girls," she snickered.

"Shit no. Let's go." We headed for the Union, parked and lay down along the riverbank. It was a perfect spring day in Iowa City. The sun was high in the sky and the river rippled and shimmered as lily pads floated and ducks swam by. Holly pulled out a neatly rolled joint and we each took a toke. Then we fell silent. I was thinking that this would be one of the last times I'd lie by the Iowa River next to Holly, watching the water roll by.

"The next time we're near a river, it should be the Seine," Holly proclaimed.

"Paris! Yes, of course! We'll go to Paris, like we always said we would. But when?" I sat up and looked at Holly.

"I don't know, but soon. Maybe after graduation." Holly pulled my wrist toward her and noticed the time on my watch. "Shit, we should get back. The mysterious os awaits us. Unless you want to blow it off." Holly smiled mischievously, but we got up and headed for her bike.

"No," I protested, "I must uncover the secrets of the os. The wonderful wizard of os! I'll ask for a heart, no a brain, no, no, an orgasm! That's it, I'll ask the wizard for a full vaginal orgasm, not one of those inferior clitoral ones!"

"How about if you go and hear all about the os, then I'll sit close to you later and learn by os-mosis."

"My kingdom for an os!" I shouted back.

"The newly liberated Os-ie and Harriet show. With the Beaver, of course."

"Wrong show."

"Right context, though." We laughed and bounced down the

sidewalk toward Holly's motorcycle, arms linked, singing at the top of our lungs, "We're off to see the wizard, the wonderful wizard of os. Bec-os, bec-os, bec-os, bec-os, bec-os of the wonderful things she d-os . . ."

On our way to the Women's Center, we cruised through town past Seiferts where something in the window caught my eye. "Stop. Holly, we have to stop at Seiferts for a minute." She pulled the bike over and shut off the engine.

"We're going to be late."

"I know, but look." I pointed at the window.

"Hats!" We yelled in unison and bolted into the store. Ten minutes later, we emerged with two hats for our trip to Paris. Holly bought a gray beret and I chose a navy suede cap that blew off twice on the ride to the center.

We were late, and the women in the room were already deep into a discussion of the female reproductive system. The shades had been drawn and the room was dark except for a big screen where a four-foot close-up of a woman's vagina was projected in full color. It was quite an imposing sight, a sight we tried not to laugh at as we stumbled to the back of the room. We slouched against the wall and tried to maintain our composure as a woman doctor from University Hospital continued her lecture on the wonders of the female anatomy. Her presentation was supported by dozens of huge, color slides that left absolutely nothing to the imagination.

After what seemed like an eternity, the lights came on and we were instructed to team up in groups of three. Holly and I clung together and Robin, who had exalted the os—joined us. She was sullen and full-figured, with short-cropped red hair. I was amazed by her skin, though. It looked translucent, as though it had never seen a moment of sun. We pulled up our rugs and pillows and the doctor handed each of us a plastic speculum. Holly and I—

"Hold it, hold it!" Zoe said. "Don't say another word. We need props!" A few seconds later the clear plastic speculum appeared in the doorway. The jaws of the speculum opened and closed and Zoe sang as she came around the corner, "Let me entertain you, let me make you smile . . ."

Jess laughed. "Hey, show a little respect," she said. "This was like a spiritual awakening for some of those women."

"I know, I know. I'm sorry, but I couldn't resist. Go on. Please."

An examining table was set up in the front of the room and Maureen, a hairy woman, naked from the waist down, lay on it and spread her legs for all to see. I felt my face flush and focused my eyes above the table on the macramé wall hanging. Holly seemed mesmerized and watched with full attention as the doctor showed us how to insert the speculum and work the catch to lock it in an open position. Holly grabbed my arm and forced me to look and I gasped with shock and amazement at how far the speculum opened things up. The doctor invited us to line up and, using our flashlights, to discover for ourselves the wonder of the os.

I stood at the back of the line and when it was my turn, I peered in quickly. Expecting the worst, I was surprised to see a tiny hole in the middle of a dome of flesh. It wasn't magical or mysterious. And it didn't make me feel particularly powerful. Holly was more enthusiastic and after the viewing, she felt compelled to read out loud every word in the handout about the fabulous os. Once everyone had seen Maureen's os, the doctor invited each of us to experience the wonder of her own os. I looked at Holly in a panic, but she was already untying her shoes and pulling off her jeans. Somehow I wasn't surprised; Holly was never modest about disrobing.

I was one of only three fully clothed women in the room, but that was all right with me. I had no interest in baring my os for anyone. The doctor distributed hand mirrors to each group and as Robin and Holly prepared for the viewing, I had to look away. It was just too much. The room was filled with half-naked women with their legs spread open. I was afraid I'd have nightmares forever. I sat in a huddle while Robin and Holly took their flashlights and exchanged views. Robin was a veteran of os discovery and had already seen her own dozens of times. But Holly squealed with delight when Robin handed her the mirror. She demanded that I come and take a look, and told us she couldn't wait to turn her mother and sister on to their os. I had to laugh out loud at the thought of showing my mother hers. I was convinced Celeste had never even seen herself naked, and I was sure she'd faint at the sight of her os!

Finally, os viewing came to an end and the pencil-thin woman who had skewered the advertising world announced that it was time to put out our dishes for the potluck. I'd brought my usual fare, potato chips with sour cream and onion soup mix. But as I surveyed the spread of food, I realized my choice was completely inappropriate. There were no hot dogs or baked beans, not even any potato salad. Instead, the women had brought organic corn casserole, whole wheat bread pudding, bean curd dip, beets and wild rice. Everything looked and tasted like dirt. Even Holly, somewhat of an organic gourmet herself, called the food bland and the presentation unappetizing. We ate my chips and dip and Holly's carrot cake with thick cream cheese frosting.

After dinner we were summoned into the living room again and the shades were drawn for the final presentation. Holly and I sat close to the door, planning our escape if things got boring. But boring was hardly the word to describe what happened next.

Once everyone was seated on the chairs and floor, a scruffy, tough looking woman in a leather jacket and torn jeans burst into the room. She told us she was a representative of the most important and liberated group of women in the world, a group called SCUM, the Society to Cut Up Men.

For the next half hour she bellowed and preached. She told us that men are egocentric and incapable of love, friendship, affection or tenderness. "They're worthless," she said, "and overwhelmed by a sense of animalism." She claimed that men have a crudely constructed nervous system that is easily upset by the least display of emotion or feeling, so they try to enforce a social code that ensures a perfect blandness, unsullied by the slightest trace of feeling.

Holly and I kept looking at each other, half astonished, half afraid of what might happen next. When she told us that sex is a solitary, non-creative waste of time and professed that women could and should condition away their sex drive, leaving themselves cool and cerebral and free to pursue truly worthy activities, Holly became visibly agitated. And suddenly, like a shining beacon in a dark room, she stood and objected, loudly. I held my breath as she talked.

"Listen to yourself! Can you hear how bitter and stupid you sound? By raising men to such a glorified position of evil, don't you understand you're empowering them even more? Do you really believe that men are so smart and together that they could wield such power over us, or over anything for that matter? What you're saying is ludicrous. More importantly, we aren't so different, men and women." The SCUM woman tried to interrupt, but Holly shut her right down.

"We've been listening to you rant and rave for an hour. I think you can shut up for a minute and let someone else offer an opinion. We may be men and women, but we're all human beings, and much more alike than we are different. And if we are ever going to be truly free, men and women have to work together. The poet Rilke said that 'the great renewal of the world will perhaps consist in this, that man and maid, freed of all false feelings and reluctances, will seek each other not as opposites, but as brother and sister, as neighbors, and will come together as human beings, in order simply, seriously and patiently to bear in common the difficult sex that has been laid upon them.'"

I was so proud of Holly that I jumped up and started clapping. Several other women clapped too, but most only stared at us like we'd just spit on Gloria Steinem. After her tirade, Holly's face was bright red. She turned and grabbed her pack off the floor and I grabbed mine, too. We bolted out the door just as the SCUM woman warned the rest of the women in the room to watch out for unenlightened daddy's girls like us who were under the evil male spell.

Holly and I ran out to her motorcycle, exhilarated by our stand. The sky was clear and filled with stars. We hopped on her bike and with our hair blowing and fire in our spirits we headed toward The Barn. When we got to the bar, Bret, the owner, bought us kamikazes and we began drinking in earnest.

"I think this night deserves a toast." Holly raised her glass and I held mine even higher. "Here's to you and me, two real women who have no desire to join the Society to Cut Up Men because frankly, the man hasn't been born who can keep us down! And we don't need a bunch of pseudo-sisters telling us what to do." Holly leaned back, put her feet up on the bar stool between us and lit a cigarette. The bar was crowded with farmers and fraternity boys, and soon the stripper, Amber Lyn, arrived. Bret turned the lights down and moved the pool table out of the way so he could fit more chairs, and Amber Lyn started taking off her clothes.

Holly nudged me and yelled over the music. "Just think, Jess, that could have been us up there."

"We'd have better costumes."

"Wait till she gets down to her pasties. Say, Jess, there's a guy over there who's been watching you since we came in."

"Where is he?"

"The one in the plaid shirt and glasses."

"He's cute." I fluffed my hair away from my face.

Holly laughed. "Don't bother. He likes anything with breasts. Word from the dancers is that a pencil gives more pleasure."

I slugged her playfully, then turned and surveyed the room. "Do you think we could get the women of America to shut off the sexual faucet like Lysistrata did, until the men in charge end the Viet Nam war?"

"It could never happen here," Holly said. "Not as long as there are women like Amber Lyn around."

"Fighting for peace is like fucking for chastity. What can it hurt? I think you and I should start."

"I already have, by default," Holly said.

Bret came up. "I think you girls should both be up there."

"You do?" There was delight in Holly's eyes.

"I'll give you each $50 if you dance."

"Do you want us to dance or do you want us to strip?"

"Both would be great."

"Only if we can do it together." She hadn't forgotten how to tease.

"If you do, I'll give you each $75." He made us another round of kamikazes. "Come on," he said, "what do you think?"

Holly and I looked at each other. Then we put our hands together and gave the Athenian women's oath: "'I will withhold all rights of access or entrance from every husband, lover, or casual acquaintance, who moves in my direction in erection . . . I will fire my husband's desire with my molten allure—but remain, to his panting advances, icily pure. If he should force me to share the connubial couch, I refuse to return his stroke with the teeniest twitch. I will not lift my slippers to touch the thatch, or submit sloping prone in a hangdog crouch.'" Bret walked off, shaking his head. Holly and I held up our drinks and clinked glasses.

"'If I this oath maintain, may I drink this glorious wine.'"

"'But if I slip or falter, let me drink water.'"

"'A-MEN!'" We each took a gulp and laughed. Amber Lyn was into the last hot minutes of her strip tease, down to her g-string and bra. Holly explained how there was always a question of whether or not her g-string would come off, in defiance of the law but to the delight of the customers. Bret left it up to each dancer to decide, but there was a cash or drug bonus if she took it all off. Amber Lyn's act was getting steamier and the guys were yelling louder, so Holly and I took our drinks outside and sat at a picnic table.

Holly held up her glass for another toast. "Here's to us, two women on their way out of this tight-butt little town and on our way to fame and fortune in the real world." We toasted loudly.

"Have you made any plans for after graduation?" I asked Holly, realizing how little we'd talked about the future. Holly said she wanted to write poetry and plays. She said she'd considered graduate school but couldn't bear living like a pauper for two more years. I told her I didn't care where I worked, as long as it was in a city, the larger the better. "Here's to big plans in big cities." We toasted again and I slammed my glass down hard on the picnic table. Holly followed, slamming her glass even harder.

We talked about dream jobs and the more we drank, the more animated we became. Finally Holly said, "Why don't we move some place together? Who better to start the ultimate adventure with than my favorite pal!"

"That's a great idea! Here's to Holly and Jess together in the big city!" We toasted. I was glad she'd brought it up. Even though I imagined myself free and working in a big city, I was afraid to go alone.

Holly confided that since freshman year, she hoped we'd end up somewhere together. "I can work anywhere. Until I get something published, I'll work in a photo studio or something. It'll be great!"

"We should find a place together. To start out." I knew there was no way I could live in the kind of funky hovel Holly would pick. "We could rent a studio, month to month, until we get settled, then we'll each find our own place, close together."

"You too high class to live with me? God, Jess, you've become such a snob!" Holly poked me and laughed.

"I didn't say that. We have different tastes, that's all. I'm not a snob. Well, maybe a snob in training." I stuck my nose in the air and took on a stuffy accent. "I will have my maid, Monique, arrive at your home the day before I do, with Lysol and a broom in hand, to assure that your level of sanitation is adequate for my presence."

"Monique won't have time to be your maid, she'll be too busy as my assistant, proofreading my scripts and scheduling my signing dates!"

"No way. She'll leave you to join me in Monaco to tend to my personal needs at the Palais Royale where I'll be writing an exclusive, behind-the-scenes story on the real Princess Grace and Prince, Prince, oh you know, Prince what's his name."

Holly jumped in. "But Monique will get tired of pampering a snobby reporter for the *National Enquirer* and she'll return to me, hiring a helicopter to drop her on my Nile houseboat where I'll be translating ancient philosophers."

"*National Enquirer*, hell. I have my heart set on becoming a reporter for *Teen Beat*! I'll finally get that interview with David Cassidy I've been after all these years." I faked a swoon.

"And I'll end up writing greeting cards. Who cares? At least we'll be out of here and on our own!"

I raised my glass and slurred, "Here's to being out of here and on our own!" We slammed our glasses together, spilling most of what was left in them. "Oops! We may be getting the slightest bit hammered!"

Holly tipped her head and rolled her eyes, "Think so? Let's see." She tried to bring her finger to her nose, but poked herself in the eye instead. "Yep, I'm hammered. Hey, we haven't set a date for our graduation trip to Paris."

"Paris, here's to Paris!" We touched glasses carefully and began talking dates. I fished in my purse for my checkbook. "Let's see, here, yep, here's a calendar, right here in my checkbook. Isn't that convenient, I think that's so convenient."

Holly grabbed the checkbook, looked at the month of June and circled the third week. "That's it, the week we go to Paris. Can you make it? Maybe you and Monique have other plans?"

"Give me that and quit blubbering. Third week in June. It's a fuckin' date. Here's to Holly and Jess in Paris!" We toasted again and the bar lights came on. Frat boys and farmers streamed out. We stood and weaved.

"Shit, we have to go home. What'll we do?" I looked at Holly's eyes. They were glazed over.

"Just remember this, my friend. You must vow to 'withhold all rights of access or entrance from every husband, lover, or casual acquaintance' who moves in your direction in erection."

"But the Athenian women want to get laid."

"In that case, we must take matters into our own hands."

"The os the os, my kingdom for an os." Laughing, we stumbled onto the street, put on our new hats and got on Holly's motorcycle. I don't know how we made it home alive. By the time I inserted my key into my apartment door, we were both on the far side of drunk and headed toward a long dreamless night and deadly hangovers. After tripping around the room for a half hour, we crashed with our clothes on, head to toe on my bed at the Mayflower.

When I came to consciousness the next afternoon, my new suede cap was pulled tightly over my head like a helmet, making my incredible headache unbearable. Holly was gone, but she'd left a note. I'll never forget what it said.

Jess,
I'm off to work at The Barn—hope Bret hasn't fired me. We didn't dance, did we? No, I remember. Lysistrata and the os. I had a great time and I'm paying for it with a killer hangover. Now I know why they're called kamikazes. I can't wait to see what it costs to fly to Paris. I'll call you with the details.
     Holly
P.S. *Teen Beat* phoned while you were sleeping. They're looking for a reporter to cover the high school prom circuit. I told them you'd already taken a job with the *National Enquirer*.
Kiss, Kiss

Zoe ran off to relieve her bladder, instructing to Jess to stir the stew. "I want to hear about Paris!"

There was no Paris, Jess thought, as she stirred and watched the liquid bubble up and evaporate. We did take a trip, though, that nearly ended our friendship. The phone rang as Zoe reappeared. "Here, stir away. I probably ought to get that." Jess picked up the kitchen phone. "Hi. What's the matter? No, I can talk.

Hold on a second, I'll go to my office." Jess mouthed her sister Kayla's name to Zoe, took the phone into her office and closed the door.

CHAPTER TWENTY-FOUR

Jess sat at the desk in her Aeron chair and used her foot to swing herself back and forth, looking first at her wall of awards, then out the window at the streetlight illuminating the mist. Kayla was frustrated and angry. Their mother had been recovering from her second hip replacement. Bert's Alzheimer's disease was progressing and the doctors were recommending that he move into a nursing home. Even though Celeste couldn't care for him any longer, she wouldn't hear of it. Jess tried to pay attention, wondering why she felt so pressured. It's because I can't take on another battle right now, she thought. Kayla described in detail the facilities she'd visited and the merits and failings of each one. This one smelled the worst, the other one had a waiting list, the third was too expensive. Jess sat, half hearing.

"Wait!" Jess shouted suddenly. "Not you, Kayla, I just remembered something. Go ahead, I'm listening." Jess sat up and began paging through her day planner. She knew she'd taken notes that night. Eric told her the demographics and she'd written them down in her planner. While Kayla talked, Jess turned every page from January through the end of the year, but there were no notes about ProbTech.

Kayla continued for half an hour, until they decided a visit from Jess was necessary so they could present a united front. Jess called her mother and tried to sound reassuring when she asked about Bert's health. When she broached the subject of a nursing home, Celeste came up with reason after reason why it would be a horrible idea. Jess finally gave up and promised to visit soon.

In the kitchen Zoe added more spices to her concoction. She took a taste, watched it simmer. She could hear Jess talking through the bedroom door and was jealous that Jess had a sister. She'd always wished to be connected to a sister who'd share her secrets and dreams. As she tasted the stew a thought occurred to her. Maybe I have a half sister somewhere. My father is probably married with children. The thought excited, then angered her. "Damn you, Holly. Why didn't you leave me a clue?"

Glancing around Jess's kitchen, she noted how generic and unloved it felt, how the dining room with its windows opening toward the bay looked pristine, unused. Like my mother's house, she thought. It was nothing like Adam's place, a vintage two bed-room brownstone. Adam's platform bed and Zeke's pillow bed filled most of one bedroom, the other served as den, study and playroom. He'd splurged the year before and bought an over-stuffed couch at a Macys' sale. Then Zoe brought her desk over and he pushed their desks together so they could face each other while they worked or studied. "Damn you, too, Adam."

Zoe unwrapped her new candles and as she arranged them on Jess's table, she remembered dinners with Adam's family, his sis-ters, Amy, Angela, Anna and his brother, Allan. The thought of their names made Zoe grin. They were always loud, always laugh-ing, they teased each other and seemed to say exactly what they felt. And Adam was always warm toward his mother. Unlike me, Zoe thought. She suddenly missed watching Adam play with his mustache as he read and the way he curled around her when they slept. Why did you do it, she pleaded silently. It could have been so good. Now what am I supposed to do? She turned down the heat on the stew and went to the sofa. She sat heavily and looked at her mother's things strewn everywhere. She sighed, lifted *Sexual Behavior in the Human Male* from the coffee table, then spotted *The Courage to Be*. She picked it up, noticing its well-worn cover. "The courage to be what, Mother?" she asked. "Confused, alone, with no answers in sight?" She threw the book to the floor where it landed next to *The Wisdom of Insecurity*. Zoe smiled at the juxtaposition and reached for another journal. She thumbed through it, looking for a date.

June 15, 1972

Paris will have to wait; neither of us had the money anyway— what else is new? But that's all right, we've been liberated at last! We're here in San Francisco, for a long weekend. We checked into this cheap residential hotel near downtown called the Post Club. It's full of travelers and people trying to find work, costs $8.00 apiece, which includes breakfast. But the rooms are prison cells, eight feet by twelve, with one twin bed and a dresser.

From our window we can see Trader Vic's, and tonight we stood watching beautiful women accompanied by successful men as they climbed out of limos to enter the glitzy world of fine dining. Jess says someday she'll climb out of one of those limos. I'm sure she will.

I feel like I can touch the place where I might finally feel at home, like this city is ready to welcome me, that all I have to do is open my arms and it's mine. Good night!

June 16

I have to write fast, because we're getting ready to go. This morning we woke late and hurried to get breakfast. Vasily runs the Post Club, he's a greasy man with disheveled dirty hair, a dark, pudgy face, sleazy to the core. He serves meals in the basement;

it's grungy, old, and painted an awful yellow, aged to putrid. There are tables packed close together and vinyl chairs with chrome legs—reminds me of the Pit in the Iowa Union. Anyway, this morning Vasily was making his way around the tables, sizing up all the young, braless women, and making sure everyone at breakfast had actually paid for a room. Obnoxious creep, I thought, as I loaded my plate with French toast. Jess and I sat at a table and looked around. "Look at that guy, Jess. What a sleaze."

"You could probably ski in his hair."

"Can you imagine sleeping with him?"

"I can't imagine taking his temperature." We sat, eating our first breakfast in San Francisco. Jess had her maps and bus schedules spread over the table, and we were going over our plans for the day, when I felt an odd sensation and looked around for Vasily. But he'd gone into the kitchen. Jess said we should visit the Wharf, Alcatraz and Ghiradelli Square. As she talked, I looked up and this time I saw her. It wasn't that I noticed what she looked like, as much as I noticed how she was looking. At me, with an intense gaze. When her lips turned up at the corners, I looked away. Jess was talking, saying something about going to the St. Francis Hotel for cocktails later, to toast our arrival, but I hardly heard her. Those eyes unnerved me.

"Do you want to go to Golden Gate Park today or tomorrow? There's an exhibit at the art museum there that I want to see, but today's the last day. Are you going to help me with this?" The stranger approached. She was slim with dark hair, her eyes were a deep blue.

"You two look like you might need some help."

Jess looked up and gave her a grateful smile. "Oh, would we! There's an exhibit at the park that's closing—"

"There are only two places in San Francisco you must see," she said. Full lips framed perfectly white teeth. She was looking at me. "The Legion of Honor Museum and the Cliff House at sunset."

"What's the Legion of Honor Museum?" I asked, trying to sound casual. She looked at me and I knew that she knew.

"A museum housing some beautiful sculpture by Rodin."

"I wrote a paper on him for my art history class." Sealed.

"If you like, I can show you where it is on the map."

"That would be great," said Jess. "Maybe we can plan a stop there."

"Oh, let's go," I said. "Even if we have to skip Alcatraz."

The stranger laughed. "Here it is," she said, pointing. "Let me show you how to get there by bus. It's not easy, but it's worth the trip."

Jess invited her to sit with us. Her name is Rachel. She's been living at the Post Club for a month while she writes articles about the art scene for a small alternative press in Los Angeles. The pay isn't much but she gets to travel, and she's been to every major city in the country.

"There isn't much you can do with a master's degree in art history, unless you teach."

"We're going to get jobs right away. We have bachelor's degrees—in English."

She smiled and wished us luck. We said good-bye and promised to see her later. I want to know how soon that is! Jess is ready—must go.

Later

Today we took buses and cable cars and climbed hills and saw old buildings with quaint Victorian facades. We went to Fisherman's Wharf, then to the gardens in the park. We vowed that we'd move here as soon as we scrape enough money together. It was at the Legion of Honor Museum where we cemented the vow. Jess fell in love with Rodin's sculpture *The Kiss*. I loved *The*

Bronze Age. We sat on a bench together, looking up at the bronze male nude.

"I feel like all my life has been a climb to this moment," Jess whispered, as if she were in church. There are times when she voices something I'm feeling, and I really believe that we see the world with the same eyes. Other times I'm sure we aren't even from the same planet; but today we were partners, sharing the same vision.

Jess wanted to go for a drink at the St. Francis Hotel during cocktail hour—we'd heard they had free hors d'oeuvres. But we missed our bus and got back to the Post Club too late for Jess to shower, so she was pissed. As we left, we ran into Rachel, who asked us where we were off to. Her eyes were playful, less intimidating than before. I asked her if she wanted to come to the St. Francis with us, but she declined. Jess seemed impatient to go— or was she angry that I'd asked Rachel to have a drink with us? Rachel said that some hotel guests were going to a dance club at 7:45, and she invited us. I told her it sounded fun and that we'd try to make it. We said good-bye and Jess dragged me away. As we walked out the front door, I turned and saw her watching us. Watching me. I blushed, then made Jess promise we'd be back in time to go dancing.

The bar in the hotel was crowded with young office workers who, like us, were there for dinner at the price of a cocktail. Jess and I were able to snag bar stools, and she guarded them as I went to the buffet and loaded two small plates as high as I could. When I came back there was a man in my chair, talking with Jess.

His name is Doug Harding and he's an account executive in a big San Francisco advertising firm. He's attractive and older, maybe 40, with dark wavy hair. He has that air of sophistication a man has when he knows he's attractive to women, which made me suspect that he sleeps around.

I kept an eye on the time while stuffing my face and listening to Jess trade exquisite flatteries with Doug. Tonight I wanted her to fail at flirting, put her foot in her mouth, drop a meatball on her lap. I wanted him to disappear, because Jess was acting like someone I didn't want to know.

They talked about the advertising business and I couldn't even feign interest. Jess was enthusiastically describing an idea she had about one of his products, Nair Hair Removal. She thought the ads ought to have a more feminist tone and should try to sell Nair as a kind of liberation from hair as opposed to getting rid of something unsightly. I couldn't follow her line of reasoning, but he said her idea was brilliant, given the changes women were making in their lives. And of course during this, he cleverly managed to slip into the conversation how much money he'd brought into the agency the previous year and where his sailboat was docked.

I continued eating, but my mind kept wandering back to the way Rachel first looked at me. I wanted to be with her, talking about Rodin. I wanted her to look at me like that again. I was daydreaming, eating a chicken wing and trying not to look too barbaric, when Doug asked Jess if he could take us to dinner the next night.

"Oh, I'd love to, if it's all right with Holly." They turned to me. I put the chicken wing down and took a gulp of my gin and tonic.

"I have a friend I'd love you to meet, Holly. A junior partner from the law firm that represents us. What do you say? There's a great little Italian restaurant up the street. You girls would love it. It has the best wine list in the city." Jess was giving me one of those please-do-this-for-me looks, so we scurried to the powder room for a powwow.

"Jess, I don't want to spend my last night in San Francisco with two strangers!"

"Holly, this could be our big break. He can find us jobs at the drop of a hat."

"At the drop of our drawers is more like it."

"The guy's happily married for Christ's sake. He told me so."

"Great."

"Really. His wife's out of town and his kids are with their grandparents."

"How convenient."

"No, you idiot. I'm telling you, he really likes me. He's interested in my ideas about his products."

"And a little fuck on the side wouldn't be bad, either."

"It's not about fucking. That's the trouble with you," Jess whispered, as a middle-aged woman came into the bathroom and entered a stall. "You think everybody's out to get laid. You don't trust anyone. He wants to have dinner with us. He's bringing his friend. How dangerous could that be?" She handed me her lipstick and I dutifully applied some.

"It's just that I thought this was our trip. Our big time to be together."

"We are together, we'll be together all day tomorrow. Look, if you don't want to go, we won't. It's up to you. I won't go unless you do." I said nothing and she worked to persuade me. "Just remember, one of the reasons we're here is to find prospects for work. If you want a decent job, you have to make the right contacts. 'It's not what you know, it's who you know,' remember? Do you think somebody's going to come knocking on our door at the Post Club?"

I laughed. "You're too damned practical." I handed her back her lipstick, which she promptly dropped into her handbag.

"That's why you love me." It was true, of course. I can't see past the borders of my own mind, but Jess is always staring down the future.

"All right. I'm yours."

"Good. You won't regret it. Who knows? Maybe this friend of Doug's will turn out to be the man of your dreams."

"I doubt it." I looked at my watch. "Shit. I want to go to the dance club. Can we go now?"

We hurried back to Doug, who called his friend and set up our date for the next night. It was just after 8:00 when we got back to the Post Club and the hotel clerk told us Rachel and the others had already gone. I felt as though the last lifeboat just left without me. Jess and I were wondering what to do, when a small, young man with short, dark, curly hair came up and introduced himself. His name is Louis. He's an expatriate from Chile whose father disowned him, he didn't say why. He has a little sports car, and he offered to take us for a ride, so we squeezed into the front seat of his Corvair convertible and took off.

We sped into the night and as Louis drove us across the Golden Gate Bridge we sang songs, cracked jokes and shouted into the wind. Driving around Sausalito, we vowed to live there ourselves some day. When we got back to the Post Club, I told Jess I wanted to read in the lobby. So here I am waiting to see if Rachel comes in. Am I nuts? I think I have a crush—on this girl!

June 17

Rachel did come back. We sat for hours in the lobby and talked about art and life and all the wonderful rest. She asked me to go with her to a painting exhibit she has to review today.

"I can't. Jess has our whole day planned sight-seeing."

"Well, then how about meeting me for sunset at the Cliff House?"

"I'd love to. Yes! Oh shit, I can't. We're supposed to have dinner with some . . . friends of Jess's."

"If you change your mind, I'll be there at sunset." I crawled up to our room at 4:30 and pushed Jess out of the way to make room on the bed. I'm beat, but Jess has another whirlwind tour planned for the one-tenth of San Francisco we missed yesterday. Why do we have to see the Mission District? What I really want to do is sit in a quiet place and contemplate Rachel. I have to figure out how to get myself out of this dinner. The tour bus awaits. Wish me luck.

Later

We're back from a day of death marching in neighborhoods I hope never to see again. While Jess showered I wandered out, walked by Rachel's room and stood outside listening. I heard a radio playing and almost knocked, chickened out. Jess just admonished me to hurry. She's being a real jerk and has ordered me to wear a dress. I have to shower.

Now I'm ready and she has to curl her hair! Fuck this. Two guys we don't know, on our last night in San Francisco. They're going to bore us to tears and Doug's friend is probably a geek. I want to wear Jess's new suede hat but according to her, this won't be a hat place. I don't want to go, I want to meet Rachel at the Cliff House. I want to watch the sun set over the ocean, I want——oh, God, what do I want?

Listen to what Jess just preached: "If you want to stay in Iowa City your entire life, don't go. If you want to move back to Chicago and become a high school teacher, don't go. If you want to curl up in a ball and shut yourself off from the world, don't go. If you want to languish in the Midwest and never venture out of a safe quiet little life there, don't go." Fuck her. I'm going.

June 18

I had the most exhilarating night of my life, and I want to kill Jess Martin.

We left the Post Club and didn't speak all the way to the restaurant. Jess had insisted that the guys not pick us up; she didn't want them to know we were staying at a cheap hotel.

We entered the restaurant with its mahogany bar and linen tablecloths. It was a dark and masculine place, a place where I imagined large deals were cut. We spotted Doug and his friend, a handsome man with wavy blonde hair and glasses, seated at a table in a far corner. Too handsome, I thought, and I shook my head in my mind as the maitre d' came to guide us to the table. He reminded me of my date to the toga party freshman year. Only then, I hadn't a clue as to why he would never be interested in me. Now I did. He was trying very hard, just like me, to be somebody he wasn't. I imagined him paired up with Louis from the Post Club, that would be a match made in heaven.

I sighed as we approached, realizing the pained conversation we'd have trying to find common ground in a sea of mistaken cues and misinterpreted meanings. Neither one of us could be who we were, and we'd spend the evening faking it in front of two other people who didn't have a clue it was all a facade. We'd perpetuate the illusion with studied savior-faire, and when it was over we'd go home and vow never to allow ourselves to be put in that situation again. But the next time somebody needed to be impressed, or taken to dinner, or around town, a friend would think of us, single us, and invite us, and we'd reluctantly go. We'd carry on inane conversations with our date, who would be either not a bit interested in us because they were in the same situation themselves, or the poor date would wonder what was wrong with them, that the only live response they got was a peck on the cheek at the end of an excruciatingly dull evening. I sighed again, audibly this time, as we approached the table.

"He's cute," Jess whispered, as if that should be enough to last a lifetime.

Doug took hold of Jess's two hands, clasped them in his and told her how great she looked. He introduced me to John Fowler and my suspicions were confirmed when his eyes met mine. The sun would burn out before this man took a woman to bed. He must have sensed my uneasiness because when we spoke, I could tell that he knew I was as uninterested in him as he was in me. Somehow, he understood. I wanted to blurt out, "I have this great guy I'd love to introduce you to!" Instead I behaved myself, sat politely down and ordered a glass of wine. I kept looking at my watch, wondering what time the sun would set.

Doug told us about his family, how he and his wife had an open marriage. "Love without jealousy," he called it. He said they'd based their relationship on a book called *Open Marriage*, by two therapists who'd done research into alternative ways men and women were relating. Jess seemed impressed when he told us that one day he looked forward to being a house-husband and taking care of the kids while his wife finished her master's degree and started a career. Open marriage also meant open sex, or as he put it, the freedom to explore relationships outside the marriage.

After half an hour listening to Jess and Doug explore marriage, sex, and the freedom to express yourself while John and I listened uncomfortably, Doug turned to John and asked, "What do you think about all this?" I looked at John and wondered if he was going to play along or if the man had any real balls.

He took a sip of his wine and cleared his throat. He looked right at me. "I think you should follow the dictates of your heart, no matter who you love. But if you love someone, I would think you'd want to be with them, and no one else." I knew it was time to find out if I had any balls, or ovaries, so I did the next best thing to following the dictates of my heart—I excused myself and went to the ladies room.

I looked at myself in the mirror and said, "You are ridiculous." I paced the area in front of the sink, back and forth like a cornered rat. "What are you doing here? I asked myself. "And who are you doing it for?" I put my hands on the sink basin and leaned into the mirror. "You idiot, you idiot, you idiot," I said to the image looking intensely back at me. I turned and paced again. I couldn't stay, I couldn't go. "No Exit." I laughed. I thought of Sartre's play and wondered if this was what hell was like. Was I to be sentenced to this room, pacing in indecision forever? No, because Jess walked in.

"Where have you been? The guys want to order dinner."

"I—I—I lost my earring."

"It's on your ear."

"Oh."

"What is the matter with you? You've hardly said a thing to him. Don't you like him?"

"I like him fine. It's just that I—he's not interested in me."

"You haven't given him a chance."

"That's not the point." I turned on the faucet and started running water over my hands. "How about if I just left? How about if I left you with both of them—you could take your pick—"

"That's a great way to spend our last night together."

"This isn't together, Jess."

"You agreed to come, so you'd better put up a good front. That's all I have to say." She turned to go.

"That's all that matters, isn't it? That it looks right."

"You should have stayed home, you know that? I'm sick of dragging you around with me, when you can't even appreciate an opportunity, let alone do something about it. Why don't you go back to the hotel and vegetate, since that's obviously what you came to San Francisco to do."

"I don't want to do that."

"Then come out and act like you're at least alive."

"I'll be right out. Tell them I'll be right there."

"Okay." She left. I knew I had to leave. But where would I find the nerve? I looked around the room. Nothing there. I dug in my purse and found a deposit slip, pulled it out and wrote her a note—

> Dear Jess,
> I'm sorry to have to do this to you, but I have to leave. I'll explain why later, but I can't stay. I don't mean to do this to you, but try to understand. I know you won't, but try anyway. It's not against you; it's for me. Please forgive me in advance.
>
>   Holly

I folded the note and gave it to the waiter, with instructions to give it to Jess after I'd gone. I hurried out the front door and ran back to the Post Club as fast as I could.

I went to our room and stripped off the dress, nylons, earrings and heels. I found my best pair of bell-bottom blue jeans, the ones where the butt was exactly the right degree of worn. I pulled out a tight pink ribbed T-shirt and tucked it in. I looked at my watch, then cranked my head out the window to see how much light I had left. I had to hurry.

I put on a pair of sandals and stood on the bed to see the back view. I turned and looked at my ass and almost fell off the bed trying to get the right angle. It looked great. I jumped off the bed for another look at my face and ran a comb through my hair. Then I held up a pair of peace earrings, then a pair of Jess's earrings, decided on the peace earrings and slipped them through the holes. I stood back. Then I saw it, Jess's cap, sitting on the bed, blue suede and the perfect complement to my outfit. I grabbed it, put it squarely on my head and opened my arms, admiring the total effect. I shook my head in wonder that I could look so good. "Dressed for the kill."

I ran downstairs to the lobby and asked the desk clerk how to get to the Cliff House. While he was writing directions, Louis came out and offered to take me. I told him I owed him my life, hopped into his car and we peeled off.

When Louis dropped me off, I stood for a few minutes across the road from the Cliff House. There was nothing past the west side of the bar but the majestic Pacific. The sun was low in the sky and had started to cast its golden glow. My legs started to shake. I felt dizzy. Oh, my God, I thought, what am I going to say? Fortunately, I didn't have a lot of time to think about it, because the sun was fading fast. It was now or never.

I walked across the road, each step a victory of passion over fear, and entered the Cliff House. It was big, earthy and warm, with thick ferns everywhere. The bar had a beautiful light wood finish and was bound by shiny brass railings. Inside, tables were crowded with people looking through the grandest picture window on earth. Outside was a balcony overlooking the Pacific herself.

"May I help you?" The bartender was friendly, older.

"No, thank you. I'm looking to meet someone."

"There are plenty of people here looking to be met." He smiled.

"No, there's someone here already, someone I know . . ."

"I see." And he smiled again.

I blushed, then hurried into the large dining room and looked around. She wasn't there. So I did what I'd been programmed to do since Jess and I started traveling together—went to the ladies room. I checked my reflection in the mirror, gave myself a talking to, then started out, bolstered. Just go, I said to myself, as I stood before the rest room door and my uncertain future. Suddenly a gaggle of girls came giggling through the door and nearly knocked me down on their way to primp. I hurried out through them and looked around the bar. No sign of her. What was I to do? I couldn't go back to get a drink from the bartender—he'd only chuckle under his breath.

Then I saw her, standing on the balcony, staring out. The wind was blowing her hair and she looked positively heroic with her face to the wind and the sun, like a character in an Ayn Rand novel. I caught my breath and went out. She didn't see me at first, then she turned and smiled. At me.

"Nice hat," she said.

"Nice face," I said, before I could edit myself.

She smiled a dazzling white, intimate smile, as though she knew everything I was thinking and approved. "Thank you."

I walked to her and we stood shoulder to shoulder, listening to the waves and watching the sun sink lower. Words seemed superfluous. Finally, she took my hand and said, "I want to show you something." We walked hand in hand down the stairs at the side of the balcony, down many steps until we reached the beach, where she led me to some rocks out of the wind. My hand was clammy and I was afraid she'd notice, but instead she took it and kissed the back of it as she led me down to a space between several large boulders.

It was moist there and slightly cold. She took a blanket out of her pack and spread it ceremoniously on the ground. I sat on it and tried to steady myself. She sat next to me and looked at me with her steady gaze—I was startled by the intimacy of it. I looked down at her mouth. Her lips were parted slightly and looked pliant and inviting. I blinked, then turned away, afraid she could read my thoughts.

"What's wrong?"

"Nothing," I said, "That's just it. Everything is right, everything is so right I . . . can't believe it." Was I going to cry? I bit my lower lip.

I mobilized all the courage I could summon and turned my

face up to hers and didn't hear the wind or the waves any longer. I could only feel my face nearing hers, until her breath was on my mouth. Then her lips were on mine and mine on hers and there was a long blonde hair in our kiss, and she laughed and took her finger and drew it away from my face and with it all the ugliness, shame and confusion of the years of "Don't do that. Nice girls don't do that. Straight girls don't do that, you don't do that." I was doing it, and it was pure and clean and right.

Her lips were soft, her kisses light but deliberate, soft pecks that lasted longer with every return. I loved the delicacy and the softness, but I wanted more, and matched her kisses, but with more pressure and more need. I put my hands around her head and pulled her closer to me, tentatively probing her mouth with my tongue, searching for answers to all the years of questions.

We tumbled to the blanket with the kiss. She was on top of me, then she started to break away. I couldn't bear her leaving my lips, so I held her head and whispered into her mouth, "Your lips are so soft, I can't stop kissing you." But she pulled away, and her eyes bore through me. Her glorious mouth whispered the words, "I want you."

With a steady grip she followed the contours of my body and dipped into the waistband of my jeans, slowly pulling up the edges of my pink T-shirt and slipping it up over my breasts until my nipples were in her hands and she was circling them between her fingertips.

She was kissing me again, her lips growing fuller with each kiss, until I felt that she would devour me. I ached to be devoured. I wanted to kiss her until I understood every nuance in her kisses, but the tenuous balance couldn't last, I couldn't wait a second longer. And she knew it. With strong, sure hands she undid the snap, then the zipper and pulled my jeans to the middle of my thighs, and I thought, it's going to happen now. I didn't want to stop, I never wanted to stop; but I felt the crisis coming and knew it wouldn't last—the tension was building with every rich, lingering stroke.

She was breathing in my ear and I could hear her breaths getting lighter, quicker. As her fingers reached into the very center of my soul, I heard myself moaning deeply, rhythmically. I fought to keep it but couldn't, and felt the little sadness before the imminent victory. The victory arrived and I followed the dictates of my pleasure and felt my head pull back and the sound take over. From the depths of my being I could hear her voice far away, like a validation, "Yes, yes, yes." When the tremors stopped, I lay there breathing like a woman saved from drowning. And then the calm. I felt her hand release me and when I opened my eyes, hers were looking into my soul.

"Oh, shit. I'm sorry. I wanted that to last—forever." She laughed, and her hands followed the curves of my body, up and up, until she was wrapping her hands around my head and pressing her mouth to my ear.

"It doesn't have to be over yet." And I blushed!

"You're right." We went on, until the hunger had risen and been satisfied again and again and again.

It was dark when we finally abandoned our enclave and hurried back to the Post Club, to her room, where we spent the night in a long embrace. In the morning, I woke up and saw Rachel sleeping peacefully, beautifully, then I looked at the clock radio. It was after 10:00. Jess and I were supposed to leave for the airport in half an hour, so I darted out of bed and threw on my clothes. I saw Jess's hat on the floor, picked it up. I wrote Rachel a note, placed the hat on the pillow next to her, and vowed to remember the sight of her sleeping for as long as I lived.

I sang in the elevator, every muscle in my body felt relaxed, aligned. But I stopped when the elevator door opened onto our floor. I treaded slowly toward our room, stood in front of our door. What would I tell Jess? I walked to the end of the hall and back. I felt the deep shame rising in me like a wave, drowning out the memory of the night. I paced to the end of the hall again, then looked in the dirty mirror across from the elevator. "Nothing happened," I said to it. "Nothing happened." I walked into the room. Jess was neatly packing her red Samsonite. "Hi."

She didn't turn and look at me. "It's about time."

"I know."

"You better not make us late." I started throwing things into my blue Samsonite, trying not to bump into Jess. We danced around each other, not speaking.

Finally, Jess stopped and faced me. "Where were you last night?" The phrase rang over and over in my mind. "Well?"

I tried to stare through the bottom of my suitcase and remembered my note saying I'd explain everything to her. I could feel my face get hot and with it the fear and shame. I felt the trap snapping shut in my mind, the trap that came up now, like an echo and a command: No, no. I couldn't tell her where I was. I couldn't bear the look on her face, the look I knew would be there if I told her the truth, the thoughts she would think about me, the ugly shameful thoughts. If I told her, she'd walk out. She'd leave me and we'd never move to San Francisco, and the only person in the world I ever really cared about would be gone because she would hate me for what I was.

"Well?"

I could choose an immediate death, or a slow tortured one. I chose the latter. I made the choice and felt my own self-loathing as the completeness of the night vanished and I returned to the carefully constructed split my mind had had years of perfecting. The preciousness of the night drained out of me as I took the path of denial.

"Are you going to tell me?"

"Wherever it was, it doesn't matter," I said.

"I sat up all night worrying about you and I want an explanation."

As I gathered my toiletries off the bureau and threw them into the bottom of my backpack, I dropped a bottle of shampoo and it spilled on the floor. "I had to leave. That's all." I grabbed a towel and started mopping up the goo.

Jess stood over me, watching. "That's not good enough."

I looked up at her. "Can't we just drop it?"

She went back to folding her clothes. "No, we can't drop it. You can't do this to me—leave me alone, then stay out all night, without even a phone call to tell me you're not coming in. I have you laid out in a morgue murdered somewhere, I don't get a minute of sleep, and you come sailing in here like you haven't done anything wrong."

"Jess, I'm really sorry, I didn't mean for you to worry—"

"Then you should have called."

"I didn't think of it." I wrapped up the shampoo-soaked towel and set it in the sink.

"You didn't think of it? You didn't think of me."

"I'm sorry." I felt the familiar pressure of numbness creep over me, the clamp on my psyche that always kept me from losing control.

"I don't believe you."

I strained to keep the clamp in place. "Okay, you don't have to believe me. Now, can we forget about it?" I started making my way around the room, grabbing clothes, throwing them into my suitcase, trying to stay out of Jess's way.

"No. I want to know what the fuck was so important that you ditched me in front of those guys." She finished folding up a blouse and laid it in her suitcase. When she saw it wasn't exactly right, she took it out and folded it again.

"I wasn't ditching you. I just couldn't stay there."

"You ditched me and made me look like an absolute fool in front of Doug and—" I cut her off. I couldn't let her go there.

"Oh, I see. That's what this is about. Making you look like a fool. It's okay if I ditch you, just don't do it in front of anyone? Especially someone who can do things for you?" I slammed the lid of my suitcase, then reopened it when I saw that half my clothes were still strewn about the room. I knew this train was headed for a dark, dangerous tunnel, but I felt powerless to stop it.

"Are you going to tell me where you were or not?"

I grabbed a pair of underpants off the floor. I tried to be calm, but my voice was shaking. I took a breath and started what I hoped would only have to be a lie of omission. "I couldn't stay there with those two guys, the one talking about his goddamned open marriage, which is an excuse for fucking whomever you want, whenever you want, and the other one who was obviously not interested in women in the least—"

"How do you know? You left before we ordered the entree."

"What does that have to do with anything?"

"Everything. You had that poor guy pegged and didn't even bother to find out anything about him." She put the blouse back in and patted it flat. I watched her while I fought to regain control.

"Believe me, Jess, he isn't interested in women."

"I suppose you're an expert on that."

"I'm not an expert."

"You see, that's so like you. You're always jumping to conclusions. You make snap judgments about people and never bother to find out the truth. I'm sick of it."

I took a deep breath and pulled out my secret weapon, knowledge of my best friend's weak spots. "You dare tell me I make snap judgments? At least I can see past what brand name someone is wearing." I started throwing things into my suitcase with a vengeance.

"So crucify me for having a fashion sense and for knowing how to present myself in public." I didn't answer. "The way you dress, my God, it's a wonder you get asked anywhere."

"The way I dress? At least I don't go around pretending I'm something I'm not, trying to impress people with the faux gold jewelry and the fake pearls. Here, these are yours." I handed her the earrings she'd lent me the night before.

"Because I don't dress like a bum in training?" She took the earrings and put them away in her special jewelry pouch. "These were all right last night, but today they're not good enough?"

"I don't give a fuck what I wear."

"Obviously not."

"And that's obviously all you care about." I was angry now, and hurt, and I wanted to hurt her, too. We packed in silence until my hurt erupted into anger. My icy voice belied my true feelings. "Tell, me, which one did you end up sleeping with? Both of them, maybe?"

"It's no business of yours who I sleep with."

I taunted her. "Mr. 'Open Marriage'? Tell me, did he take you to his yacht? Did he take you to his open marriage bed? Or did he take you upstairs to the St. Francis? Ha, that's great, Saint Francis, patron saint of animals. Too bad there's no St. Jude Hotel, because that's a lost cause."

"At least I sleep with guys."

I froze. "What's that supposed to mean?"

"You just berate them."

"Only the ones worth berating."

"Oh, so there are some good ones? Like 80-year-old men? And guys you treat like brothers. You pick real winners, O'Neal. Maybe you should start sleeping with girls!" She was too close.

"Any dog would be better than the men you choose."

"At least I don't choose ones that are totally inappropriate for me."

"Fuck you."

"Are you going to tell me where you spent the night?"

Here we go, I thought. "I went to the beach."

"With whom?"

And now the lie. "By myself."

"You spent the night on the beach by yourself?"

And now a pile of lies. "I had to get away. That whole scene at that restaurant was disgustingly fake. I wanted to be alone."

"I *vant* to be alone. And you will be, Holly, because nobody is going to stomach your bullshit. And you can't even muster an apology for making me stay up all night worrying about you."

"You were only worried about how it looked to be ditched in front of Doug and his friend."

"If you think I give two shits what he thinks—"

"You give more than two shits. You wouldn't let those guys come to the Post Club to pick us up, because you were embarrassed we weren't staying at the Fairmont, remember? So you lied to him about it. Tell me, when he dropped you off, was he surprised? What lie did you tell him about that? Huh?" She didn't respond, but walked into the closet and came out winding a leather belt into a neat circle. Then she changed tactics.

"At least I'm not a disaster in social situations."

"Because I refuse to sit around and be bored by two boring middle-aged men!"

"Because you're unsociable! Because you're so goddamned inappropriately unsociable!"

"Good. Because I don't ever want to be appropriate if I have to kowtow to some asshole in a business suit who pretends he's interested in your goddamned ideas, when all he really wants is a roll in the hay and you're too stupid to see it." I sat on my suitcase to shut it and caught the corner of the bedspread in it.

"I'm stupid? You, with your grand theories and big ideas about the wonderful world you think is going to come begging on its knees to find you. You, with your theories and your quotes and your romantic notions about art and life; you make me sick with them. You don't have a clue about what's really out there. Well, I've stuck my neck out for you for the last time." Jess looked under the bed, grabbed a shoe I'd left there, threw it at me. I caught it, dropped it, picked it up, stuffed it into my suitcase.

"I never asked you to stick your neck out for me."

She continued. "Oh, no. You just never gave a thought about the consequences of what you did, and you depended on me to pick you up whenever you fell. If I hadn't shown up in that dorm room you'd probably still be there, wearing white cotton underwear and waiting for Mr. Right to sweep you off your feet."

"Shut up, just shut up."

"No." She went after me again. "I'm sick of being treated like a dunce when you're around. I'm sick of your pseudo-intellectual bullshit, masquerading as sublime knowledge. You know how to read a book, big fucking deal. That's all you know how to do, so you might as well go back to Iowa and stay there, because the world will never have you the way you are—"

"At least I don't go faking and fucking my way through it!"

"What difference does it make to you who I fuck?"

"Whether you fucked him or not I don't care, but I do know that you'd only fuck him if you thought you could get something out of him." I finally got my suitcase closed and locked. "Tell me, did he offer you a job?"

"For your information, he did."

"Oh, so the evening was a success?"

"Yes, it was."

"And what did you have to put out for it? Did you get away with a blow job? Or did he require full service?"

"You're sick, you know that?"

"At least I don't use people when it's convenient and toss them out when they can't do anything for me any more. You're a world class opportunist, Jess Martin. I can't figure out why you hang around with me."

"Why is it that everything I do is a game? And everything you do is a noble struggle, replete with heroics. You're a real magician, O'Neal. My life's a cartoon and yours is an epic novel."

"That's right. Because I can read a book. Because my tastes run wider than *Glamour* and *Vogue*. You're about this deep, Jess, you know that? This fucking deep."

"If that's what you think, consider yourself free of me, O'Neal."

"Finally."

She slammed her suitcase shut and looked around the room. "Where's my hat?"

And the final lie. "I don't know."

"It was on the bed last night. Where's my hat?"

"What makes you think I know?"

"You obviously came back to change clothes."

"I don't know."

"Yes, you do."

I grabbed my Samsonite off the bed, stormed out of the room and took the elevator down alone. I stood outside, waiting for the bus to the airport. I watched the cars whizzing by me. I thought if I could just step in front of one, all my problems would be solved. I'd never face another accusation, another confused thought. I wouldn't have to lie anymore. Just end it, right now, I thought. I wouldn't have to fight anymore, it could all be over in seconds. And so I did it . . . I jumped in front of the next passing car.

In slow motion, I felt someone pull me back. I landed with a thud on my backside on the curb. Profuse apologies and thank-yous all around to the lovely good Samaritan who saved my loser life. Another fucking lie.

Jess and I are on different sides of the bus to the airport. She's on her way back to Iowa and I'm headed for Chicago, alone. Here I sit, writing. I hate Jess for being angry at me for leaving her. I hate myself for making a mess out of the trip that was supposed to launch us into our glorious future. And I hate the lies I told her, one after another. I feel like I'm leaving hope behind. And then there's Rachel. I will remember every touch, every detail of the sight of her sleeping. Is there a book I can read that might tell me why I'm crazy? And why, if Jess Martin is supposed to be my best friend, why can't I tell her the truth?

Zoe held the book to her chest, aching to tell her mother that she understood what it was like not to feel accepted. Do people always hold back from people they're supposed to love, something as important as their identity? Zoe felt that here was something else she had in common with her mother, the feeling that there was no one she could share the deepest part of herself with.

Zoe thought of calling Adam. No, I have to figure this out on my own. No Joanne, no Adam, no Annabelle. What could anyone tell her, anyway? No one had an answer. Her parents couldn't communicate, her birth mother hadn't been able to tell her best friend she was gay. Jess was divorced. Most of her friends' parents were divorced. Zoe twisted her face toward the back of the sofa and cried. "Why do we try so hard," she whispered, "only to fail so miserably?" She thought about Adam. She remembered what he told her when he asked her to move in permanently. "If I tell you I won't leave you, I won't. What do I have to do to prove it to you? Tell me and I'll do it." But there was nothing he could prove now, after what he'd done.

Chapter Twenty-five

Jess entered the living room and saw Zoe, her face buried in the sofa pillows, a journal lying on her chest. She stood in the doorway for a moment watching Zoe, then softly called her name. Zoe turned, forced a smile and wiped the corners of her eyes. Jess decided not to ask Zoe what troubled her. I can't take on any more, she thought. I'm being pressed from all sides and now Mom and Dad are slipping, and I'm supposed to fix that, too. If I pull my finger out of the dam, the whole country will collapse.

Zoe sat up and laid the journal on the sofa. Jess exclaimed over the wonderful smells coming from her kitchen and marveled at the candles on the dining table. Zoe leapt up, happy to be distracted from her own pain. "Is everything all right with your sister?" she asked.

Jess fought the urge to confide. "My sister's fine. But my mother had her hip replaced two months ago. She's doing all right, but now the doctors and my sister think my dad should go into a nursing home. Celeste won't hear of it, so they want me to talk her into it. So far, no luck." Jess sat down in her armchair and was suddenly tired, too tired even to rise and get the drink she wanted.

Zoe went to the kitchen to reheat her concoction and chattered through the open galley window. Zoe told Jess how she heard about a resident in a nursing home; he was on a feeding tube and wasn't allowed in the dining room. He complained that his nurse was denying him food, accused her of leading a conspiracy to starve him, and stabbed her eight times with a pencil. Before Jess had time to respond, Zoe changed subjects. "Does your family know about Eric?"

"Oh, God, no."

"I've been thinking about Adam, how after what he did I can never trust him again. Do you trust Eric?"

"There's the $64,000 question."

"But do you love him?"

"Yes." Jess answered, slowly. But why do you love him? Jess could hear Holly ask. "Because I need him," she said aloud.

"You love him because you need him?"

"Look, it's hard to separate Eric from my work. And there was a time when I'd have followed him anywhere. I should have known that things never change when you're dating a married man with children."

"He has children?"

"A daughter." Jess didn't see the flash of disapproval in Zoe's eyes. "I'm always the last person in his plans. And now I'm even more of a fool. But that doesn't happen to you unless you allow it. I'm the original girl without expectations. The worse they treat me, the better I like it."

"I don't believe that," Zoe interrupted.

"Trust me. Did you read that book about women who love too much? My picture should be on the cover." Jess sighed. "You'd think that after my divorce and some good therapy, I'd know better. But I'm tired of talking about my sorry life." Agitated, Jess rose and went to the kitchen to pour herself a glass of wine.

"I read in Holly's journal that you two went to San Francisco after graduation," Zoe finally said.

"Did you read about that awful time?" Zoe nodded. "On our last night, Holly stranded me with two guys, then stayed out all night. I was so angry, I wanted to kill her. I kept seeing her murdered in a back alley or drowned in the ocean."

Jess picked up her drink, returned to the armchair and sat heavily, thinking of the trip and that last night at dinner with the advertising executive. She never told Holly about how her night had ended; remembering it, she cringed.

After Holly left, Holly's date excused himself. Then while Jess and her date were eating, his wife came in. She'd obviously been drinking and stumbled to the table. She called him a cheating son of a bitch and Jess a slut. She slapped him, then told Jess that she shouldn't feel special, she was only one in a cast of thousands of stupid whores her husband wined, dined, screwed and left behind. Jess ran back to the Post Club, humiliated and hurt. She needed to talk to Holly, needed Holly to say that she wasn't a slut, it wasn't her fault. But Holly was gone, and didn't come back until morning. When she did, she wouldn't tell Jess where she'd been.

Jess remembered their awful argument and how, on the bus to the airport, she thought their friendship was over. Jess took a long sip of wine.

"So you guys broke up after that night?"

"Interesting terminology. We didn't speak for two years. Holly moved to Chicago and met Kate. I moved to Los Angeles and thought I was climbing to the top. In reality, I began my long downward spiral."

"What do you mean?" Zoe asked.

"There were lots of temptations in Los Angeles. Unless you were centered, you were an easy target for dangerous people and deadly vices. In my twenties, I had no center. Away from Holly, who'd been my conscience, I set myself adrift in the worst place on earth. And did I screw up." Jess sighed.

"How?"

"Drugs, bad relationships, you name it. I don't know if I can even tell you about it."

Zoe came around from the kitchen and sat on the ottoman. "Jess, I'd like to know what you've been through. It's about being honest, remember?" Jess couldn't resist the open heart that sat before her.

It was an awful time. I missed Holly, though I wouldn't admit it. Finally, two years after our fight, she broke the ice and sent me a birthday card via my parent's home. I wrote back immediately and for the next three years we corresponded and spoke by phone regularly. We talked about our lives, jobs and families, but we were tentative and careful with each other; we never mentioned San Francisco. Then I got a letter from her in the fall of '77 saying she'd be in L.A. for a writers' conference. I couldn't wait to see her and told myself her visit had to be perfect.

I was desperate to have Holly back in my life and was willing to do whatever it took to make that happen. I'd begun to realize how much I'd counted on her to keep me honest and call me on my bullshit. In Los Angeles there was a lot of bullshit.

I worked all the time and had made no real friends in the three years I'd lived there. I was a good copywriter and good at the clever banter clients expect from creative agency types. But most people didn't do a line of cocaine first thing in the morning like I did. I always had my reasons; I needed a line because I had to be up for a presentation or I had to be especially enthusiastic to land a promotion. Another day it was because I had too much work to do or I needed a little boost to handle a tough client. I had a million excuses.

The morning of the day Holly arrived was no different. I ignored the little voice pleading "no," and quickly sniffed two lines. I'll quit as soon as Holly leaves, I told myself. But then I felt the first rush and the shadow of guilt drifted away. I put a vial into a small leather pouch and dropped it in my purse. Just in case.

Freshly buzzed, I hummed along to Fleetwood Mac's "Gold Dust Woman" as I looked through my closet. I decided on my Annie Hall look, baggy tan corduroy slacks, a matching vest over an off-white blouse and man's tie. My hair was still long but I'd had it brightened with gold highlights. I wondered what Holly would look like.

I poured a glass of orange juice and surveyed my living room. I'd spent a small fortune on the furniture in my apartment and wanted to show it off to Holly. I'd decorated in trendy earth tones, thick cocoa colored shag carpet, cocoa and rust Herculon over-stuffed couch and chairs, an oak entertainment center, even two original paintings—landscapes of the California coast. I arranged *Vogue* and *Newsweek* on the oak coffee table along with a couple of art books I'd bought the week before, specifically with Holly in mind. It looked like a spread out of *Apartment Life*. I was sure Holly would be impressed. She shared a flat in Chicago with roommates, and I shuddered imagining how she was living. I pictured a mattress on the floor in one room surrounded by piles of books and journals, and in another room an old couch and a desk surrounded by mismatched bookshelves.

I fluffed the pillows on the sofa bed in the guest room. I'd placed fresh cut flowers on the dresser and a copy of my favorite book, *Even Cowgirls Get the Blues*, on the desk. After a last look, I picked up my portfolio and walked into the hall. I locked the door, then slipped the key under the mat. Holly was renting a car at the airport and coming directly to my apartment around 3:00.

Even though I planned to leave work early and meet her, I didn't want her to wait if I got caught in traffic. I'd also written her a note with instructions to help herself to the wine and Brie cheese. Just the right touch, I thought, a civilized welcome to the weary traveler.

As I headed my Trans Am onto the 405, I ticked through our agenda. Holly had to be up near Malibu at 9:00 the next morning and she'd be tied up for the weekend, so we only had the evening together. I'd been invited to a party that night by a director who worked for our agency, Perry Donnely. I really wanted to go. Perry wanted me to meet a producer friend of his, a filmmaker. It was to be a casual meeting, but Perry kept telling me his friend could do a lot for me. I'd even been taking acting lessons on the side, hoping to land a role in a movie.

I was secretly glad to be going to the party, partly because I wasn't sure how things would go with Holly, and partly because I felt compelled to prove that I was a busy, important career girl who'd made it in the big city.

I parked my car and hurried into the office, into disaster. My panicked secretary met me at the door and told me all hell had broken loose with a client. He'd seen the rough-cut of a new commercial and hated it. She followed me down the hall to my cluttered cubicle and told me the client was in the editing room, waiting for me. I dropped my portfolio on the desk and headed to the bathroom. I told myself I needed a little boost to get me through this crisis and locked the stall door, poured out a line on top of the toilet paper dispenser and sniffed it quickly. I checked my nose in the mirror and headed out to face the day.

The next time I looked at my watch it was 2:30. I'd been in meetings or on the phone for over five hours, and the day had flown by. At 3:00 I slipped out, after giving my secretary strict instructions on what to say and to whom if there were calls.

Leaving early was verboten unless you were deathly ill, everyone was expected to work late. Most of us were either single or divorced and we all either drank heavily or used drugs. Working into the night, sharing pizza, booze and an occasional line, we'd formed a sad little dysfunctional family.

After fighting my way through the snarl of Friday afternoon traffic, I arrived home around 4:00 and heard music through the deck doors. James Taylor was singing "Sweet Baby James," and my stomach jumped with excitement as I flew up the stairs.

Holly was curled up on the sofa, one of my art books in her lap, looking small and beautiful. Her blonde hair was in a shoulder length perm, but everything else about her looked the same. "Hi," I said, "You look wonderful." I wanted to pick her up and swing her around the room. Instead, I stood and stared.

"You look pretty good yourself." She stood and came toward me. We hugged awkwardly; I was reluctant to let go, but Holly released me and gestured toward the room. "And this place, it's fabulous, it looks like something out of a magazine."

"Thanks, I like it, it feels like home. I am so happy to see you. Did you get some wine?"

"Yes, thanks, let me pour you a glass." Holly turned toward the kitchen.

I dropped my portfolio. "No, sit, I want to wait on you. I never get to play hostess." I practically pushed her back onto the couch, then headed to the kitchen alcove to get wine, cheese and crackers.

"With a place like this, I bet you have dinner parties every weekend."

"Almost never. I work most weekends. Well, I've had three dinner parties. All disasters. I wish I'd learned to cook." I poured the wine, set out the platter of cheese and crackers, sat down on the end of the couch and kicked off my shoes. It felt good to tell the truth. I don't need to impress Holly, I told myself. I can relax, just be me. "How about you? Do you have dinner parties?"

"Not counting my roommates, not a one. Problem is, I don't have a table. It's hard to have a dinner party without a table." Holly raised her glass and smiled. "To future dinner parties."

The late afternoon sun rippled across the room while Holly and I caught up. We talked and laughed and when I checked the time, it was after 5:00. "Shit, we have to go. We'll be late for the party! I have to change."

"What party?"

"It's a long story, I'll tell you on the way."

"Can't we blow it off?" Holly hadn't moved from the couch.

"I'm sorry, we can't. Perry is a director for my agency. It's an important party. Business, you know." Holly protested again. "But I want you to meet my friends. I've told everyone about you. And it's free drinks." I saw a scowl form on Holly's lips, then watched her check it.

"God, how many disastrous evenings have we spent together with people we didn't like just to get free drinks. Jess, we can buy our own drinks!"

"It was a joke, Holly. But he's not a bad guy and this really is important. There's someone I'm supposed to meet. I hope you don't mind. Too much?"

"I was hoping to spend an evening with you." This time Holly didn't try to hide her annoyance.

"I couldn't say no to Perry. You'll have fun, I promise. And if you don't, we'll leave. Fair enough?"

Holly agreed without agreeing, and I dressed quickly in a black denim jumpsuit with tiny silver studs at the sleeves and around the cuffs. I finished off the outfit with a big turquoise bracelet and turquoise earrings, then slipped into the bathroom, closed the door and did another line. That's when I noticed

Holly's carry-on bag with the brochure sticking out of the pocket. I pulled it out and read the front panel. "Women Writers Weekend Retreat." Below the title it read, "Get back to nature and release your creativity with other free-spirited women." There was a photograph of women cavorting in a pond surrounded by trees.

"Can I go like this, or do I have to dress up?" Holly hollered to me as I returned the brochure to her bag.

"What do you have on?" I said, checking my nose.

"Jeans and a black turtleneck. I guess they didn't make an impression."

"You look great," I said, as I emerged and headed for my closet. "But, here, this will look great on you." I pulled out a vest in shades of purple, green and black with rhinestone buttons. "I always wear these earrings with it, too. Wear them if you want, but the ones you have on look fine, too." I didn't want to be too pushy, but I did want Holly to look her best.

"Jesus, some things never change. I've been here less than two hours and you're already dressing me. Give me those earrings." She took out her silver hoops and put on the beaded earrings. "Do I look L.A. enough to meet your friends?"

"Smashing." I closed the door and locked it as we headed out to the car.

"If I'd known we were going to be on the social circuit, I'd have had a few more drinks."

I pulled a bottle of wine out of my bag. "Ta, da! There's a glass in the glove box. Plus, if you dig in my purse you'll find a little pouch filled with real treats. You still do drugs, don't you?"

"That depends on your definition. I get high now and then, on pot. I haven't done any serious drugs for a while." She dug in my purse and found the pouch. "Coke! Even if I knew where to get it, I couldn't afford it." She opened the lid and looked into the vial. "I think I'll pass for now."

"Okay, but fill the spoon for me and hold it under my nose." Holly obliged and I took a quick snort as I turned onto the freeway and headed toward the hills.

"Fill the glass with wine and we'll share. How's this for groovy living?"

"Pretty damn hip." Holly took a sip, then handed me the glass. She turned up the radio and we sang along with the Doobie Brothers. Holly dipped another spoonful of coke for me as I drove. It was a beautiful evening and I felt happier than I had in years. The sky was clear and the sun glistened across the waves. We were singing and everything seemed light and positive. Just having Holly with me made me feel stronger, more complete. I wanted to tell her, but it sounded too weird, so I asked her about Chicago and her life there.

"Graduate school is time consuming, teaching is stimulating, but I covet the time I have off when I can concentrate on writing."

"Are you seeing anyone?"

"Not really. I told you I live with two friends, Andrew and Kate. Andrew and I have talked about having a baby together. But it's mostly talk."

"A baby! That's pretty radical. Are you in love with this guy?"

"I adore him. We might even get engaged when I get back."

I took another swig of wine as I tried to conjure up a guy named Andrew. "What does Andrew look like? What does he do?"

"I'll show you his picture when we get back to your place." Holly seemed anxious to end the conversation and turned up the radio.

"Hey, don't you love this song?" We sang along with "50 Ways To Leave Your Lover" as we started the climb up to Perry's house on Mulholland Drive.

"So my mother got engaged?" Zoe interrupted.

"She wasn't engaged. It was part of her cover-up."

"She still wasn't leveling with you about being gay?" Jess shook her head.

"I'm not sure she was even being honest with herself. And I didn't exactly make it easy for her to open up to me. I was more interested in showing her my facade of a life than finding out the truth about hers."

Perry had invited nearly 100 people to this party. I knew some of them from work, but most were acquaintances and associates of his. He seemed to know everyone. Perry was in his 50s and married. They lived in Palm Desert and he went home on weekends, but during the week he worked and partied. He'd been a well-known director on the TV circuit before he became a commercial director. He had the inside scoop on the stars' lives and was good friends with a few aging actors. I was impressed.

On three occasions, after we'd been drinking, Perry had offered to introduce me to "his people" in Hollywood, so I could get a "real" writing job or break into acting. Everyone I knew in advertising spent a lot of time talking about getting jobs in the TV or film business, but none of us ever did anything to move ourselves in that direction. The only catch with Perry's offer was that I'd have to move into his apartment in the Valley and take care of his needs, as he put it. He was looking for a live-in girlfriend during the week and made no secret of it. He'd support me and let me drive his second Mercedes. All I had to do was give him sex on demand. I'd have my weekends free when he headed to Palm Desert to be with his wife. So far I'd said no.

"So tell me, who else will be at this dinner party?" Holly asked, flicking ashes out the window.

"Perry, he used to direct for Norman Lear's shows."

"Who's Norman Lear?"

"Get serious. Don't you watch TV?"

"Hardly ever."

"He's offered to get me a job in TV, but I'm not so sure I want that life. Anyway, three other guys from my office will be there. Kyle, who just got divorced and is quickly becoming an alcoholic. Jamie's also divorced, also a drinker and heavy drug user, but one of the wittiest writers I've ever met. And Bob, he's an account manager. He's in his 40s and has been married and divorced a couple of times. He's suave and sexy, wears great suits and lots of gold chains. Women love him. Roger Burns will be there, too. He's a marketing vice president from Clairol. He's 43, perpetually tan, and has the most beautiful blue eyes I've ever seen. He lives in Malibu. You get the picture."

I hoped I'd sounded hip, but telling Holly about my friends made me feel hollow. I wasn't going to tell her that I'd been sleeping with Roger for the past six months or that he wasn't yet divorced from his second wife. Besides, I was more impressed than in love with him, because under the business banner he'd taken me to the most expensive restaurants in L.A. And since Clairol had a permanent suite at the Beverly Hills Hilton, we rendezvoused there regularly. It was exciting at first, a sizzling affair with a powerful, handsome man with lots of money. But the last few times Roger and I met at the Hilton, he was different. We did a lot of coke and he'd been rough and more sexually demanding.

I knew my affair with Roger was a mistake, that if I wasn't careful, it could cost me my job. But I was too afraid to end it with him, at least until after I'd been promoted to another account. Clairol was one of our agency's most important clients and Roger had the power to make my life miserable or get me fired. I'd seen him do it to other people who'd worked for him. There was no one I could confide in who could help me decide what to do. I couldn't tell Holly. It would be too humiliating to admit to her how badly I'd compromised myself.

Unfortunately, early on I'd entertained Roger with exaggerated stories of Holly and my past adventures, so when he heard she was coming to town he was especially anxious to meet her.

"Will there be only guys at this party?"

"There will be plenty of women, most of whom I won't know. They'll be bimbos, models and actresses. But you'll meet Patsy. She's a year younger than we are, a designer and surfer. We're friends at the office and we party after work. Patsy's from L.A., so she has lots of friends and I get the feeling she's not looking to add to her collection. Oh, Bob is bringing his latest girlfriend, a wanna-be actress. And when I told Perry you were coming, he insisted I bring you along so he could give you a proper L.A. welcome."

"Sounds interesting, in an L.A. sort of way," Holly commented as I stopped the car on the top of the hill.

"What do you mean?" I asked defensively. "L.A. people aren't all bad."

"I didn't say they were. If they're your friends, they must be nice people." I turned off the engine. Holly started to get out when I grabbed her arm.

"They're not really close friends," I stammered. "I mean, we work together and we hang out a lot, you know how it is."

"Look, I'm sure they're fine people. Let's go in and have a good time." Holly started to get out of the car.

"Wait, I need another line of coke."

"You just did one."

"I know, but, shit, it's been a long day and I need to loosen up. Social situations always make me a little nervous, okay?" I dipped the spoon in and sniffed hard.

"Since when?" Holly asked.

"Since always. Okay, let's go. Look, if this gets boring, say you have a headache and we'll leave. I'll take you to one of the cool clubs on Sunset Boulevard." Holly agreed and we headed up the walk. "You won't believe the view from Perry's house. You can see the entire valley from there."

We entered the party, which was already in full swing, even though it was only six. Perry greeted us dressed in white jeans, a colorful Mexican top with a scarf tied around his neck and no shoes. He was perfectly tanned and his hair looked freshly permed and tinted. He gave me a big hug and kissed Holly squarely on the lips.

"Welcome to the top of the world. Everyone's already here, you're late. Shame, shame, Jess." Perry told us that people had been arriving since four and they'd already gone through three cases of champagne. Then he darted into the living room and announced our arrival. A man dressed only in a g-string and bow tie appeared with a tray of champagne. He introduced himself as Perry's menial, Jason, and offered us a glass. Then, before I could warn Holly, Jamie came up and whisked her away with a promise to show her the real L.A. on Perry's expansive deck.

I entered the living room where Bob was snuggled up on the sofa with his perfectly coifed blonde, Mandy. Kyle was on the phone. They were the only people I knew of the 50 or so there. Perry was doing a line of coke at the coffee table.

"Where's Patsy?" I asked.

Perry finished his line and took a deep breath. "No one seems to know. She left work early and no one's seen her. A tryst in a cheap motel, perhaps? But, Jess, remember, my offer still stands. Just say the word."

Not wanting to offend Perry, I flirted with him until Holly returned from her tour with Jamie.

"Is this guy Jamie for real? He's already invited me to the

Hollywood Bowl for the jazz festival, invited himself to visit me in Chicago and informed me that the last time he had sex was in September. Not much subtlety there."

"None. But if he didn't ask you to have his children, he's clearly not that serious about you."

"Jesus, is that what I think it is?" Holly pointed across the room to the glass-topped coffee table with its huge mound of cocaine and dozens of straws arranged around it.

"It's a party. This is how we party in L.A. I think I'll sample the goods."

"How can you eat after all that coke?"

"That's another thing about L.A. people, Holly dear. We don't eat. We talk about eating, we even cook sometimes—usually a barbecue—but we rarely actually put any food into our mouths."

I sat next to Bob and Mandy and did a line, then took Holly on a house tour until I spotted Roger Burns on a purple love seat in a corner. He was making out with a black girl in a white gauze outfit and didn't see us. I pointed him out to Holly.

"He looks like a movie star. Who's the woman?"

"Don't know, but I intend to find out. Come on."

I plastered on my best L.A. model smile and strolled across the room. "Roger, hi. It's great to see you so relaxed." He stood up and I planted a wet kiss on his lips. "This is Holly."

"The infamous Holly. I feel like I already know you." He kissed her hand. The black girl didn't budge. She was stunning and obviously interested in Roger.

"Who's your friend?" I asked, not looking at her.

"How rude of me. This is Shawanda." She nodded but didn't speak. "She's a model and we've just met. She was kind enough to keep me company while I waited for you to arrive. But now you're here, aren't you? Sit, please."

I shot a nasty look at Shawanda, and Holly and I took seats across the table. I immediately reached out my hand and took Roger's in mine. I dominated the conversation, filling him in on my day.

Roger and I weren't going together. In fact, I should have been happy that someone was available to take my place, so I'd be off the hook. But I wasn't. Female competition always brought out the worst in me and I felt compelled to win, even if I didn't really want the prize.

Roger asked Holly about her life and she told him about wanting to write. He said he'd wanted to write when he was our age and actually had a screenplay optioned. Shawanda still hadn't spoken, which annoyed me. She kept her eyes on Roger, smiling smugly as though she had a secret, or perhaps the key to his apartment in her pocket. I downed my drink and told Roger that Holly and I needed our glasses refreshed. We stood to leave when Roger interrupted with a stern tone. "No, you can't leave. This party is just beginning. Holly, I've heard a lot about your adventures with Jess. I'll bet you wouldn't mind a little adventure while you're here in L.A., would you?" He turned and winked at me.

"Well, Mister . . ."

"Roger."

"Well, Roger, I'm here for a writers' conference, which is an adventure to me. And tonight, I was hoping to spend time with Jess so we can catch up and do a little reminiscing."

Roger looked unfazed. "Jess, sweetheart, you're always up for adventure. Later then, right?" He glared at me.

"Roger, I'm sorry, but we've made plans for later this evening. You understand." I gave him a pleading look.

"Well, Shawanda and I are very disappointed." He put his hand on hers and she smiled coyly. "We'd hoped the two of you would join us over at the Hilton for drinks and a more intimate party."

"We'd love to, but I promised Holly I'd introduce her around." I shot Holly a look and she finished her drink.

"It was great to meet you, Roger. And you, too, Shawanda. I hope you get your voice back soon," Holly said as she set her glass down on the table. I fought to keep from laughing as we raced to the bar for more champagne. I knew I'd pay later for abandoning Roger, but with Holly by my side, I suddenly didn't care. "Boy, Roger thought he had the makings for a real fantasy tonight."

"His own private Mod Squad: one black, one white, one blonde! God, what is it about us that inspires weird sex?" I asked." We passed by the bar and got two more glasses of champagne, crossed to the living room and sat next to Bob and Mandy. Then I snorted another few lines.

Suddenly a song blasted out of the speakers so loud I had to cover my ears. "Chicago, Chicago, that toddlin' town . . . Chicago, Chicago, I'll show you around . . ." Everyone looked to the top of the stairs, where Perry stood in a pink nightgown and feather boa. He mouthed the words to the song as he sashayed down, looking like a cross between Carol Channing and James Caan. Kyle and Jamie let out whistles and everyone cheered. Holly seemed stunned by the attention. She might have been a little embarrassed, too, but I was too high to tell. Perry came to the bottom of the stairs and took a seat between Holly and Mandy. He sounded very affected and very gay as he made a toast to Holly and wished her a fabulous visit.

I did another line, desperate to keep the buzz going in order to ward off the discordance I felt. Jamie and Kyle got drunk, Bob and Mandy got cozier and Perry became more obnoxious. No matter what direction the conversation took, Perry interrupted with a tasteless gay joke or some bit of gossip about this or that movie star, who was, as he put it, "a closet queer," or "a total flaming fag." I'd never heard Perry sound so mean-spirited.

"This town is swarming with queers, Holly. It's a goddamn shame. At least they used to keep their sexual antics to themselves, but now it's turned into a friggin' movement. Gay rights! What in the hell are gay rights, the right to fist fuck at will?"

"Perry, that's hardly cocktail conversation," I admonished.

"Oh, is Miss Iowa embarrassed? Sorry. As I was saying, Holly—"

Kyle interrupted. "What's your problem, Perry? This love-hate thing you have with faggots is really old. After all, you're the only guy here wearing a feather boa. Though, I admit, it looks quite stunning on you." Jamie laughed.

Bob chimed in. "Is that gown chiffon or taffeta? It's you, Perry, really it is!" Jamie, Bob and Kyle all laughed. Holly didn't.

"How about those Dodgers?" I interjected, trying to steer clear of disaster.

"It's football season, Jess, dear," Perry corrected me. "It's 'How about those Rams?' And most of them are queers, too. I'll bet you didn't know that did you, Holly? Not like your Chicago Bears. Oh, no, they're real men. What do you think Holly, is homosexuality a lifestyle decision or a genetic defect?" Perry turned to Holly and stroked her arm with his feathers.

"It's a disease that should be punished by slow torture and death," Holly stated calmly in her most cynical voice.

"My, my, methinks thou doth protest too much!" I jumped up from the table and brushed the end of Perry's boa in his face, trying hard to distract him and stop the evening's downward swirl.

"Come on, Perry. Didn't you say something about music and dancing?"

"Yes, but first dessert! Sit back down while I arrange things!" With a flourish, he was gone.

"God, who wound him up?" Kyle commented to Bob.

Jamie chimed in. "He's such a closet case, and he hates himself for it. What a fucked up life."

Perry waltzed in carrying a candy jar filled with Quaaludes. "All right, children, dessert is served. Help yourselves, but remember to share." Jamie and Kyle grabbed a handful of ludes and left the sofas. I scooped out several and put them in my pocket. Perry sat back down and turned to Bob's girlfriend who was sitting to his right. "So you're a model, Mandy? Mandy the model, isn't that perfect. I'd love it if you'd critique my runway walk."

While Perry was rambling, a distinguished-looking silver-haired man came through the living room door, a tall blonde woman on each arm. Perry jumped up to greet him. It was Mickey Frisk, the producer Perry wanted me to meet, the reason I was at the party. When he entered, all eyes turned toward him.

More people had arrived for the second wave of the party, mostly music company types and their dates. Mickey was surrounded by a throng of guests, but I wanted to wait until he was alone before I made my move. Holly went to search for some aspirin, and I went outside to the pool where the band had set up. I found a table and opened my vial. Holly found me there and I offered her a line of coke.

"No thanks, I need to sleep tonight." I sniffed a spoonful.

"You don't have to worry about that. I have Tuinals at home, they'll knock you right out."

"Thanks, but I also need to be up early."

"Tell me more about your writers' retreat."

"It's for women who are working on a novel or a play. They gather at this sort of camp. Did I tell you I'm working on a new play about Frau Lou?"

"Who?"

"Frau Lou and her relationship with Nietzsche."

"Cool! When can I read it?"

"When it's finished. Listen, Jess, don't be offended, but can we split?"

"You don't like my friends, do you?"

"It's not that, it's just that . . ."

"They're not usually this way, I mean, they're usually funnier. I think Perry was showing off for you. I've never seen him act so weird. I mean, he's always outrageous, but he's so cruel tonight. He's usually bright and witty and much more fun." I broke a Quaalude in half and offered one to Holly. She declined, so I took the entire tablet.

"Don't you do any psychedelic drugs like acid, mescaline, or MDA?"

"Never! We have too much work to do and you can't work and trip at the same time. Coke's the thing. I can work all night on a few lines."

"Are you sure you can handle all that?" I didn't answer her, just nodded. The band had started playing a Bruce Springsteen song.

"Let's have one more glass of champagne, just the two of us, then we'll go. It's so beautiful out here, don't you think?" Holly reluctantly agreed and went to get the drinks.

I was glad to have a moment to myself and leaned back to enjoy the music. I was very high and noticed that my heart was beating double time. I can fix that, I thought, pulling another Quaalude out of my purse. As I downed it, I saw him. It was Rob. He was only a few feet away, talking to a petite black haired girl with huge breasts. Rob, with his shoulder-length blonde hair and tight jeans. Rob, with his cool attitude and nasty temper. He looked great as usual, in jeans and a denim vest with a faded tie-dyed T-shirt and boots. He was sharing a joint with the girl, who couldn't have been older than 19. I watched them and fumed.

Rob and I had met at a bar in Santa Monica where Patsy and I stopped regularly for a drink after work. He played bass guitar in the band performing there, and during the break he bought me a drink and charmed me. For a few months I met him at his gigs and would sit at a table watching while he played. Afterward, he'd take me back to his place where we'd smoke pot and have frenetic sex till dawn. We spent every Saturday night together. For a while.

But women loved Rob and were always throwing themselves at him. I was incredibly jealous and went out of my way to make sure everyone around knew I was the girl he took home at night. After a set, I'd always plant a big kiss on his lips when he joined me. That really annoyed him. Whenever I got possessive, Rob got annoyed. After a while, everything I did bothered him. The more I wanted him to myself, the farther he moved away from me.

The last time I slept with him, I ended up cutting up two of his favorite T-shirts in a jealous fit when I found a note some girl had given him. He told me it was time to cool our relationship and immediately went on the road with his band, promising he'd call when he got back. Four months had passed and I hadn't heard from him. Now, seeing him with a girl sent me over the edge. Suddenly, I was the wronged woman.

"What's the matter? You look positively white." Holly sat down and handed me a drink.

"Shit. See that guy over there? I can't believe him. He was supposed to call me."

"He's too cute."

"And boy, does he know it." The ludes had kicked in and I was talking loud and slurring. "Robby Bedell, a ladies man and a big fucking liar."

"Cool it, Jess, he'll hear you. We should go."

"Not till I tell mister too-cool asshole what I think of him." I pulled the pouch from my purse and clumsily unscrewed the lid to the vial. My hand slipped and I dropped it on the floor. "Shit.

Hold this, I have to find it." I squatted and lowered my head to look under the table, but saw no sign of the vial. "Shit, fuck." I raised my head too fast, and came up so dizzy I could barely see.

"Jess, your nose is bleeding," Holly whispered as she handed me a napkin.

"Oh, it does that all the time. I'm allergic to this L.A. smog. Shit, I can't believe I spilled the rest of my coke."

"Come on, Jess. Let's call it a night. I'll drive. Let's go back to your place." Holly looked nervous.

"Fine, but I'm driving and we're not leaving until I speak with Mr. Bedell."

"You're too high to talk to anyone."

I was already standing. I picked up my drink and swayed toward Rob. Holly followed reluctantly. "If it isn't Mr. Bedell."

"Jess, hey, what's happening?"

"What's happening is nothing is happening. You said you'd call the minute you got back. Yes, I believe those were your exact words. Don't tell me, you meant to call, but, let's see, you couldn't find a dime. Is that the story this time? Well, here's a dime." I started to dig in my purse, but spilled my drink instead. Holly was at my elbow, trying to pull me back.

"Hey, Jess, I've been busy. You know how it is."

"But you weren't too busy to call what's her name here. Excuse me, what's your name? I said, what's your name!"

"Pam. Rob, can we dance?"

"Pam. Well, sweet Pam, watch out. Old Rob here is a real lady killer." They started off and I started after them. "No, I really mean it, he tried to kill me once. He had his hands around my throat and he said that if—" Rob turned into me.

"Shut up Jess," he said, glaring at me. "You're so fucked up you don't know what you're talking about." He grabbed Pam and they moved away, but not before I threw the rest of my drink at his back.

Holly dragged me toward the front of Perry's house. I was angry, hurt and so high I was close to losing control.

"Wait. I have to talk to that producer guy, Mickey Fist, or Frisk or whatever the hell his name is." I weaved my way back into the living room with Holly right behind.

"This isn't the time to talk to anyone. We need to go."

"There he is." I had spotted Mickey holding court in a corner of the living room, and made a beeline. "Mr. Frisshk," I slurred. "I'm Jess Martin, a good friend of Perry's. I've been dying to meet you. Perry thinks we should work together." Mickey turned and looked at me, then turned back to the two gorgeous boys he had been talking to. "I'm an actress. I'm studying acting." I continued, trying to get his attention as Holly stood by, horrified.

Mickey Frisk turned back toward me. "Perhaps you hadn't noticed, but we're having a conversation here. And I'm sure you're a spectacular actress," he said in a mocking tone. "Why don't you just show us your breasts and let us be the judge." He winked at the boys who had to stifle their laughter.

"Show you my breasts? What does that have to do with acting?"

"Everything in my business, dear. If you have a beautiful cunt and big breasts you can be a deaf mute for all I care. In fact, that's a great idea for my next movie. What do you think boys? "Adventures of a Deaf Mute Nymphomaniac.""

The men laughed and I quickly turned to leave, nearly running over Holly. "Let's get out of here. He's a fucking porn producer. Fuck. I can't believe it. Show me your breasts. That asshole. That fucking asshole. Let's go."

"Yes," Holly said, "but give me the keys."

"No way. You have no idea where we're going," I argued.

"I drove to your place today, and I'm sober. Did you do another one of those Quaaludes?"

"What if I did? I can still drive. I'll just do another line and it'll perk me right up. Come on." The car was at the end of the drive and I opened my door and got in.

"Jess, this sucks. I don't want to get on the freeway with you. You're too high."

I started the car. "Get in or I'm leaving without you." She stood her ground. "Okay, okay, I'll take Highway One, we'll stay off the freeway." Holly relented, climbed in and we started down the hill. "Light me a cigarette, will you? Can you believe Rob? Fuck, why do I always fall for total assholes?"

"I don't know, Jess. That just seems to be your nature."

I took the cigarette from her. I knew she was annoyed with me, but I didn't care. I was speeding down a mountain on a train without brakes. "So you think I'm a jerk, too. Thanks a lot. Shit, I dropped my cigarette."

I took my hands off the steering wheel and raised my butt off the seat. Holly tried to grab the wheel, but it was too late. The car swerved out of control and careened on two wheels sideways up onto the sidewalk, then back down again, as we flew from side to side. I grabbed the wheel and turned it hard. The car plowed into a light pole, sending Holly onto the floor and my head into the rear view mirror.

Neither of us moved for several minutes. Finally, I raised my head and tasted blood. I reached down to where Holly's head was, next to my foot. "Holly, Holly, are you okay? Shit, Holly, talk to me. Please, say something!"

"Fuck you, Jess Martin. I told you I should drive," was all she said.

Suddenly, someone knocked on my window. It was a guy and girl in leather biker jackets. "Open up." I rolled down the window. "Are you okay? Man, your head is cut. Is she okay?"

Holly raised her head. "I'm okay."

"Your car is fucked up, man, and you're hurt. I think you should go to a hospital."

"We're okay, really. Thanks, though." I tried to open the door and couldn't. "Holly, see if your door will open." It did and we tumbled out.

Holly looked at me and shook her head. "Jess, he's right. You might need stitches."

"We can take you," the girl in the leather mini skirt offered. She said it was a short distance to a hospital with a good emergency room. Her boyfriend, Mac, had two fingers sewed back on there. "Remember that, baby?" While Mac and his woman reminisced, Holly and I surveyed the damage. The front end of my car was wrapped around the pole. The engine was steaming and making weird noises.

"I can't leave it here, can I?"

Holly took my arm and led me to the couple's van. "We don't have a choice, you're bleeding all over the place. Let's go to the hospital, then we'll call the police or a tow truck. You need to have that cut looked at."

During the 10-minute drive to the hospital, Holly and I sat in silence. I was too high to speak. My head was killing me and I was embarrassed and humiliated. I had wanted so much to show Holly that I was making it on my own and this was how it was going to end. Before we entered the emergency room, Holly made me throw out the Quaaludes and coke I had stashed in my purse.

Once I was in an emergency room bay and the doctor was stitching my head, Holly called the police, who came and took our statements. Holly said that she'd been driving and she was so lucid and convincing, the cop didn't even ask her to take a Breathalyzer test. She told them a cat ran in front of us and when she swerved to avoid it she lost control and had driven onto the sidewalk. I was so grateful to her for taking care of everything. But I was too high to say it.

Finally the doctor finished, and when I could stand up without feeling dizzy, we called a cab and headed back to my apartment. I was pitiful, mumbling on and on to Holly about how sorry I was, how I hoped she'd forgive me for ruining the evening. The cabby finally closed the divider, tired of hearing my pathetic comments.

"Stop apologizing, Jess, you just got a little too high." Holly was being kind. I knew she knew I was a mess.

"I wanted you to have such a good time and I ruined it," I whimpered.

"I had a fine time. I can't imagine what else we would have done. Okay, the car wreck wasn't fun. Next time, maybe you'll let me drive. But we survived and that's what matters."

"You had a rotten time. I'm sorry."

"Jess, stop it. You showed me a good time—"

"No," I interrupted, "I didn't and you know it." The cab stopped in front of my apartment and I fumbled in my purse for money. Holly handed him a bill, told him to keep the change and we made our way inside. I was still dizzy, but grateful for the painkiller the doctor had given me to stop the throbbing in my head. "Do you think I'll have a scar?"

"Probably not one anyone will see. It's pretty far back on your forehead." Holly checked the bandages as I unlocked the door. "Does it hurt?"

"Nothing like before. He gave me Percocets. Do you want one? They really work."

"You'll need them tomorrow. I have a feeling you're going to have one hell of a headache."

Holly got me a glass of water and I sat on my beautiful new sofa and tried to make sense of the evening. "Thanks again for dealing with the police. I'm sure they'd have busted me if they knew. It would have been so humiliating."

"It seemed like the right thing to do." She sounded tired and distracted. "So, does the sofa in my room turn into a bed? I'm exhausted and my ribs are sore. I'd love to go to bed."

"Fine, let's go to bed. I'm beat, too." I helped her pull out the sofa bed and asked her to wake me before she left. I stumbled into my bedroom, closed the door and dropped onto my bed. The Percocets combined with the Quaaludes and the booze put me out immediately.

The next morning Holly woke me gently. I was in a fog until the events of the evening came rushing back. "Jess, I have to go. Registration is at 9:00. How do you feel?"

I touched my head and winced. "Terrible. God, Holly, do you have to go so soon? We hardly had any time to talk." I reached up and she held my hand.

"I know. But we had fun." I knew she was lying. "The towing service called, they have your car. I left the address on the kitchen counter." She handed me a glass of juice and a pain pill.

"Thank you, God, I'm a mess." I was suddenly panicked. "Can't you please stay?"

"I really have to go. I'll call you later today and maybe we can meet for breakfast tomorrow before my first session."

"That would be great. Have a good time."

"I will. Hey, please take care of yourself, okay?" Holly waved from my bedroom doorway.

"I will, I promise." When I heard the door close, I swallowed the Percocet, buried my face in the pillow, and cried myself to sleep.

CHAPTER TWENTY-SIX

Zoe had sat silently through Jess's story, hardly believing that what Jess was telling her could be true. When a few moments passed and Jess hadn't spoken, Zoe blurted out, "You're lucky you didn't die."

Jess nodded. "The accident totaled my car. But as scary as that was, it wasn't enough to make me give up drugs. It wasn't until Jamie died a year later that I finally saw where I was headed. He was killed as he drove the wrong way on the freeway. He plowed into another car, slaughtering three people. The autopsy found cocaine, Valium and twice the legal limit of alcohol in his system." But even without the drugs, Jess thought, I couldn't find my way, especially with men. In a town like Los Angeles, if you look pretty but feel worthless, you draw bad men like a magnet.

Zoe struggled for something to say. She was trying to reconcile the Jess who sat in front of her with the one she'd heard about in the story. "How did you finally stop?"

"I changed jobs, friends, moved to another apartment."

"Why did you do all those drugs, Jess?"

Jess took a long swallow of wine and emptied the glass. "I thought I was worthless and tried to prove it. Why does anyone self-destruct?"

Zoe shook her head in disbelief and Jess was sorry her answer had been so flippant. "Why would you ever feel worthless?"

"When someone you love abuses your trust . . ." Jess's voice trailed off.

"What do you mean?"

Jess took a breath. "They say it's supposed to get easier to talk about with time . . . but it's still hard. I was sexually abused. As a child. I didn't even remember it until after I was married."

"I'm so sorry." Jess nodded. "It was someone you loved?"

"My uncle."

"Uncle Jack?"

Hearing his name in this context made Jess sick to her stomach. Even after all this time. "Yes."

Zoe reached over to Jess and squeezed her hand. "I'm so sorry that happened. That should never have happened to you."

"It should never happen to any child. And it does and it does." Jess searched for more wine in the bottom of her glass. But it can never happen to me again, she reminded herself. Jess recaptured her stomach and took a breath. She felt lighter having admitted her secret to Zoe. Then came the pang of regret. Secrets shared could always be used against you; it was time for a change of subject. "You know, your mother was lucky to meet Kate when she did. They had a healthy lifestyle compared with the people I knew in the 70s. While I was partying and doing drugs, they were writing plays. Holly wrote, Kate directed. They made an amazing team."

"But she still hadn't told you the truth about who she was?"

"She wasn't telling me. Maybe she was afraid I wouldn't accept her. Maybe I didn't want to know. I guess I suspected it, though. It's like the elephant in the room. You tiptoe around it until one day someone yells, 'Hey, there's a damn elephant in this room.' That's how it was with us. I went to visit her once, before she told me she was gay. It was the most bizarre visit."

"You have to tell me about it. But first, let's eat. I'm starving and dinner is ready." Zoe ushered Jess into the dining room. She lit the candles, poured Jess wine and water, and set before Jess an odd looking, but delicious smelling vegetarian dish. Zoe dimmed the lights, sat down and held up her water glass.

"To new friends," she said, with a twinkle in her eyes. "Us." They clinked glasses and Zoe looked into Jess's eyes and smiled fully. The intensity of the connection clogged Jess's throat and she blinked back tears. Zoe sensed her discomfort and changed the subject. "So, you did finally meet Kate?"

"Barely. It was the year after Holly came to see me in L.A., and I'd just stopped doing drugs. I had a client meeting near Chicago. I was looking forward to meeting Kate and Andrew, and relaxing in a better environment than the one I'd been in, where I wouldn't feel the need to run to keep up. But Holly had other plans.

"In fact, she'd bought a new outfit so we could spend a hot night on the town. She picked me up in a limousine, wearing tight purple spandex pants and a tube top with sequins all over it under a sheer voile top. I hardly recognized her! I'd written her that Brad and I were taking disco lessons—he's my ex-husband, but we weren't married yet. She figured I'd want to go dancing."

"This is our limousine. One ride only," Holly laughed. The driver took my bag and opened the door for us. We climbed in and leaned into the upholstery.

"Holly, I can't believe you. Where did you get that outfit? It's so unlike you."

"Don't you like it?" I wasn't sure how to answer. "You're about to find out that the Midwest has just as much to offer as L.A."

She opened the refrigerator and pulled out champagne and two chilled glasses. "Ready to party?"

"I . . . sure, of course, if that's what you want."

"I figured it would be fun to check out the scene in my city, unless you don't want to?" She didn't want to and I didn't want to, but neither of us would say so.

Holly popped the cork and poured each of us a glass. We toasted to good times. I took a sip, then looked at Holly and smiled. "I can't wait to see your house."

"You will."

"I want to meet Andrew. You're engaged, right?"

Holly swallowed hard. "Kind of. Well, we go on and off. I mean we're still talking about having a baby, maybe . . . someday."

"And your other roommate, Kate, the director. She sounds interesting."

"You'll meet them. But tonight we're staying at the Ambassador Hotel. It's in the middle of everything that's happening; I reserved a room." I was surprised. "Andrew has to work, Kate has rehearsal and I want to show you a night on the town, Chicago style."

"Sounds great," I lied.

As the limo sped toward downtown, we sipped champagne and joked about the Playboy Club and the disastrous time we tried modeling. Safe topics because they were in our past. And because we each needed to perpetuate the lies we were living. We were in our late twenties and we talked about how John Travolta was hot, and we agreed it wasn't the Beatles that were more popular than Jesus, it was disco.

We dropped my bags off at the hotel, where I changed into an appropriate disco outfit, a long-sleeved, rust-colored leotard and a swirling black nylon skirt that wrapped around my waist. Holly couldn't believe that I happened to have just the right outfit. I didn't mention that I was only wearing what everyone was wearing.

"A girl should always be ready for an evening out," I teased her, blending my blush.

"Listen, you need to know something. I've invited a couple of guys from my dad's office. They're no great shakes or anything, but one of them has a membership to Faces—"

"Faces?"

"The hottest disco in Chicago. You'll love it. But these guys, I'm warning you, they aren't exactly what you'd call cool."

"Are they ugly? Stupid?"

"No, they're just guys, if you know what I mean."

"Just guys are okay."

We left the hotel and took a cab to Faces, where we met Allen and Chip. Allen was Italian, with slick, dark hair, combed straight back and large, weepy eyes. He wore black gabardine pants and a silky polyester shirt, gold necklaces, a diamond pinkie ring, and a big diamond-faced Rolex watch. His shoes were shinier than a pair of patent leather pumps. Chip was a younger, shorter version of Allen, and a little less studied. He had on the obligatory polyester shirt, but his had gold threads in it, and he wore it with jeans. He had on black platform shoes that were so high he tottered.

Allen slipped the host a bill, which got us a table next to the dance floor. Faces was Chicago's quintessential disco—dark burgundy walls, a big dance floor with mirrors everywhere. The walls and ceiling were mirrored, a large mirrored ball hung from the ceiling, even the dance floor was mirrored. We sat with our drinks, watching as the strobe lights kept time to the dance beat and illuminated the dancers dressed in full disco fashion. Most of the men wore polyester suits with open collared shirts, their lapels were so wide they disappeared off their shoulders. Most of the girls wore swirling skirts like mine, and everybody looked very high.

People were indiscreetly snorting cocaine at the next table, and somebody at another table was inhaling amyl nitrate. It was a total boy-girl scene, dating and flirting and dancing. I could tell

Holly was uncomfortable. I sat sipping my drink and watching Chip try to appear taller; I swear he was a foot shorter than me. Chip finally asked Holly to dance, and they gyrated together on the dance floor. When they returned, Allen brought out a vial and offered it to us.

"No, thanks, I think I'll pass." I looked away, feigning interest in the dancers. Staying clean was a daily struggle.

"You passing up drugs, Jess? I can't believe it." Holly looked up at me and smiled quizzically.

"I have work to do tomorrow, otherwise—"

"Oh, come on," Allen coaxed, "a little won't hurt you." I refused again, but when he passed the mirror to me to hand to Chip, I couldn't resist.

"Maybe I'll do one little line. I wouldn't want to be impolite." I made a small line, snorted it, then handed the mirror to Chip. Holly passed. A Donna Summer song came on and the four of us danced. After an hour, Allen decided we should move on to a bar called the Baton.

Chip seemed horrified. "Isn't that a drag show?"

"They're female impersonators," Allen said. "It's a great time." I looked at Holly who smiled and looked away.

We walked the two blocks to the Baton, and when we entered, the small room was crowded and smoky. Allen and Chip paid the cover and we were seated at a tiny table in the front row over to the side. "Barbra Streisand" stood on-stage lip-synching to a song from "Funny Girl;" the crowd was going crazy. Men and women came to the stage and stood in line to hand her bills. Chip and Allen went to the bar to get us drinks, probably afraid of being propositioned by a man if they went solo.

The place was filled with a bizarre mix of straight couples, as well as men with men and women with women. I was afraid to ask what Holly thought. Instead, I tapped her arm and yelled into her ear. "Our dates are really unique."

"You have a problem with the O'Neal dating service?" she shouted back. I laughed. "What's the matter? You haven't taken to one of our escorts yet?"

"I'm dying to take Allen back to California with me. He'd be one of kind there."

"Oh, he's one of a kind here," Holly shouted back.

I was beginning to feel comfortable with Holly when the guys returned with our drinks. We sat and sipped them as "Bette Midler" came out to a roaring crowd and started to lip-synch to "Boogie Woogie Bugle Boy." I thought the show was a blast. I'd never seen one, and I laughed at the irony of sitting with two guys from the suburbs drooling over the drop-dead gorgeous pre- and postoperative transsexuals.

Unfortunately, I was beginning to feel the need to get higher, and asked for another line. Allen handed me his vial and I headed to the women's room. When I got there the door was locked, but a sign on it read, "Real Women Only." Amused, I stood and waited. I was in a short hallway near the rest rooms and telephones, standing next to two guys who were making out. One was dark and nondescript, but I was struck by the other one because he was over six feet tall and had bright red hair. When a guy came out of the men's room, they entered together. I waited until "Judy Garland" came out of the women's room, then went in and did two lines. My old friend took the edge of strangeness off the evening. I looked into the mirror and promised myself I'd stop again as soon as I got back to L.A. When I came out, our dates were complaining about the crowd and wanted to go some place quieter.

"Why don't we go to our hotel for a drink? We'll sit in the Pump Room. Jess, you'll love it." Holly seemed eager to leave, and to the strains of Aretha Franklin singing "Natural Woman," we hailed a cab and went to the hotel.

We'd ordered our drinks when two women came in from the dining room and greeted Holly. They asked how her writing was going and told her they were celebrating an anniversary. She didn't ask what kind and didn't introduce them to the rest of us.

"How's Kate?" one of them asked.

"Fine. She's in rehearsal for the Frida Kahlo piece at Links Hall," Holly said, stirring her drink.

"Say hello to her for me."

"Sure."

"Who were they?" Allen couldn't resist. I knew exactly what he was thinking.

"Some friends of my roommate's." Just then one of them came back and handed her an earring.

"Holly, I've been carrying this around with me for weeks. You left it at our house the last time you came for dinner." Holly's face turned purple as she took the jewelry.

We finished our drinks and the guys left us at the elevator, but not before Allen offered to get an extra room. When we got upstairs Holly and I talked for awhile, but not about anything personal. Was I going to tell her I was having trouble giving up drugs? Was she going to tell me she was gay? I went to sleep that night, feeling estranged from Holly and from myself.

I'd be spending the next two days in Milwaukee, but made Holly promise to show me where she lived when I came back through Chicago. She agreed and saw me to the train.

On my return, she was late picking me up from the train station, so I only had a little time to visit before I had to leave for the airport.

Holly, Kate and Andrew lived in a huge three-bedroom apartment in the Wicker Park area of Chicago, a pretty rough neighborhood that Holly claimed was beginning to gentrify. Their home looked like what it was, a haven for three artists who chose to earn a meager living so they'd have time to create art. Andrew had started making furniture and his tables and chairs were everywhere, along with Holly's and Kate's books, plays and posters from various productions. It looked eclectic and lived in, but Holly hustled me through so fast I don't remember much else. She made certain I knew that there was a Kate's room, an Andrew's room and a Holly's room. In the living room she introduced me to Kate, an imposing woman with the brightest blue eyes I've ever seen. She greeted me warmly, but Holly whisked me away so quickly, we barely had time to speak.

After that, Holly took me to the garage to meet Andrew. He was sculpting a tall metal structure. He was very tall with red hair, and when he took off his safety glasses, I told him he looked exactly like a guy I'd seen at the Baton two nights earlier. He started to answer me enthusiastically, then stopped and looked at Holly. She was beet red and said nothing. We left and I knew everything.

Jess sat, twirling the stem of her wine glass. "Later, I found out that no one knew about Holly's real life. She'd kept being gay a secret from her family and from her straight friends. Andrew was a front for her. Her family thought she was living with him, and of course they disapproved even of that. Kate was semi-reclusive herself, but she knew the psychic drain Holly's world-juggling act caused. Holly didn't see it herself for a long time. Years later, she told me that during those years she felt like she was suffocating.

"So I knew then, but I didn't say anything. Holly and I had officially grown up," Jess said, in a self-mocking tone, "we'd become expert at covering up."

"Where's Andrew now? Maybe I can contact him?"

"I'm sorry. Andrew died of AIDS in the late 80s."

"Kate's dead, Andrew's dead. You're the only one who really knows." Jess nodded, but didn't speak. Zoe finally broke the silence. "When did my mother finally tell you about Kate?"

Jess started to answer when the doorbell interrupted her. Startled, she made a move to stand, then froze in her chair.

"Were you expecting someone?" Zoe asked. "It's after 10:00." Jess sat perfectly still, but her heart was pounding. She didn't answer. "Do you want me to get it?" Zoe started to stand as Jess jumped up.

"No, I'll get it." Still, she made no move toward the door.

"It's him, isn't it?" Zoe asked, a note of disgust in her voice.

"Yes."

"And you're going to let him in?" Zoe was standing now, too, staring hard at Jess.

"I have to deal with Eric my own way. This is probably a good time for you to go to bed." The bell rang again and both women jumped. Jess moved toward the door.

Zoe turned to her. "Why are you doing this, Jess? You know where he's been. I think you should tell him to go to hell."

Jess spun around. "It must be nice to be young and have a perfectly clear view of things. Someday you'll realize that everything isn't black and white. In real life everything is gray."

"This is black and white and you know it." Zoe grabbed a journal, turned and walked down the hall.

Jess watched Zoe enter the office and close the door, then she moved slowly to the front door. Her heart was pounding and her mouth was dry. She should tell him she knew about Harper, that she was tired of playing this game.

She opened the door. Eric stood there looking gorgeous, a lighted cigar in hand, his blonde, gray-streaked hair disheveled, polo shirt slightly askew, smiling his three-scotch smile. "Hi, Jess."

He stuck his head in and looked around. "Your little friend gone to bed?"

"Yes, and I was just headed there myself."

"Perfect." He grabbed her around the waist and pulled her close. She could smell the alcohol on his breath and the strong scent of cologne, obviously recently applied. Jess pulled away, closing the door behind him. "Is the bar still open? I'd love a drink? I've got so much to tell you. It was a very interesting trip." Eric took off his coat and laid it on the chair, then followed Jess into the kitchen.

"Where were you tonight?" Jess asked coolly, pulling the bottle of scotch from the cupboard. Eric was already filling a glass with ice.

"The club. I worked out, had a couple drinks at the bar next door." He sounded convincing. "I have to tell you Jess, this Hong Kong trip was a real eye opener. We think too small at our firm, and we're losing out on business in the international marketplace. We ought to be strategizing with every one of our clients on how they can take advantage of global markets. The opportunities are infinite. I tell you, Monday morning I'm going to get face time with John and Barry and pitch them on the idea. This is big, Jess, very big." He paced, dropping ashes on the floor as he gestured with his cigar. He continued talking loudly and enthusiastically about important changes in Africa, Asia, Russia, the huge opportunities on every front.

Jess poured herself a glass of wine and leaned against the counter. This was a scene they'd played out dozens of times. Eric and his brainstorm in need of a sounding board. Jess played the audience role perfectly, commenting now and then but mostly listening, nodding until he wound down. Tonight Jess wasn't hearing his words. She was too busy imagining Eric with Harper, her sitting attentively, listening, admiring. Did they have sex? No, that wasn't Eric's style. He'd take it slow, impress the hell out of her, bask in the light of her adoration a while before he actually plucked the fruit.

"And you're going to be a big part of all this, Jess." The sound of her name startled her, and she looked to Eric. "I'm going to open an international office, probably in Hong Kong, maybe one in London. This will be your big chance to get international experience. You know, that's all you're missing to make you real VP material." He stopped pacing and stood near her, leaning against the counter.

"You'd want me to manage the creative team at an international office from here?" Jess asked, trying to understand exactly what he was proposing.

Eric took a drink of scotch and a puff of his cigar. "Of course not, the company would move you. And I'm not talking only about creative. I think it's time you broadened your view. How does VP and General Manager sound?"

"You're kidding, right?" She felt a flicker of excitement. "I mean, it'd be a terrific opportunity." He's reeling me in, she thought. And she took the bait. Suddenly, Harper and the ProbTech account didn't matter. With Eric's help, she could move up. A vice presidency. And so many problems would be solved if she left, moved somewhere new, started over. Again. "But surely there are more senior people than me who'd want this job."

"Maybe. But no one with your creative sense and a feel for how this business works. After all, you've learned from the master." He laughed, then went on. "Plus, you're great with clients, and you're ambitious as hell. That's something I've always loved about you." He took another sip of scotch, savoring its flavor and her attention. "There will be a lot of competition for this opening," he said, then swallowed the last of his scotch and pulled her close. "But then, you have the inside track." He said it with a wink, and Jess didn't resist as he pushed her against the counter.

She moved into his embrace and wondered what it would take, what she'd have to do to get a VP title in front of her name. At that moment Eric turned to kiss her, and she knew exactly what was required.

CHAPTER TWENTY-SEVEN

Zoe sat on the sofa bed, fuming. Even though the office door was closed, she could hear Eric's deep voice beyond it. She began stuffing her clothes and books into her backpack and when her photographs slipped out, she looked hard at Adam's picture. She needed to talk to him. Even though he'd slept with Meredith, at least he didn't lie to her about it. She quickly dialed his number, got his machine and left Jess's number. She hung up and was sorry she'd called. He was probably at Meredith's.

Zoe put her head on Jess's desk, too dispirited to cry. She lifted her head when she heard Jess and Eric talking softly in the hallway. You're no different from the rest of them, she thought. You're as full of compromises and lies as my parents. She put on the Woodstock documentary to drown out their voices, now coming from Jess's bedroom. She crawled under the covers and tried to find some comfort in the pages of her mother's journal.

June 18, 1982

I'm on a plane to Sioux City to be a bridesmaid at Jess's wedding. I feel like such a shit. A failure as a human being, an undeserving wretch.

When the invitation arrived, addressed to "Holly O'Neal and

Guest," I didn't show it to Kate. So when I was throwing clothes into my suitcase, in a last-ditch effort to leave on time, she picked up the invitation from the top of my dresser and handed it to me.

"This says it's for you and a guest. Why didn't you invite me?"

I grabbed the envelope out of her hand and looked at it as if that were the first time I'd seen it. I threw it into the suitcase and turned away to answer her. "I knew you wouldn't want to go. You hate this kind of thing."

"Maybe I would. Why didn't you ask me?"

"I'm sorry."

"She still doesn't know about us, does she?"

"I haven't told her yet."

"How much longer are you going to do this, Holly?"

"I don't have time for this right now."

"Jess is your best friend, isn't she?"

"She was. Is. We're as different as two people can be. But I'd do anything for her. Don't ask me why."

"You'd pretend for her? When are you going to tell her?"

I grimaced as I tried on the thought, then immediately discharged it. "I don't know."

Kate crossed her arms across her chest. "I just can't understand what you gain by lying. Aren't you proud of who you are?"

"When I'm with you I am."

"You of all people, deserve to live honestly."

"But if she knew—"

"If she knew, she'd either accept you or reject you. If she rejects you for loving me, she's not worthy of you." Then she said the words that made it clear. "Holly, if you don't ever risk being wrong, you'll never be right."

I know she's right, I can't risk losing anything. But Kate knows completely who she is, and accepts that, so no one can shake her confidence in herself. "Who made you so smart?" I asked her.

"I did," she answered, and I bounded into her arms and felt as loved as I imagine any human being has ever felt. And free, so free.

Thirty thousand feet up and I keep flashing back to the disappointment on Kate's face. My life has gotten smaller and smaller, and I wonder if that isn't because I'm such a coward. I keep people at a distance so I won't have to explain myself to them. "Just say it," I can hear Kate say. She can say it. Why can't I? What would happen if I told Jess? How would I tell her?

I just came back from the rest room where I practiced in the mirror: "Jess, I'm gay." Too cold. "Jess, I have something I want you to know about me, and that something is I sleep with women, well, one woman, Kate." No, she doesn't need to know about my sex life. "Jess, I know you're not going to believe this, but I'm gay. I have been for a long time now." No, she'll think I've always wanted to sleep with her. "Jess, fuck you, I'm gay, okay?" That's more like how I want it to be. I want not to care what Jess thinks of it or of me. But it does. Because what if she rejects me? What if, what if, what if? I can feel my stomach knot.

I think about Kate and how much she loves me, so much that she's willing to take me as I am—imperfect and cowardly. And in spite of her usually tough demeanor, I knew I'd hurt her when she found the invitation. Why am I protecting anyone else, when look what I've done to Kate? I'll tell Jess the minute I see her.

Later

I'm sitting on the hide-a-bed in the Martin's den, trying hard to focus, reading the titles off the rows of *Reader's Digest Condensed Books*. I turned off the light and tried to sleep by practicing my yoga breathing. It didn't work. The air in this den is stuffy and thick, and even though it's June, the windows are closed and locked.

I didn't tell Jess the minute I saw her, I didn't tell her at the rehearsal, and I didn't tell her at the dinner. I wish I could forget all of it, especially what Jess said to me on her front porch a half hour ago. "Maybe you should apply that to your own life."

I miss Kate—it was a mistake to come here alone—I feel so estranged from Jess. It was such a bizarre day; it felt weird from the minute I arrived at her folks' house in Clear Lake.

I got out of the rental car and Jess clung to me almost desperately. I wanted to feel good about seeing her, but it seemed like we were in two different universes. Which we were, the universe of the wedding and the universe of the homosexual. She showed me her ring. "A full carat," she gloated. Jess met Brad in L.A. a few years ago. He's a real estate agent in Santa Monica, I guess his father is one, too, and they're making a killing. So Jess is still on the fast track.

I got ushered into the house by Jess and her sister, Kayla, where Jess mocked her wedding gifts. So far she's unwrapped two macramé plant holders, a large floating candle, a zodiac wall hanging, a crocheted toaster cover, two sets of flowered towels and a big sunburst wall clock. She said she'll have a garage sale when she gets back to L.A., or maybe just donate the stuff to the Salvation Army. She'd hoped for cash, so she could buy her own china in her colors—salmon and seafoam green. Despite the gifts, everyone was in a festive mood, and I rationalized that I shouldn't spoil the fun by telling Jess I was in love with a woman.

We drove around drinking wine—Jess, Kayla, and me—and doing last minute errands. For once, Jess wasn't her usual organized self. She complained about not having had time to buy her dress in L.A., so she was forced to go to a local place, Lana's Fashion Farm—what a name—and buy a dress that needed major alterations. (Kayla and I are wearing chiffon things in shades of green, with capes—one of those looks-great-going-down-the-isle, never-wearing-this-again kind of dresses.) Jess's dress wasn't ready, so we have to go tomorrow, the day of the wedding, to pick it up. That was bad enough, but when we went to get the flowers, Jess went ballistic. She'd ordered white gardenias and calla lilies, but her order had been cancelled for some reason and they offered her daisies and tulips. Kayla knew a florist in another town, so the problem was resolved. But Jess only became more short-tempered and edgy as the day wore on.

Her mood worsened when Brad, his brother, Carl, and his best man, Judd, were late for the wedding rehearsal. We stood around at the church until the minister said we'd better start. Just as Jess's dad was about to walk her down the aisle they sauntered in, smelling of alcohol. Brad was all smiles and played "mister charming," kissing all the women, looking the men straight in the eyes and giving them the warm handshake. He apologized for being late, but I don't think he meant it. Then he took his place next to Jess at the altar and we finished the rehearsal.

In the car on the way to dinner, he acted like it was Jess's fault he'd been late. They argued in the car, but Brad turned up the music and since I was in the back with Carl and Judd, I couldn't hear what they said.

At the country club, I went downstairs to the rest room. As I rounded the corner on my way out, I saw them. Jess took Brad's arm as he walked by her.

"Please Brad, don't be mad—this night means so much to me. I know this is a nightmare for you but—"

"What is your problem?" He pulled his arm out of her grasp. "Jesus, I'm here aren't I? Why the hell are you still whining?"

"You were supposed to be back early and everything went wrong. The dress wasn't right and my flowers didn't get delivered because you gave them a bad credit card." Tears filled Jess's eyes.

"It's never enough, is it? No matter what I do, you're never satisfied. What exactly is it you want from me?" He glared at Jess who stared back, her lips trembling.

"If you'd just treat me like you loved me. I was so embarrassed today."

He grabbed her arm and pushed her to the wall. "Let me tell you something. You dragged me into this stupid little town for your fairy tale wedding. You want to talk about embarrassed? This is a trailer trash circus." He twisted her arm. "I don't want to hear anymore about how I should act. Not one word. And no more whining. Got it?" He put his face close to hers and then his fingers were on her face, moving her mouth. "Say it, 'No more whining.'"

"Stop it, you're hurting me."

I had to say something. "Leave her alone."

They both turned toward me and he let her go.

"Just a little misunderstanding," he said. Then he left, but not before he berated her one last time. "Better fix your face, your mascara's running. I'll be in the bar."

I ran to her. "Are you all right? Did he hurt you?"

"We had an argument, that's all."

I tried to take her arm, but she pulled away. "That looked like more than an argument. Are you hurt?"

"He gets this way sometimes when he drinks. It's my fault, I've put a lot of stress on him with this wedding. We should have gotten married in Los Angeles." She wiped the tears away and straightened herself.

"Let me see your arm."

"It's nothing."

"Your arm is red. Are you sure you're all right?"

"Drop it."

"Jess—"

"What?" She was cold and accusatory in a way I'd never seen before. I couldn't say what I felt. I let it go.

"Nothing. Never mind."

After an hour of cocktails, we sat down for dinner. It was painful to watch the toasts and feel the goodwill and know that for Kate and me, life would never be like that. Most of the people in that room would view my life as a failure to measure up to the standards set by generations of family tradition, a failure to participate in what parents have children for, to have children of their own and leave a legacy. Seeing the warm conviviality in that room, I was jealous of Jess for the validation she was receiving.

Later, back at the Martins', Jess said she was tired and went upstairs to bed. Everybody else was drunk and happy, or drunk enough to think they were happy. Bert, Jess's dad, offered us all a nightcap. We sat in the kitchen, and did a postmortem on the dinner. When I finally made my way to the hide-a-bed, I noticed Jess sitting on the front porch.

"Jess . . .?" She jumped, startled, and wiped away tears. "What's the matter? What is it?"

"I . . . don't know."

I sat down next to her and felt her body tense. "It's okay, cry if you want. I think it's allowed the night before your wedding."

"It's such a big step. After tomorrow, that's it, there's no turning back."

"Are you sure you want to go through with this?"

She moved away from me. "What do you mean?"

"There's no rule that says you have to get married tomorrow. If you're not sure, you can wait."

She got defensive. "Of course I'm sure. Of course I want to get married. It's all this pressure and being here in this house . . . I'll be fine."

"Okay. But be honest with me. Did Brad hurt you?"

"He would never hurt me." She said this slowly, with daggers. I tried to lighten the conversation.

"It's just that you know how much I hate violence. I can't even kill spiders."

"We had an argument, okay? It was my fault anyway, coming to Iowa to have this stupid wedding."

"Please Jess, don't lie to me if it's more than that. You know what they say about lying. Every time you do it, you lose a little blood."

"Well, maybe you should apply that to your own life."

"I never lied to you," I said, lying.

"Yes, well, try that line on someone else." What could I say to that? We sat—neither of us said a word for several minutes. Then she got up and said she was going to bed. I stayed on the porch steps, cursing myself.

I tossed in bed and realized there would never be a right time. I debated whether or not to call Kate and ask her what I should do. But I knew what she'd say: "Be honest." I made my ten thousandth vow. I'd tell Jess the first moment I could.

I don't want to be at this wedding. How long will I give this marriage? A year? Two? No matter what Jess sees in this guy, he's a loser. I don't care who his father is or what his prospects are. I wish Kate were here.

June 20, 1982

I'm going home and I couldn't be happier. I never want to see Iowa again. The wedding is over, and I made my peace with Jess.

The morning of the wedding, I woke up to the smell of coffee and bacon frying. I went into the kitchen and Celeste and Bert and Kayla were there, showing the wear of too much celebrating the night before. Jess was still upstairs, and I cursed myself for not immediately marching upstairs and telling her about Kate. But Bert offered me coffee, which I accepted, and a bit of "the hair of the dog," which I declined, and it was easier to sit and chat about the rehearsal dinner than face Jess. When she came downstairs, she'd practically lost her voice and hardly spoke. She barely looked at me.

We went to the church, where Kayla stuck close by Jess. We got dressed and I could feel myself getting caught up in the wedding frenzy again. How easy it would be, I thought, not to say anything, to just let it go.

I found myself with Jess, alone in the bathroom before the ceremony. She told me how important it was that I was by her side on her wedding day. It was the perfect time and I started to tell her, but then her mother walked in.

So finally, we were standing at the back of the church, Jess and I, before she was to walk down the aisle. Bert had gone off for a final smoke, and Kayla ran to get Kleenex. We were alone. Her face was turned toward a big stained glass window. She looked absolutely regal—beautiful, soft, expectant, yearning for a future of fulfilled promises. But her lower lip was trembling. I walked up to her and felt my own knees wobble. It was now or never.

"Jess, stay right where you are. I have something to tell you." She made a move toward me, but I stopped her. "Don't move and don't look at me. I've got to say this and if I don't say it now, I never will. We talked last night about telling the truth. And about lying. You were right. I have been lying to you. For a long time. I can't do it any more." I touched her arm, covered with makeup to hide the bruise where Brad had twisted it. She winced, pulled away and made a turn toward me.

"Don't—"

"Don't say anything. And don't look at me or I won't be able to finish. Let me finish." This is about the truth . . . I love you and I need to tell you the truth . . . I'm gay. Okay?"

"What?"

"Do I have to repeat it? It was hard enough saying it once." She took a moment, then twisted her face and moved away from me. "You're the first person I've ever told this to—"

"That you're in love with me? Holly, how could you do this to me? And now?" It took me a moment to realize what she thought I'd said. "That's so like you, always picking the worst time to throw something like this at me—"

"Wait a minute, Jess! I'm not in love with you—"

"You're not?"

"No! I'm in love with Kate. I love Kate. And right after I see you get married, I'm going home to her. I've waited 10 years to be able to say it, and I said it to you, and you know what, it's not so bad. The sky didn't fall. Lightning didn't strike me dead. You know what else? I'm free. And I want you to know, that if you ever need me, I'll be there for you. All you have to do is ask." Then I giggled. "God, I did great. That was great."

Jess looked at me hard, like she didn't know what I was talking about, but I didn't care. Then she smiled quizzically and said, "Well, God, what am I supposed to say? I guess—congratulations. If you're happy, I'm happy for you." I kissed her cheek, told her I loved her, then Bert came and we started down the aisle. I was beaming. But when it came time to make her vows, Jess had almost lost her voice. Her "I do" was a small quiet squeak.

But I'm free. I'm finally and forever free.

Zoe closed the book, turned over in bed and cried. Her mother may have been free, but she'd left Zoe with a hole. And Jess was the only person who could tell her what she needed desperately to know. Her mother was dead, but somewhere she had a father.

"You were born one month early." Joanne had told her that; it was one of the few things she knew for certain about her birth, and she clung to it. Jess hadn't mentioned names of Holly's boyfriends, except for David Delaney. And she seemed certain he wasn't Zoe's father. If Jess did know her birth father, why wasn't she talking? Was she trying to protect Zoe? Or maybe she was trying to protect her father? But Jess had no right to protect anyone. If she knows, I have a right to know, too, Zoe thought. She circled and circled the unanswered questions, then rose and went into the kitchen for a glass of water.

She saw Jess sitting alone on her deck, smoking a cigarette. Zoe brought the water out and sat in the lounge chair opposite her. Jess didn't speak or even look up, she just sat with her feet up to her knees, staring out at the bay. Her hair had loosened from the barrette, a large, dark brown strand hung over one eye. They sat in silence while the dark October night enveloped them.

"I was just thinking that maybe my father is someone very important. I mean, maybe he's a scholar, an ambassador, or a musician. Maybe he'd like to know me. Maybe he has a wife who can't have children, and they've tried and tried and she can't have kids . . . maybe they adopted. And maybe if he knew he had a child, he'd want to know me."

Jess stared past Zoe while she talked. When she finished, Jess shook her head slowly. "You've got to give this up, Zoe. You aren't going to find your father."

"If you knew, would you tell me?"

"It was such a long time ago."

"Then you do know. It isn't right, you know, to keep it from me. I have a father and I deserve to know who he is. He exists, if he hasn't died, too."

"Nothing good can come from going down that path. It'll only bring you more pain. Haven't you had enough?"

"How do you know?"

"I guess I don't," Jess lied.

"The pain of not knowing is the worst pain of all. You don't understand anything about me; I've tried to explain myself to you, and you haven't listened. When are you going to start listening to me? I want you to tell me everything. You said you wouldn't lie to me. I want the truth. I deserve the truth." Jess's lips formed a straight line against the battle raging inside. She looked at Zoe with cold eyes. Zoe didn't notice and pressed on.

"What makes you think you have the right to be the gate-keeper? Does it give you a feeling of power? Well, it's all a facade. You don't have any real power. You let that guy come over here, even though you knew he'd been with someone else. Did he tell you where he'd been? I heard you in your bedroom. You fucked him, didn't you? Why did you do that? It's amazing what a good show you put on, but that's all this is. The car, the hip job, the mar-ried boyfriend. All show. I don't know what my mother ever saw in you."

Zoe's words stung Jess, then they settled in and joined the chorus of voices already playing in her heart. There was Celeste's voice, the voice of perpetual disappointment. There was her father who spoke the words of unconditional love but who was always away. There were voices of so many men, enamored at first, then unsatisfied, abusive. All the voices melded together and formed a dark, empty pond, a pond without life, without hope.

Jess finally took a long drag off her cigarette, turned her head and spoke. Her voice was cold and emotionless. "You want to know who your father is?" She paused, then continued. "He's nobody. You don't want to be protected from this, all right. The night of that Hawaiian party, Holly had sex with two guys, two strangers. They were two nameless guys we met there. We made a fire on the beach. There were four of us. I went off with one of the guys. I don't know what happened to Will. But Holly stayed behind with the other two boys, and later she told me she had sex with both of them. We didn't know their names, we didn't know anything about them except that one of them turned out to be your father. Holly made me promise never to tell. I vowed I wouldn't. Are you happy now?"

"But maybe—"

"No. I am not going to help you find one of the two men who gave you half your genes. Because that's all he did. The link breaks here, Zoe. Give it up. Paul and Joanne parented you, not perfectly, but the best they knew. Your father is Paul. Your mother is Joanne. I'm going to bed. Good night."

Jess left and Zoe gripped the edges of her chair. She felt sick, but forced herself not to run to the bathroom, not to purge herself of the horrible truth. Two guys, one of two strangers, was her father. The thought disgusted her, and she despised her mother. For all her high talk and the search for her own truth, she had sex with two guys on a beach. Willingly, Zoe thought. And from that, from that, came me. Zoe's mind raced to make sense of it. But all she could think about was her mother, being careless and thoughtless. I am the product of nobody, she thought. I am nobody. Reeling, Zoe lurched to Jess's office. She wanted to scream, but all she could do was cry.

CHAPTER TWENTY-EIGHT

Jess went to her bedroom and closed the door. She slipped her nightgown over her head and watched her hands shake as she struggled with the buttons. Lying face down on her tousled bed-clothes, she smelled Eric's cologne on her sheets. The scent usually made her feel close to him, but tonight it left her lonely and iso-lated. She sat up, turned on the television, channel surfed. Disgusted, she threw the remote across the room. She kept seeing the disillusionment on Zoe's face. What have I done? she thought. Jess remembered her promise to Holly, now broken. The voices started in her head; their accusations broke through the noise of the television and filled the room. Jess pressed hard on her tem-ples, trying to fend off the guilt of betrayal and the feelings of worthlessness. She had to do something. She turned the covers back, got out of bed, put on her robe.

She hurried into the living room and began putting Holly's journals into the box. If I can make it through this night, she thought, things have to get better tomorrow. I'll be able to think, I can make a plan with a clear head. She quickly lined the bottom of the box with the journals, then began putting in the books, *Sexual Behavior in the Human Male*, *Sisterhood is Powerful*.

Jess picked Holly's dog-eared copy of *The Courage to Be* off the floor. She sat back and examined its cover, remembering how the book was rarely out of Holly's hands freshman year. She read the jacket comments under a photograph of Professor Tillich: "This book is concerned with anxiety and its conquest. It is also concerned with the meaning of 'courage' in the history of Western thought and with its roots in the ground of reality."

She opened the book and slowly turned its pages, noting Holly's yellow and green highlighter markings and the comments she'd inked in the margins. At the end of the book, tucked deep within its final pages, was a piece of ruled notebook paper, tightly creased. She removed it and unfolded it carefully, then sat back on the sofa and read.

November 20, 1969

I'm sitting in the dark in my room—there's a slit of light from the kitchen seeping through the crack in the door. One candle is burning, just enough to write. Jess says she'll help me through this, she's going to save my life. We're going to find the baby a home and no one has to know but us. I should be happy. And I am—for that

But I lied to her. I told her I don't know who the father is; I told her that I had sex with those two guys on the beach when she left with what's-his-name. Of course she asked, but I couldn't tell her the truth. I couldn't say—"It was your uncle." She'd never forgive me and now I can't forgive myself. What kind of a person am I, if I can't tell Jess the truth? Jess, who is the first person I never wanted to lie to and promised myself I never would.

How can you admit something that's so awful you can't believe it yourself? How would I explain it? I wanted him to, then I didn't want him to but I let him do it anyway, and then I hated him for it and hated myself even more.

I play it over and over in my mind. How he came into the bath-room where I was crying, how he was so nice to me at first, how he told me not to worry. He said the kiss wasn't my fault, that I wasn't queer. He talked to me like a real person. He rubbed my shoulders, touched my face. But then he started to really touch me. I asked him to stop, he didn't, he just kept telling me I was pretty and smart. He told me there was a way to prove I wasn't that way, and I knew what he meant, and I let him go on for a while. Then I couldn't, I told him I wanted to leave. He said that if I did, he'd have to tell Jess and I was afraid of what he might say, and even more afraid of what she would think of me.

Finally I got scared and tried to push him off. I cried out for him to stop and he got angry and covered my mouth. "Shut up, you little bitch, they'll hear you." I was on the floor, my cheek was against the cold porcelain tub. I can't stop hearing his voice. I hear it everywhere, over and over: "Shut up, you little bitch, they'll hear you."

It's going to be a girl and I'm going to name her Zoe. She'll take all the bad and make it good. As for me, my life is now a lie and I won't ever write again. Because if you can't live with the truth, then nothing has any meaning at all.

Shocked and sickened, Jess crumpled the page into her palm. A voice deep inside of her wanted to scream out, "No, not you, I won't let it be you!" She pulled her arms around her stomach, hugging her waist. She moaned softly, tears filled her eyes. "Oh God, not you." She sat back as tears streamed down her cheeks; she thought of Holly and Zoe and of her own unforgivable sins. She opened her fist, flattened the page, read it again. She stared at it until bitterness overwhelmed her.

CHAPTER TWENTY-NINE

The note still clutched in her hand, Jess stood and stumbled to her bedroom. She closed the door and curled up on her bed, trying to breathe, to think, to understand. Uncle Jack. Holly. Zoe. She closed her eyes but couldn't shut out their faces, the swirl of remembered features.

Jess opened her eyes, sat up and stuffed the journal page into her robe pocket. Grabbing the box of photographs from under her bed, she flipped through them until she found it—it was a photo of her uncle and Shelley at the party. He wore tan pants and a Hawaiian print shirt. He had a lei around his neck and he was smiling. His arm was around Shelley, his hand gripping her shoulder, pulling her close to him. That wavy hair. Those hands. The thought of them touching Holly sickened her. She forced herself to look, hoping it wasn't true. But Zoe had his nose, the same wide forehead. Jess sat, staring at the photograph, shaking. "You bastard," she said the words out loud. "You fucking bastard."

The next picture was of Holly. She stood under a lantern by the pool, wearing the soft pink dress Shelley had made for her, the breeze blowing her hair. She looked young, innocent and ripe for abuse. She held a drink toward the camera in a mock toast to Jess, who remembered taking the picture. "You were barely more than a child," Jess whispered, holding the pictures side by side. She put the photographs back in the box and slid it under her bed.

She was sitting on her bed, staring out, grief-stricken, when Zoe knocked. Jess opened the door and Zoe rushed in, breathless, crying, her hands gesturing, shaking.

"I don't . . . want . . . to . . . be . . . alive," she stuttered. "I don't want to live in this fucked up, no good, terrible world. I hate this, I hate this, I hate this!"

Jess wrapped her arms around Zoe and pulled her close. "I'm so sorry." Zoe's body quaked. Jess led her to the bed and they sat together. Her head rested on Zoe's; Jess smelled her fresh, sweet hair. Zoe's loud sobs soon turned to hiccups, and Jess went to get her some water. She wanted to comfort Zoe, but how could she? Her own heart was a muddle of anger, sorrow and guilt. Was there anything she could say to Zoe now? Was there any way to soothe her?

The women sat together on the bed until Jess located the remote and turned to an old movie. They watched Greer Garson comfort a sleeping Ronald Colman in "Random Harvest." Jess remembered seeing the movie for the first time in the small den of her parents' home in Clear Lake. It was the tiny, dust and book-filled room where Uncle Jack slept when he visited.

Jess watched Zoe's face reflected in the mirror above the dresser across the room. Seeing her uncle's features she was both mesmerized and repulsed. He was there in the profile of her nose, her forehead; even the hairline was his, the straight line of hair with the perfect peak at the crown.

But the connection was intense, too. This was Holly's daughter and her own cousin. Part of her wanted to reach out to Zoe and tell her the truth. But how could she now, knowing how her uncle had violated Holly? She needed time to sort out the guilt and regret that consumed her. Another wave of revulsion came when she remembered what she had told Zoe about Uncle Jack. "When someone you love abuses your trust . . . I was sexually abused . . ."

She tried to remember Uncle Jack and Holly the night of the party on the ride home, but no images came. She'd been so angry with Holly and with herself, the rest of that night was a blur.

Then it struck her: You never told me, Holly. What must your secret have cost you? And when I finally told you about my own private hell, you kept it even then.

Jess couldn't bear her ruminations another second and got out of bed. Zoe stared at Ronald Colman, lost in his amnesia, looking forlorn and confused. Forgetting the past seemed a blessing. Jess went into the bathroom, wet a washcloth and pressed its warmth into her face. She looked at herself in the mirror. What was she going to do now? She was sorry she'd been so open with Zoe. You always pay for intimacy, she told herself, there's always that price.

And there was Eric. She was ashamed that Zoe had seen her in her weakest moments with him. "Why am I still doing this," she whispered into the washcloth. She thought of Holly, always so strong. Where did she get that? Jess wondered. I've always let myself be buffeted about, carried away by any wind that blows hard enough.

Her skin pink from the hot washcloth, Jess retrieved a towel from the rack. She held it to her face, then let the tears pour into it. "I'm sorry, Holly," she sobbed. The ache of her betrayal brought more tears. And now she had inflicted pain on Zoe, whose only crime was that she wanted to know her mother and father.

What would she tell Zoe? She'd come to Jess because she wanted to know who her birth father was. Should I tell her who he really is? Jess wondered, folding the towel back into place without any answers. As she opened the door, she prayed a silent prayer. Holly, please, please help me. Help me make it right.

Zoe had the covers to her chin, eyes staring at the television screen. Jess crawled in beside her and they watched the two lovers enter their small cottage by the bridge on their wedding day, unaware of the dangers ahead. Jess broke their silence and turned to Zoe. "Do you want to talk?"

"Not really."

"I do. I need to apologize to you. I should never have told you about your father."

"You mean my fathers? It's what I came to hear."

"I hope that's not all."

"My mother is dead and I'll never know who my father is. That's what's important."

"That is not what's important."

"Now, everything's a jumble; I have more questions, I . . ." Zoe's voice trailed off. They sat quietly, trying to focus on the details of the movie story. Finally, Zoe spoke. "My past adds up to a big zero. My father is nobody and my mother is nobody, either. I'm so fucking alone. I hate this world and everything in it."

"I'm sorry."

"I'm the one who should be sorry. What was I thinking? My mother abandoned me and my father is nobody. I'm so stupid; I should have believed my birth certificate: 'Father—unidentified.' That's what it says and it's true.

"All my life, I dreamed that there must have been this great romance between my parents and for some reason, some really good reason—a reason beyond the love they had for each other—they couldn't be together. Maybe his parents had forbidden the marriage because he was from a foreign country or was a different religion. Maybe my mother was a dancer or an actress, and her career came first. What bullshit! What a stupid fairy tale! My mother was a lesbian and my father is one of two strangers. I came from nothing."

"That isn't true."

"I always wanted to feel special. But I know that being wanted by your real parents is the most important thing. It's a fucking ironic joke now. I couldn't be less special. I'm just who I am and this is my life."

"You're wrong about that." Zoe pouted at Jess's words. "You're very special. You are the daughter of the most amazing woman I've ever known. You have Holly's honesty and her sense of right and wrong. I see it in everything you do and in everything you say." Jess spoke softly, but Zoe turned away.

"I want to tell you about something that happened to me. I want to tell you so you know what kind of friend she was and what she did for me. Your mother was the most important person in my life. I loved her more than I've ever loved anyone. As weak-willed as you think I am, I was a thousand times worse before your mother saved me." Jess took a breath. "I married the wrong man."

"Brad."

"Yes." Zoe sat up and looked at Jess. Jess turned down the volume on the movie and told her story. "I remember everything about that day . . ."

It was a Wednesday, early in the morning in the late fall. I woke from a fitful sleep when the clock radio blared music. I even remember the song, it was Joe Jackson singing, "Steppin' Out." I didn't move. I had to lie perfectly still so Brad would think I was still asleep, even though every part of me wanted to scream out in pain. My whole right side throbbed. I heard him stir and held my breath as he slammed at the radio, cutting off the music. He threw the covers back and stumbled to the bathroom, closing the door behind him. Still, I didn't stir. It wasn't until I heard the water running in the shower that I finally took a breath.

Slowly, I tried to move my right arm, but a bolt of pain shot through my body. Better to stay still until he dresses and leaves, I thought. I heard him humming. A few hours earlier he'd nearly killed me and now he was humming. What had started it? I tried to think through the pain. Of course, it was about my plans with Holly. She was coming to Los Angeles to meet with a director who wanted to produce one of her plays. We'd made lunch plans, plans I didn't share with Brad, couldn't share with Brad. I didn't share anything with Brad anymore.

When Holly called the night before to confirm, he'd answered and she'd told him the truth: we were meeting for lunch, she was looking forward to seeing me. Sweet Holly wouldn't understand about Brad and me. How could she? I'd been lying about my life for four years. I'd told her that we were happy, my marriage was great, we were in love.

It hadn't been so bad the first year, an occasional slap, a couple of bruises, an irrational outburst in public. Then Brad's dark side moved in permanently, and the past year had been a living hell. His real estate company had downsized, he'd taken a job with a small local firm and hated it. He was always in a foul mood, he had a drink in his hand whenever he was home and took all his anger out on me. I was never sure from one minute to the next what would set him off.

I had no friends anymore, Brad had made certain of that. He was jealous of everyone, even my women friends. And I'd gone through three jobs since we were married. I quit two because Brad was jealous of someone I worked with. I'd been fired from the last one because I'd taken too many sick days—too many days hiding at home, waiting for the bruises on my face to heal. For the past six months, I'd been selling ads for a community newspaper. It gave me the flexibility to take days off when I needed. That was my life.

Lying in bed, I thought about the day when Holly had called to tell me she'd be in town. My heart soared and for one brief moment I remembered the Jess that Holly knew. That Jess was bold and strong, she laughed and danced, she was ambitious and willful.

That Jess was gone. In her place was a weak, frightened shell of a woman who fabricated stories to keep everyone from knowing the truth. That particular day I looked pretty good, despite the months of abuse, so I figured I could get away without her suspecting. There were no noticeable bruises that a little makeup couldn't camouflage. I could spend two hours over lunch reminiscing with Holly, keep up the facade, further the myth. How hard could it be to pretend for a few hours? She wouldn't have to know the truth, and it would be so good to see her again.

But Brad had gone wild after Holly told him about our plans. He called me a slut and a lying whore, and put his fist through the wall in three places. He was especially threatened by anyone from my past who cared about me. He ranted about our planning a secret liaison, accused me of wanting Holly sexually, then he claimed Holly and I were meeting a gang of men to engage in perverted sex.

After a while I stopped listening, stopped being present. I shut down and just took the beating. I never cried out or screamed anymore when he hit me, I just huddled up and made myself as small as I could and tried to disappear. There was no use trying to protect myself from his blows, I couldn't get away from him anyway.

But this time, my subservience made him angrier. That's when he grabbed my arm and flung my body with so much force I thought I'd split apart. I fell forward and my face hit the arm of a chair. The pain kept me awake most of the night, but I was afraid to get up and take a pain pill, afraid if I did, he'd wake up and start again.

Suddenly, the bathroom door opened. I stiffened and slowed my breathing so he'd think I was asleep, a deceit I was skilled at. Drawers opened and closed. He dressed.

Finally, he was ready to leave. I could feel him standing above me. My heart was beating so hard I was sure he could hear it. And with a few words in his charming voice, he made sure I stayed a prisoner. "I'm sure you don't feel like going anywhere today. I'm taking your car in to have the oil changed. I'll call you later." He turned and walked out of the room. I lay perfectly still. The door downstairs slammed shut, I heard my car engine start and him drive away. I was finally alone.

I managed to sit up, holding my arm as still as I could to keep the throbbing to a minimum. My head hurt, too. The night before it had been impossible to keep track of exactly where the blows were landing. From the pain in my forehead, I was pretty sure a few had made their way to my face. I staggered to the bathroom, turned on the light and nearly fainted from the sight in the mirror. My right eye was a deep shade of purple, from the bridge of my nose past my temple. There was dried blood in my hair.

My vision blurred and I caught myself on the towel rack on my way to the floor. I sat with a thud and lowered my head to my knees. I tried to breathe steadily, to pull air into my lungs and push out the pain. Again and again I breathed, trying to bring myself back to life one more time.

My head felt clearer after the deep breathing, and I pulled myself up to the toilet seat. I reached to the medicine chest for the painkillers I'd gotten the time when four cracked ribs had sent me to the emergency room. Then, I'd told the doctor I was in a biking accident. When he saw the bruises on my side, he seemed to believe me and prescribed something with codeine. I'd been careful not to take them all. It made sense to save a few, to plan ahead.

I washed my face carefully and tried to rinse the blood out of my hair, then wandered out to the living room to survey the damage. The holes in the wall were fist size and evenly spaced above the couch. Nothing else appeared to be broken.

I called the office and told the receptionist I was too sick to come in. She sounded sympathetic, but I could tell she didn't believe me. I hung up the phone and, holding my arm, filled the teapot with water, turned on the stove and slipped out the sliding glass doors, desperate to breathe fresh air. The Los Angeles sky was clear blue and without a cloud, but the yard looked as unloved as I felt. The geraniums were overgrown and leaves covered the top of the pool. It had been months since anyone had been swimming.

Four years earlier, Brad's parents made the down payment on the house as a wedding present, and I thought I'd finally arrived. My life is good, I'd thought, I have a three-bedroom house with a swimming pool. But it wasn't good; it was never good. From the beginning it had been a struggle, now it was unbearable. After pouring myself a cup of tea, I returned to the patio and curled up on a lounge chair, pulled my robe around my legs. The sun felt kind and forgiving. It wasn't long before the painkiller kicked in, and I dozed.

A few hours later, the phone rang impatiently, again and again, waking me from my sleep. It took me a while to remember that the answering machine didn't work anymore. Brad had thrown a tantrum and smashed it the week before. Then, he'd been angry because he thought Kayla and I spent too much time on the phone.

I stood up quickly. My head spun and I almost fell. Then panic took hold. I had to answer the phone; it might be Brad and he'd be furious if he thought I wasn't home. But as I picked up the receiver, I remembered Holly and our lunch date. I couldn't talk to her now.

I held the phone to my ear, but said nothing. I figured that if it was Brad he'd say something so I'd know it was him. It wasn't Brad; it was Holly. I listened while she said my name two or three times, then I hung up without a word. It was the only thing I could do, I told myself. I had to keep my secret.

I checked the clock. 10:00. The codeine was beginning to wear off and the throbbing pain had returned to my arm. I was on my way from the bathroom after taking another painkiller when the phone rang again. I picked it up.

"Jess, Jess, I know you're there. Why won't you talk to me?" It was Holly again. I slammed the receiver down and sat on the side of the bed, tears filling my eyes. I cried, half out loud, "I can't talk to you. Don't you understand? Go away. Please go away and leave me alone. There's nothing you can do. It's all ruined, and there's nothing anyone can do."

I curled up in bed, covering my battered body with the blanket and pulling the sheet completely over my head. Lying there in a pale pink cocoon, I convinced myself that Holly would never understand. She couldn't stand cruelty of any kind. But then, Kate adored her. They shared everything and treated each other with love and respect. Everything Holly told me about their relationship had been good and healthy. Everything I told Holly about Brad and me had been a lie.

I slept again, this time for more than an hour. It was the sound of pounding on the door that finally woke me. I lay still, trying to get my bearings, remembering other times when Brad had forgotten his keys or been too drunk to unlock the door. I lay quietly, listening, fearing. But it wasn't Brad's voice I heard. It was Holly's.

"Jess, open the door. Jess, please open the door, I know you're in there. The woman at your office said you were too sick to work. Jess, please open up. I need to see you."

She sounded frantic and kept beating on the door, but I didn't move. Lie very still, I told myself, and she'll go away. They'll all go away, then the pain will go away and you can slip off and die. But Holly kept pounding. Then I heard a loud thud and a crash, and suddenly it was quiet. She'd broken the windowpane and was unlocking the door.

"Jess, it's me. Are you here, Jess?" I could hear her moving from room to room, calling my name. Finally, she was in the bedroom. "Jess? Jess, are you okay?" I felt her hand on my shoulder. I didn't move. She pulled the sheet away from my face and gasped, horrified at the sight. "Oh my God, Jess! What has he done to you?" She turned me toward her. "Oh, Jess, you're so hurt." I couldn't speak. I couldn't cry. She hugged me, but I couldn't hug her back. Finally, she pulled away and looked at me. "You're getting out of here. Right now."

"No!" I tried to shout, but my voice was hoarse, small. "I'm not going anywhere. I want you to leave." I sat up to show her the door and winced from the pain in my arm.

"You're crazy if you think I'm going anywhere without you. Have you seen your face?"

"You have to go. Please. You don't understand." I was holding my arm, trying to stop the shooting pain.

"I understand that you need help and I'm not going anywhere until you get it. Where can I find a suitcase?" Holly was up and opening drawer after drawer, pulling out my clothes and throwing them on the bed.

"This isn't what it looks like. We had a little fight. It was my fault. He didn't mean to hurt me."

Her anger was clear and determined. "That's bullshit and you know it. He beat you, Jess. He beat you black and blue and you're not staying here another minute." She found a duffel bag and began stuffing clothes into it. "Get up. You have to get dressed." I didn't move. "I'm not kidding, Jess, get out of bed. We're leaving and if you won't get dressed, I'll drag you out of here in your goddamned robe."

She kept up her whirlwind of activity, while I mumbled in protest. "You don't understand. It's complicated. I can't go." I tried to gesture with my right arm but the pain was so intense, I let out a loud cry and fell to my knees.

"What is it? Your arm?" She knelt next to me.

I was crying and could only nod. I tried to gesture toward the bathroom and managed to say the word "pills." Holly jumped up and ran to get them. She helped me sit up on the bed and held the water while I drank. There were tears in her eyes as she sat next to me and put her arm around my waist.

"God, Jess, I'm so sorry. You're right, I don't know anything about your life. But I do know that I love you too much to see you in pain. I can't bear it; I won't let you stay here."

Tears were tumbling out of my eyes so fast I thought they'd never stop. I couldn't talk, I couldn't think.

Holly got up, moved across the room to the closet and found a pair of jeans. She helped me put on one leg at a time, slowly and deliberately, being careful not to jar my arm.

"We'll go to the emergency room, unless you have a doctor you'd rather see. You can stay with me at my hotel. Is there money in the house? Do you have any money, or does he control that, too?" She asked question after question. I knew they were probably important questions, but I was in a stupor from the pills and lack of sleep and could only nod and point.

Holly took care of everything. She found my checkbook, packed my bag and helped me with my sweater. I watched her tie my shoes and wanted to tell her how sorry I was that I'd made such a mess of my life, how much I appreciated her help, how glad I was that she was there. But no words came.

Once we were in her rental car, I began to feel more lucid. The pain had subsided for the moment, and I was able to point Holly in the direction of my doctor's office. "Pull up to a pay phone," I said between swollen lips, "and let me call my doctor. If I tell him it's me, he'll see me right away. We've been through this before," I admitted.

"Okay, but if he can't see you right away, I'm taking you to the emergency room. Your arm is probably broken." Holly pulled into a convenience store and went in while I made the call. Afterward, waiting for her in the car, I felt strangely calm. Finally, someone knew the truth. Not just someone, Holly. I had no idea what I was going to do, but I felt better knowing she knew. I remembered the abortion in Chicago 20 years earlier, and the night in L.A. when she covered for me with the police and got us home safely. On the surface, Holly sometimes seemed indecisive, but inside she was a rock. And that day, I desperately needed her strength.

Holly opened the car door and handed me a bag. "Here, I brought you a soda, some pretzels and a couple of apples. Have you eaten today?" Holly closed her door and opened the Coke.

"I'm not hungry. Thanks, though. Dr. Kalish says to come now and I can go right in."

At his office, I told Holly I wanted to see my doctor alone. I didn't tell her I'd lied to him and said I'd been in a car accident. I couldn't bear to have Holly witness my cowardice firsthand. She protested, but I persisted and she finally relented.

In the examining room I kept the lie going, saying as little as necessary while Dr. Kalish poked and prodded around my shoulder. "It's dislocated, that's why it hurts so badly. I can reset it, which will hurt even more for a few minutes. But then it can begin to heal. Think you can stand a little jolt?" I nodded and he called the nurse in to help. It took only a few seconds to snap my arm back into place, but the pain was so intense, I screamed. After he gave me a shot for the pain, Dr. Kalish dismissed the nurse.

I sat, staring at the floor.

"Jess, I think we both know that you weren't in a car accident. I'm worried about you and want to help. I have friends in the police department and I know of a women's shelter where you'd be safe—"

"It's nothing like that," I interrupted. "I'll be fine. Thank you for fixing my arm." I stood up and turned to get my purse. I couldn't look at him.

He turned me around gently and handed me a card. "If you change your mind, this is my direct line and my home number is below that. I'll give you a prescription for codeine because your shoulder will hurt tonight. Do you have somewhere to go where you can get some rest?"

I nodded. "My best friend drove me here and she'll take care of me." I felt small and pitiful as I walked out of his office. When I saw Holly in the waiting room, I tried to regain my composure.

"What happened?" She jumped up when she saw me.

"Nothing much. My shoulder was dislocated, but Dr. Kalish and his nurse fixed it. It hurt like hell for a minute, but he gave me a shot and now I can't feel my feet touch the floor. Want me to drive?" I asked, trying to lighten things up.

"Not on your life. I may never let you drive again. I'm right outside." Holly helped me to the car and I noticed a bag from Macy's in the back seat.

"You went shopping while they were torturing me?"

"The mall was across the street, and I thought you needed a little something to cheer you up and cover that shiner," she said, pulling the bag into the front seat.

"Don't tell me, you bought me a mask. I hope it's a clown face with a big a red nose." As I talked, she pulled a navy wide-brimmed felt hat from the bag.

"I figured navy was good with jeans, right? And hopefully it'll make you feel a little less vulnerable. Here, let me put it on you." I fought back tears as she gently placed the hat on my head and pulled the brim down stylishly over my bruised eye. "It's you, don't you think?" She pulled the visor down so I could see myself in the mirror.

It was a beautiful hat, but I could still see the bruises and the sight made me wince. "Thanks. I may never take it off." I choked out the words, then gave her a hug with my good arm and tried not to cry.

"Okay, enough of this." She wiped her eyes and started the car. "I'm staying at the Marriott and I have two double beds. We can call room service and relax there."

"Holly, thanks, but I have to go home. It's not as bad as it looks and I can't abandon him." It was almost 1:00 and I thought that if I was lucky, Brad wouldn't realize I was gone. I'd talk to him; we'd make a plan, maybe go through counseling or a trial separation. He'd feel terrible once he found out about my arm. Maybe that would shock him into changing.

Holly turned the engine off. "You're kidding, right? You're not thinking about going back there?"

"He's my husband. We have to work this out and make some decisions, together. I'm not going to walk out on him."

"Jess, there's nothing to work out. The man beat you, and I'm guessing this isn't the first time. He deserves to be walked out on."

"You don't know what it's like. He's been under a terrible strain at work. Things will get better now." Holly didn't say anything, just stared at me. "I'm not going to fail at this marriage. You don't understand what it means to be married. It's a commitment: 'until death do us part.' It's not something you give up on," I argued.

"I know exactly what that kind of commitment is all about

and what it isn't about is being beaten until you bleed. Jess, don't you see this isn't about failing? He isn't worth it."

"You don't know anything about Brad, you've only met him once. He's not always this way and he loves me. He just feels insecure right now, and he's got a bad temper." Even I was having a hard time believing my story.

Holly started the car and pulled away. "You're coming with me and that's final. You aren't thinking straight and you need some rest."

"Holly, you might think you know what's best, but you don't. Please, turn around and drive me home. My arm is fine and I can sleep all afternoon there."

"I'm not taking you back there." She sped up.

"Goddamn it, Holly," I pleaded, "I have to play it out. Turn around, now!"

"No. You're not thinking straight."

"Brad won't understand. If I'm gone all night, it will only be worse." I felt the fear creep into my voice. I pleaded. "Holly, my marriage is the most important thing in my life. If I lose it, I'll have nothing. Please take me back. Please, please . . ."

"I'd never forgive myself." Holly kept driving and looked straight ahead. The freeway entrance was less than a block away.

"Stop and I'll walk home. I'm getting out." I moved to open my door, hoping to shock her so she'd stop. She went faster.

"Fine, jump. But I'm not stopping and I'm not slowing down. Jess, you're marriage isn't worth saving. The man beat you and now you're threatening to jump out of a moving car. Let me help you. You've got to let me help you."

As she drove the car onto the freeway, I felt my resistance fade. I began to sob. I was confused and overwhelmed and didn't have the strength to fight Holly.

"We'll go to my room. You can take a long, hot bath, and put on a thick terry robe. We'll order some food and talk about what to do next. Besides, you're too tired and overmedicated to have the kind of conversation you need to have with Brad."

The thought of confronting Brad scared me more than I wanted to admit. A night in a warm bed by myself sounded safe. But a wave of fear changed my mind. "God, Holly, you don't understand. If I'm not there when he gets home, he'll freak. He does have a horrible temper, he's liable to drink himself into a frenzy. He'll drive around—maybe he'll come looking for us. Last night on the phone, did you tell him where you're staying?"

"I'm sure I didn't. But I'll have the desk clerk change the name I'm registered under. Brad won't find us and if he gets drunk and gets himself into trouble, that's his problem, not yours." She turned onto the exit ramp. "It's time you started looking out for yourself." I tried to imagine what that would be like. I couldn't.

At the Marriott, we gave my bags to a porter and went inside. When Holly asked to change her reservation, the desk clerk looked confused. I raised my hat so he could see my bruised face. He obliged and asked what name we'd like to be registered under. "Monique. Monique Chantecler," Holly said, and turned and smiled at me.

"Very well, Ms. Chantecler. Welcome to the Marriott. I hope your stay will be a pleasant one." He gave Holly two keys and directed us to the elevator. The porter followed with my luggage.

Holly drew a hot bath for me, complete with bubbles, and left a soft terry robe next to the tub. After the bath I tried, without much success, to cover the bruises on my face with makeup. When I emerged, I was greeted by a smiling Holly and a table filled with food. It looked like she'd ordered everything on the menu. There were steaks, vegetables, salad, three desserts and a bottle of sparkling water. She opened the bottle and it made a soft fizzing sound. "Sit. Eat."

I sat down, trying to remember when I'd last eaten. It seemed like weeks since I'd had anything close to a normal appetite. As I sipped the water, I tried to sort out my feelings. Part of me was relieved to have a safe place to rest and grateful that Holly was with me. Another part felt only fear, fear of Brad and the beatings that were surely waiting for me when I returned home. But sitting in the big terry robe next to Holly, the most overwhelming feeling was despair. Absolute and total despair. It was a sadness that went so deep I feared it would consume me. After a few comments about the food, I ate in silence. Holly quickly sensed my depression.

"Jess, you can talk to me, if you want to." She was so eager to help. But that made me even sadder, because I knew that no one could help me. It was much too late.

"Thanks, I'll be okay. It's great to see you, though, and I am hungry. Thanks for getting all this food. You haven't told me anything about Kate and the play?" It would be easier if we could feign normalcy, if we could talk about something else. Anything else.

Holly told me about her life with Kate. She entertained me with stories from her Off-Loop productions and finally a success with a script someone wanted to do in L.A. Holly chatted through the afternoon about her life, her art and her relationship with Kate. Every time she tried to turn the conversation back to me, I balked, and she realized I wasn't ready.

Slowly, I began to feel stronger. Then, as we sat together in that room in the Marriott, I found myself trying to reassemble the facade. I had to convince Holly that I'd be okay. I needed to show her that my life wasn't the disaster it appeared to be, so she'd go home and leave me to mend the torn fabric of my marriage one more time. I'd become a master of denial, and I hoped that once again I could push on, find something in the future to focus on, some small thing that would get me through.

But this time it was harder. I'd finally admitted the truth to someone, and I wasn't sure how to cope with that reality. My first instinct was to lie, to pretend, to put on a happy face and make things appear to be different than they were. I was particularly good at that. But this was Holly, and she would be harder to fool.

Holly asked about my job. I tried to sound excited as I talked about the challenges of ad sales and played up my few success stories. But it didn't take a rocket scientist to see how far I'd fallen down the corporate ladder, and I knew Holly saw through my false enthusiasm. I tried to conjure up good stories about my life, but after a while even I found it tiresome.

"What's on television? I'm tired and I'd love to doze off to a movie." It was early evening, but I was exhausted. Holly flipped through the channels and I stopped her on an Audrey Hepburn movie. "Oh, God, it's 'Breakfast at Tiffany's.' Have you seen it? It's so sad when she pushes the cat out into the rain."

"I'm not big on old or new movies. But believe it or not, I do know who Audrey Hepburn is." She turned up the volume and curled up next to me. "Who's the guy?"

"George Peppard. They were so romantic. The end always makes me cry." I remember watching until Holly Golightly throws the wild party in her tiny apartment. Then I was asleep.

Jess was quiet and Zoe reached out and took her hand. "I'm so sorry that happened to you."

"It was your mother who saved me. Do you see how much she did for me? Do you understand what an extraordinary person Holly was?"

"Yes."

The phone rang, startling them. "There's no one I want to talk

to," Jess said, as the phone continued ringing. The machine in
Jess's office picked up and the two sat, listening.

"Hello. This message is for Sarah Ryerson . . ."

"Adam!" Zoe leapt off the bed as Jess handed her the
portable phone. She waved to Jess, then moved into the hallway
and closed the bedroom door. Jess was left suspended between
the past and the present where she remembered, in horrible detail,
the dream she had that night.

Jess and Holly were wearing flowered muumuus and drinking
champagne out of wide rimmed glasses. They were at Woodstock
with Uncle Jack and Shelley. The crowd was loud and rowdy and
people kept bumping into Holly and Jess as they moved back and
forth, screaming for Janis Joplin to take the stage. Then Holly was
topless and, unlike the grubby looking people around them, she
looked fresh and innocent. Daisies were braided into her long
hair.

Holly took Jess's hand and they moved through the crowd,
which parted for them as they walked toward the stage. They
climbed the stairs, and people along the route smiled knowingly.
When they arrived on stage, George Peppard was waiting for Jess.
Holly gave him Jess's hand and waved as Kate came from behind
some curtains and whisked her away.

When Jess turned back, the man whose hand she held wasn't
George Peppard; it was Brad, and he was wearing his wedding
tuxedo. Then Tyler appeared, Tyler from the Hawaiian party, the
boy who pinned her against the sofa, who raped her. Tyler sneered
and hurled insults. Jess looked to Brad for protection, but he held
her hands, laughed, and pulled her toward him. Then as Tyler
moved to grab her, Jess pulled away from both of them and ran.
She ran until she could no longer breathe.

Suddenly she was in Clear Lake, in the middle of a cornfield.

She was running home. She was late for supper and her dress was torn, the brown and blue plaid taffeta dress Celeste had made for her 10th birthday. She came to the end of a row of corn, gasping for air. There was her Uncle Jack, standing like a giant in front of her. No matter where she turned to run, he caught her with his strong arms, laughing, tickling, moving his hands over her body.

He pushed her to the ground. Jess tried to kick him away, but he grabbed her leg and laughed. She tried to scream, but no sound came out of her mouth. He kept laughing. Then Brad appeared, in his tuxedo. Jess was lying in the field in her taffeta dress and Brad was telling her uncle not to worry, because she wasn't any trouble, she wouldn't make any noise. They laughed together as her uncle moved over her, ripping her dress, pulling at her under-pants.

Jess yelled out, "Stop it! Stop it!"

Zoe came rushing in from the hallway. "Are you okay? What's wrong?"

Jess was flushed, her heart was racing so fast her ears rang. Zoe looked alarmed, but Jess took a breath and reclaimed her composure. "I'll be all right."

But Zoe quickly said good-bye to Adam and climbed back into Jess's bed. "Please, please tell me what happened."

"I remembered a nightmare."

"From that night?"

"Yes."

"Do you want to tell me about it?"

"I can tell you that it was your mother who awakened me from that terrible dream, from a lifetime of terrible dreams." Zoe looked with intense, questioning eyes as Jess finished the story.

I was screaming and crying in my sleep when I heard Holly's voice, calling to me, trying to wake me. "Jess, it's me. You're dreaming. It's okay; you're okay. You're here with me; you're all right now." Holly held me in her arms.

I was wet with sweat and my heart was pounding. "Oh, God, Holly. I can't do this anymore. I can't, I can't." Great rolling sobs sent shudders through my body. "I can't do it." Over and over, the same words came pouring out. "I can't, I can't."

"It's okay. You don't have to. It's over. You don't have to do it anymore." Holly cradled me as I cried.

Finally, fully awake, I pulled away and fought back tears. "But I've been doing this my whole life. I feel such a desperate need and I fall so hard. I go too far, I get hurt, and when it doesn't work out I always blame myself."

Holly took me in her arms. "All that's over now. No one can hurt you. You're safe." We sat on the bed, her arms around me, my head buried into her shoulder. I could hear the music rise as the final scene of the movie played out. And for the first time in my life, I felt safe, truly safe. I fell into a deep, heavy sleep.

I awakened the next afternoon feeling like a rock had replaced my stomach. Everything seemed cold and real and I felt sick and frightened. I knew I had to face the truth but I had no idea how to do it. Holly ordered breakfast and I ate silently while she read the *Los Angeles Times*. I looked out the window at the Hollywood Freeway and watched as thousands of cars made their way through the mire. Finally, I just started talking. Holly listened. I said the words, but it felt like someone else was speaking. My voice was low and flat.

"The night before last, I tried to hide behind a chair, to make myself so small he couldn't hurt me. But he came after me, swinging, trying to find an open place to strike. In my mind I kept hearing the words, 'He's going to kill you. If you stay here, he's going to kill you.' The truth washed over me, but I felt powerless to do anything about it. I think I believed I deserved to die, that it was my fate.

"For a long time, I tried to be optimistic, I tried to change myself so he would change. I told myself it was his job, that he'd be happier once he was making money again. Then I thought it must be me. I nagged him too much. I was too possessive. If I'd learn to cook, he'd be happier. If I kept the house perfectly spotless, he wouldn't get so angry. If I worked harder, made more money and didn't spend so much, he wouldn't hit me. But nothing I do makes Brad happy, and he never misses an opportunity to tell me how worthless I am. I've been living a lie. My whole life is a lie."

"Jess, I understand," Holly said. "Until I met Kate, my life felt like a lie. For too many years I didn't understand what I was lying about. I'd always felt like I didn't belong, like I was invisible. I truly believe it was some kind of fate that we were thrown together freshman year. Let's face it, we were both misfits, orphans in a way, set down in a world we weren't prepared for. We needed each other. We still do."

"But you faced the truth and found Kate. And she loves you, the real you. No one has ever loved the real me. Who could, I'm such a fake." I didn't want to cry, but I felt my eyes burn and quickly turned away.

"Jess, you're not a fake. You're a survivor." Holly's voice sounded so sure and wise. Then it cracked a little. "And I love the real you." I turned back and felt two huge tears roll down my cheeks. "You love so fiercely it makes my heart ache for you. I want so badly for you to find someone who is worthy of that love. And as sure as I found Kate, I know you'll find someone who deserves and appreciates who you are." She stopped for a moment, then went on.

"Do you know that you were the first person who ever loved me? For who I was. As different as we were, you still loved me, and your love gave me the strength to love someone else. I hope you find strength in my love for you." She reached out and took my hand in hers. "Someday you'll appreciate who you are and what you've come through.

"Besides, you're smart and funny and so beautiful. And you understand the world out there." She gestured to the window and the maze of freeways filled with cars on the horizon. "You flourish out there. Do you know how incredible that is? And you have a huge heart, Jess. Hell, yesterday you almost had me feeling sorry for Brad because he'd lost his job! You may have the biggest heart in the whole damn country!" We both laughed.

"Seriously, Jess, once you get your life back together and put this behind you, you'll find someone who will love you like you've never been loved before."

I turned and hugged Holly long and hard. She knew exactly what I needed to hear, and I never loved her more. After we wiped away our tears, I gave her a serious look. "Maybe I should try women. I've never had much luck with men."

She shook her head and grinned. "Sorry, Jess, you're about as heterosexual as they come, and believe me, I know. Don't give up, though; he's out there somewhere. But right now, I think you need to concentrate on you. How about if we go out and find a place for you to live that's cheaper than the Marriott?"

She stayed in town and helped me begin to piece my life together. We didn't find a place for me to live that day. Instead, Holly and I bought a California map. The next week she drove me to San Francisco and helped me find a safe place to heal.

"If it weren't for Holly, he would have killed me." Jess fell silent and Zoe reached up and hugged her. "It was so hard for me when Holly died. She was my rock." Jess choked out the words.

"I know."

"That night and for the weeks and months that followed, Holly helped me take my power back. I visited her and Kate often, and seeing them together, I learned that it is possible to love someone and trust them to protect you. That's what love is. Being honest about who you are and showing that to someone else, weaknesses and all. If the love is true, they'll love you for your strengths and protect your vulnerabilities. Which is a contradiction to everything else we learn in this world." Zoe smiled and nodded.

"You know, Zoe, if Holly were here today I think she'd tell you not to be afraid to let people into your heart. You have a strong sense of yourself, even if you're not feeling strong right now. If you ever do marry Adam, or anybody else, I believe you can stay centered. Just be careful not to lose yourself." Jess said, more to herself than to Zoe.

Zoe's eyes were wide. "That's my biggest fear."

"If you respect who you are, that won't happen. And you have that. I can see that spark in you, like your mother had. She was strong and you are, too."

The two were silent as they sat side by side, wrapped in a flower garden of sheets and blankets, surrounded by memories of the past. Finally Zoe spoke.

"Adam is going to pick me up at the airport tomorrow. I didn't tell him about the baby. I'll do that when I see him. He hasn't been with Meredith, he's been staying with a friend."

"That's good news."

"I'm still afraid."

"Of course you are. But now you have me."

Jess cradled Zoe until "Random Harvest" ended as Ronald Colman remembered his past, embraced his future and the credits rolled across the screen. Then she turned off the television and pulled the blanket over Zoe. When she was certain she was in a deep sleep, Jess rose. She took her robe off, hung it up. When she did, she felt Holly's journal page in the pocket. She took it out and buried it deep in a box in a corner of her closet.

Jess had her answer now. Yes, Holly believed that knowing and living the truth were what mattered most. But Holly had kept the secret, and now Jess understood that some truths should never be told. She wanted to protect me, Jess thought. She never told me because she loved me and wanted to protect me from her own shame and from the horror of my uncle's evil act. To tell Zoe the truth about her father now would only hurt her more. Jess vowed to protect Zoe's innocence as fiercely as Holly had protected hers.

Jess climbed into bed next to Zoe. She pulled the covers up and turned out the light, grateful for the warmth of Zoe's body next to her, and for the feeling of safety and safekeeping that seemed to wrap around them—as if Holly's spirit was in the room, smiling on them.

CHAPTER THIRTY

The next morning Jess awakened abruptly with a vivid memory. She recalled exactly where the page from her day planner was, the page with the notes from her dinner with Eric, the page that would prove whether or not she was losing her grip.

Zoe was sleeping soundly and Jess slipped out of bed quietly, trying not to disturb her. She showered and dressed in slim black jeans and a gray cashmere turtleneck. She tied her boots, then quickly pulled her hair back into a barrette. She brushed a bit of blush on her cheeks, closed the door to the bedroom, and made her way to her office.

The book, *22 Immutable Laws of Branding*, was staring at her from the bookshelf. She remembered tearing the page from her day planner and using it as a bookmark when she flew back from a meeting in L.A. She pulled it out and there were her ProbTech campaign notes, tucked between pages 66 and 67. She read through them. "Objective—to sell software . . . Execution—magazine, radio, in-store promotions . . . Target Audience—35 to 45-year olds." She read it again. Eric had told her the audience for the campaign was Baby Boomers. She hadn't been wrong. He made the mistake. Or was it a mistake? Jess folded the paper and stuck it back into the book. It didn't matter.

Jess thought of Harper and the conversation she'd overheard. She remembered how small she felt when Eric left yesterday afternoon, how worthless when he left her bed last night. Then, when she thought of her day with Zoe and the sweet and bitter memories of Holly, she felt a quiet calm. She knew exactly what she had to do.

She picked up the phone and began dialing Eric's pager number so he could call her back. Then she put the receiver down. "Not today," Jess said out loud. She called information and got Eric's home number. She dialed the number slowly, savoring her power as it rang. Rosemary answered and Jess asked to speak to Eric. When she asked who was calling, Jess said in a strong voice, "Jess Martin."

There was a short silence, then Rosemary asked her to wait. Jess sat smiling, imagining the two of them sitting in their Pacific Heights condo, reading *The New York Times* and drinking fresh-squeezed orange juice. She heard his voice, strained, anxious. "Jess Martin, what a surprise." Then under his breath, "What the hell are you doing?"

Jess answered simply. "I have two questions. I want the truth. Did you meet Harper for a drink last night?"

There was a long silence on the other end. Then Eric said, "Yes."

"Are you giving her the ProbTech account?" Another long silence.

"Yes." Eric had more to say and began to protest, but Jess had heard enough. She moved her finger to the phone cradle and pushed the button long and hard, cutting him off, cutting him out of her life. She calmly hung up the phone.

She stood, smiled, and let her hair lose from the barrette, shaking it free to fall softy around her shoulders. The phone rang until the answering machine picked up. It was Eric's voice, but

Jess couldn't hear a thing he was saying. She'd already closed the door.

The sun blazed through the kitchen windows, and Jess hummed as she boiled water for tea. The day lay ahead of her. Maybe she'd go to the park. Maybe she'd call Dan. No, she needed time, time to make a simple plan. She located her teapot, then spotted an unopened package of herb tea bags in the back of her cabinet. While the tea steeped, she went into the living room to finish packing up Holly's box. She wanted to treasure its contents one last time.

She finished stacking the books on top of the journals, then the lighter objects, the Hogs Head Pub ashtray and Holly's army jacket. She packed the Irish coffee mug from the Cliff House, the plastic speculum, Holly's blue felt hat, the package of sparklers. With the box nearly full, she went to her room and gently woke Zoe.

Zoe showered and dressed. When she came into the kitchen, she looked radiant. She wore the rayon print dress she'd bought on Haight Street, Holly's love beads and the purple knit rolled hat Jess had given her. Jess made a wolf whistle. "Talk about retro!"

Zoe smiled and sat down to eat the toast and tea Jess had set out in the dining room. They ate in a comfortable silence. Finally, Zoe spoke. "Did my mother suffer in the end?"

"I don't think so," Jess answered. "I know she had a doctor she trusted, who told Holly she'd make certain she wouldn't be in any pain."

Jess told Zoe about getting Holly's phone call, three months before she died. Holly said the cancer had returned but she wasn't going to take any more poison. "I thought she was crazy. I wanted her to live, even if the chemotherapy only gave her a few more months. But she was adamant."

Zoe ran her finger slowly around her teacup. "I wish I'd been there."

"There was nothing you could have done. Holly had made up

her mind. I couldn't even change it, although I tried. I flew to Chicago and showed up at her doorstep in a rental car with a dozen hats. I told her to pack up, I was taking her on a road trip into our past. I was willing to try anything to convince her to live.

"We drove to Iowa City and visited our old haunts; the ones that were still there. We went to the Union, Magoos, the Pentacrest. I even dragged her to a football game. It was ironic and sad, so many places had been torn down or transformed. Little Bill's was gone, but the Mill restaurant was still there. Things and Things and Things, the hippie store where Holly bought our first hats had become a 7-Eleven, The Barn still stood but had been turned into a sports bar, the Gaslight Lounge was a Gold's Gym. Some things actually improved; a large women's health cooperative had replaced the small Women's Center, and there was more diversity in the student population. Seiferts was gone, but Iowa Book and Supply had grown and taken over its building.

"Did you have a good time? I mean, did it at least lift her spirits?" Zoe looked hopeful.

"I think so. But it wasn't long after that she really began to fail. I wanted to be with her at the end, so I took a week off and flew to Chicago. I would have taken a year. I spent a few days there, but Holly became obsessed with finding you. She sent me to Minneapolis to 'work your magic with the authorities,' as she called it. But there was no magic that could penetrate the Catholic Charities. After my meeting with them, I called from the airport to see how she was feeling and she insisted on hearing the news: even under those extreme circumstances, her birth daughter's records would not be released without her daughter's written permission. All we could do was to wait to see if you responded. When I arrived back at Holly's apartment, her niece met me at the door. It felt like a mortal wound when she said the words 'she's gone.' Her ashes are scattered in a rose garden in Chicago. Along with Kate's."

"It's all my fault," Zoe choked out.

"No. You had no way of knowing. You can't be blamed for that."

"Maybe she would have agreed to the treatment, maybe she would still . . ." Zoe was near tears.

"Oh, Zoe," Jess said softly, "there was nothing anyone could have done. Not even you."

Zoe sat looking out the window toward the bay. "It's so sad, what happened to my mother."

"Yes and no. Holly found Kate, who helped her find herself. That's wonderful. What's sad is the short time they had together. But no one gets to choose that part." The women finished their breakfast in silence, each transformed by the memories they'd shared. Finally, Jess stood and began putting the dishes in the dishwasher. Zoe followed, carrying her plate.

"I guess it's time to call Joanne, she usually calls on Sunday morning. If I'm not there she'll worry."

"What are you going to say?"

"She'll want to know where I am and if I tell her, she'll want to know why. If I tell her why, she'll take charge and want me home immediately. Well, I'm going to stand up to her. Even though that will only put her into motion—she's such a control freak." Zoe went to Jess's office to make her call, and Jess returned to the living room to finish packing Holly's box.

She arranged the last few items and picked up the lid from underneath the coffee table. As she went to place it, an envelope taped to the inside of the lid caught her eye. Inside she found a note in Holly's sprawling hand and the silver peace sign on the leather rope that Jess had given Holly when she was pregnant and making her journey home at Christmas. Jess put on the necklace and read the note.

Dear Jess,

This container holds either junk or treasures—you decide. I put them together to remind you of how important you are to me. And to thank you for the miraculous trip down memory lane last week. You pulled me back from the brink of the abyss, once again. How do you say thank you for gratitude of the soul?

I want you to know that the times I shared with you were always memorable and I believe as honest as either of us dared to be. We have bled, both of us, for many years and in many different ways, and so the joys we share together are always a great and deep pleasure for me. Every inner battle we've survived is a testament to our each achieving some miracle of spirit. The miracle is that we overcame what fate handed us, to become the vision of ourselves that we held somewhere in our deepest souls. What's more wonderful is that we were able to acknowledge that vision in each other when we were young, however feeble and maligned those youthful attempts were. We have won, even if no one else ever knows it.

Promise me that you will keep yourself far away from the abyss. And thank you again for helping me find my way back from its edge.

I love you forever,
Holly

"I can't believe it!" It was Zoe, rushing into the living room, oblivious to the tears in Jess's eyes. "I'm blown away! I called my mom. I told her about the baby and do you know what she said? She told me I needed to go home and talk it over with Adam. She said she'd support me no matter what I decided."

Way to go, Joanne, Jess thought.

A horn sounded outside and Zoe went to the window. "Hey, the cab's here already."

"You called a taxi? I wanted to take you to the airport."

"I'd rather say good-bye to you here. I want to remember you in this place."

"You look so strong and beautiful, just like your mother. I want a picture." Jess got her camera and took a quick photo of Zoe at the door. They stood together where Zoe had knocked so persistently two days earlier.

"I put my card in the front pocket of your backpack with my home, work numbers and e-mail address. I expect to hear from you soon."

"Jess, I want to tell you something. I know I'll never find out who my father is, and that's all right because, thanks to you, I do know who my mother was. Thank you for that." Zoe gave Jess a huge bear hug.

As they walked out Zoe insisted on carrying the box and her backpack to the waiting taxi. When the driver tried to put the box in the trunk Zoe refused him, and placed it carefully on the seat. Jess grabbed Zoe and gave her a final heart-to-heart hug. "You take phenomenal care of yourself." She watched as Zoe climbed into the cab, next to the modest cardboard box. "I love you, Zoe."

"Me too, you." Jess reached inside the window and gave Zoe a kiss on her cheek. As she turned to go, Zoe whistled from the cab as it backed out of the driveway and headed down the street. Zoe whistled again, then stuck half her body out the window and shouted, "Hey, call Dan! Remember what they say about a boy who loves dogs!"

Jess laughed, then waved as the cab turned and disappeared down Potrero Hill, into the sunny Sunday morning.